A SLOW COLD DEATH

Susy Gage

Published by Bitingduck Press
ISBN 978-1-938463-37-2
© 2012 Susy Gage
All rights reserved
For information contact
Bitingduck Press, LLC
Montreal • Altadena
notifications@bitingduckpress.com
http://www.bitingduckpress.com
Cover image by Dena Eaton

Publisher's Cataloging-in-Publication
Gage, Susy [1971-   ]

A Slow Cold Death/by Susy Gage –1st ed.—
Altadena, CA: Bitingduck Press, 2012
p. cm.
ISBN 9781938463372

[1. Detective and Mystery Stories, 21st century—
Fiction 2. Murder—Academic setting—Fiction 3.
Espionage—Academic—Fiction   3. Physicists—
California—Fiction. 4.Canada—Quebec—Rollerblading—Fiction   5. Research laboratories—Rivalry—Grant proposals—Fiction 6. Astrobiology—Ice
core samples—Fiction] I. Title

LCCN 2012941373

For Ozy, because sometimes denial really is a superpower;
and for Skaludy, my first fan

"The balance sheet for the universe makes the crucial distinction between a universe that will expand forever into a slow cold death, or on the other extreme one which will fall back upon itself in the big crunch" –Prof. John Learned, University of Hawaii

Disclaimer

None of these people are real, and none of these events actually happened, except the part about the mallard. Any resemblance to real people or events is a concidence or a product of your guilty conscience.

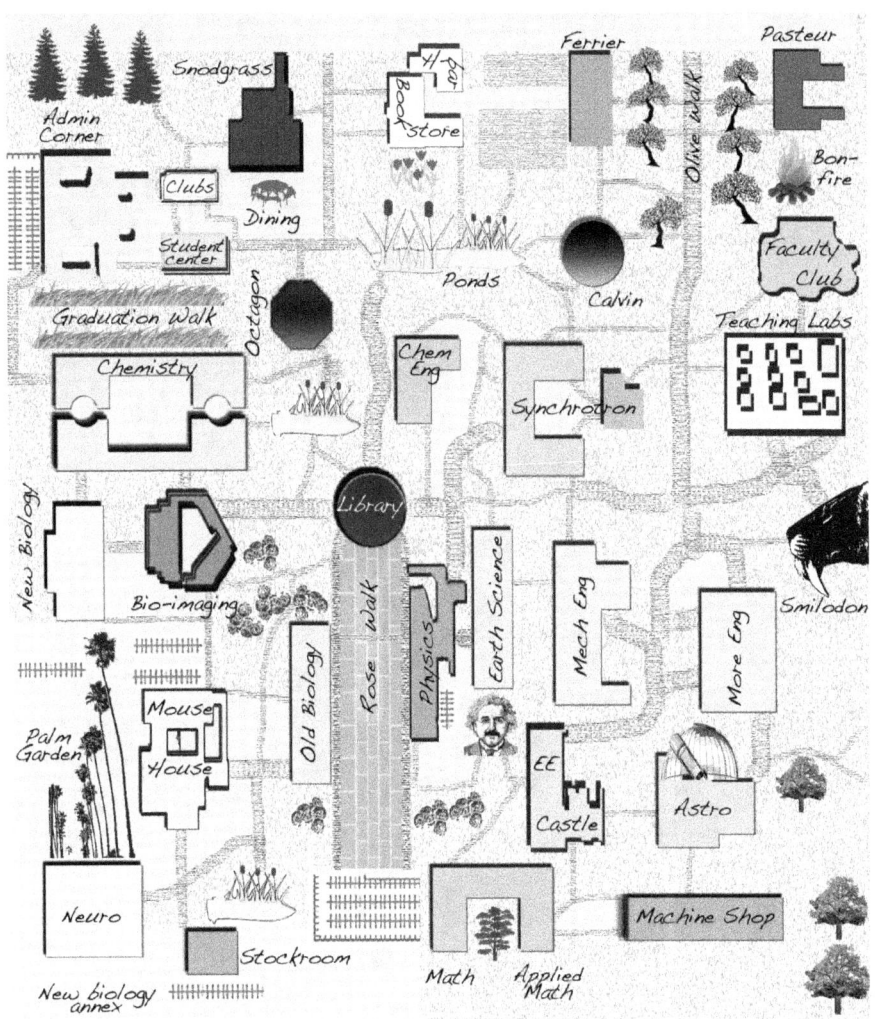

Ferrier: the Ferrets. Color: black. Motto: "The tooth shall make you free."
Pasteur: the Buboes. Color: maroon. Motto: "Considère-moi comme une peste."
Calvin: the Thorns. Color: ecru. Motto: "Barefoot through adversity."
Snodgrass: the Snots. Color: green. Motto: "Yeah, we're the dumb ones."

PROLOGUE: 1991

JACOB SILVERMAN HATED GRADUATIONS.

They made him feel like a piece of infrastructure, paraded around in a silly costume for the benefit of students who had bugged him for four, eight, sometimes as many as thirteen years in the case of his least-favorite PhD student. His gray and red academic regalia was sweltering, and at ten o'clock on this ninth of May in beautiful Pasadena, California, it was already over one hundred degrees.

So while the campus of the Superior Technological Institute was being strewn with roses and computer cables for the big day, he strapped a water bottle around his waist, laced up his hiking boots, and headed into the foothills alone. The air grew cooler and cleaner with every mile, and there were no sounds besides the humming of insects and his own footfalls.

When he was struck from behind, he thought at first of a landslide, raising his arms to protect his head. Then a second blow fell between his shoulder blades, accompanied by a distinctly human grunt.

Tumbling over the trail's edge to the chaparral below, he thought for a crazy few moments that he would survive. The sand was soft and welcoming and he dove into it hands first, images flashing in his mind of his family, then his mother, then himself marching into the police station to file a report. There weren't very many people who would have an interest in killing a physics department chairman, even if his department was the best of its kind in the world.

But the sand was slippery on the steep slope, and he accelerated as he slid, grasping more and more desperately at cacti and manzanita trees that tore from their moorings under his speeding weight. His last hope was that the murderer's identity would be as obvious to his colleagues as it should be, and then he broke through the underbrush to plummet two hundred feet to the canyon floor.

ONE: RIGHT BACK WHERE I STARTED FROM

MAUPERTUIS WILL TELL YOU many things, but pay him little heed."
Alexander Kuznetsov's too-formal English made him seem even creepier
somehow. "He was shot in the chest on the freeway last year, and he hasn't
been the same since. He'll die long before he gets tenure."

Lori recoiled instinctively from the heartless words, forgetting she was
still wearing her rollerblades. She scrambled for balance, clutching the wall,
leaving a streak of sweat on the department head's beige paint.

The last time she had stood in this room she had been sixteen years
old, pursued by a reporter into Silverman's office for some bullshit feel-
good story about the youngest graduate of America's best science university. Valedictorian, a single A- (organic chemistry) the only flaw on her
record, three papers published as an undergrad. It should have felt like a
triumph, returning to the place that had been her home and to one of the
most coveted positions in all of geekdom. Only a hundred and fifty people
in the world could claim the title of professor at the Superior Technological
Institute. An even dozen could claim to be professors of physics in the
department that had housed Millikan, Dirac, Einstein, and Feynman.

But something had been wrong since the moment she arrived half an hour
ago, and it wasn't being number thirteen. The department she remembered
so well had become a ghost town. The secretarial cube farm was closed
and dark. Half of the rooms had no names on them. The only person here
at nine-thirty on a Wednesday morning was the new chairman, who had
skipped her interview out of pure spite and whose welcome sounded more
like a death threat.

She took a deep breath and tried to channel Silverman. Kuznetsov never would have been hired if his predecessor hadn't died in a freak hiking accident, and she returned his sneer with one of her own. "In that case, is there anyone *alive* I should meet?"

"We didn't expect you until next week," he replied coldly, as if her early intrusion were a personal insult. "I understand your research group will be joining you?"

"Just one postdoc."

"We must talk." He rose to his feet, brushed past her and headed down the corridor, not even giving her a chance to change her footwear.

She half-marched, half-rolled after him, noticing that even with hundred-millimeter wheels she was a head shorter. Kuznetsov was a bit scary looking, clean-shaven and deathly pale with slanted gray eyes and a neat cap of silver hair. He wore a suit and tie and there was a trace of Russian in his voice, but so slight it sounded fake at times.

He led her down two flights of stairs (she stepped sideways, clinging to the handrail) and across the tiny campus, past the thirteen-story library that gleamed like mylar in the sun, and to a completely remodeled bookstore with a café called the "H Bar and Grill."

The place depressed her. They had obviously tried to make it fancy, but it was a faux gourmet rip-off, with tiny portions and inedible baked goods. The new layout of the bookstore was wretched, too—there were no longer any books. Instead there were shelves of electronic gadgets and their assorted accessories, all branded and logoed and arranged by color-code for each of the four STI Undergraduate Houses. Lori felt as if everything she held sacred had been turned into a bauble.

Slurping loudly on his four-dollar latte, Kuznetsov told her that she should fire her current postdoc and replace her with the incoming crop of his hand-selected superstars. Of the six first-year students, he expected Lori to support at least three, all of them string theorists. Now that she'd made her presence in town known, she was "invited" (no choice involved) to spend the weekend in Palm Springs at the new students' retreat, where he would introduce these people to her.

"As close as you are to your tenure review, stick with what you know," he told her with a muffiny grin that showed decayed stubs of teeth, stigmata no doubt of outdated Soviet dental practices. He tried to convince her that trying to set up an experimental lab before tenure was too risky, that she shouldn't even bother. Everyone at the interview had said the opposite. Besides, if she was supposed to stick with what she knew, why abandon her Canadian postdoc? Fang Li was a theorist, and she was good, and Lori refused to have her callously jettisoned.

"As you know, STI only allows postdocs to have that status for five years," Kuznetsov pursued, leaving her no room to reply. "Your Canadian has but one year left—for her to leave her country would be unwise."

Lori groaned audibly. She had told Fang to make sure she had her green card—after all, she had done her PhD at Chicago: she knew the U.S.—but being the impractical flake theoretical physicists all were, she'd never done it.

After all the grief of last year, Lori had wanted to leave Canada so much that she hadn't stopped to wonder what STI really wanted from her. She had thought they were being generous when they gave her credit for all five years she'd spent as an assistant professor, offering to give her tenure after only one year if things went well. That was the ultimate sign that she was so out of touch that she no longer understood anything that mattered. It was the first rule of this place—trust no one. But she had signed a contract, and now she was here, and had to avoid becoming a pawn for the losing side.

She didn't even bother to argue. Paying for his students was out of the question, no matter how brilliant they were, but let him entertain his silly hopes if that made him happy. The first thing she needed to do was to find out who was responsible for space allocations, and whether the experimental lab they'd promised in the letter of offer was real or a lie.

He continued to chew with infuriating slowness, so finally she got up, excused herself without veiling her sarcasm, and skated out the door.

All of her luggage was still on the moving van, which had left her this morning with the only means of transportation that could fit in a carry-on. Perfect for the flat bike trails of Montreal, her custom carbon-fiber speedskates were about as appropriate in the Los Angeles foothills as swim fins on a gymnast. The three-mile descent to campus had been terrifying, done mostly backwards and involving one face-first crash onto someone's lawn.

But the campus was smooth and flat, the only obstacles a few fallen fruit on the Olive Walk and string trimmers wielded by the eternally zealous campus landscape crew. She gave the gardeners the finger, sprinted past the cafeteria, twisted around the library, and flew up the wheelchair ramp towards the physics building. The tiny campus had been made entirely accessible five years before—she knew for whom, and she knew he'd graduated, so she truly wasn't expecting a guy in a wheelchair to be in her way right at the top.

Swallowing a *holy shit,* she turned a hard left (always easier) and bumped down the short flight of stairs to execute a not-so-nice front T-stop just in front of the rose bushes. She then had to grab onto them to keep her balance, and swore for real this time in every language she knew as the thorns tore through her wrist guards. She sat down hard on the pavement.

There were too many people watching for this hour of the morning, and all of them were laughing.

"Lori Barrow returns in style," called a kid sitting on the library steps. "Nine point five."

"Nine point four," commented the guy in the wheelchair who had spun himself around in a tight radius. "Deduction for cursing." He sped down the ramp and over to where she was sitting. "'*Tabarnak de câline de binnes*'?" he smirked, offering her his hand to pull her up. "*Qu'est-ce que c'est que ça?*" His eyes sparkled with laughter, but his face looked tired and too old to be a student's and his French was straight from the *grandes écoles* of Paris.

"*Crisse de tabarnak,*" Lori replied, exaggerating her best Quebecois accent. "You must be Louis Maupertuis."

TWO: THE MOST LOGICAL COSTUME

EXCELLENT! YOU SAY MY name even better than Murray Gell-Mann." Louis didn't look as if he had any intention of dying young. He was tan and grinning, with sun-bleached curly hair and a T-shirt that read *String Theorists Have P-Branes*. His grip was strong as he pulled Lori to her feet in a single motion that was surprisingly graceful. "What's it like being back?" His English was as casual as his French was snobby, without any trace of a foreign or regional accent.

"Like being Rip van Winkle, that's what," she griped, sticking one foot behind her so she wouldn't trip again. "Everything has changed, I recognize nothing, and I hate it all. The coffee shop employees are so mean they wouldn't fill my cup."

"That's weird, they're usually very nice." His bushy blond eyebrows knit into a scowl and he lowered his voice. "Unless you were with Kuzno?"

His obvious loathing only made Lori's vision of the department even murkier. She half expected him to say that Kuznetsov didn't have long for this world. Instead he just explained, "No one will serve you if you're with that son of a bitch. He's abused all the waitstaff in a five-mile radius." He glanced at her feet, then her head. "Why don't you change your clothes, and we'll go get some coffee somewhere else."

Lori was suddenly conscious of the immodesty of her skinsuit, her backpack stained with the mud of a winter that would never end, smelly wrist guards now splotched with blood, and the number "116" still stuck on her helmet from last month's marathon. "Er, well..." she tried. "I don't exactly have any other clothes. I'm not really at work today—I just came down here to check the place out and was hijacked by Kuzno."

Louis grumbled like a grouchy old dog. "Exactly what I was trying to prevent. You have to tell me what he said—but not here. The bushes have ears." The way he glared at the nearest rosebush made Lori half expect it to reply, but it stayed stoic as he spun around and headed for the edge of campus.

She thought she knew where he was going and followed eagerly. The first Peet's outside Northern California had been on the corner a block from the astronomy building, and as long as it was still there, all was right with the world.

"Is Kuznetsov evil?" she asked.

"He's more than evil," retorted Louis, who pushed the way obsessed people walk, flying down the bumpy sidewalk with apparent disregard for fallen grapefruit and ficus pods. "He is the enemy."

Lori had never seen a wheelchair like that before, with a frame crafted with minimalist titanium simplicity like a racing bike, a really low back, and fancy expensive wheels of the same brand she used to have. "Nice wheels," she remarked, "but I sold mine with that type of spokes. They're really hard to true, and they break a lot, especially on a mountain bike."

He looked briefly surprised. "You're right, actually. I paid a fortune for these, and they break all the time."

"I can show you what the national team guy taught me." She hopped off the sidewalk and skated in the street, which was grapefruit-free and put her closer to Louis so she didn't have to shout. "As soon as the moving van shows up with my truing stand, that is."

"You true your own wheels?"

"Always. Usually in my office—it relaxes the brain." She braked at the red light on Lake Avenue, scanning the unfamiliar storefronts. Cell phones and chic clothing, a fancy supermarket and a cheap department store—nothing to hint that they were two hundred yards from the greatest concentration of geniuses in the world.

"Suddenly I feel like a loser theorist," said Louis, who was about the best example of loser theorist she'd ever seen. Seriously, "P-Branes"?

"Even a theorist can use a truing stand," said Lori, without really meaning it. Most of them couldn't handle a screwdriver, but she was an exception and she hoped Louis was too, in case she needed to recruit him for her new lab. "By the way, how did you recognize me like this? I was hoping to stay incognito."

He laughed. "Lori, you're wearing your skinsuit, helmet, and a number in eleven out of the twelve images that appear under your name in a Google search."

"Do you realize," she rattled off in a single breath as they took turns pushing the button for the green light, "that when I last left STI, the Internet was just a bunch of physicists posting their preprints and half a dozen newsgroups of which I was a founding member of half? The computer lab on the library's first floor had nothing but six amber-colored monitors and a printer for testing your LaTex because you couldn't visualize it on screen. Can you imagine that there was no C++ standard? That the most common operating system on campus was MS-DOS?"

"Wow, you should teach a class in Ancient Geek History. And I think I know who you were on *alt.tasteless.*" The light changed at last. "Where do you want to have breakfast?"

The heat was oppressive and the air smoggy. It took her a moment to catch her breath as they slowed down to navigate the commercial center and another moment to remember what September was like in Montreal: Cold. Always cold. The only safe month in Montreal was July, and it was all alone, a sad pitiful little month standing up to eleven cruel others. "I don't know. I think I want to go to Peet's, unless it has changed. I know nothing anymore. Even the tutu-man is dead!"

Peet's had changed—it was now part of a brightly colored bagel shop that had certainly not been there before. There were a ton of people milling about and hogging the sunny spots, but Louis seemed to think it was worth the crowd and found them a place in line for both bagels and coffee. "It's OK, Lori," he said without any trace of irony. "We'll make another."

"What? Another tutu-man?" Lori balanced on one foot and fought with the buckle of her skate. "You can't just make them like, like—"

"Like ice cubes? I choose my analogy carefully. There are simple ways of turning a sane, healthy physicist into a gibbering lunatic; it's as well defined as a phase transition. First, he has to be appointed to a high-ranking position and then thrown out like an old rag."

Lori was starting to see the picture. "Second, he has to sue and be granted tenure." Finally free of the first skate, she started removing the second. "Third, he has to then decide to spend the next eighty years hanging around campus wearing a miniskirt and swim sandals just to annoy the university, calling it 'the most logical costume for males in a hot climate.'" She shoved the skates into her bag and took out her cheap rubber flip-flops, feeling the blood return to her toes one by one.

"Now I wonder who is on stage one?"

"I may be immature, Louis, but I am not stupid." With the skates off, she was right at his eye level and gave him a steady glare. "I know perfectly well that string theory is for losers and that we were hired to drive Kuzno and his flunkies out."

They had reached the front of the line, but Louis appeared rather stunned, so Lori just stepped in front of him and ordered herself a breakfast sandwich on sesame and the largest coffee they had.

"And what would *he* like?" asked the saleslady, looking askance at Louis.

Lori was somewhat appalled, but honestly her new colleague was doing very little to dispel the image of being a drooling dement. "I think he wants a lobotomy. Hey, Louis! Earth to Dr. Maupertuis! Are you going to order something or are you just going to sit there?"

He got himself coffee and a bagel but didn't snap out of his fugue until they were outside settled under a tree at one of the rickety wire tables. "Lori," he said quietly, stirring a packet of sugar into his coffee, "you should really, really not say those things out loud in public."

"Huh? What?" To humor him, she lowered her voice. "Does Kuzno have spies? I thought everyone hated him."

"They do, but they'd be delighted to see his wrath directed elsewhere." He added another packet of sugar without tasting and continued stirring. "It's not a joke, I'm afraid. We really do have to get rid of him, and because he's tenured, it's not easy."

"So we have to drive him mad?"

"That's an option."

"Or kill him?"

"That's going too far."

Maybe he's the one who shot you! she thought, but suppressed the idea quickly. Perhaps he had post-traumatic stress disorder and was a little paranoid. Lori groaned silently to herself—she couldn't bear any more lunatics. She'd left Canada to get away from lunatics, both those she loved and those she loathed. "He told me I should give up trying to do experiments this year," she informed Louis, trying not to regret her past life, which already seemed so far away. She forced herself to think of the sun, the heat, and the roses; the roses in Montreal were sad, fuzzy things, all spindly branches with chronic fungus infections from being kept under styrofoam shields all winter long.

"He did *what?*" Louis clearly intended to leap to his feet but had forgotten he no longer had the axonal connections to do so, and nearly fell forward before slapping his hands on the table in a gesture half of self-arrest and half of outrage. Coffee jumped out of both cups.

"See what I mean?" he demanded in a low voice. "He's the spawn of Satan. You have the infrastructure grant for the collaborative center now. If you start moving right away, you'll have experimental results in three months. If you miss hiring the incoming students, you'll have nothing for a year. Don't let him foist his loser theorists off on you, and don't let him make any excuses for not giving you lab space appropriate for your microscopy and lasers. And don't let him make you fire Fang Li. She's one of the best young theorists there is."

Lori's mind was spinning. He knew too much already. "The theory students this year are losers?"

"You'll see for yourself. They want to do string theory, but he can't afford to hire them so he's trying to make you do it. Did he say anything about lab space?"

"Nothing immediately realizable. He promised me space in the new building."

"He lied. It's been taken by biology even though the building won't be finished until after you get tenure. You need to look in our basement."

The choice of breakfast hadn't been the best. Lori had forgotten how hot and dry California was, and now she was feeling a bit ill and stricken with a raging thirst. "I don't know who or what's in the basement. That's where the electron microscopy used to be." She remembered she had an apple in her backpack and pulled it out, caressing it gently. A Quebec McIntosh, smuggled unwittingly into California on the airplane, a relic of *les produits de chez nous.*

"Used to be?" Louis hadn't touched his coffee or bagel up until this point. He seemed to suddenly notice they were there, tasted the coffee, made a face, and picked up the bagel. "Still is."

"Still is? You mean van Gnubbern hasn't retired yet?" It took her a long, long moment, and rather pitying look from Louis, before she realized the truth. "Oh, no." She bit a huge chunk from the apple. "No, no, no," she garbled, chewing. "Kuzno I can handle, but van Gnubbern taught me how to do electron microscopy when I was a freshman. He got me on my first paper. Forcing him out would be like stabbing my grandpa."

"That's why you were hired," he said with no trace of emotion. "We all know Lori Barrow can stab her grandpa."

That was too much. Lori could leap to her feet, so she did, and threw her empty coffee cup on the table. "Fuck you, Louis. You're an asshole!"

He seemed genuinely delighted at this. "Why, thank you, Lori. You don't know how much that means to me. But quit it with this *Louis* nonsense: I'm Lou."

"As in *Le Grand Méchant?*" she asked automatically.

"Oooh, I like that." He gave a toothy grin. His canines seemed particularly long. "They of course hired *me* because I'm an asshole. Didn't even have to do a postdoc. You know I'm younger than you are? By three years and eight weeks. Unfortunately, a random act of L.A. street violence made me *hors de combat* for most of the last year."

Without any idea why, Lori sat back down and burst into tears into what remained of her McIntosh. The words that came with the tears were hopefully as unintelligible to him as they were in her own mind, a mix of how she didn't want to know about him, she didn't want him to know about her, and for God's sake she didn't want to hear anything at all in French.

Lou waited patiently and handed her a napkin. "Sorry about that," he said perfunctorily.

She listened in horror as the phrase she had hated all of her life came out of her own mouth. "You're just a kid, you don't understand," she sniffled. Not surprisingly, he looked as outraged as she felt. "When do you come up for tenure?" she tried to amend.

"Not for four more years," he admitted.

Lori took a shaky breath. It was hard to explain to someone who hadn't been through it yet what the tenure process really meant. After six years, a professor went through a grueling procedure of preparing a dossier containing her entire life's work, including research, teaching, and "service" to the university and community—which could mean everything from hosting high school students to being on committees to preparing a display for a museum. To this were added long, meticulous reports from at least three scholars in the field who had to claim that the candidate was, or at least would become, a world-class expert in some desired field. The whole package, which could easily be upwards of a thousand pages, then passed from the departmental tenure committee to the faculty-level committee, to the university-level committee, and finally to the president of the institution. Usually…but not always…the higher-level committees supported the department's decision, but secret enemies could derail an application at any stage.

During the twelve to sixteen months that it took for the entire process, everyone started to look like one of those secret enemies.

If your tenure was refused, you had to leave the university. There were no second chances. The level of ignominy depended upon the school, but in the very best case, a professor refused tenure would start the process again at a new institution at least one step down on the prestige scale. For a lifelong overachiever, it was a big fat F—and a new beginning in what was often a miserable bumfuck place, with trailing spouse and children angry at the move, and competing for jobs with bright-eyed optimists ten years younger.

In the worst case, it meant you were forty, unemployed, and unemployable. It had happened to people she knew, too many to count.

But if the answer was positive, a tenured professor could be as big a pain in the ass as she wanted. Nothing short of a major felony could get you fired, and sometimes not even that. Most people—especially most young professors—didn't understand that winning tenure was less about being a great scholar than about convincing your colleagues that they wanted you down the hall for the next sixty years.

Lori had fled Canada after submitting her dossier but before the university had reviewed it, and STI had asked her simply to hand them the same dossier to put through their process. It was as close to being hired with tenure as she could expect, but it was still light-years away. For the next year she had to please everyone—or go down in a (hopefully figurative) duel to the death with Kuzno. She was certain now that someone had set this up on purpose, and there weren't a lot of choices for who the mastermind might be. Only four of the Twelve were full professors with the right to sit on a tenure committee.

"You don't understand," she insisted again. "I am just hosed. I'm going to end up homeless in Santa Monica giving handjobs for change, or dead and washed up in the drainage ditch like Silverman."

"No, no, of course not," Lou said reassuringly. "I'm sure they'll give you tenure even if you fuck up." He showed the ends of his teeth in a villainous grin. "You'll just have to take the place of the tutu-man. As of this morning, you even have the costume."

THREE: A NEW SPIN ON BOSON

CAROL NEARLY CHOKED ON her protein shake when she saw Lori Barrow's name on the weekly Astrophysics mailing list. It took her three days to get up the nerve to send her an e-mail.

They'd gone to graduate school together in Minneapolis, Minnesota, and Carol felt as though she knew Lori intimately even though she feared that her colleague wouldn't remember her at all. Lori, of course, had been the star, worlds away from the nameless, faceless sea of mediocre students whom the elite clique always called *bosons.*

Carol hadn't even known at first that the word referred to a type of elementary particle, a type that had spin zero or one rather than one-half, which naturally had made things even worse. "What's a boson? *You* are!" echoed in her head as she composed her e-mail message, trying to remember with equal vividness Lori's small acts of kindness and reassurance that had often warmed Carol's heart and kept her going the way nothing else would have.

In a way, then, she was contacting her to thank her; in another way, deep down where she was ashamed to admit it, she was contacting her to show off. For a boson, Carol had managed to make something of herself. She worked four-day weeks as an engineer for the Lobo Peak Rocket Lab and pulled in nearly $200,000 a year. Her husband, who was one grade above her in the department next door, made even more. They had a mid-century modern style house in the foothills, a small plane that they took to the beach on weekends that weren't too foggy, and a full-time caretaker for their show ducks and Australian shepherds.

Nonetheless, she was astonished (stupefied!) when Lori replied to the message almost immediately, saying that she wasn't officially working until Monday and that certainly she'd be free on Friday for lunch. Nothing could beat her amazement, though, at seeing her old classmate roll into their driveway at two thousand feet elevation on a pair of bright orange rollerblades.

All her old feelings of inadequacy returned as she watched Lori bend over to undo her skates, flexing six-pack abs that showed through her shirt and thighs even more perfect than they'd been when she'd won the Minnesota cross-country collegiate mountain bike championship. It was as if the laws of aging didn't apply to her, as if no matter what happened in the world, Lori Barrow would always be sixteen. Carol was about ready to regret the invitation when Lori stood up, spotted her at the end of the driveway, and ran down in just her socks to kiss her on both cheeks and exclaim, "Carol, my God! You look wonderful!"

Carol took a deep breath and then relaxed into a laugh. Up close, Lori was as human as the rest of them; she looked fatigued and even had some gray in her light brown hair. The house and garden were having their mesmerizing effect, too, and Carol waited for her to take in the yard before she launched into her explanations.

"It's a California chaparral garden, designed by the native plant nursery," she said. "This keeps the live oaks happy, because that way there is no summer water, and it's more ecologically friendly too. This oak here is probably three hundred years old. You can see the way they had to cut away the walkway to accommodate the growth. It's very low-maintenance, I leave all of the leaves in place." She was gratified by Lori's effusive praise, which prompted her to continue, "The kennels are back here. I have an Aussie Shepherd bitch and some pups that are almost ready for sale, and yes, these are the duckies: that's Weber, Henry, Billie, and Bob."

Lori, of course, appreciated immediately that "Henry" was a unit of… inducktance. "That's good. The puppies are killing me! The cuteness is lethal. Do you have a boyfriend? Any kids?"

"No kids," said Carol, "but I am married." She flinched instinctively, since the Lori she knew would have berated her mercilessly for selling her soul to the State and her body to the Man. At least she hadn't changed her name—but mostly because his name was kind of silly. Bob Drift was a good name for a guy who looked at transport in ice floes, but she didn't want to be a Drift. Dugoni she was born and Dugoni she would stay, even if the nickname "Dugong" hadn't remained in third grade where it belonged.

But it had been fifteen years, and by now even Lori would know that ideals won't warm your toes on a winter's night or rub your back after a hard day. "Is he a physicist?" was all she asked.

"A former student of Professor van Gnubbern at STI," Carol said proudly. "We work in the same colony, but different cells. In fact, he's trying to hire one of his advisor's old students right now."

"Van Gnubbern?" Lori wondered idly, running her hand along the thickly curling trunk of the wisteria. "I thought he hadn't had students since I left. …What a beautiful house."

"Well, it seems to me it was a huge project Bob wanted this guy for—he has all his own money and everything. Even the colony manager interviewed him." Carol felt, as always, like a boson.

"Hmmm," Lori mused, and Carol could almost hear the gears whirring in the conspiracy lobe of her brain. "Bizarre. …I love the way the rear windows open into the garden. It's as if the outdoors were part of the living room."

"Yes, we looked and looked for weeks, and then when the agent brought us here I just knew. I stood rooted to the spot, crying, 'It's mine!'"

She laughed nervously, a bit taken aback by her classmate's look of envy. She remembered hearing something about what had happened to Lori in Canada and suddenly felt very guilty. "But go ahead and get comfortable. Sit in a chaise longue or in the hammock, and I'll go get our brunch. You must be starving if you came up that hill on rollerblades."

Carol hadn't known what to serve for lunch, so she'd just bought some prepared trays of fresh fruits and vegetables, bread and cheese. Back in graduate school, when she had been bulimic, she'd been too caught up in her own anxieties to notice how healthy women ate. Now she had a psychotherapist and a personal trainer, but it was still rare that she had to choose food for someone else all by herself. She was immensely pleased that Lori was happy with the food, and she watched Carol serve herself with what could only be described as compassion.

"You look really amazing," Lori repeated. "I'm so glad you managed to conquer your demons, get your degree, and come out here. I mean, of all the people in our class, who would have thought it would be the two of us sitting in California, rich and powerful and gloating?"

Carol laughed easily. As a boson, she couldn't expect real confidences from Lori, but they could certainly play remember-when. "What ever happened to Radhika?" she wondered.

"Radhika dumped me like a rotten potato when I took a job in Canada," Lori declared too cheerfully. "She said, and I quote, 'If I ever see snow anywhere again, even on a remote mountaintop, it will be too soon.' She lives in Darwin. It's hard even to have conversations by e-mail with the time difference. It's about been reduced to 'Don't envy you, going surfing, neener.'"

"Darwin? Where's that? What does she do there?"

"Northern Australia. Femtosecond spectroscopy."

"Good for her."

"For dumping me, or for Darwin?"

"Darwin, of course!" Carol exclaimed, but Lori didn't seem too upset. "I mean—she's Hawaiian. Come on! She was completely traumatized by Minnesota—Canada would have killed her. Absinthe—you remember Abby?—She's a lawyer here in town. She does IP issues for STI."

"Are you serious? Oh man, she's richer and more powerful than all of us. Hey, the women in our class rock." Lori helped herself to handful of baby carrots and stretched herself out in the chaise longue while she munched. "Too bad about most of the guys, though. I heard from Gus the other day. He's at a government lab in Texas, and he hates it. Says it's like San Quentin. They get the anal probe every morning when they go to work; the guards search the scientists and take away their pocketknives even though they're coming onto labs with nuclear weapons. It's not quite that bad at the LEPERLab, is it?"

"I hate that name!" Carol felt her face grow hot. "I always say 'Lobo Peak' or the 'LPR Lab.' I don't know if it's that bad; it comes and goes. Usually when there's a crackdown I take a personal day off and miss out on the worst of it." She stood up to gather up the trays. She'd had enough to eat, and had to fight annoyance at Lori for making all that Carol had accomplished suddenly seem hollow and vain. She knew that the professors on the STI campus saw the rocket lab as a bastard step-child, despising them for their militarism and limits on intellectual freedom, but she hadn't expected Lori to have assimilated the attitude quite so quickly. The rest of the world only saw the glamour: it was LPR who landed things on Mars. "Hey," she suggested suddenly, "do you want to help me deadhead the roses?"

"You bet I do!" exclaimed Lori as if she hadn't touched plants in years. Maybe she hadn't.

"What's it like in Montreal?" Carol asked.

"Freezing," said Lori. "Dank, wet, humid, cold. I tried to have a garden, believe me." She took the shears that Carol handed her, and they both went out back past the kennel to where the rose bushes were.

Carol put on a baseball cap to shield her face from the sun and a pair of leather gloves; the only pair she could offer Lori were her husband's and much too big. "This is my favorite cultivar," she said, touching an intricate cluster of mauve petals. "Lavender Pinocchio—I got it at the Huntington last year at their sale. Here, sniff."

Lori breathed it in like a victim rescued from smoke inhalation. "Oh my. Oh, that's amazing. The only things that grew in my yard in Montreal were dandelions and some sort of pestiferous ground ivy. Sad to say, even that was so much better than the snow that I thought they were beautiful."

"You probably learned to speak French," said Carol, who had never learned anything in a foreign language except *Apaga la pinchi soplador de hojas.*

"Mmm," said Lori. "I did. But now I can't speak it without weeping."

Carol opened her mouth but then shut it again. She didn't need to give any pruning advice—Lori was doing it exactly right, removing the dead flowers and the suckers, cutting just at the right spot as if she had the mind of a rosebush and could feel exactly what would make it bloom again.

That was always what she had admired about Lori: her easy expertise with absolutely anything mechanical or physical, from screwdrivers the size of the head of a pin to the two-ton electron microscope she'd moved with a forklift. Everyone had panicked when it started to fall, but Lori had moved the vehicle an infinitesimal nudge to one side, and it stood right up again. If it had been anyone else, the thing would have crashed to the ground, probably destroying the building in the process.

Now Carol risked making Lori mad with an insensitive comment, but curiosity had gotten the better of her. "Yeah," she said sympathetically. "I heard Roger died." Actually, Absinthe had told her that Roger drowned himself because Lori wouldn't go out with him, but such details were unnecessary.

Lori stuck the pruning shears into her pocket and ran her arms around the rosebush, checking the symmetry perhaps, but she appeared to be embracing it. "He jumped off a bridge," she said. "In February."

The February part seemed superfluous until Carol thought about the water underneath being frozen, and then she shuddered. "That's horrible. Why?"

"Why?" Lori didn't sound angry, just tired. "Because he had major depression; because he'd had it since he was fourteen; and because I was so arrogant that I thought I could help, that after not even speaking to him for ten years I could appear out of the blue and make everything better with my stupid advice." She sighed and moved over to the next rosebush, a China white.

"Careful!" Carol cautioned automatically. "You deadhead those gently, the buds only." She was still on her first rosebush, but then, she had never moved so swiftly as Lori in anything. "You can't blame yourself for someone else's illness," she said after a long moment. "You know that I was pretty messed up back then in graduate school. You couldn't cure me, but all the times you were nice to me counted for something."

Lori looked baffled, as if searching her mind in vain for the shared memory. "I was *nice* to you?" she muttered, looking the other way and turning a bit pink.

"Yes, you were! All I ever got from the rest of them, including Abby, was 'Just eat!' or comments about my fat butt, or cruel songs about me throwing up, or offers of a home lobotomy."

Lori laughed mirthlessly. "That's what Roger needed. A big, fat lobotomy. And there I was telling him to stay away from the doctors." She turned her head away and Carol closed her eyes, afraid to see Lori cry since she knew there could be no greater humiliation than to break down in front of a boson.

But Lori didn't cry, she only sneezed, and then she started laughing and sat in the grass. Henry the duck ran over and bit her ankles, but she didn't seem to care.

Carol came and sat next to her, and they howled in remembrance of the absurd cruelties and ridiculous obsessions that had run their lives for more than half a decade.

"Maybe he needed five hundred milliCoulombs of happiness!" Carol suggested. "Do you remember that?"

"Poor Roger." Lori was still laughing. "He had such a phobia of psychiatrists that you had to laugh. Who would ever know that federal regulations limit not the voltage in volts, not the current in amperes, but the total charge in milliCoulombs delivered to your brain during electroshock therapy?"

"And remember when we all visited him in the mental hospital? We tried to give him his homework, and he yelled, 'I will never be happy, never!'"

"'Not unless it's five hundred milliCoulombs of happiness!'" they both chorused, rolling on the lawn.

"It inspired Kurt so much, that's what he called his rock band after he dropped out," Carol reminded Lori.

"Oh man," Lori gasped, "I am so glad I'm not in grad school anymore. But you know what?" She tugged at the grass. "I hate the people I work with. We're all so shallow—we'd watch babies being trampled and just think 'How will this affect my grant proposal?'"

"You need friends away from work." Carol couldn't believe that she was giving advice to Lori or, even worse, that Lori just nodded in response. "If I were with engineers all the time, I'd go crazy. I know it's different for you because you have to work so hard to get tenure, but you have to give yourself some 'me time' now and then. I'm almost ten years older than you, you know."

Lori half smiled and half frowned, as if not sure whether she was being called a kid or a not-so-old lady. "I know."

"And I've found that one of the most important things in the desert is to take care of your skin. My friend makes organic natural sunscreen; I'll give you some. Would you like a duck-egg facial?"

In an instant they were giggling in the way that Bob hated, rooting in the duck pen to get that morning's eggs and cracking them in a little bowl to smear all over their faces. Carol had never heard Lori giggle, but right now there was nothing more fun than playing at being shallow SoCal girls and letting the thick, gooey duck egg stretch away the decade that had passed since they had last met.

"You deserve to be happy," said Carol. "You deserve to find someone who loves you."

Lori laughed and smiled and hugged her—things she wouldn't have done for anyone back in graduate school, not even for Radhika. The charm lasted until she left, but once Lori had washed her face and strapped on her orange skates and disappeared, Carol figured she'd never see her again unless it was in a TV broadcast from Stockholm.

FOUR: POUND PUPPIES

WORSE THAN THE DREAM about having signed up for a class and forgetting to do the homework was the dream about being in elementary school again. Lori had only begun to have that dream after turning thirty, and for some reason the imagined humiliation was overwhelming. She'd be squished into a little desk, knowing full well she had a PhD in physics, but somehow no one else would realize it and would continue to make her recite the multiplication table.

The situation could have felt comparable, crouched in the backseat of an ancient Honda Civic driven by a Russian postdoc, on her way to Palm Springs and the new student retreat. She was sandwiched between between the Father of Quantum Gravity, Professor Rose, and his wife, with her first advisor, Dr. van Gnubbern, riding shotgun. Seatbelt-less, knees hitting her chin, she was a kid again, but it made her feel warm and fuzzy the way nothing had since she had left the embrace of STI sixteen years ago. She could forget how she was supposed to betray and stab van Gnubbern, and recall the kinder and gentler physics department of days past, where they were all just there to learn and play the occasional prank.

This same weekend, she knew, the incoming freshmen were off on a deserted island being picked for their Houses.

"Do they still do the Selection the same way?" she wondered out loud, remembering her night in a pine tree thinking there was a bear lurking below. "With the tents that are impossible to pitch and starting fires by rubbing sticks?"

"They've made it easier for the younger generation," sighed van Gnubbern.

"At least they're left in the wilderness with nothing but a topo map and a compass, I hope!"

"Well, sure," said Rose, "but they have their cell phones now."

"Last year they manage to get pizza delivery," chortled the Russian postdoc.

"Lori, you were the last of the true Buboes," said van Gnubbern wistfully. "Do all of you remember the papaya incident?"

"Exaggerated," Lori protested.

"You didn't rappel off the library carrying a twenty-pound Mexican papaya?"

"Sure I did. But the part afterwards is apocryphal. Does anyone remember what we did to the elevator in the physics building? I remember it breaking, but I can't remember why."

"You weren't just riding on top?" Rose suggested.

"It's the Fucking Ferret Freaks who do that."

"An obviously unworthy prank," Rose smiled ironically. Seventy years after he had been a freshman, he still wore a black sweater with a tiny embroidered ferret clutching a capital letter Φ in its paws. "I seem to recall that you were going to try to disguise the elevator as a classroom, so that people would seat themselves and then panic when it began to move."

"That's right!" Lori couldn't believe she'd forgotten that one. "The cable broke when we dragged the desks in there. I still feel bad when Lou has to wait five minutes before the thing starts working."

There was a slightly uncomfortable pause, followed inevitably by the rush of gossip that only physicists could provide about an absent colleague. Most of it was rubbish, the sort of "he's so brave" nonsense that made Lori's stomach turn, but she listened assiduously for any real information.

"Can't say he's not dedicated. He managed to finish his big NSF proposal in the ICU," commented Rose.

"Even better, it got funded." Van Gnubbern sounded envious. "Maybe I'll try writing my next grant in a morphine haze."

"But he had to spend the money right away, so he kept on grad students rather indiscriminately," Mrs. Rose observed. "They were really a handful for a while from what I hear."

Van Gnubbern made a snort of disgust. "I refuse to believe that second-year physics graduate students need close supervision. They're adults, and all they do for the first two years is take classes, especially the theorists. Why, Lori here was only thirteen years old, and I used to leave her alone at the microscope all day long in that cold room in the basement. She worked until her fingers were blue. I had to buy her a parka."

"Is that why you used to walk across campus in the parka?" murmured Rose. "I thought you were concealing something."

"I probably was," Lori admitted. Only a small stab of remorse assailed her as she casually asked van Gnubbern, "Who does the microscopy now? Do you have any students?"

"You were my last and best," replied van Gnubbern. "No one funds that kind of thing anymore. If I want to do a little electron microscopy, sometimes the technician in the basement helps out, but mostly I do it myself."

"The problem, Bert," Rose persisted, "is that the grad students *are* adults, and they have adult problems. You can't just fail them out, or they'll have you in court. That one of Lou's we couldn't shake, he kept coming back wanting to re-do his thesis proposal even after he'd clearly failed. And then there's the woman—"

"That's who I was thinking of," his wife admitted. "Maybe now that we have a female faculty member we can prevent some of that."

"Oh no!" Lori blurted. "Don't palm off the nutty nymphos on me!"

They all laughed, but in a good way. "You haven't changed a bit, Lori," said van Gnubbern.

"Of course I haven't."

"But you must," Rose warned. "Things are different now. Don't fail anyone; don't insult anyone; and for heaven's sake, don't sleep with anyone."

"And please no killings," added van Gnubbern. "Unless we order them, of course."

That was in somewhat bad taste, and everyone grew quiet. Lori turned to look out the window—the desert had changed as much as she had, and as much as she could never be a careless little Bubo again, nor would the broad expanses of sand between L.A. and Palm Springs ever recapture their wild barren beauty. The dunes were now pockmarked with hideous mini-mansions, each sporting a lawn and a swimming pool. Not even God knew where the water came from. Mega shopping malls, flat and reddish like Kaposi's sarcomas, sprouted within SUV range of what had once been ghost towns.

Palm Springs was teeming with human activity, but at least it was torrid. Lori liked torrid. Even the concept of torrid was reassuring since it could never, under any circumstances, be applied to Canada. The very first thing she did when they arrived at the hotel was put on her bathing suit, walk slowly to the pool in the unbelievable heat, and bounce about for a while. She didn't even bother to swim, just enjoyed the feeling of her unsubmerged parts desiccating and baking instantly before being plunged into the warm water yet again.

She didn't feel like changing into real clothes, but was still a little needled about the idea of her blue and orange Roller-Montreal skinsuit becoming the next tutu-man costume, so she waited a couple of minutes in the sun to dry out before putting on a pair of jeans and T-shirt ("MIT" on the front; "they're losers, STI" on the back) over her bathing suit. It turned out to be the perfect outfit, because the first order of fun in the pound-puppy show was a game of Strip Integration.

They were in a big theater room with padded carpeting, foldy chairs, and a deep stage with velvet curtains. There was seating for about five hundred; it was hard to gauge how many people were there—or which of them she knew—since everyone was so scattered about. The six-foot whiteboard and laptop projector on the stage seemed too technological for the setting, as did the six new graduate students, whom the stage lights rendered paler and geekier than usual. Clutching the famous *Table of Integrals, Series, and Products*, they would write a chosen problem on either side of the whiteboard and two professors would start solving it simultaneously. The last to finish had to take off an item of clothing.

Rose and Kuzno were at each other's throats by the end of it, scowling and slashing with their pens. Lori was pleased to see the department head finally reduced to his half-length European style bathing trunks while Rose still sported his "What Part of [the equations of General Relativity] Don't you Understand?" T-shirt and Bermudas. Cheers and jeers erupted from various parts of the room, presumably reflecting the two professors' research groups, but whether their loyalties lay for or against their bosses Lori couldn't tell.

Rose held his signature pink pen aloft and began to re-don his clothing. "Who's the next challenger?"

"That is so demeaning and sexist," snapped a voice from behind Lori's shoulder.

Lori spun around to find a woman of twenty-five, give or take, with two sharp little pigtails poking out of the sides of her head. The pigtails alone had been dyed bright orange; the rest of her head was an ordinary brown. She had braces on her teeth. Student? Postdoc? Secretary? Paramour? "What, you think there should be a women's division?"

"There's not a single woman here who would take part in such a humiliating exercise."

So of course Lori got on the stage, waving her arms and challenging the Father of Quantum Gravity to an integration contest. Half in jest, she asked for special dispensation as a member of the "unfair sex." "At least give me the pink pen."

"No way," Rose objected, hugging it to his chest. "It's lucky."

A chant of "Barrow, Barrow, Barrow" started up in the opposite corner from the pigtail girl. She didn't know any of her fans; from this distance, they all seemed to have ridiculous hair, curled or dyed bright colors or extraordinarily long.

If she'd known she'd be up against Solomon Rose, she would have studied. And she lost. It was close only because she moved a little quicker and the pink pen seemed to be running out of ink, forcing him to stop and shake it now and then. In the end, she was left in her bathing suit (one-piece and black, thank God) while he retained his tie and a single flower-topped rubber slipper in addition to the Bermuda shorts.

"Cheat! Cheat!" yelled the weird-hair gang. "He dropped an *i*!"

"Complex analysis is all just fun and games till someone loses an *i*," Rose scolded through the microphone as his group came up to crown him champion. He had apparently won for years in a row, because the crown was some kind of deformed quasi-religious relic chosen just for him—a crown of thorns made of plastic roses. It sounded as if a group of students had found it one year in a gay sex shop in town and bought it assuming that Rose would win the contest as usual.

"And now," Rose continued, beaming from under the crown, still wearing only one flip-flop, "I'd like you all to meet Lori Barrow, the newest member of our faculty. She was an undergraduate here, a Bubo of course, and is famous for many reasons. I'll only mention the good ones." The weird-hair contingent hooted and cheered horribly. "First of all, she was the youngest undergraduate to ever finish a physics degree at STI—though only the second-youngest to ever matriculate. I'll leave it to you all to look this other person up. Second, she once rappelled off the library, dangling from her ankles and carrying a papaya about yay big."

Lori stood behind Rose, shaking her head and making "loony" signs around her temples, but there was no stopping him.

"Now, it just so happened that the president of our esteemed institution was having a meeting with some trustees a couple floors down. He looked out just as our favorite undergrad here decided to smash the papaya all over her head. Thinking that he was seeing the remains of blood and brains, the president fainted dead away. And," Rose concluded over the laughter, "the very next week announced his retirement! We now have a new president— and no more rail around the roof of the library. With that, Lori." He handed her the microphone.

It was all a bit overwhelming, and gazing out over the shadowed faces she suddenly felt shy. She stammered a few lines about her research; was sure she'd made a terrible gaffe by saying she looked forward to working in the basement, allowing van Gnubbern to see her treachery from a mile away; and then gave up before she lost her composure completely. "But this day is for the students," she said, only slightly hypocritically. "I understand you've been preparing skits for a while, so come on up."

Relieved to get off that stage, Lori went to go sit with the hair gang in order to find out who they were and how they knew her, but they dashed out of the room snickering before she could get near them. She returned to her old seat near the ponytail girl—a mistake.

"Can't you make them stop?" the girl whispered right in Lori's ear.

Lori jumped. "What? Who?"

"Didn't you see them leave? They're going to do something really cruel. It's just so wrong."

"I'm sorry," said Lori, who by now was so curious that she had no intention of stopping anyone. "It's not my position to tell them what to do. I don't even know who they are."

"They're the Maupertuis group," whispered the girl, "as am I," she added with a little whine, as if used to always being left out.

Aha, Lori thought, so you're the problem child. "Where's Lou?"

"He's not here. I'm sure he's home sick, and he has a phobia of freeways. So do I, you know: I have a restricted visual field, and the motion makes me so disorientated."

Do I need a tattoo on my forehead saying *NO TMI*? Lori wondered, tuning the girl out by thinking of how Roger used to lecture people who used the word *disorientated*, explaining with a delicate shudder that *disoriented* was a perfect synonym without containing that discordant extra syllable.

The skits mostly went right by her, since she didn't know many people and was a little clueless when it came to sexual innuendo. It was obvious, though, that everyone was afraid to make fun of Kuzno. His group, all Russians, performed a song about neutron stars that was kind of cute but reeked of censorship.

That only made it more obvious that what came next was trouble. As soon as the Russians had received their polite applause from the audience and praise from Kuzno, the lights went out. Shadows could be seen moving about the stage, and a couple of spotlights lit up the strategic figures.

The smallest male member of Lou's group had tied orange yarn to the sides of his head (since the rest of his hair was green, the effect was quite odd) and was sitting on the edge of the stage holding a teddy bear and sucking his thumb. Worse, the tallest member was teetering on some kind of platform shoes, and if this weren't obvious enough, had a sign hung around his neck reading HEAD. Lori watched him intently, but he stood off to one side, arms folded, expression grim.

Then the spot moved off towards the center and the guy with the longest hair, an immense tangle of chestnut curls, swaggered to center stage waving a sheaf of papers in one hand, a coffee cup in the other, and laughing a villain's cackle. "With this NSF proposal, I own the department! You are all my slaves, you are mine body and soul!" He gave a resonating ominous laugh, like something from a 1940s film noir.

Then there was the sound of a gunshot off-stage. The villain screamed, dropped the papers, and somersaulted into the stage wings.

The guy in front with the pigtails took his thumb out of his mouth, threw down the teddy bear, and grabbed the sheaf. "Hee hee hee," he giggled in a falsetto. "I got the proposal! I got the proposal!"

The spotlight turned from the thumbsucker onto the HEAD, who slowly, slowly unfolded his arms and started to move towards the papers. "Oh no you don't, my pretty," he drawled. "It's all mine, after I have my way with you—"

Not surprisingly, the lights and sound went dead. There were some scuffling noises, mutters of "Oh yeah, who says?" and, strangely enough, an indistinct woman's voice. The woman held the microphone when the lights were restored on the now-empty stage. She was a very young woman, younger than any of the grad students, and not anyone that Lori could place.

"Well, everyone," she declared cheerily, "I think that was our last skit. The buffet will be served in the courtyard between six-thirty and nine-thirty. Please take the opportunity to get to know your colleagues. And welcome to the entering class of future PhDs!"

What a crock, Lori thought. She turned around and noticed that the pigtail girl was crying. Not in the mood for any more TMI, she got up and ran.

It was still hot out. Students and professors arranged themselves under parasols by the fountain, helping themselves to fruit salad and tostada fillings. Lori filled her plate with salsa and jalapenos, an old summer camp tune running through her head: *I love you California in the summer when it's hot*....In the English part of Montreal, a buffet meant little sandwiches on white bread held together with mayonnaise, potato salad drowned in so much mayonnaise that the potatoes looked like clams, greasy chips, and cheap pastries. There had been months where she would have mugged someone for a hot pepper.

She realized now that of course she knew who Lou was. The combination of the way Americans butchered his name and the lack of his trademark long hair had confused her, but of course someone who'd come to

STI as a professor at the age of twenty-eight was known throughout the field. She still didn't think she'd ever seen him in person, but she had once spent an hour on a train with a graduate student who raged nonstop about the asshole jerk in their group who was nothing but a lazy theorist and who kept insisting the data were inconclusive, thus forcing hardworking experimentalists like himself to return over and over to the South Pole. Somehow, this bum of a theorist kept winning all the awards and getting all the recognition while he suffered, froze to death, and got called "Beaker" by the scientist-hating hardhats at the Pole.

Ordinarily this would have been a forgettable conversation, but it had remained in her mind all these years (when was it? Four years ago, maybe) because the guy had had dirty, somewhat bluish, four-inch fingernails. Of course he had caught her staring, and told her that at the South Pole, something about the cold and altitude made people's fingernails not grow. Somehow, this had inspired him to swear not to cut them until he finished his PhD.

"So what does the asshole theorist do?" he sneered, clacking the appendages together. "He tells me if I don't cut my nails, he won't cut his hair, and we'll see who gets the most chicks! There's plenty of girls who like long nails, right, baby?"

Lori had fled the compartment retching, and even now in the heat of the desert she shivered to remember it.

Sweeping away the memory, she went up for seconds and looked around for a group to join, thinking that she should at least try to meet the new students even if she didn't hire them. She couldn't just hide behind van Gnubbern—he was not really her colleague. Physics had been different when he was getting established, when all a theorist needed was a pencil and a sheet of paper. Now it took two million dollars of NSF money and your soul.

"Dr. Barrow!" bellowed a voice from a large table. It was the guy with the curls, the one who had played Lou in the skit.

Lori took her plate over but didn't sit down, thinking it might be disreputable to be seen with them. There were four of them, the three from the skit and a Chinese guy who listened carefully but didn't seem to speak.

"Hi, everyone," she said, struggling with the line between formality and over-friendliness. "Um, thanks for cheering for me. I didn't have a chance against Professor Rose."

"You were *awesome*," said the fake Lou, slapping the table the way the real one always did. "Especially since you shut up Marybeth." He shoved a fragment of tostada into his mouth.

"Marybeth," squeaked the guy who'd played her. He was still carrying the teddy bear. "Oh, poor Marybeth."

Lori waited a minute for explanation as to who Marybeth might be. When it wasn't forthcoming, she demanded bluntly, "Who?"

"'That is so demeaning and sexist,' they all mocked as a chorus, doing a very good job of capturing her strangely raspy voice.

"Oh," replied Lori. Not even mildly interested in what this crew knew about that sad and sorry girl, she asked, "How'd you know who I was?"

There was a pause—then the table erupted in howling laughter. "How did we know who you *were*?" squealed the guy who'd played Kuzno. "Oh! She asks it with a straight face!"

Lori felt her cheeks get hot and made a show of sniffing her fruit punch. "What's in this stuff? Damn." Her stomach began to get the better of her social insecurities, so she finally tugged over a chair and pushed her way in between the Chinese student and the Marybeth. "At least tell me who you guys are," she commanded, chomping into a Serrano chili. "Since I don't know your names, I keep thinking of you as the characters you played, and it's screwing with my mind."

The fake Lou cackled. "Weren't we the best?"

"Till we were interrupted—"

"By that bitch—"

"Kuzno's 'wife'—"

"Formerly his *under*graduate assistant—"

"Say it all together, kids: EEeeeeeeewwwwwwwwww."

"I'm Sam." The fake Lou offered Lori his hand. His voice must have been a fake too, because when he was himself he had a New York accent. "Did you like my Demon Laugh? And the Memorial Walk?"

"Awwww," said Lori, not sure if she was being sarcastic or not. "Isn't that sweet? You've immortalized his swagger for posterity. I haven't heard him laugh like that, though."

"You will," promised Sam. "That he can still do. The Walk is trickier. Ideally, it's done with a twenty-ounce coffee cup with no lid, and you can't spill."

"We felt so bad when he was paralyzed that we all grew freaky hair." It was the first time the fake Marybeth had spoken in a normal voice, but he addressed his teddy bear instead of Lori. His own hairdo was a rather simple bowl cut, but dyed a scary transgenic green. At least the yarn was gone. "'Cause he cut all his off in the hospital." He clammed up again and had to be prompted gently for his name, which was Brian. "Or Brain—I'm dyslexic," he offered cordially.

The HEAD, who had blond dreadlocks and was eating pineapple squares out of a bowl with his fingers, was next. "I'm Alexander. They made me play this vile role—" he pointed at the sign still around his neck—"because I have the same first name as our six-foot-eight embodiment of departmental evil." He put a hand on Lori's shoulder, and after glancing around once, brought his pineapply lips all the way to her ear and barely expelled air as he spoke. "I know for a fact that Kuznetsov was stealing Dr. Lou's pain pills when he got out of the hospital. Fact."

"To take himself?" Lori wondered. "Or to sell?"

"No, dummy," he said out loud. "To fuck our boss up so he could get his cash and *us*."

"You guys are scaring me," she admitted.

"Be scared," said Brian. "And take our advice—don't hire just anyone because you have money. Otherwise you end up with—"

"Marybeth," they all squealed at once.

"The first-years are right behind us at that table," Sam pointed out. "There are six of them, waiting to be adopted." He folded his hands into paws and panted.

"I know," replied Lori, who didn't really need the visual. "I even know their names."

"But are they any good?" Alex quizzed.

"On paper, well—"

"Never mind on paper."

"I'm not sure yet," Lori admitted. "I'm still feeling kind of traumatized."

"Let us do it!" They were the first words out of the Chinese student's mouth.

"Yeah," said Alex. "We'll go talk to them, and then we'll tell you who's good and who sucks."

Lori had a feeling that this was a very bad plan, but she was certainly not up to speaking to the first-years tonight. All she wanted was to bounce a bit in the swimming pool, drink some more fruit punch, and crawl off to bed.

Fortunately, the pool was all the way around on the other side of the hotel, so she could sneak off without anyone stopping her. The boisterous voices became more and more remote, and she started to relax as she thought that no one would be in swimming and that she would be left alone.

But no, there was one person there, swimming laps ceaselessly and seemingly without tiring. He was an excellent swimmer but didn't seem to know how to do flip turns: he did them funny and pushed off the wall with both hands.

It was Lou, of course. Refusing to acknowledge the presence of anyone or anything, he continued swimming, and finally Lori slipped into the water and swam beside him. The pace seemed easy at first, but after twenty minutes or so she was getting pretty tired. Radhika always told her that her technique was wretched and that she relied on brute force and ignorance.

That combination did at least get her to a pause. "Aha," said Lou, emptying out his swim goggles. He peered at her intensely before replacing them. "Thought it might be you." His chest was tan and muscular without any trace of a scar.

"What are you doing out here? You missed the skits and everything."

To Lori's immense surprise, he grinned and treated her to a perfectly executed example of the Demon Laugh. "Are you kidding? I was the one working the spotlights. Weren't they wonderful?"

"The spotlights or your students?" It was hard to imagine what was wonderful about implying that he had been shot on purpose, or that the department head had raped Marybeth.

"My juvenile delinquents. I'm so proud."

If they had been grad students, the workout would have been immediately forgotten in a passionate exchange of intimate details about their fellows—who was smart, who was dumb, who was slutty, who could not be trusted. Lori felt poignantly how different this was. As the only two non-tenured members of the faculty, she and Lou were there to judge each other, not only to decide whether they could tolerate working together for a half-century but whether they could remake a dying department in their image. They weren't in direct competition—if they succeeded, the university would almost certainly tenure them both—but they were in a lot of trouble if they couldn't get along.

"You seem to enjoy being a pain in the ass, Lou," Lori remarked in her best older-and-wiser tone. "That's fine if you're smart and productive enough to justify it, otherwise…"

"Otherwise you'll try to kill me, too?" he wondered, with an expression she couldn't read because of the goggles. "Just do a better job than the first guy, OK?"

Lori hid her shock by pretending she hadn't heard that and by reminding him that they were there to exercise. "Another thousand meters?" she suggested, looking at her stopwatch.

In the end they swam much further than that, forgetting for a blissful hour that they were STI's youngest physics professors as they reveled in the warmth of the water and the glint of the setting crescent moon in the clear desert sky.

FIVE: YELLOW JACK

LORI GOT MARYBETHED.

She was going to slap Lou. He had asked her to come in really early so they could arrange their teaching assignments for the term, since he had a big meeting with the lawyers for the NSF subcontract all the rest of the day. Nothing was going to get in the way of that meeting, which had apparently been delayed several times already, usually due to his own health. Not by any means a morning person and still sleeping on the floor because the moving van had been delayed somewhere in the Midwest (weather already), she had only motivated herself out the door and down the hill by thinking that she would be teaching physics at Feynman's university.

There was hardly a course that she hadn't taken as an undergrad, and every one had been such a classic that it seemed heresy for her to even imagine taking one over. Rose, of course, taught field theory and general relativity. If anyone other than Kuznetsov had non-equilibrium statistical mechanics, the world would come to an end. Senior/ graduate quantum mechanics was and had always been van Gnubbern's, and she was already preparing to betray him once; that was enough.

There were always the freshman and sophomore classes, which would put her in contact with another generation of Buboes, Ferrets, Thorns, and Snots and show how undergraduate life had been transformed by such recent inventions as the Internet. There were at least three tracks for Physics 1, including the honors section, which was usually not worth it because the students, 80% Bubo, thought they were above going to class and would leave tape recorders or nothing at all (were tape recorders Ancient Geek History now?). A regular section could be fine, since the "average" STImpy was still in the top 0.5% of graduating seniors.

So long as it wasn't Physics P. She recalled with a shudder of horror, almost not braking in time for a stoplight, that Solomon Rose had told her the new administration had insisted upon the creation of a remedial physics class for those who came unprepared (unprepared! To STI!) or more to the point, those who were (his words) "kind of hopeless."

The class was 100% female and 80% Snot. Call it prejudice, but to Lori's mind the residents of Snodgrass would never be good for anything except working at the gym. If Lou so much as breathed the words *Physics P* to her, she was going to put a bullet in him. Another one.

Lori had arrived way too early—she was getting better at descending, even though it turned her feet to hamburger—and had changed and washed her face in the downstairs bathroom. There would never be a women's room on the theory floor. Wearing normal clothes and having tucked her skates away in her backpack (washed of its Canadian dirt), she mounted the stairs like a responsible and grown-up physics professor, albeit one with slightly bloody socks.

Lou's office had been open and his light was on, and—pleased that he was early, too—she'd marched in without knocking. She froze as she caught sight of the orange pigtails.

Marybeth was printing something from Lou's computer and jumped slightly when she saw Lori. "Dr. Barrow!'"

"Ms Coleman," said Lori curtly, thinking, *Oui, on se vouvoie, ma 'tite maudite.*

"I was just printing out some stuff for the meeting this morning. But I really wanted to talk to you."

That's when Lori started to smell a set-up, because as eight o'clock came and went, there was still no sign of Lou, and Marybeth was begging her for a job.

Ordinarily, Lori could handle this situation just fine. But interspersed with the desire to do experiments, Marybeth offered details of a childhood and adolescence so horrific that it was like a sick joke, the blind crippled kid who got cancer for Christmas.

It couldn't possibly all have been true. There were contradictions right and left—Marybeth had allegedly survived 9/11 as an infant—but if even 10% of the abuse she described were remotely plausible, it was a miracle that she was alive, free, and in graduate school. Besides, the tone of her voice was all wrong: she sounded blithe and flippant, emphasizing each horrific event with a slow, grating enunciation of every word. It was enough to make Lori want to pour acid in her own ears, but some horrible fascination kept her rooted to the spot.

"This is a souvenir from my mother!" cried Marybeth, raising a left arm that presumably was supposed to be scarred and twisted in some way, but which looked perfectly normal. "She didn't approve of left-handers, so when she caught me writing with my left hand she broke my wrist in seven places. It still doesn't move right, and so I write with my right. I'm actually perfectly ambidextrous, but I can't write in cursive. I got away from her when I was fifteen, but I was homeless in Santa Monica for seven years...."

A train wreck would have been more pleasant. It was such a relief when Lou showed up that she didn't notice at first that he was covered with dust and furious.

"You guys are in *here*!" he exclaimed, talking way too fast. "Dammit, Lori! I dialed your number but never thought of calling my own. The elevator is now officially out of order." He held up his hands to show them how dirty they were.

"What did you do?" Lori inquired, impressed. "Climb the cable hand-over-hand?"

"Yeah, right. It was a lot less dignified than that. Christ, I have to print out the proposal budget and look over it. It made no sense at all to me last night."

Interrupting herself in mid-tale, Marybeth was suddenly all business. "*I* did that, Dr. Lou," she declared proudly, holding up the printer output. "And then what I did, I underlined the people in red, the numbers for the first year in blue, and the overheads in green. I made a copy for everyone, I re-did all the figures for the raises...."

She only knows one pronoun, Lori thought, feeling the ball of horror in her stomach slowly begin to dissolve. Clearly those two didn't need her and she could leave, but she stayed anyway, uncomfortable somehow with the fact that Lou didn't know anything about his own budget. The administrative part of proposal writing wasn't Lori's forte either (pronounced with a silent *e* because it was a French word; Oh Roger, how I miss thee!), but she had always had help from secretaries who were trustworthy, not Marybeth.

"I am such a retard when it comes to arithmetic that it is not even funny," grumbled Lou, dusting off his white shirt. Marybeth stood far, far away, as if he were trying to hit her. "See what happens when I attempt to look respectable? But seriously, it seems as if the subcontract to the LPR Lab is too big. I'm not going to have enough left to support my group."

"I recalculated it, and it's because of the overhead expenditures, I put those in green," Marybeth repeated in her strident voice.

Lou finally acknowledged Lori. "Oh my Gawd," he said, establishing once and for all that he was a native of Southern California. "Barrow, I am so sorry we missed our meeting. This department is too flaky to get us courses to teach, because if you cross the old guys, watch out. Look, fast: you can take graduate level classical mechanics or Math Methods, easier for me if I do MM since I did it last year."

Lori enjoyed making prof-talk too fast over Marybeth's head. "Classical uses Goldstein?"

"Of course. First class is Wednesday. Can you handle it on such short notice?"

"No problem. I have my notes from sixteen years ago—if the moving van shows up."

"You're my hero. Do it well and I will kiss your feet."

"Ew! Anything but my feet, I have blisters the size of a loonie. Good luck with the lawyers, rich boy. Don't let the LEPERLab bleed you dry." She wanted to make eye contact, to try to signal Don't trust Marybeth!, but he was already absorbed in the color-coded printouts as his student explained once again what she had done.

There were two messages on her office phone. The first, strangely formal and sheepish, was from Lou: "This is Lou Maupertuis, you know, your new colleague. It's five to eight, and if you would come to the south stairs, I could use your brain or brawn or both." The second (At last!) was from her movers, Les Déménageurs assidus. "*On s'en vient chez vous cet après-midi,*" said a working-class Montreal voice, already sounding so foreign. "*Tcheke pour qu'il y ait pas de neige dans ton stationnement.*"

She laughed. Making sure her driveway was clear of snow for the moving van was a request she would have no problem fulfilling. Teaching a graduate-level class at STI was another matter, but it was exactly the kind of challenge that filled her with joy. Leaving the building in a state of euphoria, like a kid let out of school, she stopped at the bookstore for the newest edition of the textbook by Goldstein.

The book was so heavy that it made her tip forward twice on the way home, and she didn't attempt the driveway at all. This way she would appreciate Goldstein even more, like everything that had cost her an effort to haul or drag or push home. She had just made herself a peanut butter sandwich and settled down to refresh her memory of tensor calculus when she heard the grinding of gears in the driveway that told her the stuff had arrived at last.

She'd moved the cheap way, getting one-third of the space in a truck and five hours to unpack it herself before they took it away to its next desti-nation. Living in a split-level with the house down the stairs didn't make things easy, though, especially because it was nearing one hundred and ten degrees in the sun. She was recovering from Canada, but this was ridiculous. She was lucky not to be a furniture person—there was a bed (single) and a coffee table, and apart from that it was sports equipment, tools, and books. Five bikes, spare wheels, the work stand, and all of the tools just got shoved into the garage to be dealt with later. She'd forgotten how many books there were, though, even with all the physics texts being sent directly to work. After the dozenth trip down the stairs and her half-dozenth glass of lemonade, she started to wonder if Roger's old linguistic treatises really had that much sentimental value after all. She hadn't wanted to leave anything of his behind, but face it, he had read some dull shit, half of it in Finnish, Urdu, or Serbo-Croat.

She imagined he was there with her—he would be telling her all about the history of the boring books, each with its story or purpose. He would talk about the time he was in Prague and met Vaclav Havel, and had wanted to ask a question about *The Garden Party* but had forgotten the neuter plural declensions in the instrumental case. Naturally this would be exaggerating for dramatic effect, since Roger never forgot his instrumental plurals, even though he sometimes forgot how to find his way home on the metro. They would have a clever method to pass the boxes down the stairs, minimizing the number of steps they each had to take in the hot sun.

Actually, it was Radhika she wanted for this, Radhika who, like a mango tree, thrived better the hotter it got. The swimmer with biceps like coconuts who would take three boxes of books or more, limited only by the length of her arms. She, who used to get so pissed when guys would offer (insist!) to help her carry things but had learned to say sweetly and patronizingly, "Oh no, it's much too heavy for you." There had been a time, in the first year of grad school, where Lori had had to force her to go to the gym instead of studying all night, but no doubt she was incredibly fit over there in Darwin. Her shoulders were probably bigger than Lou's, even.

It was a good thing she didn't like Lou, because this brick path would be really something for him to navigate. The tree roots had grown under it and destabilized all the bricks, which wobbled and broke loose under her feet like decayed teeth. She should fix them anyway, even if he was a jerk.

She was pathetic. It was one thing to be a sixteen-year-old virgin, quite another to be a week away from thirty-three (Lou wouldn't even be thirty for nine weeks!) and to have had only two partners in her entire life, both of them classmates from graduate school. Why did it always seem as if her last real emotions had been felt in graduate school?

By the time she was done, the sun was starting to set. It was cooling off a little, and she was out of lemonade. The tree in back still had lemons, but she needed sugar— she needed groceries, period. Now that she had the mountain bike with the trailer she could roll into town and get everything; it was just too bad she lived on top of the hill.

When the phone rang, there was a long pause after her "Hello?" She figured it was a wrong number or telemarketer and was about to hang up when a man spoke.

The voice made her blood run cold in the summer twilight. She had forgotten how militaristic the United States had become, and hadn't heard a tone of voice like that in five years. "Is this Dr. Lori Barrow from the physics department at Superior Technological Institute?"

She had to fight the instinct to deny it. He was obviously a cop. "Who is this?"

"We need you to come down to St. Vitus's Memorial Hospital. There's been an incident."

It wasn't the police station. It wasn't the police station even if the guy was a cop. "An incident? Was anyone hurt?"

Her heart thudded against her ribcage even though, honestly, what did she care about anyone in this town? "We're not sure yet," he said at last. "We need you to drive down here and talk to us."

Drive, of course, being Angeleno for "displace by any means." Hesitating between her road bike (faster) and her winter bike (worth fifteen dollars at best, in Canadian), she chose the latter. The rate of bike theft in this town wasn't astronomical —who would bother when there were Lexus SUVs to steal?—but the hospital was in a crummy neighborhood and losing her racing bike would be a tragedy. She'd built it herself from parts, including the wheels; it was a work of art.

Not so for the rusty, salty wreck that she'd ridden for five winters. It wasn't even salt they used on the roads there but what they called *calcaire*, chalk dust that encased everything in a whitish cast. The drivetrain barely turned, and there was a big hook off the left handlebar that she'd installed to carry her Christmas tree each December, which she didn't bother to remove even though it threw things a little off balance. It was going to be an adventure coming back up the hill, especially since she'd brought the trailer for groceries, but it certainly got her down and for now that was all that mattered. Consumed by curiosity, she avoided the slow roads with the speed bumps and barreled down one of the main drags, the beginnings of rush-hour traffic going at the same speed three feet to her left.

The whole thing seemed surreal from the moment she entered the building. The emergency room used to be open—she remembered sitting there once with a broken finger and giving her medical history to a kindly nurse who wrote everything down. Now the receptionists were behind bulletproof glass and seemed unable to hear or understand anything, pushing insurance forms at her without listening to her explanation of why she was there.

Finally she felt a tap on her shoulder and turned around to find Kuzno. He was accompanied by a couple of doctors in scrubs and a fat guy with a LEPERLab badge whose role was unclear but who spoke with the cop voice she'd heard on the phone. "Follow me," he commanded. "We're in here."

The interview was surreal, too. They kept treating her as if she were an undergrad, asking if she thought "it" could be an undergraduate prank, if students had been known to "make use of biohazardous materials."

"I can't form an opinion unless I know what happened," Lori kept repeating, wondering how on Earth they could imagine she had the pulse of the STImpy student body in 2007.

Things gradually became clearer as they reluctantly parted with the details. It seemed that several people—the group of lawyers and LEPERs who had come for the grant proposal meeting—were walking past van Gnubbern's lab in the basement when they stepped in a puddle of pink liquid. The technician ran out, screamed that the freezer holding the biosafety level-3 samples had exploded, and called an ambulance to take them to St. Vitus's.

Lori realized suddenly why they had called her. She had been van Gnubbern's last student, and probably the last person at the university to go into the old BSL-3 containment lab, so long ago yet so clear in her mind. "The BSL-3 area is tiny and attached to the electron microscopy room," she recalled. "That was so the guy who was there before van Gnubbern could look at his viruses without having to carry them down the hall. He was working on"—the words came out before she could stop them—"yellow fever."

"Yellow fever!"

And then she was in a gown, mask, and gloves, being ushered into a quarantine room where they had put the remnants of the morning's leak. There were a couple of fifty-milliliter plastic Falcon tubes containing some viscous, watermelon-colored gunk and a whole bunch of smaller tubes in a plastic rack, the tape labels little more than dust after twenty-five years in the minus-eighty degree freezer.

It certainly looked like the samples she vaguely remembered, but pink liquid was pink liquid; it could have been fruit punch for all she knew. "Unless you want me to put some under the electron microscope," she offered excitedly, thinking, Maybe you can come home again.

"Oh no!" Kuzno exclaimed. "We'd better leave that to the experts."

And what am I? Just a theorist. "Well," she said to one of the doctors, deliberately turning her back on the department head, "if you want to titer it, any hepatic cell line will work, HepG2 cells if you have them."

"How do you know this?" Kuzno sounded panicked.

There were many possible responses, but she chose the most obvious. "I'm an experimentalist now, Dr. Kuznetsov. One thing that isn't right, though—the BSL-3 facility was always under negative pressure and the doors are sealed underneath. Stuff can't just leak out."

There was another one of their long pauses, and no one said anything until they had left the quarantine room and disposed of their "contaminated" gowns, masks, and gloves.

"We better let her talk to Jim Kalb," said Kuzno.

There were several long minutes of ridiculous discussion about whether it would be safe for them to go into the quarantine rooms. Finally the MDs decided that it wasn't, since even if yellow fever wasn't spread person-to-person, there could have been "other things" in the samples.

They were wrong, of course, but there was no point in arguing, especially because Jim was a lot easier to deal with behind glass. He was a creepy-looking guy, in his forties, with a scraggly little beard with pimples between the hairs. It was quite a few moments before Lori realized that the parka he was wearing had been *hers*, the one Dr. van Gnubbern had bought for her so long ago, now faded from a pale blue to a scabrous off-white. What looked like a trail of nacho cheese dust trailed down the front. He also had a scarf, little mittens, shorts, and sandals.

"Aha!" Lori exclaimed. "You must be the electron microscopy technician."

"I'm a lot more than that," spat Jim. Flecks of spittle stained the glass.

She jumped back, feeling as if she were at the zoo. "I just meant," she stammered, thinking, Watch out, or I'll tell them the samples contained rabies.

"I have a PhD from Chicago," he declared. "I do everything for the basement labs: electronics, programming, microscopy—"

Repulsively, Kuzno came to her rescue. "Yes, and Dr. Barrow is a new professor in our department, so I'm sure you will be able to be of great use to her," he interrupted dryly. "To begin, we were just wondering what exactly came to pass this morning."

Lori recollected herself quickly. "Right. First of all, what were the lawyers even doing in the basement?"

"Ha!" Jim rejoiced. "That was Marybeth. She wanted to use the color printer that Bert—Dr. van Gnubbern—has down there."

So they were on to the next cage, containing an even worse animal. After the histrionics of this morning, Lori expected some elaborate tale, but Marybeth didn't even try. "*He* made me go in the basement!" she whimpered.

"Who did?" Lori and Kuzno wondered at once.

Marybeth made pointing gestures at the wall to her right. "Dim Bulb!"

Lori bit back a laugh at the nickname, but didn't buy Marybeth's explanation for a second. "You and all the lawyers?"

"He said he wanted to show us something."

It was clear who the liar was. Sick of the zoo spectacle, she was ready to go home and write her lectures in peace, but got the final shock of the day passing by the last isolation room.

Absinthe McRae hadn't finished her first year of graduate school. She hadn't even passed the qualifying exam. Sexually harassed by a professor and stalked by at least one fellow student, she had left bitter and angry, threatening to become an intellectual property lawyer and spend her life rich, successful, and happy while the rest of them languished as postdocs. If Carol could be believed, Absinthe had held true on this threat.

So here she was, pushing forty but just as slim and blond as ever. No doubt she had had Botox, because her look of *My God, it's YOU!* fixed itself to her face and froze there.

"Hi, Abby!" Lori exclaimed. If only she had a bag of peanuts! "Isn't this cool? We're all in California now. Bummer about the yellow fever."

Laughing cruelly to hide her utter confusion at the day's events, she left the high-security hospital, got her bike, and set off in search of a grocery store.

SIX: PLEASE SLAP ME

THAT WOMAN IS A menace! Oh my God, I thought I had gotten away! What's her body count now? Five?"

Carol held the phone away from her ear. Absinthe should have been an opera singer: she had the voice for it. "Abby, it's not Lori's fault that—"

"That I'm locked up in the hospital with yellow fever? Less than a week after she's back in town!"

"You don't have yellow fever," Carol reminded her. "It's just a precaution. My husband is down there too, remember. I have to figure out how to get his car home—"

"We're *all* down here!" howled Abby. "She manages to slime the whole department, practically, then walks by and smirks at us like we're in the pound! Remember how her parents died under mysterious circumstances when she was only twelve? And her least favorite professor washed up in the arroyo the day she graduated. Remember that? Silverman, the department head. And we were there when her worst enemy just happened to die in grad school. And now Roger!"

"Lori loved Roger," Carol objected, before she remembered that she didn't really want Abby to know that their old classmate had come to visit her. Even though she'd only spent a year in their program, Abby had established the friends Carol was allowed and forbidden to have. Admiring Lori from afar was grudgingly accepted, talking to her had to be done in secret, and having her over for brunch and landscaping would have been no less than a scandal.

Abby was too mad to pick up on subtleties, though. "Oh yeah, that's why he's fine till she comes to town, then BOOM! What was that song I made up in grad school?"

Carol winced. Most of Abby's cruel songs had been about her. "I don't know. Not 'Death and Lori'?"

"Ha! That was a good one! But I was thinking of—" she began, and then from her room in St. Vitus's, Abby burst into what had to be the cruelest of her songs: "The Freaks in Our Class." Resonating through Carol's LPR Lab phone, to the tune of "My Favorite Things," came the old forgotten words

"Lori's a killer and Roger is crazy
I'd transfer out if I wasn't so lazy
The students have scurvy, the profs smell like pus
Tell me, why's grad school so vile and heinous?"

"I don't really want to be reminded," protested Carol, who was feeling guilty about gabbing on the phone at work. "I'm the one who spent eight years there." Even though in principle she was the one who had succeeded, Carol was still intimidated by Abby, who had always been everything that was more perfect: taller, thinner, blonder, smarter, fitter, and more social. She had not dropped out of grad school, no; she had left in disgust to do better things.

"I don't know how you did it." Abby was not in the least envious. "I should just refuse to have anything to do with the physics department! Last week I did a contract for the new animal facility. STI has gone totally bio, and they have monkeys and all kinds of terrible things. The vivisectionists were creepy as all get out, but at least they knew how to dress and talk.

"I'm telling you," Abby was calming down a bit, no longer shouting. "I was having flashbacks the instant I stepped into that building. These *mutants* came running at us out of the basement, a guy in a puke-jacket dragging this girl by her pigtails, holy guacamole! Then they make us walk through the basement and start screaming that we all have a disease. They called an ambulance, for Pete's sake! I had to ride here in an ambulance with the mutants!"

Carol found herself unable to suppress a laugh. It was an awful lot like some of the things that had happened in grad school. "So it really is physics," she mused, "not just the school we went to. I kind of like the idea of refusing to work with the physics department. Say you were traumatized as a child by a physicist."

"As soon as this one is over, believe me."

Carol was taken aback. "I thought it *was* over. My husband said it was over. He got his contract through to hire the guy."

"Huh?" Abby sneered. "We didn't have our meeting, stupid. We didn't even make it upstairs."

"I don't know!" Carol was *not* being a boson this time. "I spent all morning running around with the paperwork so Bob could hire this guy. He's supposed to start on Monday."

"If you didn't get the principal investigator's signature," said Abby casually, "it's illegal. But," she added brightly, "I *so* don't care! He's a mutant too!"

Carol really needed to get back to work, but long experience had taught her that blowing off Abby was not allowed. Containing her impatience, she promised to go to the gym and day spa with her friend the moment the victims were released, and then finally hung up and sprinted out the door to the All-STUMPs Meeting about the Polar Institute Proposal.

Of all of the STUMPs—science, technology, upper management, principals—everyone but upper management was on "soft money," meaning that they had to find a project or projects that would agree to cover their salaries. They said it had been a fine system when there were billion-dollar missions, but Carol never saw that era, and now it was a lot harder. Their overheads, which paid the managers, were so high that the average project couldn't even support a full person.

In the six years she'd been here, things had gotten noticeably worse. When she was hired, she had been split fifty-fifty between two charge accounts, called SLAPs for science lead authorization for project. Now she had eight SLAPs, and it was hard to do the accounting—she spent at least an hour every Thursday afternoon trying to make sure she was charging each project fairly. She still always felt guilty, thinking she really wasn't contributing anything to anyone because she was split too many ways.

Of course, it was different if you had your own money. Anyone lucky enough to win a proposal could choose how much time he or she worked on that project, up to full-time if there was enough to go around. She didn't know anyone of her generation in that situation, though. Writing a proposal at the LPR Lab was an organization-wide effort, and you had to have influence with upper management to get a science role. People like her made copies, typed out the "compliance matrix" so the investigators would know if their proposal contained everything it needed, and proofread it if they were lucky.

She was hoping for a proofreading SLAP, since two of her current projects were probably going to disappear. Drop below 80% coverage and you'd be laid off after a week. That was another thing that had changed since she'd been hired—it used to be a month.

The Polar Institute Proposal was huge. Six hundred million dollars, and control over not just the big experimental physics projects but the new Polar Astrobiology Center as well. The managers presenting at the meeting spent over two hours reciting the proposal requirements to a packed room,

Between the heat and the excess carbon dioxide, Carol was practically asleep by the time the excitement began.

The lab's chief scientist stood up. He looked too much like a teenager, skinny and platinum blond with a pointy nose and a squeaky voice—it was hard to take him seriously. He actually tried to argue in front of all the employees that the LPR Lab was not a credible leader in astrobiology, the search for life on other planets. "We don't do biology here!" he squealed. "We're not *allowed* to do biology here! We had an astrobiologist, and he left without even starting his experiments. He abandoned a hundred pounds of Antarctic ice cores in the freezer. If we could analyze them, we'd win this proposal hands down, but we can't because of our own rules and bureaucracy!"

Everyone sat up straight, waiting to see what would happen. There were intakes of breath. But it ended as quickly as it begun—he was shuffled off the podium by two men in turbans, and various other managers tried to make things right.

"We will win," declared Carol's colony manager, Ellis D. Tripp, "because of our *organization*. No university has the time, the resources, the people to respond to this proposal the way the LPR Lab can."

This was apparently not enough because the Lab Director stepped in. He was a tiny olive-skinned Iranian with thick glasses and an even thicker accent. Dr. El-Something or Something El-Something… Carol could never remember, it seemed the director was changed monthly under directions from Washington.

"We will win," declared El-Something, raising his hands for silence, "because we are the *best*. I wouldn't trade all the resources of STI for one single LEPER!" Balling his hands into fists, he started them on the chant, "Four three two one, send a rocket to the sun…."

The noise became unbearable as the room took up the cry. Carol hated this kind of thing. It was pathetic to see chubby middle-aged engineers in cheap suits acting like they were in the Marines. Having just spoken with Abby didn't help, Abby who parodied everything and would no doubt be whispering something like, *One two three four, I'm a fat and sweaty bore…*

All she'd wanted was a SLAP, but it looked as though she'd be stuck here for the rest of the day and probably end up with nothing. *Five six seven eight, see the mutants froth with hate.*

When the meeting finally ended, it was not yet four o'clock and her boss told her to go ahead and go home. Knowing she would be spending the evening alone, she took advantage of the remaining daylight to head to the foothills, where there was a four-mile jogging trail up Lobo Peak. There weren't any wolves that she'd heard of, but there were definitely bobcats and mountain lions.

Part of the fun of working here was the contrast—right by the rocket science lab was real wilderness where you could still get mauled by a bear. Of course, they'd had a lot of problems since 9/11—the reinforced fences would let the deer in but not let them out. The generation of deer born on campus was excessively tame and aggressive, stealing food off people's tables while they were eating lunch and once even tripping a cyclist and killing him. Now no one was allowed to bicycle on lab.

Officially the employees were supposed to get around on little yellow go-carts driven by trained personnel, but Carol didn't like them. They were noisy and stinky and the brakes didn't work on hills. She could usually get away with walking (not jogging), so she held her head high and tried to look official as she strolled past the guard gate and out into the park.

During her run, she realized that her husband's car gave her an excuse to try to get the other side of the yellow fever story. Sitting on an outcrop looking over the valley, she took deep breaths of the clean air above the smog, then pulled out her phone. She dialed Lori's office number to tell her to pedal up from campus and wait outside the guard gate, where the guards wouldn't see her. Carol would come by with Bob's car and then walk back for her own.

In a moment of inspiration, she asked if Lori would like to go out for Mexican food and dancing afterwards. Not only did Lori accept, but she suggested a club where the last band of the night was their old classmates in *500 milliCoulombs of Happiness.*

Kurt, the band's drummer, and Andrew, who played the bass, had not been among Carol's closest friends in grad school, but they had had boson status in common. They had spent many long hours on the steps of the physics building discussing the relative merits of dropping out or seeing things through. Although fate had drawn them all to the West, she found it hard to go to see them play now that their dreams had come to fruition. Kurt had rejected her in grad school to pursue Absinthe, and a few months ago when Carol had gone to his show he'd still been chilly and standoffish. It hurt to imagine the way he would act once he found out that Abby, too, now lived in town—even though Abby loathed him with a spitting passion, calling him Ginger Snapped.

In some deep uncharitable part of her mind, Carol knew that things would be different with Lori. Men reacted badly to her, since she had a way of making them all feel clumsy, hopeless with tools, and all-around stupid. Even if a guy ever did think Lori was cute, she would remain blissfully unconscious of the fact or make puking noises like a ten-year-old. Of course Carol was married, and had no intention of ever doing anything to hurt Bob. Still, it might be fun to spend just one evening with her own private wingman.

SEVEN: ROSE TO THE OCCASION

Lori's undergraduate House took nothing more seriously than a good prank, and everyone knew that once a Bubo, always a Bubo.

If pressed, she might try to argue that this wasn't so much a *prank* as an *investigation*. After all, she wasn't a kid anymore. She had a mere twelve months to go before her tenure review…eleven months and three weeks as of tomorrow. Nevertheless, her heart skipped excitedly and she cackled to herself as she flew down the hill on her road bike, Goldstein bumping on her back in case it turned out the building was quarantined and she was forced to study in spite of herself.

Naturally the building was wide open. University biohazard committees were notoriously lax, and STI's was one of the very worst. Where else could a thirteen-year-old freshman practice electron microscopy on live viruses left behind by a tropical disease expert who hadn't even labeled the racks? So there were six people in quarantine at St. Vitus's hospital right now, waiting out the three- to six-day yellow fever incubation period while the mystery liquid lay untouched and potentially virulent in the basement hallway.

No one had tried to mop it up; probably no one had even passed this way since the incident. It was a remote corner of the basement, and she would imagine that the only ones ever around were van Gnubbern and the horrible Jim, and even they probably never went into the virus room. The group of lawyers and LEPERs would have had absolutely no reason to pass this way unless someone (Marybeth) had lured them here.

The BSL-3 lab itself was very secure. It had a double entryway with an autoclave built into the inner door as regulations required. Lori made a quick dash to the pharmacy in town, returning with latex gloves, a make-shift lab coat, a bucket of bleach, and rubber boots. She poured just enough bleach into the puddle to neutralize anything horrible, then prepared to look inside the room. The outer door opened with a key and the inner door with a passcode. Keys, of course, did not stop Buboes since lockpicking was the first Pasteur House initiation rite, one that she had taught with glee as an upperclassman. The passcode was even less of a problem: she had set it herself to the reciprocal of the base of the natural logarithm many years ago.

She sloshed through wetness all the way through the entryway. The first thing she did when she entered the room was sneeze three times. The room was hot and it smelled. The second thing she did was bash her nose against something that shouldn't have been there. The third thing she did was leap back in a surge of pure instinct, scrabbling backwards through the inner door as a crash shook the room.

She felt the vibrations dampen slowly under her feet, and after a long minute of standing in the dark reached one arm back into the room and switched on the lights.

What shouldn't have been there was the door of the ceiling-high cryo-genic freezer, which had come loose from its hinges and made a valiant attempt to crush her. It now lay on its side, still unstable, so she cautiously rolled it over until it rested harmlessly against the wall.

It took a few minutes for her heart to stop pounding, but there were no other heavy loose items to be seen, so she continued her inspection. The puddle arose from rack upon rack of tubes of all sizes filled with liquids of various pastel hues, mostly pink and yellow but with a sampling of blue and a couple that were green. Only the far corners of the room had escaped the flooding, and they were littered with dirt, plastic tubes, and dead crickets. To the left was a bench with the same fluorescence microscope she had used as a student to check the quality of her samples before bringing them to the electron microscope. On the far wall was a biosafety containment hood bearing an inspection sticker from her senior year of undergrad.

It was impossible to tell if anyone had been in there recently, since the liquid and the falling door would have erased any traces. It also didn't look as if the freezer had suffered any catastrophic failure; it had simply come unplugged and the door forced off by a quarter-century of accumulated frost. She turned off the lights and left the inner room as she'd found it.

It remained to be seen what had allowed the liquid to escape under the outer door. To be honest, she wasn't expecting much—rotten wood, decaying rubber, broken hinges, or any sign of the decades of neglect that had made the rest of the lab such a shambles.

But she saw, when she crouched all the way down by the outer door, that the bottom inch of it was clean. The rubber seal had been recently torn away and the paint was covered with scratches as if attacked with a dull pocketknife or sharp nails. Even if the freezer failure and falling door had been an accident, the release of the puddle into the hallway had not been.

There was a scuffling behind her in the inner room. Lori hunched into a ball and covered her head, expecting to be struck or kicked or shot. After several minutes passed peacefully, she got up and abruptly flicked the inner-room lights back on.

A huge rat gave her a peevish look before scurrying away under the biosafety cabinet. She laughed nervously with relief, unable for a long moment to appreciate the irony that she was less afraid of a rat lapping yellow fever juice than of her own colleagues.

She had no reason to be scared, she told herself over and over while trying to slow her heart. So far as she could tell, no one in the department had committed or even threatened an act of violence. She shouldn't let Lou's students and their creepy skit go to her head, or Marybeth's wretched stories, or that rabid Dim Bulb. The falling door had been the inevitable result of decay, and the scratches no doubt were made by rodents.

But why was it that Lou seemed incapable of starting his research project, of holding that one meeting that would open the subcontract and turn on the grant money?

The old Lori would have burst into his office, no doubt giggling, demanding gleefully whether all the times he had been sick matched up with when he was trying to schedule the meeting. The new, grown-up Lori, this stranger in her own body, knew enough about loss to realize that this would be too cruel. By all accounts, Lou had handled a devastating injury with almost superhuman strength. After getting out of the ICU he had spent only three weeks in a rehabilitation center in Downey, sending e-mails to his students every day, and had come back to work right after. He asked for no special treatment, no teaching relief, no re-set of the tenure clock. More than one person had seen him sneak off to cry, and everyone had seen him pee his pants—including Absinthe, who concluded that he was retarded. If he had gotten sick a lot, it was no doubt because he hadn't let himself heal, body or spirit, and insisted upon doing everything as before despite physical challenges that she couldn't even imagine. She couldn't even find words to think about it since all the terms had either been tainted by PC (call me *special* and die!), were utterly meaningless (*exceptional* was her favorite, referring to both ends of the curve; it gave her visions of the two tails of the Gaussian looking over the big hump and waving to each other), or were tasteless and crude (she thought of her *alt.tasteless* days with a pang of guilt).

On the other hand, if her suspicions *were* justified, it would be even crueler to say nothing.

Well, she couldn't save the world. The best thing she could do for the health of the campus community would be to put all of the tubes and liquids in the BSL-3 lab into autoclave bags and sterilize them. She spent several minutes feeling like a disgrace to her House for not having brought a camera, until she remembered the built-in webcam on her new laptop. She snapped photos of the puddle, the freezer, the samples, and most of all the torn-up edge of the outer door.

Biohazard bags were easily begged and borrowed from the building next door; the rest of the task took all day. The autoclave would only hold a single bag at a time, and there were hundreds of tubes, racks, and vials that were potentially pathogenic. She spent the down time between runs mopping the floors with a dilute bleach solution, testing the old equipment for functionality, and occasionally running down the hall to see if perhaps van Gnubbern—or, God forbid, Jim—had returned from quarantine.

It was late afternoon before she finally had enough and went next door to the library to write her lecture. There was still no one in the physics building, which gave her the willies, and she suspected the theorists might be hiding in the library out of fear of yellow fever. Besides, she had always liked the library. Each subject was on a different floor, so each floor had a personality as distinct as the research field it represented. The couches were different (biologists seemed to actually sleep in the library on occasion), the décor was different (chemists loved posters with fancy graphics), and, of course, on the physics floor they had the best computers.

They were all there. It almost looked like a party. At the long, low table that usually displayed the new journals, Lou's group and Rose's two students had spread out all their papers and were discussing renormalization of the vacuum in loud whispers.

"Day-um, Dr. Barrow," said Sam-with-the-curls as she went by. "What happened to you?"

Lori looked down at her clothes. Despite the disposable lab coat, which she had autoclaved, she was covered with dust, dead bugs, bleach, and the remains of things too horrible to mention. "Be grateful," she said. "I just cleaned out the lab in the basement."

The table grew strangely quiet, and she met Lou's eye an instant before he laughed so maniacally that the undergrad librarians screamed and hugged each other. "Hi, kids," he called, giving them a little wave. "Physics is bad for the brain! Lori," he whispered, "you are a fucking genius. Sol and I have just concocted a Fiendish Plan."

Sol? Professor Rose, of course. Was he on their side as well? Or was it an uneasy truce?

"Of course, we were merely theorizing while you were working," said Rose with a knowing smile. "Isn't that always the way it works?"

"How can it be that she's only been here for a week, and already she's a step ahead of me?" Lou exclaimed, sounding immensely pleased.

"Because you don't take steps at all, Dr. Lou," Sam reminded him.

"So she's one gear development ahead, then, if you like. Barrow walks only slightly more than I do—she's got quite the assortment of bizarre vehicles."

"You ain't seen nothin' yet," said Lori. "But how did you even know? Did you see me at the hospital yesterday?"

"Of course, with your trailer and the rocket launcher. What was that thing?"

She didn't answer the question. "I didn't see you."

"I was being discreet."

"Discrete as opposed to continuous?" asked Brian the dyslexic Brain.

"Lori," said Professor Rose, rising to take his leave with his hand on her shoulder, "you will own us all, body and soul. Just don't waste any time," he warned Lou. "You only have three months."

The delinquents lost all control the instant Rose was gone. "Eeeeew, he's got yellow fever now!" said Alex, the HEAD.

"Barrow," groaned Sam, "take a shower."

Brian jumped up and did a little dance. "Ooh ooh ooh, yellow fever," he sang in a whisper, drawing more odd looks from the volunteer librarians. Lori had been one once on this very same floor.

She was going to take a seat and demand details of the Plan, but Lou was already putting his notebook and journal articles into his bag. "It's time for me to go to the gym," he said. "Lori, if you don't mind walking across campus with me, there's something I'd like to ask you."

The students elbowed each other and cackled suggestively, but Lori and Lou ignored them. They took the huge, slow-moving elevator down into the courtyard and crossed the campus, past the teaching labs with their marble sabertooth cat replica, and across the street to the path that led to the new gym. The sun was just beginning to set, casting long shadows in the shimmering heat.

Right outside the pool fence, Lou spun around and pointed off to the north. "Here's my question," he said. "What do you see?"

"Huh?" Lori saw foothills. "I see a habitat that, ten thousand years ago, supported sabertooth cats."

"Who's there now?"

She shrugged. "Dunno."

Lou grinned and snapped his fingers. "And that's my answer. STImpies don't even acknowledge the LPR Lab."

Was *that* what this was about? She finally realized there were a few white buildings dotting the hillside, the management center of the Lobo(tomy) Peak Rocket Lab. "Of course not!" He knew who she was from *alt.tasteless*, so she added, "They're just a bunch of fucktards. Don't say 'L-P-R': it's the LEPERLab. Even faculty aren't allowed up there any more without some kind of armed guard."

"Right. Closed, secretive, militaristic. But very powerful, and very rich."

"Rich only because they have a 250% overhead rate so their grants have to be big enough to cover it."

"But the kind of physics I do, they control." Lou spoke so softly that splashing from the pool and the *boing* of the diving board drowned out some of his words. "They determine access to the South Pole because they're the only ones with the budget to support the trips. Because of that, it's their fucktards who do the experiments, instead of smart people. And sure, I'm a theorist, but you can't be a theorist with crap data. With their budget and our overhead, I could send six experimentalist graduate students to the Pole instead of one—you say *LEPER*? That's good! —and get fifty times the data. We could say whether there is physics beyond the Standard Model, definitively, within five years. Whether the universe will die a slow, cold death or whether it will contract."

"What does that have to do with me?" Lori wondered. "Or yellow fever?"

"Aha, well. That's where Sol comes in. A true genius, and truly on your side. There were some people who didn't want to hire you, you know..." A pair of undergrads—Ferrets, because they were all in black—had paused to listen to their conversation, but instead of lowering his voice, Lou raised it. "They said you were trouble, and he said, 'I got the Nobel Prize for causing trouble!' Solomon Rose, Physics, guess the year," he added for the benefit of the audience.

"Cool," said the Ferrets, and they didn't leave.

In a moment of drama, Lou extended his hand and cupped it over a particularly vile stain on Lori's T-shirt. "Sol pointed out that the LEPERLab's mortal weakness is that there's something it fears irrationally."

It was a sensual touch, and she was flustered for just a moment before giving a one-word answer that applied as well to the stain on the T-shirt as to what was under it. "Biology."

"Damn," said Lou, letting his hand drop. "Between you and Sol, I feel slow. That's right, they're afraid of biology. But you're not, and now the microscope lab and the BSL-3 are yours for the asking; van Gnubbern will never go down there again. I'll pay for the renovations because Marybeth did make a mistake with the budget, so I'm richer than I thought."

"You're doing so well for your age," said Lori with mock condescension. "But we can't talk here." She'd be surprised if those Ferrets hadn't concocted a torrid affair by Monday, and even the mention of BSL-3 around STImpies was asking for trouble. "I'll take my shower, and you go work out. But wash that hand first or we'll have an epidemic."

She didn't trust him. It was almost clear what he (and Rose?) wanted: she would take over the microscopy and BSL-3 lab and do something that had to do with rocket science and the South Pole. This would somehow lead to Lou's being able to decide which experimentalists in his field went to the polar station to collect the data he desired. It was that last link that made no sense to her, but she had never known anything about the rocket lab projects. STI rarely, if ever, bothered with them.

She had one more biohazard bag, into which she crammed all her stained clothes before taking a long, hot shower and changing back into her bike shorts and jersey from that morning. The gym was nice, she had to admit, even though it now had rules (No bare feet!) and assigned hours for different kinds of music to accommodate the different generations. Classical early in the morning, for the real geezers, rock and pop in the daytime, and "oldies" from the eighties and nineties for people like her who had nearly-standard working hours.

It still nagged at her that the pink liquid incident seemed to have given her everything she wanted, or was supposed to want. She no longer had to expel van Gnubbern; he'd been grossed away. Surely Lou wouldn't hot-agent his own co-investigators and lawyers?

Why had he been so dusty yesterday, anyway? Was the elevator truly broken? She hadn't checked. Or was he perhaps less disabled than he let on?

That last was easy to check in the gym, and she put her suspicions to rest very quickly. Being paralyzed from the waist down was not something you could fake, and his legs really didn't move at all. He had to pick them up with one arm to be able to move himself from his chair to the weight bench, which looked hard, and he lost his balance now and then, letting her know that his lower back and abs were pretty good but not perfect.

She never had any qualms about staring, so she stared, only half-heartedly playing with the free weights. Lifting weights was dull.

He was not at all offended by her curiosity, and after finishing his military press and hopping back into his chair, he asked almost playfully, "What's my level? Can you guess?"

It would have to be kind of a wild guess, since he was wearing a shirt and she hadn't seen him do sit-ups or anything. "T10 or T11?" she hazarded, drawing her hand across her abdomen, right over her bellybutton.

"Legends never lie! Barrow knows everything." He reached for a pair of 35-pound barbells, which he lifted onto his shoulders and over his head. "T10 complete. I was very lucky, really. It could have been much worse."

Lori wouldn't do that with any barbells—she'd be afraid of getting a concussion. "Yeah, it's a good thing you've got nothing in your chest but a hard lump of basalt."

He acknowledged the comment with a raise of his eyebrow and continued lifting without dropping the weights on his head. She hadn't noticed before, but his eyes were blue. "A useful trait to have," he assured her. "Here's another legend: can you still do fifty pull-ups?"

"It was never fifty," she objected, but finally let herself be talked into going over to the chin-up bar to see what she could do. At least he knew how to speak French, because for the last five years all sports were Quebecois and there was nothing that inspired her quite so much as a good cry of "*Triche pas!*"

EIGHT: JESUS AND ALEXANDER

IT WAS THE BEST birthday ever.

Lori had not liked being a kid, and even now, nearing her mid-thirties, she had never been in a situation where she was considered too old instead of too young. Each year brought her more accomplishments, more success, and fewer people who could tell her what to do.

Until Roger's death, she would have said that each year had brought more happiness. Now she was just confused: she still didn't know whether coming back to California was a humiliation or a victory, whether she was a failure as a Quebecoise or a resounding success as an Angeleno. It was as if she had lost her connection to Quebec when she lost him, no longer cared about integrating into that small, closed yet warm community of French-speaking Canadians where she had for a while thought she felt so at home.

But could she ever feel so at home as she did at STI? She had all the keys. She knew all the passwords and the underground passageways. She was enough of a legend that new Buboes pointed her out and first-year graduate students didn't dare approach her unless they were introduced by those older and more jaded.

Her thirty-third year had also brought her something she had never had before: an experimental lab. Not just any experimental lab, but one where she could, if she wanted, grow yellow fever, rabies, and HIV. Dr. van Gnubbern presented her with a door plaque reading "BARROW LAB" and another for indicating biohazards and chemical hazards.

"I'm so glad you came back," he said, clearing his throat as if he were going to cry.

"Of course, you'll be the senior author on any electron microscopy work," Lori promised.

"Oh, Lori," sighed van Gnubbern, "I'm tenured, I don't need it. If I take the pictures myself, you can put me on."

Lou's delinquents, accompanied by two of the first-years and Marybeth, went all out. They gave her a home-made watercolor for the lab entryway showing a bunch of plague bacteria framed by her all-time favorite Pasteur quote: *Le microbe n'est rien, le terrain est tout.* They even brought a cake. They couldn't eat it in the biohazard lab, of course, so after hanging the picture they all trooped upstairs to the conference room. Alex let the two first-years take seats first so that he could point at their heads from behind, and mouthed at Lori, "The ones who don't suck."

The ones who didn't suck were a tall, broad-shouldered Chinese guy named Chi-Ming and a skinny, long-nosed platinum blond whose exact likeness adorned every wall of honor at STI. It was as if the University's first president had reproduced by binary fission, spawning generations of clones of whom the last was the twenty-two-year-old in front of her: Walter W. Waddles IV. You could never go wrong with a Walter W. Waddles; his grandfather, Junior, was in Applied Physics and in Lori's day had been the most beloved of all the professors.

She was grateful for Lou's students' efforts. It appeared that they had learned as painfully as she had that a professor couldn't just hire anyone and let attrition do its work. She'd had her own share of Marybeths early on, one of whom had submitted a paper to a major journal before Lori had had a chance to realize that whole sections of the article were plagiarized. She caught it just in time; twenty-four hours later, and there would have been a scandal that might have cost her job. Her next hire was picked with extreme care and was first-rate, but so far any attempts to bring Fang Li to California had been futile—she seemed to have dropped off the face of the Earth.

Lori cut herself a slice of cake and was about to take a bite when the significance of the lemon-yellow cake with extra dark devil's food frosting hit her. "This color scheme is not a coincidence," she announced.

The problem children, who had been restraining themselves, shrieked with laughter and danced around. "I looked up yellow fever on the web," said Brian, "and it said when you have it, you turn bright yellow and throw up black, so I thought..."

"Mmmmm," sighed Lori, spooning the black frosting into her mouth. "Thanks, guys. I can't believe I'm having a lab-warming already. This was really nice of you."

"The Boss's idea," Sam admitted. "You should have heard him laugh as he painted that quote. The cake was an afterthought. Tolja she'd figure it out *and* eat it anyway," he cackled, accepting the dollar bills that Alex and Brian slipped him.

Lori hadn't seen Lou in a couple of days. "So where is Le Grand Méchant? Being discrete again?"

All heads swiveled to point at Marybeth, who scowled and sulked and twisted her face into a sobbing-toddler grimace, but without tears. The first-years looked appalled, but Lou's students snorted in disgust. "Tell her, Marybeth."

"So I made a mistake in the proposal budget," Marybeth snapped, still with this horrible look. "I accidentally put someone from this department as part of the LEPER subcontract, and the LEPERLab took the money last week, somehow, when they were all being quarantined. It's not my fault. If it wasn't for me, the proposal never would have gone in at all!"

"So he's at the LEPERLab trying to get the money back," Alex explained. "He never signed off on the budget, so it's totally illegal, but LEPER is such a morass of bureaucracy that once they have the money, you're hosed."

"How much did they steal?" Lori wondered.

"Two hundred thousand," chorused the guys, with a glare for Marybeth.

"But—" Lori stopped herself. Two hundred thousand dollars sounded like a lot to the kids, but it was nothing compared to six hundred million. Surely Lou wouldn't waste days— *days!*—up there just on a slim chance to get such a pittance back.

But of course the students didn't know about the Fiendish Plan. The Plan had sprung into existence within the last twenty-four hours, and the best birthday present of them all was having been picked by the two most ambitious members of the department to join their plot to upset the LEPERLab. The three of them were going to submit—and win!—a six hundred million dollar Polar Institute Proposal, giving them control over physics and biology at the South Pole for the next seven years.

It no longer mattered that she didn't trust Lou or that Rose had a reputation of grinding his students and colleagues to hamburger. They seemed to share her vision for what the department had to become and were ready to move quickly and ruthlessly. Now that things were beginning to take shape, Sol had decided that it all must be done in the utmost secrecy. The LEPERs would never imagine that a tiny university like STI could make a bid to control the PIP, and they would submit their usual perfectly organized but scientifically weak proposal. STI's proposal, if done right, would hit them out of left field and astound the reviewers with its simplicity, its lean science team, and its rock-hard data.

They had an incredible amount of work to do and less than three months to do it in. Fortunately, Sol was good at reading through the mass of requirements and making a simple list of what had to go into the proposal. They had fifty pages maximum to describe the science, twenty pages for management, the budget, and then all of the usual "bullshit" parts: facilities description, personnel and CVs, institutional signatures, and on and on. The list was exhaustive and painful, including the final requirement: fifty copies to be delivered to Washington, DC by December 21 (how much would a package like that weigh?).

But better to slog through it all themselves than to risk another Marybeth "mistake." Lori's role was both harder and easier than that of her two colleagues. She would be spared her share of the bullshit in exchange for handling ice cores under highly sterile conditions—the BSL-3—slicing them ultra-thin, and imaging them with electron microscopy.

"You're the only theoretical physicist in the world who can grow yellow fever," Lou had said by way of explanation of why they had chosen her.

"I had this in mind when I voted to hire you," Rose elaborated. "In fact, I think I've had this in mind since you were an undergraduate. Physics departments have been in crisis for decades because they don't want biology—but 'astrobiology' is physics, and the PIP will finally allow us to do real physics with a real experimental component again."

What that might mean for Kuzno, Lori didn't know, and she didn't really want to speculate. If she was going to do her part, she needed experimentalists and she needed them now. There was no way she could slice, image, process, and write everything in the time they had all by herself. Of course, she had to get the ice cores first—maybe that was what Lou was up to today; she could only hope. It would take a lot of discretion to be able to sneak something like that past the LEPERs.

No one was touching the yellow fever cake. She was the only one who had taken a slice. "All right, back to work," she announced, turning to the first-years. "When can you start?"

Like true STImpies, they chorused "Now!" and that was good, but it remained to be seen what she could get out of them.

"OK," she declared, standing up. "The first thing to do is to start getting you guys trained on the microscope. The second is for me to beg, borrow, steal, buy, build, or conjure a microtome of the appropriate size." How would they keep the identity of the samples a secret? She would have to talk to Dr. Rose about that. She wasn't secretive by nature, which would make this even more difficult. "Also, if we're not going to get our renovation money, we'll have to renovate the bio lab ourselves. That'll give you a chance to demonstrate your experimentalist skills. Sam, would you come downstairs with us please?"

"I'm a theorist!" Sam objected plaintively. "You don't expect me to touch the pus?"

"No," she promised. "I just want to ask you some questions."

She wasn't sure why she had chosen Sam over any one of the others. She hoped it wasn't because he'd played Lou in the skit, because she'd have to watch not to let slip things that were for his boss's ears only. The secrecy was already weighing on her.

Annoyingly, Marybeth also followed them down the stairs. "I can do experiments, too," she insisted.

"If so, I'm sure I can find something for you to do," said Lori generously, thinking, *Sweep the floor.*

"At least I'm not afraid to come down here any more," wailed Marybeth in her piercing tone. "Now that *he* is gone."

"Who?" Lori asked quickly.

"He stalked me for a year!" She paid no attention to the incredulous looks from the first-years. "He put a video camera outside my house! Every time I called the police, they said there wasn't enough evidence."

Sam let out a low sigh of disdain, almost a growl. "She's talking about Dim Bulb."

"Dim Bulb is creepy," Lori affirmed. "He foamed at me like a mad dog. But what do you mean he's gone?" She had been afraid she'd have to fire him.

"Don't you know?" Sam exclaimed. "He's the one who got Dr. Lou's money. He works at the LEPERLab as of this week."

"The prosecutor said he had already raped seven girls." Marybeth stopped at the entrance to the basement and looked all around her before daring to head towards Lori's lab.

"It's worth two hundred thousand just to be rid of him," Lori muttered.

Dr. van Gnubbern was at the microscope, which was lucky. She left Marybeth and the first-years with him for a tutorial and dragged Sam into the antechamber of the BSL-3.

"I knew you'd make me touch the pus," he shuddered, looking around at the biohazard signs, the autoclave, and the five fresh new lab coats she had hung in the entryway.

"Get a grip, there's no pus in here. I just have to ask some questions or my head will explode, and I want to be able to do it without traumatizing anyone. So don't repeat this conversation." She took a deep breath and put a hand against the autoclave as if for moral support. It was still warm from her last bags of horrible detritus. "I think my first question has already been answered. There's no way Marybeth would have been in cahoots with Dim Bulb."

Sam seemed to realize they were going to talk conspiracy theories, and his face brightened. This was good; the students had to have been speculating like crazy long before she ever came to STI. "Not a chance. You heard her. She sued him, and then she sued Dr. Kuznetsov for not taking her seriously. She tried to have them both arrested. This was all when Dr. Lou was in intensive care. When he got better, he made her stop."

"OK, number two: is everything Marybeth says a lie or just an exaggeration?"

He was silent for a long moment, glancing at the door as if he intended to run. Finally he asked, "Did she tell you gnarly stories?"

"She told me she was abused by her parents."

"Is *that* what she told you?" Sam looked repulsed. "Ew."

"Yeah, ew."

"No, I mean *eeeew*. She told me she had had cancer, and a friend of mine died of cancer. She told Dr. Lou she'd been a ventilator-dependent quadriplegic for two years until she miraculously snapped out of it. It's all lies. It has to be."

"Ugh!" Lori's shout resonated around the tiny room. "That *is* vile. She's like some kind of twisted chameleon. I don't want her to know the stories about me."

Sam laughed nervously. "You can't help that. You're a legend."

"I don't want to be a legend!"

"No? I thought everyone did. Dr. Lou sure does. I think he doesn't even mind being a gimp if it contributes to a legend."

"Oh, really? Well, so you know, I didn't murder my parents twenty-one years ago. They died in a random act of L.A. street violence. Which brings me to my last question."

Sam had grown pale and put his hand on the wall as if he were going to throw up or pass out. "Barrow," he said finally, "I can't take the smell in here."

"Would you rather be overheard?" Lori cracked the door and listened, but there were no spies, and she heard the murmur of van Gnubbern's voice one room over. "OK, you must have speculated, all of you. Who shot Lou? Was it random or not?"

Sam took deep breaths of the fresh air through the crack. "He thinks so," he said finally. "He was just driving to his parents' in Malibu. He never saw the guy; police never caught him. Why?" he asked at last, clearly reaching for his last bit of courage. "Do you suspect something?"

"I don't know if I do or not," Lori sighed. "That's why you can't mention this to him. It's just that…people keep getting in his way, and he is kind of arrogant and overbearing—"

"Ha!" Sam laughed too loudly. "Kind of! You didn't even know him before. You didn't even see him with that Beemer he had. Man, he still talks about it."

A Beemer and Malibu, Lori thought. That explains a lot. "Did he wreck it?"

"Oh, no, there wasn't a scratch on it. The ambulance driver said he'd pulled it perfectly off the road, downshifted and cut the engine, and the first thing he said when they got to him was 'How's my car?'"

"That's what I would have done. Not bad for a theorist."

"Yeah, but you know, theorists don't shoot people. We can't—we would miss, or push the wrong button, or whatever. Besides, my boss might be an asshole, but the rest are ten times worse. Look at Kuznetsov. Dr. Lou never dated any nineteen-year-olds, and he always supported the people he hired—almost too much, if you know what I mean."

"So I'm paranoid," said Lori. "That's good. But just so you know, the elevator cables were on the point of breaking, just about five feet above the top of the box—where people have a tendency to stand and spray-paint 'Fucking Ferret Freaks.' I don't think any undergraduate would cut them, but I think someone did, and they've now been fixed with a video camera placed in a strategic location. That's my contribution, but if anything else funny happens…"

"I'll come running to tell you," finished Sam.

He continued to stand there until she realized he was waiting, like a kid, for permission to leave, which she dutifully provided. Mind still not at ease, and annoyed about having missed the training session, she went to see if she could at least tell something about the capabilities of the new students. She still needed to see Rose and try to get some idea about a microtome and about the diameter of those ice cores.

The students had gone. That was the trouble with first-years—they had classes and had to study. So she went next door to the biology building with a vague memory of something called a cryoslicer that kept things cold while sectioning them with a retractable blade.

It was here that she finally appreciated how much STI had changed, and how the mutation of her own research interests was a reflection of something much bigger. At this school where three-quarters of entering freshmen were physics majors, it was biology that had a whole new annex with four buildings. The Imaging Center housed an opulent computer lab containing two poster-sized color printers, all inside a glass atrium opening onto a square lined with transplanted palm trees, so new that their leaves were still tied in ponytails. One floor down was fluorescence of every kind, and the sub-basement boasted a microscope facility for new and experimental types of microscopy that hadn't even been theoretically conceived when Lori was a student.

No one knew her—all of the professors were her age. No one knew what she was talking about when she said "cryoslicer"; she finally found an old guy who told her to try the mouse house. That was another new building, with its own private parking lot. The door to was key-carded and had an alarm, but she waited until someone came out so that she could slip in.

Everything was shiny, new, and smelled of paint or varnish or mice; students milled around with rodents in plastic breadbox cages. The corridor was wide, as if for gurneys, and in one room there was an operating table with an overhead light that was almost exactly one-third of the expected size.

She was just wondering what that could be for when she saw it: two tittering grad students in lab coats and gloves with a wide-eyed monkey strapped to a stretcher held between them. A metal probe the size of a carrot protruded from the poor animal's brain, surrounded by a bloody and poorly stitched wound, and for the brief instant that Lori looked into its eyes she saw hatred for herself and all of her species.

Not caring that it made her look like an intruder, she turned and ran, back to where the walls were crumbling and the freezer doors fell off and dead crickets piled up in the corner. Dashing up to the fourth floor, she stopped dead in the hall when she saw her own horror mirrored in the wide-eyed gape of Solomon Rose.

"Is something wrong, Professor Rose?" she wondered.

"Every morning," the Great Man began in a labored voice, "of every day, the university should hold a moment of silence in which we all bow our heads and say, 'Thanks be to God that I don't work at the LEPERLab.'"

NINE: I'M NOT YOUR SONYA

LORI RISKED DESTROYING BOTH her circadian rhythm and her bank account by returning Radhika's birthday phone call in Darwin, Australia, catching her on her lunch hour by calling just before eleven at night in California. She felt guilty for how little they seemed to share lately, but the absurd time difference and the amount they both worked made weeks and months go by without any real communication.

It was only now, five years after they'd broken up, that Lori was beginning to appreciate how much Radhika had meant to her. In grad school, she had almost resented her for always being around, ruining Lori's hard-earned reputation as a cold-hearted, asexual physics robot and forcing her to feel emotions when all she wanted was to do some homework. But they had kept each other sane, and in all the time that had passed since, Lori hadn't found a single other person with the patience to share her life. She and Roger had never moved in together, never even seriously considered it, but she and Radhika had spent twenty-four hours a day together for a total of over six years without ever growing sick of each other's presence.

The same thing that had brought them together drove them apart: snow. They had been recruited to Minnesota by fancy theory fellowships when neither had been above latitude thirty-four North in her life. Lori walked into class the first day and spotted, among a sea of six-foot blondes, a wide-shouldered brown girl in a flowered camisole whose only signs of nerddom were her glasses and the fact that she wrote with her left hand. Thinking she had to be foreign—Indian, probably, with a name like that—Lori had gone to sit next to her and asked where she was from.

As Lou had done last week, Radhika replied with nothing more alien in her voice than the San Gabriel Valley. "Dude! I'm from Kalapana, Hawaii. But I did my undergrad at UC San Diego."

Lori had been somewhat disappointed by how un-foreign that sounded, not realizing that Kalapana had been destroyed by a volcano and that Radhika had, for all intents and purposes, been raised by savages. It didn't take Lori long to appreciate just how exotic Radhika really was, as over the next two weeks she demonstrated that she was utterly incapable of dealing with Scandinavian-Americans or with any of the basic assumptions of civilization that made up the American Midwest.

The Minnesotans never knew what to make of Radhika. They didn't know what race she was, they didn't know what sex she was, and they alternately treated her like a retarded child and a royal savage. They thought she was cruel and violent because she said things like "Kill the motherfucker!" and was immune to political correctness, but nothing could have been farther from the truth. They thought she had to be a lesbian because she cut her hair short, carried heavy things, and studied physics, and so she was forced to date Lori because the men were afraid of her. They thought she was angry and bitter about life, but what she wanted was more for herself and for them than they could imagine, something far outside the boundaries of three kids, an SUV, and Lutheran church hot-dish suppers.

She had survived five years there only because she had so much work to do. With an undergraduate degree in chemistry, she hadn't been prepared for advanced classical or quantum mechanics and had had to check out beginner-level texts from the library and study them alone in secret. In the summer she would swim miles across the local lakes, braving algae and swimmer's itch; in the winter she would brood and grumble and sulk, walking through the cement tunnels to do laps in the gym pool that she hated for its crowds and its powerful bromine smell.

Lori hadn't appreciated then that Radhika had taken the fellowship in order to support her family. Their twenty-thousand-dollar a year stipend was more than their family of five had ever seen, and she managed to send at least half of it, sometimes more, back to her parents and her two young sisters so that they could eat well and the girls could think of college. Even without knowing this, it was obvious that Radhika was generous to a fault, that she placed no value whatsoever on material things, and that if you were her friend, everything she had was yours. One night they had worked late and emerged from the building to find Radhika's bike had been stolen. She said simply, "I hope whoever it was needed it more than I did," and came to school on a skateboard until she could afford a used ten-speed.

She had a temper, though, especially with anyone she considered stupid or small-minded, and there were an awful lot of those in Minnesota. It was refreshing to see her hate with an idealist's fervor those whose "truth" was a collection of platitudes about men and women, life and death, freedom and oppression. But she was always in trouble for telling people off, for "threatening" them by using "bad words," or for tearing up the creationist pamphlets left in everyone's mailbox.

Her few friends—it was Roger who started it—teased her that she had a Raskolnikov complex and called her "Radi" to emphasize the point, in some kind of bizarre anglo-hawaiianization of poor old Rodion's first name. Usually this just made her grumble that there was no fucking way she was spending eight years in this Siberian hell-hole. When Lori adopted a marmalade-colored cat, they called her Sonya. Sonya had died last year at the age of nineteen, a month before Roger, giving one farewell mew in her sleep at the foot of Lori's bed.

When Lori left Minneapolis after finishing her degree, Radi spent her last six months there completely alone. Then she fled to a postdoctoral position at UC Santa Cruz and never looked back. The move brought her reasonably close to Lori, who was at Berkeley, so they got back together more or less simply because neither one ever really found anyone else. Lori never even had a fling; she knew Radi had had a couple, always with men, but they didn't talk about it in detail and didn't consider it cheating because they never called themselves a couple. Each had been forced to move again at least every two years, sometimes closer and sometimes farther, and they both knew that a relationship forged in graduate school was more based upon shared adversity than anything else and that they couldn't force being together because one or the other would always be short-changed.

She had gone to visit Radi's family just once. As a general rule, Lori disapproved of parents, but she knew the trip would make Radi happy. The volcano had forced the family from Kalapana, and they now lived at an even more remote southern point called Na'alehu. Radi's now-teenage sisters had miles of remote trails to explore, and took them to a secret green-sand beach made of tiny particles of olivine. The silence was perfect, and every night displayed unpolluted black skies where Lori could see the Southern Cross. They avoided the usual "Where do we sleep?" awkwardness so often experienced by same-sex couples because all of the "kids" slept on a single mattress on the lanai. The scent of that pure air, filled with ferns and jasmine and grass and coconut palms, still sometimes came to Lori in moments when she least expected it.

Radi's family was poor but far from stupid, and they hadn't made her go to public school, letting her learn from books at home—usually ones stolen from the library—and the occasional private math tutor paid in homegrown fruit and fresh eggs. Radi had immersed herself in the island's richness, the same environment that had inspired Darwin, her back yard filled with beak-shaped flowers and flower-shaped beaks.

At least their postdocs had sent them to warm climates—after California, St. Louis, and then Florida—until the fateful day when Lori decided that among her five tenure-track offers, the one in Canada was the most appealing. Canada's best university was offering a great start-up package, a joint appointment in the Faculties of Science and Medicine, and a fun city where people spoke a mix of French and English that she found irresistibly charming.

Radi had been furious. "Go back to Siberia if you want, but I'm not your Sonya," she had raged, and she stayed in her industrial chemistry position in Miami until she managed to find a job in Darwin.

Australia seemed more like exile than Montreal, but Radi was Radi, and of course Oz was closer to Hawaii than the Northeast was. She liked it there, and Lori hoped she had finally managed to lose the last of her wrath at being forced to play a Minnesotan for so long.

Now Lori pulled the phone over to the bed so that she could nestle under the covers for a long conversation, but she found herself unable to say anything of substance. The Fiendish Plan was supposed to be secret; what would Lou and Rose think if it leaked out because Lori blabbed to her ex?

All this time, and all this distance, and they found themselves talking about furniture. Radi had been an experimentalist for seven years now, and she knew things about equipping a lab that Lori had never even considered.

"Do a group trip to one of those general stores for your office," she advised, "but don't skimp on lab furniture. It's the one thing I always pay full price for. If you have a BSL-3, you want to make sure none of the material in the furniture is porous, or nasty things will soak into it and start growing. You need to get chairs that are comfortable and rise to all different heights since you'll be spending long hours at different instruments. You can re-surface the benchtops yourself, but anything robust enough is going to be heavy. I'll find you the catalog number for the marble we used in Miami."

"What about a cryoslicer?"

"A what?"

"Never mind." Lori sighed and hung her head over the bed so as not to over-stretch the phone cord. "I need to be able to slice things thin but keep them cold at the same time."

"Why not use a regular microtome in a really cold room?" Radi suggested, cackling as if it were a joke.

"That's a good idea, actually, but it would have to be well below freezing."

"And it serves you right!"

Lori laughed because that was true enough, but the thought of something serving someone right led her down another trail of thought altogether. "Tell me," she said, apropos of nothing because Radi would never be confused, "do you know Alexander Kuznetsov or Louis Maupertuis?"

"Not off-hand." Radi sounded a bit defensive; she had always been known for having the inside scoop on every physicist on Earth. "I'm not so plugged in any more, way out here. Are they theorists?"

"Kuzno is. He stopped being productive years ago. He seems creepy—married an undergrad. Maupertuis is an ordinary Standard-Model theorist who only got his PhD a couple of years ago."

There were some scratching noises, and typing. "I'm thinking," said Radi. "What is it you want to know?"

"Do they have any enemies?" Lori responded promptly.

"Why?" Radi would never be confused, but she would never be fooled, either. "What are you involved in?"

"A Fiendish Plan," Lori admitted.

"And you're plotting with Maupertuis and Kuznetsov?" Radi wondered dangerously.

"With Maupertuis and Rose *against* Kuznetsov."

"All right. Kuzno, as you call him, appears to be your run-of-the-mill skanky slut. He knocked up his undergrad and married her, but then apparently she had a miscarriage or an abortion."

"That's a relief. Imagine baby Kuznos!"

"I've never met him. Maupertuis, though, I saw the last time I went to the March Meeting—but he's just a baby. He was still in grad school."

"Don't you think he might have pissed people off to get where he is at his age?" Lori hinted.

"I can find out," Radi promised. "But why?"

"No reason," Lori sighed, playing with the blanket. "Tell me about this nonporous furniture."

As Radhika babbled on, Lori thought back to her days with van Gnubbern. He had boasted then, back when he gave her the parka, that his lab was not just over-air-conditioned but perfectly climate-controlled between negative ten and positive thirty degrees Celsius. If she set it at its lower limit, she would be able to sort, slice, mount, and photograph the ice cores without them vanishing to nothing in her hands.

It would be uncomfortable—downright dangerous if you stayed inside too long. But since she had no experimental students, she was the only one who would be in there.

And, as Radhika said, it served her right. Conversation over, she hung up the phone and lay staring at the ceiling for a long time, impatient for morning to come so she could put the next phase of her plan into action.

TEN: GRAND THEFT ICE CORE

OH MY GOD, I'M going to Gitmo." Lori put her elbows on Solomon Rose's desk and buried her head in her hands.

The Great Man had a great office, the whole east corner of the fifth floor with a view of the new gym out one side and the foothills out the other. Photos of the good ol' days dotted the walls: his appearance in STI's last football match against California Bible College in 1937, a visit from Einstein, one of himself with a much younger but already miniskirt-clad tutu-man. Not even a Nobel Prize, though, made him able to offer anything better than a plastic chair for his guests to sit on. Apparently infrastructure grants had ceased paying for furniture many years before.

"No, no, no," chuckled Rose. He had just turned eighty-seven and was quite spry if rather wizened. Tiny and bald with a scabby head, he reminded Lori somehow of the flower whose name he shared, an old rose apple left to bake in the sun. "We are not *stealing* the ice cores. They are the legitimate property of my close personal friend Ben Gerson, who collected them, labeled them, and just happened to store them in the cold room in a lab that LEPER has recently consigned to—"

"To the enemy! To Bob Drift and Dim Bulb."

"Bob Drift isn't really the enemy." Lou's voice carried from over in the corner, where he was inspecting one by one the theses of the students Rose had graduated over the decades. "Even if he did embezzle a couple hundred K from me. But of course he can't know what we're up to."

"And how about Dim Bulb?" Lori wondered.

"She means Jim Kalb," Lou explained to a puzzled Rose, "that idiot from the basement. Beneath contempt. He was kicked out of Chicago the year I started—had to finish his degree somewhere in the frozen north, Fairbanks or something. It took him eleven years to get his PhD."

"Nevertheless, I don't want him spewing Lyssavirus at me. How are we going to make sure he's not there? And how big and heavy are these ice cores, anyway? We're not the most physically imposing group of conspirators, you have to admit."

The others laughed. Lori did not think it was all that funny.

"My role," said Rose, "is to act as a diversion. The LEPERLab was of course quite pleased that someone of my stature offered to give a talk on quantum gravity at their, ahem, institution this Friday. The institutionalized will thus be required to attend. A single guard will probably deliver the three of us to the lecture hall and then should leave. All you kids need to do is to make yourselves scarce, stroll casually across the lab to the cold room, and load as much sample as you can into a small and innocuous-looking cooler, something that might pass as a lunch box. Ben has sliced the cores into ten-centimeter sections and has marked the most interesting with a star. Then we shall run back to campus and install them in your lovely little Arctic lab." Rose beamed as if the idea of cooling a room to miserable temperatures had been his own, rather than a sarcastic suggestion from someone skulking in the tropics.

"You should have at least an hour to operate," Rose continued. "Make a couple of trips if you like, just don't let *them* pick you up."

"Oh, the go-tards," Lou scoffed. "You can hear them coming from a mile away."

Lori listened in slack-jawed skepticism as they explained that the LEPERs were no longer allowed to walk from building to building, under pretext of safety, but had to be shuttled around on some sort of horrible yellow leafblowers on wheels. She just plain didn't believe it when they told her that the safety issue was killer deer.

"I feel like Bigwig going into Efrafa," she groaned. She was reminded by Lou's laughter that they were about the same age and had thus both been warped as little kids by the tyrant bunnies and the terrible, terrible Woundwort. "Which obviously makes you Hazel."

"Hazel-*rah*," Lou corrected with an air of bunnylike superiority.

"A good enough analogy," Rose agreed, "since your goal will be to blend in as much as possible and not give our secret away. Lori, if you don't own a business suit, which I suspect you do not, buy one. It can be cheap, but it must be black. Try to look a little older, and study this carefully."

Lori took the sheet of paper he handed her: it was a hand-drawn topo map of the LEPERLab showing its rugged terrain, with the Drift lab perched at the top of the largest hill in between a clump of trees and a rocket-fuel lab marked *Abandoned*. She turned around to show it to Lou, but the way he smirked at her over *Unitary Theory of Two-Dimensional Quantum Gravity* made her realize that he had drawn it, that the past two days had been a mission of reconnaissance.

"If we make several trips with our coolers, how do we keep the cores cold?" Lori wondered. "Do we need a refrigerated truck?"

"Try driving one of those on lab, and you *will* go to Gitmo," Rose warned. "No, we want a perfectly innocuous California car, which we will pack with dry ice. What do you drive, Lori?"

"What, me? My disapproval of internal combustion isn't part of legend yet?"

"Hm. Lou, your vehicle doesn't have a lot of room."

"And I sold it to pay for the set of wheels I'm sitting on now."

Rose looked as if he was finally beginning to understand how sorry his accomplices were. "One of you at least has a license, I hope? I haven't driven in many years."

Lori raised her hand. "A Quebec license, if that counts. But I assume a rental car would attract suspicion?"

Lou gave a deep sigh. "Let it go down for the record that, in the interests of science, I am willing to speak to my parents and borrow their accursed SUV."

Lori had never eaten at McDonald's or been to Disneyland. She didn't have a cell phone, barely knew how to make one dial. She mowed her lawn with a little push mower from the 1950s that she sharpened herself. It was with a sentiment of eternal corruption, then, that the very next day she heaved herself what felt like ten vertical feet into the driver's seat of a monstrous white SUV.

The road seemed a hundred miles away. The cars around her looked like ladybugs. She had no idea how Lou was going to get into the passenger seat until she realized the dashboard had a huge handle, like one of the best holds at the climbing gym. It was still quite a pull-up, and he sprawled in the seat and looked around the interior of the car with disgust. "I need to learn to drive again," he muttered, "but being in this thing makes me physically ill."

"Yeah, tell me about it."

"You, because you're a budding ecoterrorist." He put one hand on her shoulder for both solidarity and balance, trying to position all body parts correctly into the seat. "Me, because someone tried to kill me in it."

"*What?*" Lori squealed, recoiling from the door and steering wheel as if they would be spattered with blood. "Everyone says you were in the Beemer."

"Well, you know STI and its stories. After what I'd heard about you, I was expecting—"

Lori really wanted to hear the end to that sentence, but Rose interrupted them. "Happy thoughts, kids! Think happy thoughts!" He buckled himself into one of the passenger seats. The interior was so cavernous that it swallowed without a trace their two industrial-sized coolers filled with dry ice. They were covered with a blanket for some semblance of discretion, and the lunchbox-style coolers were scattered over the top along with some old clothes and a couple of random items of sports equipment Lori had grabbed from her office.

She must have been nervous, because she took two wrong turns on her way up the hill. Rose chuckled approvingly as she cursed and swore her way out of a dead-end street of which both lanes were narrower than the SUV. "It's good to be a bit late," he mused. "They might let us park right behind the building. Whatever you do, don't park in Visitors. You'd have to sneak past the guard gate with your samples—curtains for sure."

The first big mistake she made was to take the right-hand lane into the control area. There were two lanes, separated by orange cones, and this was apparently the wrong one. The size of the SUV kept her from noticing right away that there were guards running towards them, and she had to brake suddenly. They all winced as they heard the coolers in the back slide around.

The guard looked at her, put his foot up on the SUV's step, and started screaming into her face. She couldn't even understand most of what he said, something about a punishment memo and her "colony manager," and it took all of her courage to remember the coaching she'd got from Rose: she slowly pointed to her STI faculty ID from her lapel. As much as the LEPERs hated to admit it, STI managed them, and she knew that the University president had more than once told the LEPER director that he could treat his people any way he wanted, but that students and faculty were not to be abused.

Then she spoke, as calmly as possible. "I'm sorry, I've never been here before. We are all faculty from the Physics Department at STI."

"We are delivering Professor Rose to his lecture, where he is going to tell the institution about his Nobel-Prize-winning work on quantum gravity," added Lou, who seemed to have a better understanding of how to talk to arbitrary authority than Lori did.

The guard peered in the windows but wasn't satisfied. He called for backup, and a second guard appeared holding some kind of poster. They opened the passenger door to reveal the great physicist.

Lori turned around in her seat and nearly screamed, thinking Solomon Rose had had a stroke. He was nodding his head slowly and the tip of his tongue protruded from a corner of his mouth. "Oh my goodness," he murmured, as if he had been asleep, rolling Lou's wheelchair towards himself. "Yes, my talk. Where do you say we have to park? Not sure if I can walk in the hot sun...."

The guards consulted the poster, which Lori guessed was some kind of VIP guide. There was nothing written on it, just photos of people among whom were all of STI's Nobelists. They seemed to find Rose among the pictures, and after glancing a few times at him, waved them through to park behind the building.

"Christ, Sol," said Lou, "you wanted to look infirm, not gaga. Skip the slobber next time."

Lori couldn't believe he could talk that way to Rose. She couldn't even do the first-name thing yet. "It worked, anyway. Professor Rose, why weren't you a Bubo?"

"Because I've always preferred to dress in black." All traces of his senility had evaporated. "Besides, in my day, Pasteur House embarrassed itself by having a most egregious French grammatical error painted right on the door."

"An *s* on an imperative for a verb in *–er*," Lou agreed meaningfully, shaking his head. "*Quelle horreur.*" Lori couldn't tell if he was joking or not.

Being allowed to park next to the building meant they were halfway there. Lori quickly lost sight of Rose and Lou in the crush of LEPERs pouring through the auditorium doors, but she wasn't worried about them; they knew what they were doing much better than she did.

As far as she could tell, there was no side door to sneak out of except an emergency exit with an alarm, so she just walked backwards through the crowd, row upon row of zombies who didn't so much as look down to acknowledge her. They were all wearing suits and had their IDs clipped to their lapels, so thanks to Rose she blended in, even though she felt confined in the jacket and dress pants. It always made her nervous to wear something she couldn't do a backflip in.

To her right as she emerged from the building was a gate topped with barbed wire, and beyond it Visitors parking. To her left was the main lab, from which a long trail of LEPERs was filing towards the auditorium two by two. They looked cheap, hot, and uncomfortable in their suits, mostly black but with the rare female presence signaled by a speck of red, beige, or mauve. Lori got a couple of funny looks, but no one said anything as she slipped around the corner close to the gate and walked up the drainage ditch past the building.

Once out of sight of the march, she figured she was home free. There was no one behind the auditorium building—nothing, in fact, but a row of eucalyptus trees and some well-tended bushes of wild rosemary. She paused to consult her map, recalling again that the Drift lab was all the way to the north.

North here meant "up a very steep hill." Lori jogged to get it over with, and she came over the crest only to encounter a yellow go-cart parked in the middle of the road.

The go-tard had clearly expected everyone to be at the talk, since his engine was off and it looked like he was finishing a burrito. He could probably be fired for that—or flogged. "Stop!" he cried, revving the thing into action with a cloud of blue smoke and a noise more horrible than a thousand leafblowers.

Lori did the only logical thing: she turned around and ran. The seams of her cheap suit stretched as she sprinted down the hill with a stride she wouldn't have thought possible, thanking God she hadn't tried to wear dress shoes. She instinctively followed the path that would have scared her the most on her rollerblades, the one with the narrowest, steepest hill and the sharpest right-hand turns, but the thing was right behind her, spewing gasoline and roaring over the feeble shouts of the LEPER driver.

At the base of the hill was a parking lot dotted with small trailers. It looked like a bad place to hide, so at the next right turn she leapt from the street into the bushes next to a tall cement building. The go-tard saw her, put on his brakes, turned the wheel to the right, and crashed.

Visions of federal prison dancing in her head, Lori breathed a sigh of relief as the guard extricated himself unharmed and kicked at his sputtering up-ended go-cart, probably swearing, but she couldn't tell over the two-stroke engine noises. She sneaked all the way around the building in the bushes, came out on the road that led to the auditorium, and retraced her initial steps as fast as she could possibly run.

The air conditioning in the Drift lab hit her like a wave, and she hid under the stairwell for a minute, gasping for breath and feeling this morning's eggs and salsa burn in her stomach. She heard footsteps somewhere in the hall, someone running, and when the door handle turned she wanted to scream—but it was Lou, apparently no more efficient at sneaking around the lab than she was.

For fun, she slipped up behind him and tapped him on the shoulder, but he didn't flinch. He just said "Good" very seriously. "The cold room should be right down this hallway." A note of amusement lifted his voice as he got a good look at her. "I like your 'Birnam Wood comes to Dunsinane' approach. Did it help?"

Lori looked down at herself and realized that she had collected quite a few leaves, sprigs of rosemary, and cactus spines. "It's not funny. I got chased by a go-tard."

"Yeah," he sympathized grimly. "They have their engines off. Come on, let's get this over with."

They each had two small coolers lined with fake ice, and managed to pack in quite a few of the ten-centimeter rounds. Before they left, Lori stuck her head into the hallway and looked around, still unnerved by the footsteps she'd heard. She didn't mention them to Lou, though, too distracted by what she saw as he latched the door. "That is an extremely dangerous handle to put on a cold room. They should be designed so you can't get trapped inside."

"Remember, Lori," he replied solemnly, "the number one safety concern of the LEPERLab is killer deer. I can assure you that the latch is entirely hoof-proof."

They went back to the car together, taking the highest road across the top of the lab and coming down as close to the gate as possible, hoping that the steep terrain would discourage go-tards. Lou enjoyed the downhill, but admitted he'd had a rough time the previous week identifying a path to the Drift lab that he could climb without falling over backwards.

Although the descent was uneventful, neither could face a second run, and they and their samples took refuge in the immense bowels of the SUV. They sat in the rearmost passenger seat and sorted the cores into one of the coolers, trying to read the scribbled handwriting on the brown paper each one was wrapped in.

They still ducked every time they heard a noise, but there was no sign of human (or cervine) life until the auditorium doors burst open and the zombie parade began in reverse.

"Hurry," Lori urged, throwing in her last few cores without inspection. "He'll be here any moment, and your cooler seems to be leaking."

Lou covered his lap with his lunchbox. "Um, no, I think that's just pee."

Rose was not at all astonished to see the job done. He gave them the thumbs-up and got into the passenger seat while Lori walked, nearly upright, through the vehicle to the front. She started the engine before the Great Man had even had a chance to find his seatbelt.

Their adventure wasn't quite over. They waved their IDs at the gate and were immediately surrounded by a throng of armed guards with baby-seal-clubbing gleams in their eyes. They made them all get out of the car and dragged out the coolers, and Lori heard "anonymous tip" and "white SUV" whispered smugly more than once. If only they'd thrown some cans of soda in the coolers and pulled the paper off the ice cores, they would have looked like so many ice cubes. Now they were going to jail and it was her fault.

"These are the personal property of Benjamin Gerson," she heard Rose say as they led her around to the passenger door where two guards were tossing every loose item they could find out of the SUV.

Inside the guard booth, behind glass, stood the person who was presumably commanding them. It was someone from the VIP list, a fat man with tiny eyes and ears and a look of twisted hatred on his face. He smirked with glee as an enormous guard towered over the ancient physicist, and Lori could see the struggle in both of their limbic systems between the joy that snapping the old man's neck like a twig would bring versus the fear of retribution for abusing a Nobel laureate.

"So," the behemoth asked dangerously, bending over to look into Rose's weathered face, "you must have a *personal property pass?*"

"Of course I do!" Rose exclaimed confidently. "Dr. Barrow, Dr. Maupertuis, do you recall where you put that pass I gave you?"

Lori and Lou gaped at each other, betrayed. *They* weren't on the no-clubbing list. *Don't hurt us!* ran in a panicked refrain through Lori's mind, but she made a show of opening her briefcase pocket, rustling through the papers until something occurred to her. She held up a yellow slip. "Is this it?"

"I think that's it," Rose replied.

The guards looked at each other, peered at the paper…and then they started loading everything back into the SUV. They even shook out and folded the blankets. Lori worked as fast as she could, picking up strewed items so as to have something in her hands, to not be left holding that piece of paper at which the fat man might ask to take a closer look. Already he was moving in their direction, but they were quicker; Lou got into the front seat so fast that she thought he might enjoy going to the climbing gym one of these days.

Weaving out past the orange cones at last, she was shaking so badly that her foot slipped off the brake and she almost ran a traffic light. She could still see the fat man in the rear view mirror, and now that he was no longer scowling she recognized him as the guy with the cop voice who had interrogated her at the hospital.

"*La voiture maudite*," Lou murmured, pulling off his jacket and inspecting a large tear in the lining, then casually using it to cover his crotch. "It's all right, Lori, *du calme*."

This time it helped to hear him speak French, since it reminded her of that cold, innocent country so far away, and of Roger who always spoke Franglais when he was nervous. She told herself that if Lou could maneuver this thing after being shot, then surely a little abject terror was no excuse, and she gave him a weak smile.

"*Je m'excuse*," she muttered as she took a side street past the football stadium, automatically choosing the bike route even though now she was the overgrown fossil-fuel-guzzling enemy. "I don't do well with authority."

"What was it that you showed them back there?"

She tried to laugh but only a squeak came out. "My bill from the bookstore. It was obvious from the Big Men On Campus poster that they don't read well, if at all, and I don't know if it's a coincidence, but the bill said 'Book, Goldstein.' Ben Gerson?"

"Ten points to Pasteur House," quavered Rose from the back seat. "I think I wet myself."

Having distinguished herself as the only member of the expedition not to pee her pants, Lori spoiled the effect by pulling over the instant they were on campus and heaving her breakfast onto the base of a sixty-foot California Fan Palm.

Sol watched her hurl, then rolled down the window and passed her the ice cores. "Go stick this in the freezer, and then I think we can all start our weekend a little bit early, don't you?"

Lori wiped her mouth self-consciously, looking at each of them in turn. They made no move to get out of the car, so she slung the lunch boxes onto her shoulders and headed towards her new "ice lab" to put the cores away.

The door didn't open when she punched in her code, making her go so far as to pull out a calculator to make sure she'd remembered the square root of the fine structure constant correctly. After three tries she realized that the code was not the problem—the door wasn't even locked.

It was almost as if there was something behind it, blocking its swing. She stepped back and gave a tremendous push, and there was a sickening thud and a gap of no more than six inches opened up. She stuck her head in, turned on the lights, glanced down, and then pulled her head out and sank slowly to the floor.

"Lori?" came a distant voice, how many times she didn't know. "Lori, what is it?"

She didn't know how long she'd been sitting there, and it took her a long moment to recognize Bert van Gnubbern, bent over her with worried blue eyes swimming behind thick glasses. "Lori?" he repeated. "Are you OK?"

She finally roused herself when it looked as if van Gnubbern were going to try pushing on the door himself. "Stop!" she yelled. "Don't touch that. Marybeth is in there. If she wasn't dead before I bashed the door open, she is now."

ELEVEN: A VERY CANADIAN WAY TO DIE

THEY SPENT THE ENTIRE weekend being interrogated. The cops didn't drag them downtown, only to the tiny campus police station, which was barely furnished and contained only one cell that they used to call the Bubo tank. The walls were made of unpainted wood and usually it was really hot inside; this late September day was no exception. Despite what she might claim to scare people, Lori had only ever spent the night in jail once before, but there was nothing she hated more than the cops.

She knew it showed. She talked nervously, her hands shook, and she no doubt came across as the most hopeless liar on the planet. It was comforting to hear definitively that the clunk on the head from the door had not done Marybeth any further damage: she had been dead for hours of hypothermia. What was less comforting was that Lori was somehow entirely at fault for the grad student's getting trapped inside the electron microscopy lab.

"What safety precautions were on the room?" they asked more than once. One of them, chubby and sitting, did most of the talking, while the skinny one stayed standing and held onto the documents and photos.

Lori thought fast. "A phone," she said finally. "There was a phone right by the microscope. She could have called Campus Security."

"A phone?" they repeated, as if Lori had said something completely outrageous. "What do you mean, a *phone*? You mean a landline?" They huffed with disdain as she nodded. "Do you know if this landline was operational?"

Of course she didn't—the last time she'd used it had been back in the previous century. "But couldn't Marybeth pound on the door and scream?" she wondered. "It was the middle of the day."

They didn't answer that question, just kept asking her if, and how, and why she'd let Marybeth work in the lab. She had to give all the details about how Marybeth wanted to be an experimentalist but carefully avoided using the words *ice core* or mentioning what the project was about. Marybeth had received no safety training, but then again, she wasn't going to be working with biohazards or going into the BSL-3.

"Would the handle on the door have been visible to someone who was visually impaired?" asked the skinny one with the photos.

That was a dumb question, of course, because there were all sorts of visual impairment, from a myope's bad resolution to central defects to colorblindness. Lori recalled with a sinking feeling her first meeting with Marybeth, though, and something about a restricted visual field. "Was she really partially sighted? I thought she was lying. I mean…"

So then they made her recite all of Marybeth's lies. It made her sick even to contemplate what might have inspired them or whether they had a grain of truth. After a while, they decided to recognize that Lori was nervous and upset, and they asked her why she was shaking.

"Because I'm hungry," she offered, so they left for a few minutes and came back with a small bottle of orange juice and a nasty muffin. The pair checked their notes as she ate, and when they started again, it was at a rapid-fire pace with no mention of Marybeth at all.

They asked why she'd gone to the LEPERLab. They asked what she'd been doing hiding in the rosemary. They showed her a picture and asked her to identify the man in it.

"Anthony Hopkins?"

They looked at each other and apparently decided she really didn't know. "Ben Gerson. Did you have any grudge or resentment against Marybeth?"

She was starting to think that this whole thing was much bigger than herself, lab safety, or even the physics department. "I barely knew her."

"What is your relationship with Louis Maupertuis?"

The way they pronounced his name made her wince. "We're colleagues."

"No more than that?" demanded the fat cop. "You didn't know him in Chicago?"

"In Chicago?" Lori echoed, searching her mind desperately for a possible trap. *Fang Li was at Chicago at the same time as Lou*, she realized, but wasn't about to share that information. "I've never even been there."

They tapped the table impatiently, looking at their notes. Lori's throat was dry, and the juice hadn't helped; it contained some sort of fake flavoring that tasted metallic. "Your employee went into your space, was trapped four hours at below-freezing temperatures, and lost her life. This is an extremely serious incident," said the skinny one harshly.

"My employee?" Lori exclaimed. "Marybeth was not my student."

"Your supervisor informed us otherwise," they gloated together, delighted to have caught her in a lie. "Dr. Kuznetsov affirms you were her official advisor as of your arrival."

"That's news to me." God*damn* Kuzno, Lori thought. "I have no idea why Marybeth thought she should go in there, or how she got the passcode. I was the only one who was supposed to use that lab."

"You could have been injured, too," said the cops.

"I have plenty of warm clothes—" Lori began, then stopped herself as she realized they had something else in mind.

They smirked pityingly, *Poor girl doesn't know what almost hit her.* "You had no business going into the abandoned lab. The falling door could have killed you."

Having spent five years in Canada, Lori had felt her blood run cold on many occasions, but none quite so icy as this. She had not told a soul about the freezer door that had come too close to crushing her two weeks ago. "Who told you about that?" she gulped, sliding her chair back.

"Calm down, Dr. Barrow." The fat cop moved to stand up, as if he were going to run to block her exit.

"I told *no one* about that—not Dr. van Gnubbern, not Lou, not Professor Rose."

"And the incident report?" demanded the skinny one, holding up a sheet of paper with its back towards her.

"Who filed an incident report?" Lori demanded.

They wouldn't tell her. They insisted she knew about it. When she protested otherwise, they claimed to have a written report showing that Kuzno had spoken to her about safety but she had been "unresponsive."

A thought flashed through Lori's mind: Would Kuzno murder Marybeth to stop me from doing experiments?

It was absurd—and yet a student was dead, and it was Lori's fault.

She wouldn't change her story, so after another long hour they had to let her go. Of course, it wasn't without kicking her a few times first: she could have been arrested for stealing from the LEPERLab, she was not to leave town, and she could expect severe repercussions for what she allowed to happen to her student in her space.

"No one's going to be using that lab again for a good, long time," they added as a parting shot.

Lori was too dejected to dwell on the fact that that sounded like a phrase drummed into them by Kuzno.

Hot, sticky, starving, and utterly demoralized, she was in no mood to be slapped on the back by Hannibal Lecter as she left the room.

"Lori!" the stranger exclaimed as if they'd known each other forever. He had a crisp Midwestern accent, more Christian Slater than Anthony Hopkins, making her mind flash between *I ate his liver* and scenes from *Heathers*.

"You must be..." she began with false certainty.

"Ben." He enveloped her hand in a massive, calloused paw and gave her a wink. "I'm here with the *real* personal property pass."

Pulling her hand away, Lori realized it now held a business card: Ben M. Gerson, Regents Professor of Microbiology and Earth Sciences, University of Southern California.

"Give me a call next week," Ben murmured as he moved towards the interrogation room. "I just might tell you why I hate those motherfucking LEPERs."

TWELVE: A BAD BULB

Twelve-thirty on Monday, and it had already been a rough week. Carol had lost her next-to-last SLAP, been forced to "testify" to the security guards about a co-worker's parking violation, and then waited half an hour at the cafeteria for Bob before she gave up and bought lunch without him.

She was picking at her sushi when she saw the ambulance pull up outside of his building. Panicking, although she knew she shouldn't, she abandoned her table and ran across the street, not caring if there were guards or police who would stop her.

Cramps of fish-flavored nausea assailed her as she stood outside the lab on the hot black asphalt of the new parking lot, painfully reminded of just how lucky she was to have Bob. He made good money, he was reasonably good-looking—the gray tooth in the front needed a cap, and she wished he would shave every day, but those were minor details—her parents approved of him, and his parents approved of her. Most men in science were so poorly socialized that even at the age of forty they all trailed after one or two unattainable female targets, PhD in physics with an Olympic gold medal and D-cup breasts.

Her terror evaporated as she caught sight of her husband striding purposefully from the building. Some EMTs followed, supporting a pale, staggering guy in shorts and a thick winter jacket and mittens. They helped the guy onto the stretcher, and before loading it into the ambulance had a conversation with Bob that Carol overheard.

"He says he's been locked in the cold room all weekend," one of them announced in a voice that carried to the small knot of gathering rubber-neckers.

"Claims you forced him to work and he got stuck with no one to hear him yell," the other added. "I think he'll be all right, but he could easily have died in there."

Bob did his best to contend that he didn't know anyone in his group had access to the lab on weekends, but it was clear that they didn't believe him, and the guy in the jacket moaned and writhed theatrically. It seemed to take forever to load the stretcher up, and in this time Carol's panic transformed into anger against Bob's newest employee. He looked homeless, scruffy and dirty with a nasty little beard, and she would bet he didn't get that way just from two days in the cold room.

As soon as the ambulance pulled away, she got up and prepared to run to Bob, but the colony manager appeared and she shrank back. The presence of Ellis D. Tripp always meant danger. She'd never been in his presence without being punished herself or being forced to explain why someone else had done something wrong.

Tripp put his arm around Bob, and Carol thought it was probably time to go home and start polishing her résumé. If Bob got fired, she couldn't stand to work here anymore, but she couldn't just quit. Not with the mortgage they had.

She sighed, looking at the ground, and then bent over to pick something up: it was a sprig of wild rosemary, out of place out here by the cafeteria and the parking lot, where nothing grew. She twiddled it between her fingers, staring off into the distance. Who would hire a pair of ex-LEPERs? Neither she nor Bob had published anything in years.

She watched Bob being led away by Tripp, with a droop in his shoulders that made her sad. There were a lot of times that LPRL made her cry, but she had never seen Bob so discouraged before. She probably wouldn't ever mention it to him, but she had had a bad feeling about this new hire from the beginning, even before catching sight of his beard and little mittens.

As a recovering bulimic, Carol knew one thing: the only thing worse than being stressed and scared was being stressed and scared with low blood sugar. The cafeteria was closed, but there should still be a roach coach down by the trailers where they put the temps, students, and those being punished. She started walking that way, thinking that she would get him a bean burrito and some fruit to leave on his desk.

A year ago—almost a year and a half ago—she had stayed home to meet the professional live-oak tree trimmers and make sure they were as professional as they advertised. That was when this Jim Kalb guy had first been to see Bob. Bob had talked about nothing else at dinner, and she wouldn't remind him now, but he had been pretty suspicious. Jim had said there was a "big proposal" going out at STI and had wanted to know if Bob could hire him if he was on it as a co-investigator. That was OK, and the colony manager had confirmed that it was all true and reasonable. The problem was that the guy had been so secretive: he'd said he was a student of van Gnubbern's, but he didn't want van Gnubbern to know that he was applying for jobs…what sense did that make? Worst of all, it hadn't sounded as if he actually *was* on the proposal, just that he wanted to be, or had "ways" to get himself on if he had to. Had he been blackmailing Dr. van Gnubbern?

But no, it wasn't van Gnubbern who had been the principal investigator—she knew that from Absinthe. It was the young guy in the wheelchair, who'd made the mistake of being crippled and trying to talk down to Abby. Carol knew from painful experience that Abby didn't tolerate physical weakness.

But Jim Kalb could certainly have taken advantage of him if his health was as bad as Abby made it sound. He could wait until the guy was in the hospital and then put his own name on the proposal. The more she thought about it, the more she started to think there was some truth to this. The meeting to open the subcontract had been delayed more than once, and all the problems always seemed to come back to Kalb. No one knew why he was on there as a co-investigator, certainly not for such a large amount of money, and no one could get him into the same room with the principal.

Heading back from the roach coach with a burrito in her hand, Carol noticed that someone or something had trampled the rosemary behind the colony manager's building. It looked like one of those safety movies about the deer attacks, but she didn't really believe in killer deer, and from up close it was pretty clear that these were people-prints. Someone had gone all the way around the building in the bushes.

Someone who was wearing running shoes and had very small feet. Putting Bob's lunch down on the curb, Carol went into the bushes and measured one of the prints against her own. Size 5 max. A kid? Kids weren't allowed at the LPR Lab, certainly not running in the bushes.

No one was allowed to run in the bushes. How had they managed to do this without being seen or picked up by a go-cart? Sure enough, she had only been there for a few seconds when one came putt-putting by, yelling at her and demanding to see her ID.

She managed to grab a small white thing stuck to the rosemary and to retrieve the burrito before surrendering to the go-cart and allowing it to take her back to Bob's building. Once free of the fumes, she turned the white thing over in her hand: a discount department store tag, $29.95 in size 2P.

There were a few small female LEPERs with bad fashion sense. But she didn't know any small female LEPERs with bad fashion sense who would wallow in the rosemary.

She left Bob his lunch, with a little note telling him to look forward to Indian food tonight, and then rode a go-cart up to the Visitors' desk just to set her mind at ease. They didn't want to show her the list of visitors from last Friday, but she said she was processing their mileage reimbursements and they finally gave in. What she thought was a vague and absurd suspicion was confirmed: Lori had been to the LPR Lab on Friday just before Jim had been trapped in the cold room. She had been in the company of a Louis Maupertuis and a Solomon Rose—the latter was marked VIP—and had been driving a white SUV.

It was easy to dismiss Abby's hyperbolic tendencies (they'd all loved the math pun in grad school), but apparently she had a point. Lori Barrow was back in town and weird things were happening. And it was hard to imagine the nefariousness of a plot that would induce Lori Barrow to even get into an SUV.

THIRTEEN: GREEN-EYED MONSTER

As SWIFTLY AS IT had come, Lori's experimental dream vanished. Both the basement labs were barred to entry, the old-fashioned keypads replaced by sturdy police locks. Like a grounded kid, she sat at her desk with a pencil, trying to be a theorist. Kuzno had told her—betraying no emotion—that she needed three theory papers before next year to earn tenure.

It wasn't equations she found herself scribbling as she stared at the page, though. Instead she stared at her bare white wall, contemplated, and scratched a series of notes.

Marybeth made a mistake with budget, $200k sent to LEPERLab, was the first. Then:

Dim Bulb hired with the money. Who hired him? Why?

Who filed the report on the falling door?(Kuzno?)

The door squeaked and slammed open. Lori jumped and shoved the paper under her computer, pretending to be typing on the keyboard.

She'd expected the cops, or worse, but it was just Lou, waving a sheaf of paper in the air.

"What is it?" Lori exclaimed, pushing away her laptop.

"Here." He slid the sheets onto her desk. "Take a look. Poincaré is right about this theorem, of course, but he does the proof in such a cumbersome way."

"What?" Lori glanced down, seeing row upon row of differential equations in small, crabbed handwriting. In ink, no less.

Her reproach must have shown on her face, because Lou got defensive. "I'm just trying to help. You need three theory papers, right? Finish this with me and that's one. In a few more days you'll have a couple more, and then we can think about other things again."

"I can't believe you can think about this at all, when—when—"

"Spit it out, Barrow."

Lori pulled out her own page of notes. "When your graduate student was murdered on Friday!"

Lou dropped his gaze to the Poincaré derivation, hiding his face. He pulled out a page and shuffled it elsewhere in the stack, as if it had been out of order. "Why would you say that?" he asked at last, in a flat voice.

Lori scrunched down to try to look him in the eye, but he stayed stubbornly riveted on the manuscript. "Because too many things are suspicious," she said at last. "Kuzno got everything he wanted. He hated Marybeth, right? Now she's gone. I refused to take his advice, and now I have no choice. I have to hire his students and be a string theorist. I can't even complain about it, because I'm in disgrace for letting a poor blind girl stumble into a freezing room."

She paused for breath, trying to think of the least-paranoid scenario. "Maybe Kuzno just wanted to get me in trouble, so he locked Marybeth in for an hour or so, not expecting her to die. What were those skits all about, anyway? Did he really molest her?"

"Those skits were a joke, Barrow," Lou growled. "My students were just taunting Kuzno."

She looked back down at her notes. "Or maybe it wasn't Kuzno at all. How about Dim Bulb? You said you didn't even remember putting him on your proposal. And now look, he went from being in the basement to having his own position, based upon Marybeth's 'mistake.'"

Lou gave a strangled laugh. "Murdering someone to get a job at the LEPERLab would be so fucking pathetic that if I thought he was even capable of it…I'd almost feel sorry for him."

"And did someone try to kill me?" She was about to explain about the falling door, but decided to try to trap him instead.

Lou glanced up at last, startled. He looked tired; no doubt he'd been up all night with his crazy French mathematicians. "Who and how?" he wondered, still without inflection.

"The door in the BSL-3," she said quickly, not giving him a chance to think.

"You mean the yellow fever leak?" Lou was regaining his composure, smirking a little. "Surely that doesn't count as a murder attempt."

He didn't know. It was a good thing, she supposed, and she needed an ally, so she told him the whole story.

This time she did get a response, if a lukewarm one. "OK, so you need to find out who submitted the incident report. If it's Kuzno, then we can panic."

"The problem is, head of Safety is Absinthe McRae. She's my sworn enemy since the first year of grad school."

Lou slapped Lori's desk, scattering pages of math. "I really don't have time for this shit. Can't help you with Absinthe, sorry—she hates me too. But if you figure out who the killer is, I'll be in my office."

He left, running over the poor abandoned math paper, which lay crumpled and forgotten like the shards of Lori's career.

Maybe he was right. Maybe she should be writing proofs instead of seeing killers behind every self-latching door. But it wouldn't hurt to go see Absinthe—and try to kill two birds with one stone, because Fang Li seemed to have found herself in Gitmo.

On Sunday evening, after another session with the police, Lori had returned home to find a weepy message on her answering machine from her Chinese-Canadian postdoc. Fang had apparently had visa problems at the border, and when she'd tried to contact STI, had been told she had no position—that, in fact, there was no evidence she ever existed.

HR couldn't help, because STI's HR was two senile old ladies who didn't even seem aware they had jobs. If Lori wanted something done, she needed the all-powerful arm of the legal office. They called themselves "Intellectual Property," but there really weren't that many inventions coming out of a university this size. Patent lawyers though they may be, the employees of IP spent most of their time keeping student pranks, faculty backstabbings, and suicides out of the newspapers. They no doubt did things even more mysterious and underhanded, but what those things might be, Lori couldn't even guess.

Taking her course text and a notebook in case she had to wait to see her lawyer of choice, she headed to the edge of campus and then one block west to the beautiful old Victorian that housed the STI legal center. The university had promised the city not to expand past its historical boundaries, but it had managed to get around that inconvenience by gradually allowing administrators and support staff to ooze, like metastatic cells, into the surrounding residential district.

An enormous specimen of floss-silk tree grew in front of the legal building. They had been imported from Brazil and looked like something out of the Jurassic. Their lizard-green trunks bore triangular, carnassial-like teeth, as if warding off brontosaurus attack. The palm-shaped leaves dropped off in the fall, giving way to pink and white hibiscus-like flowers that morphed into six-inch green footballs stuffed with soft cotton. This particular tree was in the stage between leaves and flowers, but by spring it would have all stages—flowers, footballs, cotton—and it was hard to imagine it needed such teeth to protect the hard, inedible fruit. She gave its spiky trunk a careful pat for luck and went up the stone steps to see Abby.

The secretary pointed her to an armchair and told her to be patient. She waited quite a while, solving end-of-chapter problems until she felt eyes on her. Her old classmate towered above her, pitiless gaze taking in every inch to judge whether Lori had gained a few pounds or learned how to dress (the answer to both was no). Her green poison-liqueur eyes finally fell on Lori's work, and she burst into a mad cackle that probably terrorized the parakeets feeding in the floss-silk tree.

"Well, well, well, Lori," she chortled, "It's not just about the qualifying exam anymore, now is it?"

Lori slammed her notebook shut and stood up. Abby had always been intimidating, but back in grad school Lori had had the advantage. This role reversal was downright scary.

They'd never really been friends, but as Lori took her seat in the conference room and listened to Abby's recriminations, she realized her old classmate hated her. After all these years, she was still angry that Lori had found graduate school in physics to be her natural element and that she, Abby, had been forced to look elsewhere for a career, not because she couldn't do physics—in fact, she'd been nearly brilliant—but because she couldn't deal with the social aspect.

Maybe "anti-social aspect" would be a better term. Lori did have to admit that a psycho had taken a pot-shot at Abby in graduate school, only missing her because one hundred fifty pounds of flesh, in the form of the most annoying graduate student who'd ever lived, had gotten in the way.

Still, that wasn't Lori's fault.

"You were this close—" Abby held two fingers a hairsbreadth apart, right under Lori's nose—"and I mean *this* close to being arrested. The LPR Lab wanted to press charges against you for trespassing and theft. We had to tell them that legally, they are owned by STI, so STI faculty have the right to be on their campus at any time." She chortled in a self-satisfied manner that Lori had never heard; Abby must have taken Arrogant Gestures 101 in law school. "It's just a good thing those LEPERs tick me off, or I would have let them haul you away. Then it seems you're buddies with Ben Gerson, too."

"I don't even know him," Lori protested, remembering she was supposed to call him. About what? she wondered vaguely.

"You've been here less than a month," Abby reminded her. "You've already been the target of a formal complaint, and now there's a body to back it up. I don't know why there's anyone left trying to defend you."

"What formal complaint?" Lori wondered.

"Oh, you've conveniently forgotten this already?" Abby got up and left the room, letting the heavy wooden door close with haunted creak. When she returned, she carried a bottle of water and the very thing that Lori had come here to see.

It had been Marybeth who filed the incident report on the falling door. Unable to believe it, Lori read it through several times, thinking it had to be a different event. But there it was—unsecured freezer door, falling to the ground and nearly causing personal injury.

"Listen to me," Lori hissed, examining the signature very closely so she could verify it later. There was a special curlicue on Marybeth's M. "Something is really strange here. I didn't tell Marybeth about this. I didn't tell anyone. There was no one besides me in the entire building that day, so far as I could tell. She had no way of knowing this happened, unless of course she set it up to happen."

"Marybeth tried to kill you?" Abby smiled benignly, standing up in the corner, sipping her water. "That doesn't work, my dear. Your boss, Kuznetsov, says he lectured at length about the building's infrastructure problems, but you refused to have the labs inspected before you started using them."

"Kuzno is a liar." Lori decided to play a card that made her sick, one of Marybeth's own, hoping that the version of the events she'd gleaned from student gossip wasn't too far from the truth. "He was sexually harassing Marybeth since she got here—you know that yourself. She filed lawsuits against him more than once."

It worked, at least a little. Abby stopped frothing and started thinking. "So what is it you want from me?" she inquired, plopping lazily into her leather chair. "I certainly won't be able to convince the safety committee to re-open that lab any time soon."

"I don't care about that," Lori lied. She leaned in close for dramatic effect, narrowing her eyes at Abby. "I want you to help me figure out who killed Marybeth."

Abby started to laugh, but it quickly turned into a splutter. She spent a long moment gulping water before she responded. "Ordinarily," she admitted, "I'd say you were nucking futs."

Lori waited. "But you know I'm right?" she prompted after a long pause.

"After what happened this morning at the LEPERLab, I'm not so sure."

FOURTEEN: ON TOP OF THE WORLD

CAROL FELT ABOUT INDIAN food the same way she did about anal sex—it was gross, but sometimes she put up with it because Bob liked it. When he was really down, nothing cheered him up like greasy, spicy hunks of meat.

The problem was, he didn't need cheering up. Instead, from the pappadums through the rice pudding, he gloated nonstop about his promotion for saving Jim Kalb's life.

Maybe she should be happy that he wasn't fired. At least they weren't out on the streets looking for new jobs. But something was sketchy, and Bob's mindless celebration of his reward without stopping to think about it was starting to get annoying.

The mango laasi was good. At least she had that. But everything else at this restaurant was too rich and just a little off. Even the water was bad. It had a sort of dishwasher taste; she swore she saw bubbles.

"I don't trust that guy," she interjected at last.

"Who?" Bob raised an eyebrow, chomping away.

"That guy you just hired. Kalb. He's been trying to get this job for years now. Why would he do something so stupid as to sneak in on the weekend and get himself locked in the cold room?"

"That room is not up to code," sighed Bob. "I knew that. It was just lucky I got to him on time." He reached over to pat her with a curry-smelling hand. "I'm sure he was trying to impress me, get some work done on his very first day."

"What kind of work?" Carol asked skeptically. She didn't want to spoil his dinner, but she wished he'd hurry up. It didn't feel like much of a celebration somehow. "What was he doing in there?"

Bob shrugged, taking yet another thick slice of garlic naan and sopping it into his leftover red sauce. "Just cleaning up, I guess. Gerson left a real mess in the cold room—samples wrapped in paper all over, poorly labeled, maybe dangerous. Jim got rid of most of it."

"He threw it out? What if Ben Gerson wants his samples back?"

Bob laughed nastily through a bolus of bread. "There's no way anyone's going to let him back on lab after what he did. He'd better find himself some new samples, is all I can say."

That wasn't a surprising response. Everybody knew the Gerson story, and there weren't many who felt sorry for him. He was a big shot from back East who'd been hired to start an astrobiology program at the LPR Lab, and from the moment he had arrived things had gone wrong. He complained that they wouldn't let him do experiments, or hire graduate students, or do any of the other things important biology professors did. It didn't seem like such a bad deal—he was essentially being told he didn't have to work hard and could just travel around and give the lab some credibility in biology. Finally he had left to take a high-ranking position at a university, and his criticisms had leaked around the media no matter how much both the LPR Lab and STI might have tried to cover them up.

The only reason that he'd gotten away with such vocal complaining was that he'd been a friend of the chief scientist. Anyone else would have been given a punishment memo and had his office reassigned to the trailers in the parking lot. Maybe, Carol thought, Bob was being rewarded for purging the last traces of Gerson from the lab.

It still didn't make sense. By all rights, Bob should be in the trailers too. She'd thought she'd be babying him tonight, not listening to him brag about what a hero he was.

She tried to be conversational, but the instant they got home, she locked herself in the bedroom with her laptop and started searching.

When she first pulled up Jim Kalb's history, her instinct was *There but for the grace of God.*

Kalb was a boson among bosons. He'd spent longer than she had in graduate school, being expelled for being too slow and having to change schools. Anger and frustration were understandable—Carol still remembered stealing packets of mustard and ketchup to season their ramen noodles. If she'd been single, slightly older, or uglier, what a nightmare. They all started grad school so hopeful. None of them, except possibly Lori, really understood that the PhD was only the beginning of a long, hard road.

All her potential sympathy vanished when she followed Kalb's record to his new school in Alaska. He had had sexual harassment charges filed against him several times and been arrested once for indecent exposure, and it didn't sound like an innocent sunbathing or pee-in-the-bushes type of incident. She was starting to think he'd been kicked out of Chicago for reasons other than the slow pace of his thesis research.

When Bob went to take a shower, Carol quickly dialed Lori's number, but of course there was no response and she didn't have a cell. Unable to bear the suspense any longer, Carol tried Abby.

"Oh no," groaned the sleepy voice on the other end. Abby sounded as if she were splashing in the bathtub. "Who put you up to this?"

"No one," Carol insisted. "Well... unless you count Bob. He got a weird promotion and it doesn't make any sense."

"I can't talk about it." Abby emphasized her words with a pull of a plug and a vortex of water. "This is my job, and I'll be damned to *hell* if that woman is going to ruin my career a second time."

"I'm sorry," Carol blurted automatically, shocked to hear Abby swear, but her words were to the ether. Abby had already hung up.

There was only one thing to do. If Lori hated phones so much, she was going to get a personal visit. Carol told Bob that she needed to run to the pharmacy for "something personal" and clutched her tummy, ensuring that he would ask no questions, then got in her car with her GPS.

Lori's address was already in the STI directory, and only a few miles away. It was up a street Carol had never seen before, with a driveway so steep she didn't dare take her aging Honda up it. Bob was always on her case to get a new car, but she was attached to the old gray Civic that had taken her away from postdoc hell into the land of—well, if not milk and honey, at least Soy Delicious and high-fructose corn syrup.

She hid the car behind an overgrown podocarpus and walked up the hill, bent over like the Missing Link, wondering how Lori managed to navigate it on any of her preferred means of transport.

A huge, twisted pine tree obscured the house. Carol reached into her purse for a small flashlight, only to jump as it reflected off a pair of eyes high in the tree. A raccoon, she told herself, heart thumping as she sidled up to the door.

But this wasn't the house—it was a garage. There was another building down a broken brick staircase, obscured by sharp vines that grabbed at her clothes as she felt her way down carefully wth her feet. An old oak and a thick, overgrown bougainveilla obscured the front door until she was right in front of it.

She knocked—timidly at first, then like she meant it. Lori finally appeared, still sweaty and in lycra even though it was nearly ten o'clock. "Oh, hi," she said blandly, not seeming in any way surprised. "What's up?"

"Bob got a promotion at the LEPERLab."

"Oh, really?" Lori scratched her head, puzzled.

"But it's bad. I think."

"Uh huh. Come on in and have a drink."

Carol wasn't quite sure what "have a drink" would mean, since Lori had never had a drop of alcohol or commercial soda in her life. She sat at the kitchen table and waited, mildly curious, until she was presented with a fresh, homemade, thoroughly undrinkable lemonade.

"Auugh!" she spluttered, as the acidic liquid burned her already curry-assaulted lips.

The New Lori was empathic enough to hand her a glass of plain water and a vial of a viscous substance she claimed was glucose syrup. "It's the same one I use for electron microscopy—well, not exactly the same one," she amended as Carol grimaced. "Same recipe, though." She started to babble about the relative solubility of sugars, but Carol was too impatient for that tonight.

"Bob hired this guy Jim Kalb who worked for Dr. van Gnubbern," she began, adding a bit of lemonade and a generous serving of glucose to the water. It was actually good this way. "The first weekend he was on lab, Jim got trapped in the cold room. They took him away in an ambulance this morning, but instead of punishing Bob, the colony manager promoted him."

Lori gave her a look of absolute incredulity, as if Carol had transformed into a werewolf in front of her eyes. She missed her own mouth with her glass, spilling lemonade on her cheek, and seemed utterly incapable of speech.

Finally she found something to say. "Is Jim dead?"

"Dead?" Carol wondered. "No, of course not. He's in the hospital, but he'll be just fine." She giggled nervously. "I think Bob would really be in trouble if Jim had died."

"But don't you know…?" Lori broke off, got a bit unsteadily to her feet, and lurched off to the dark living room. She returned after a few seconds with an open laptop, typing as she walked. "You don't know," she concluded, then typed again. "No, you really don't." She placed the computer on the table, then collapsed into a chair. Her computer was battered at the edges, its screen filthy. "Jesus Christ on a stick! I always thought the Coverups Office was my friend."

It was Carol's turn to be incredulous as she learned that a graduate student on campus had suffered the same fate as Jim—only she, unlike Jim, had died. There was nothing in the papers about the deaths, the poor girl had no family or friends, and so the whole thing was about to disappear down the collective memory hole.

"Dim Bulb had been harassing her, apparently," Lori mused, "which really throws a monkeywrench into the hypotheses."

"Who is Dim—?" Carol began, then realized: Jim Kalb—Dim Bulb. Always you and your epithets, she thought, growing angry at Lori. "But Kalb was a victim, too, right?"

"Maybe. Maybe he set himself up in a similar way to divert attention. It still doesn't make any sense, because everyone seems content to believe Marybeth's death was an accident. Unless Kuzno tried to kill them both, and failed with Jim?"

"Who's Kuzno?" Carol wondered.

Lori gave her a look of supreme scorn, clearly thinking that campus intrigues should be known to all. "Who's Kuzno? Only the worst department head the STI physics department has ever seen. Murder is the only thing he hasn't done—or at least been caught doing. Maybe he hired Jim and used him to kill Marybeth, then tried to off him to shut him up."

"It was Dr. van Gnubbern who hired Jim," Carol protested.

Lori jumped up and took the lemonade things, returning them to the kitchen. With her head in the fridge, she called back, "I forbid you to imply anything bad about Dr. van Gnubbern."

"Well…" Carol couldn't resist twisting the knife a little. "You have to admit, he is known for hiring freaks and misfits."

Lori pulled her head out. The fridge gaped open, empty. "Dr. van Gnubbern saved me from a life as a crack whore. If he hired Dim Bulb to give him a chance, that's fine. But if he's seen anything evil going on, I know he would have stopped it."

Carol knew it was futile to argue, and for now she didn't have any other ideas. Her phone vibrated in her bag and she leapt up, not wanting to have to explain what had taken her so long. To the list of Jim Kalb, Dr. van Gnubbern, and the mysterious Kuzno, she would have to add Bob as someone who wasn't acting right and who, just possibly, knew too much.

FIFTEEN: MY FELLOW LEPERS

I WOULD RATHER BREAK ROCKS in Siberia than have anything to do with the LEPERLab."

Ben Gerson's voice carried dangerously in the near-silence of the public gardens. It wasn't safe to talk in the physics building, so they had decided to clear their minds of death and freezing by taking a walk in the most extensive botanical garden in Southern California. Lori, Lou, and Ben appeared to be the only ones here, at the top of the steep trail that terminated in a Zen rock garden and bonsai display, and Ben made no effort to whisper as they stood on the stone path and waited for Lou to make his way up the gravel. It was a hot and windy day, small stones dancing on the path at their feet.

"And I mean that literally," the ex-LEPER continued with a hearty laugh. "Last year I got to break rocks in Siberia! A very adventuresome Russian postdoc took me to drill permafrost cores in the Arctic. Can you imagine, forty thousand years of microbial history, and you can hold it in your hand!"

Ben was exactly what Lori wanted to be when she grew up. He had the energy and enthusiasm of a boy one-quarter of his age, not to mention the crude sense of humor and the potty mouth. He was charming, personable, by far the best explainer she had ever met. A mere two hours after they'd started this afternoon, she felt as though the entire realm of astrobiology was within her grasp.

At the same time, there was something merciless about him that poor souls like van Gnubbern could never achieve. Lori got the impression that he had stabbed quite a few van Gnubberns in the back in order to get everything he'd had: an endowed chair at a big-name university back East, a research group of forty students and postdocs, and sponsored field trips that spanned the globe from pole to pole. His group had been to Siberia, Antarctica, the Galapagos, the Falkland Islands, Hawaii, Iceland, Greenland, and Alaska—and those were just the places he'd mentioned within the last hour.

"Tell me, Ben," Lou demanded when he had finally made it up the hill, "do your students love you or hate you for dragging them off to Siberia?" There was a nasty edge to his voice that Lori had never heard before.

"It depends on their temperament," Gerson replied solemnly. "Of course, I will not take anyone on fieldwork who is disruptive or mentally unstable. There have been incidents, but no one has ever been seriously injured or died in my group. This is in part because I have zero tolerance for sociopaths like James Kalb."

"Did you know him?" Lori asked quickly, before Ben could have a chance to censor his thoughts.

Ben hesitated, glanced at Lou, nodded. "I suppose I owe you the whole story... Do you want to sit under a tree while I dredge my poor old memory for the details?"

"You owe me nothing," Lou growled, "and I don't want to sit. Is this the top already?"

They were, indeed, at the highest point of the gardens, and spread out below were a dozen acres representing almost every flora on Earth. The mild California climate was kind to everything except the true tropicals, like cacao, and cold-loving species such as quaking aspen. To their right were the zones comparing Africa and South America, the succulents of remarkably similar shapes and sizes despite being genetically unrelated. Australia was just below them, mostly shielded by a forest of eucalyptus that rustled in the hot breeze. Leading off to the left were a series of traditional gardens from all of the major nations of Europe. They were standing in Japan, having passed up the path through China, and the path down the other side would take them through Thailand and India and finally to the rose garden that had helped make their city famous.

"Shall we visit Thailand, then?" Ben mopped his forehead with an embroidered handkerchief and started down the trail with a spring in his step. All that fieldwork had made him as fit and sure-footed as a bighorn sheep; even Lori could barely keep up on the downhill. He was clearly stalling for time, giving them anecdotes about various scientists who had gone mad in the field while debating which real subject to broach next. It was testimony to his charm that he was able to make Lou laugh merrily at the image of a Bulgarian geologist hallucinating on a cinder cone, throwing his crampons at imaginary Martian attackers.

Standing under a mini-plantation of rubber trees, Ben grew sober again and admitted, "Kalb has a reputation everywhere. Lou, I warned your advisor many years ago about him—I think it was even before you started graduate school. Far be it from me to tell someone how to run a research lab, but I let him know in no uncertain terms that I did not want that guy around my people at the South Pole."

They continued down the hill, Gerson a bit more relaxed as he changed the subject from Dim Bulb to the South Polar Station. He himself had never spent the winter there—"and nothing could induce me to do so!"—but for a while he had had students there every year. "The Pole is not ordinary field-work," he explained as a fragrance of sandalwood welcomed them to India. Lori didn't have to read the sign to recognize this one; Radi had introduced her to it in Hawaii. "It drives even good men and women batshit. The altitude is the equivalent of eleven thousand feet, so you spend your days in a constant state of mountain sickness, your hair and nails don't grow, you become forgetful and moody. People imagine that they will be spending a cozy winter among colleagues—this is an error. The researchers are a small minority, and the support staff despise them. Think of all of the administrators and secretaries and other fools we scarcely tolerate on a daily basis. Now imagine that they are somewhat more misanthropic and anti-social, enough so that they feel a compelling need to spend a year away from civilization. *Now* spend your days and nights locked under a dome with them, with walls the thickness of cardboard and no sight of the sun for three solid months. It is no place for either alcoholics or teetotalers, since taking refuge in booze is one of the sanest approaches to surviving August, which they call One Long Fucking Month. I would never send a student there twice, and never under any circumstances make a trip there either a punishment or a reward. Kalb was a recipe for disaster. But Lou, I have to tell you it was a mistake not to speak with your advisor earlier."

"Why?" Lou sounded distracted, occupied with navigating the paving stones. It took him a second to realize the implication and ask, "Did you talk to him this weekend? What did he say?"

"He feels terrible about what happened, and in some way responsible, which he is. He bailed Kalb out of jail more than once, and he knew about Kalb's pathological hatred for you."

Lou pulled off the trail, locked his brakes, and closed his eyes for a long moment. When he opened them again, they were fixed on Ben. "You're saying that Kalb did more than kill Marybeth."

"I'm saying it's very possible," Gerson admitted, seeming pleased that Lou had caught on without histrionics.

Lori knew Lou well enough by now that she could tell when he was emotional—his voice got very quiet, and if it was especially bad, he used too many weird French cognates.

So far, he didn't seem upset at all, just disbelieving. "Was he even around when...? I mean...it's been almost two years."

"He was hired six weeks before the attempt on your life," Lori noted. "You'll also notice we've had no more problems with the elevator since he left. I've been watching it carefully."

"Jesus Christ!" Lou slapped a feathery tree trunk next to him. "You think he'd do this to me and then fuck with the elevator? I can't even imagine that level of sadism." He looked pleadingly at Ben, obviously hoping the old man would give a different answer. "Ben, we're physicists! We don't murder each other."

"Happened when I was in grad school," said Lori, bending to examine a lotus flower. "Some squalid love triangle. Abby was involved and came a few inches from having her head blown off. They let the guy finish his degree in prison, too."

"It gets hushed up, in general," Gerson agreed. "Why do you think STI students are no longer terminated based upon the qualifying exam? And Lori, what was that incident in Montreal?"

"Which one? The rejected student who killed fourteen women just because they were women? Or the professor who didn't get tenure and shot all of his colleagues?"

It was like Strip Integration. Ben was not to be outdone. "Then there was the one in Iowa, which actually should win some kind of award, as it's the highest body count by an actual physics grad student."

"Virginia Tech, highest body count total!" Lori rejoined.

"You're making me wish I had failed geometry and gone to work for the movie industry," Lou grumbled. "I'd still be living in Malibu with my girl-friend. Do you honestly think it was Dim Bulb? What did I ever do to him?"

"He was expelled from grad school," Gerson reminded him, "and apparently he always blamed you, claiming he was forced out so you could be hired." He held up a hand before Lou could interrupt. "I know, it has no basis in reality. It also seems he was jealous of your success with the opposite sex."

"That has even less basis in reality," Lou informed him with a dry laugh.

"Kalb had his issues," Ben admitted. "I have bailed my students out on occasion, but not for the sorts of crimes Kalb was accused of—assault and attempted rape."

"Ew!" Lori groaned, making the others turn around as if they had forgotten she was there. A bunch of pieces fell together in her mind at once. "Oh my God. Jim Kalb is the guy with the fingernails." She found herself telling the story of the guy on the train, who had hated Lou then. Had he come to STI as a technician in order to concoct some sort of twisted and horrible revenge? "I never noticed his face on the train, or learned his name, and here he always had," she paused to shudder, feeling queasy, and then said, "those mittens."

Lou shut his eyes again. His face was so full of pain and horror that Lori couldn't bear it and closed hers too. When he spoke, his voice sounded hollow, as if he were speaking in a dream. "He is an evil, stupid, moronic fool," he began, drawing a deep breath. "If he wanted to take advantage of me and fuck up my life, there are plenty of ways he could have done it. He could have just put his name on my proposal—I would have been too flaky to figure it out. He could have taken 90% before I would have noticed. There's so much fun he could have had, and I would have had fun figuring it out. It's not *revenge*, what he did, it's just monstrosity."

Lori peeked at him to see that he had folded his arms across his lap and was gazing up into the leaves. "We're going to get him," she promised, sitting down to take off her backpack. It was full of photographic equipment Lou had asked her to bring, but her laptop was in there too, and she pulled up the photos she'd taken of the torn-up rubber gasket on the bottom of the door. Shielding the screen from the sun under a rubber tree, she showed them the pictures of the gouges in the rotten wood. "At least we can prove he was responsible for the yellow fever leak," she suggested.

"But why would he lock himself in a different coldroom? To divert attention?"

"That's exactly the sort of thing he would do," snorted Ben. "Too stupid to leave well enough alone. It doesn't surprise me in the slightest."

Lou looked at the ground, stopped Lori as she was about to pack up the equipment, and gestured silently for her to hand him the camera and a wide-angle lens. It was a fancy SLR that looked brand new, and he caressed them for a long while in silence before he spoke. "You guys go ahead," he murmured at last. "I want to be alone for a little while, commune with a tree, and pretend I don't belong to the human race."

"Promise you won't hurt yourself," Lori demanded before she could help it.

He glanced at her with a little smile, not at all angry. The dry air had turned his curls into a dandelion-like frizz that suddenly made him seem innocent, like a blond young Einstein. "Promise. I don't know if I'll be coming back in to work today, though."

"If the cops won't arrest Dim Bulb, I'll kill him myself," Lori reassured.

Mentally unstable, Lou was not, so they left him there among the thirsty-looking gardenias and finished descending the hill into the rose garden. Lori knew that this had to be one of the hardest days of her colleague's life and that she, too, should mourn to some extent, but what she mainly felt was relief. She was thrilled to have met someone she could look up to at last, someone who at sixty had never grown up and who had made science into the great adventure it was supposed to be.

"I don't really give a flying fuck about Dim Bulb," Gerson confessed as they passed under the trellis into the roses. The sun baked the sandy garden, and the fragrance from the crawling, climbing, and shrub roses was intoxicating. Dozens of overhead misters tried to combat the desert air, but the wind carried most of the water onto the few visitors, who hurried along the path. "He needs to stop killing off the good people, but that's not why I'm here. I need you to analyze these ice cores and win this Polar Institute proposal so that the LEPERs lose."

Gerson talked nonstop as he trotted, growing increasingly furious as he told Lori how he had become a LEPER. It took a lot to convince someone to leave an endowed professorship, and the LEPERLab had turned on all of its powers of seduction to recruit him. They had flown him out to L.A. no fewer than five times, showing him off to schools in the area like a trophy. They marveled as he described the experiments his group would do to quantify how bacteria had reshaped the Earth in macroscopic ways: from the pillars in Mono Lake to the multicolored strata in Death Valley, microorganisms had changed the geology and geography of the planet, even after they had long been extinct. Ben's goal was to extrapolate their observations to other planets in the solar system, looking for signs of bacterial activity on Mars, Venus, or the moons of Jupiter from orbiting satellites that could survey them entirely. He would go down in history as the man who discovered the first known extraterrestrial life.

His nasty surprise had started less than a week after his arrival. Rather than the fully supported research group he had been promised, he found himself in a soft-money position worse than that of an assistant professor. He was expected to abandon all of his people and write grant proposals for his own salary, laboring under the burden of a 250% overhead. "Pardon me, but I'm too goddamn old to do that shit again. Those first six years are hell."

"I understand," Lori agreed. "I'm almost through with them, and I know I couldn't do it again." They finally left the cloying sweetness of the roses and entered into the cooling shade of eucalyptus. The path was sandy, and she thought that one reason Lou had let them go on was so they wouldn't see him struggle. If he had any idea how she'd crashed, wept, and bled her way through Montreal while learning how to rollerblade, he wouldn't be embarrassed around her.

"That was not the worst part," Ben continued. "It was insulting, humiliating, and it pissed me off, but it was by far not the worst part. False modesty aside, I'm a good enough grant writer that I can pull in enough money to support myself, my whole group, *and* a bunch of shit-for-brains who sit around and smoke pot all day to get the inspiration for their newest acronyms. No, the worst part is that they didn't want me to do experiments. They wanted me to *talk* about them." He bent down and scooped up a handful of eucalyptus acorns, tossing them one by one to emphasize his next words. "Actually doing a damn thing in that fucking place is against the rules."

His anger was refreshing, and Lori really wanted to get him to name names but was afraid of making him clam up. "Is it the whole place, or just a few bad managers?" she prompted.

"The whole motherfucking place." Ben tried to stomp his feet but almost slipped on the leaves and acorns. "I would have given my right arm for a beautiful little containment lab like you have, Lori. I have been a practicing microbiologist for forty years, and I tried to grow a simple plate of *Staph aureus* while I was there. Ever have a zit? Ever blow your nose? *Staph aureus*. But it's a BSL-2 organism, so their 'safety' committee dragged me into a punishment room where some pipsqueak who had failed Micro 101 lectured me for five hours about how I was putting all their lives in danger. That leper of a colony manager, Tripp, made me walk to work for two weeks wearing some kind of Unclean sticker, and he would have done worse if I wasn't friends with the chief scientist. It was like that day after day, week after week, until all I could do was spend 100% of my time driving around the area looking for other jobs."

A row of century plants of all different ages grew at the entrance to the gardens. The youngest looked like nothing more than overgrown aloe vera; as they moved along the row, a few brave specimens were shooting up their twenty-foot stalks, which swayed in the wind. The stalks would bloom in early spring, and then the plants would die. Nearest the entrance, flowers still stood around tangles of dead leaves, dried and brown and curving over the entryway like a gate.

The campus was hidden from view by the immense trees of the movie-star neighborhood. Lori paused before they began their two-block journey home to say, "I don't have that containment lab any more, you know. Until we get Dim Bulb arrested, Marybeth was my fault."

Ben put his hand on her shoulder and for the first time spoke in a whisper. "I hear that you're not discouraged by something so minor as a padlock."

"You're right, but sneaking into the lab won't work. If we want to submit a proposal, Kuzno has to sign off on it, which of course he won't do if we were in the lab against the rules. And what if..." She didn't want to sound paranoid, but it had to be said. She stayed rooted to the spot, delaying their return to where the walls and rosebushes had ears, and whispered, "What if Dim Bulb wasn't acting alone? What if Kuzno put him up to it?"

"Well." Ben seemed to consider this seriously. "You have a point. There was a bomb placed in my car while I was interviewing, and this was before Dim Bulb was hired."

Lori couldn't believe Ben had kept an item so juicy from them this whole time. She was opening her mouth to shout when he interrupted.

"Do recall that the Enemy School is located in South Central. The police refused to take it too seriously, saying it was a local punk. But it's thanks to the fact that the bomb was made by an idiot that I'm here talking to you today."

"Honestly, I don't have much desire to do experiments until these people are locked up."

"Hmph." Ben looked disappointed. "Well, if you want to get Kalb off the streets, I think you need to use the LEPERs for that one."

SIXTEEN: SKELETONS IN THE CLOSET

BOB WASN'T THE ONLY one to have received a mysterious LEPER promotion. Jim Kalb had been promoted, too, and now he was Carol's boss.

First he took her to task for her lack of productivity. He told her to stop trying to get administrative SLAPs and to do "what she'd been hired to do," which was lab work.

There was nothing she would have liked better, but there wasn't any lab work to do. Jim reassigned her office to a dusty nook next to what used to be the electron microscopy room, and told her she was now the "imaging technician." There was no desk except the one the microscope was supposed to sit behind—the microscope itself was being used to prop open the door. Dozens of dusty old posters hung from the walls, showing close-ups of insect heads, mineral grains, or miniature electronics.

Jim didn't offer to help with getting the room back in order. What he did give her was a wrung-out, reeking parka "in case it gets cold in here."

She didn't like Jim, but honestly, this wasn't the worst thing that had happened at the LEPERLab. If she could drum up some business here at her "imaging center," maybe she'd be back on track to being a scientist again instead of just a secretary.

This brief surge of optimism rapidly evaporated as she called around to the technical groups she knew, asking if they needed any electron microscopy. Everyone—absolutely everyone—told her to try back in three months after the big proposal had gone in. Even the people who usually welded parts for the rovers were all on board for the astrobiology effort, writing or proofreading or running budgets. No doubt Jim had known this; he had probably deliberately set Carol up to be laid off when she couldn't get a SLAP.

She also wasn't sure if the microscope worked—or even if there was electricity in the room. The lamp she unearthed in the corner didn't respond when plugged in, and neither did her cell phone charger. After dozens of calls to Facilities, a pimply teenager dropped by with an Ethernet cable and explained to her thoroughly and at length how it should be plugged into her computer and into the wall, but that was it. She was still sitting in the dark with a two-ton instrument as a doorstop.

At least she had Internet. It wasn't long until she gave in to the temptation to try to find out more about the people who knew too much.

The thing she found the most horrible was that no one seemed to care about the dead graduate student, Marybeth Coleman—Carol made a point to remember her name. There had been absolutely nothing in any of the papers, or on the TV news, or anywhere. Even if the university didn't want to publicize the accident, there should have been someone somewhere who wanted to celebrate her life.

Or not. She was just another failure. With a pang of guilt, Carol thought back to when there had been a shooting in their class in Minneapolis—everyone was just relieved that Absinthe wasn't the one who died. The guy who'd been killed had been a boson with too much interest in a woman way beyond his reach, and people had cared more that Lori would be arrested than about him. Carol had to admit she, too, always forgot his name. One of the apostles, wasn't it? John, or Matthew…She hadn't much cared for him either, but no one deserved to end up dead.

Marybeth didn't seem to have had a web presence, either personal or professional. A search on her name showed that she had been an undergraduate at UC Santa Cruz and that her STI thesis advisors were first Kuznetsov, then Maupertuis, and finally van Gnubbern.

Van Gnubbern's webpage was nothing more than the institutional front page with his picture and a "recent publication" with himself and Lori Barrow in 1988. Lori's web site wasn't much more informative: a few links to her site in Canada and a page about the class she was teaching. When Carol went to the Maupertuis site, she stopped and gaped, not sure which image affected her more.

No matter what Abby said about Maupertuis now, the old version of him was exactly her type, except maybe for the dorky T-shirt with Maxwell's equations on it. Tall and almost unbelievably good-looking, he wore tight jeans, an earring in one ear, and a smile saying *Don't you all wish you were me, suckers?* He had his hands on the shoulders of two equally tall guys next to him, and the shorter members of his group—an Asian guy and a round little nerd—crouched in front looking so much less cool.

Three feet to one side stood the strangest woman Carol had ever seen. When she moused over the figure, hovertext confirmed that this was none other than the poor frozen Marybeth. Everything about her seemed incongruous and wrong. She was at least in her mid-twenties and had a drawn look and big circles under her eyes that made her look even older. But she had her hair in little pigtails and was clutching a pink cylindrical pencil bag and a stuffed salamander. Her dress was a cross between a bathrobe and a nineteenth-century ball gown, made of flimsy cotton that revealed she wore no bra (but needed one) and ringed with lace at the wrists, neck, and ankles. Where had she even found such a thing, Caol wondered, and what brain hemorrhage possessed her to wear it in public?

Eyes half-closed, Marybeth was giving the group of guys a sideways glance of hope, envy, and fear.

Maupertuis's personal link was a bandwidth hell of photographs of all kinds. Carol's LEPER connection was too slow to deal with most of it, but she did find a couple pictures of Marybeth. There was one of her in the passenger seat of a black BMW in a parking lot with palm trees, where she looked terrified. There was another of her on a horse, wearing a helmet and foam pads on her knees and elbows but actually smiling in a way the other pictures would not have suggested was possible.

Carol was staring at that image, trying to penetrate somehow into the dead girl's mind, when she recalled that the library had a legal database accessible only from campus computers. Her fingers quivered with excitement as she logged in, but half an hour later she was bored to tears and making faces at the monitor. The database only reported cases that had been settled in court, and if it could be believed, STI and the LEPERLab combined had had only four cases against them in the past decade. Two of them were about parking.

She was about to give up and try to call Lori when she had the brilliant idea of searching through the newspaper archives instead. The problem was that "Marybeth Coleman" was a distressingly common name, and the database included every little local rag from Imperial Beach to Eastport, Maine. Even "Marybeth Coleman—obituary" gave her over one hundred hits.

The more obscure names gave less data but nothing of interest. Van Gnubbern had given a series of lectures on how everyone should be a scientist—whoop de do, no they shouldn't. Maupertuis had been in a bunch of plays when he was in high school and undergrad, and had been valedictorian of the Faculty of Arts and the Faculty of Science at the Enemy School. Neither of them featured in the papers at all for the past three years, thanks to the powers of the STI coverups committee.

To Carol's surprise, "Kuznetsov" returned thousands of hits, and at least one of these Kuznetsovs led an exciting, evil life. Her heart leapt into her throat when she saw "Kuznetsov named in wrongful-death lawsuit," but it turned out to be an S. Kuznetsov from somewhere back East.

She continued reading some of the stories at random, until something occurred to her. Weren't people named Alexander often called Sasha?

"S. Kuznetsov" was a physics professor and department chairman. And he had been sued after a female graduate student in his department disappeared, presumed killed. Her body had never been found, but the suit claimed that she had asked for protection repeatedly from the department head, who had "mocked" her.

It was either his brother or a coincidence too horrible to be true, but it still didn't make sense. If that was their Kuzno, he had been at a state school—a top school, but still a big public university. Disgraced professors didn't get traded to STI from places like that; it was the other way around.

That incident was seventeen years ago. Just to reassure herself, she looked through the campus directories for the beginning of the nineties.

And there he was. *Sasha (Alexander) Kuznetsov, Principal Engineer, Lobo Peak Rocket Lab, September 1990.*

It was before there were scientists, so he was an engineer. Continuing through the years in the hopes that something would emerge, Carol found that Kuzno had left the LEPERLab for campus right at the time that the Science Colony was formed—almost six years after he was hired. The person who was the obvious choice for physics department head, Walter W. Waddles III, had become a LEPER.

It was almost like an exchange of hostages—Kuznetsov for Waddles. But what could that possibly mean? And why hadn't the campus known to keep him away from the children?

She was scribbling madly on a piece of paper, trying to put it all together, when the dusty old phone on the microscope began to ring.

Somehow, even though most of the time she couldn't use a phone to save her life, Lori had found her. Not only that, but Lori knew that Carol was now the "leader" of electron microscopy at the LEPERLab. She even knew the make, model, and year of the poor instrument being used as a doorstop, and when it had last been operational.

Carol's annoyance faded as Lori began to provide useful information. She said there was nothing wrong with the microscope at all, but that the wiring in the room wasn't set up to handle it. It had apparently been sitting on the floor for nearly a decade, when all it really needed was to be plugged in.

"I can bring you the ice cores!" Lori suggested excitedly. "That way I don't have to wait to have my lab reopened before we start."

It was a good thing Carol was sitting down, because the audacity of that would have knocked her off her feet. "I can't do that!" she cried. "I'd be in direct competition with the LEPER effort." And now here she was, saying "leper" with the rest of them.

"Hogwash!" Lori scoffed, in a tone that made the euphemism worse than a swear word. "Carol, how many times do I have to tell you that the LEPERLab does not exist? We are the same institution. I can give you a charge number right out of my start-up funds. What do you call your funding authorizations, again?" She gave a scornful snort. "A WHAM or a PUNCH or something?"

"A SLAP," Carol admitted, so busy slathering over the thought of a real live charge number that she didn't even get annoyed at Lori. What a sad, Pavlovian creature she had become.

"Right." Lori laughed uproariously at the stupidity of LEPER acronyms. "So I'll SLAP you and everything should be fine. The only one we're in competition with is the LEPER principal investigator."

"OK, I guess, but just one more thing. What if the LEPER principal investigator is a murderer?"

There was a momentary surprised pause—but Lori would never be nonplused for long. "Then I'll give you a few video cameras to catch him with," she promised with a conspiratorial chuckle.

SEVENTEEN: FIRE AND ICE

IT WASN'T EXACTLY THE kind of theory she was supposed to be doing, but by the end of the week Lori had made real progress on the astrobiology project. She was just now starting to get what she thought was a good conceptual grasp of what was important about the microorganisms—"microbial communities"—in the ice cores.

Ben Gerson had been a godsend in helping her formulate the questions to be answered. There were key ways to image the traces of life in the ice in a way that astrobiologists could understand and appreciate. The students were useless to her at this point; Lori realized that what her infinitely long education had taught her was how to dig through the scientific literature for jargon, techniques, and open questions, adjusting what she did and how she did it so that the experts in the field could interpret the results at a glance.

The trouble was, she knew exactly what images she wanted, but the actual data collection was still out of reach. Even though Carol had been assigned the old LEPER microscope that had once been van Gnubbern's, Lori didn't have a lot of hope for that. That scope had always been delicate to handle, which was why van Gnubbern had given it to the LEPERs in the first place—and face it, Carol was a boson. It was more likely that any progress there would infuriate Dim Bulb and make him do something stupid, and that his arrest would exonerate Lori.

But so far, no luck. Besides, if Dimmy was only a henchman for Kuzno, then the real problem was right down here on campus in Lori's face.

She didn't even know what level of evil she was dealing with. If Kuzno had just been trying to get Lori into trouble and had killed Marybeth by accident, a simple murmur of *I know what you did* might be enough to scare him straight. But if he had shot Lou, and set up the falling door, and then deliberately wiped out Marybeth just to keep Lori from doing experiments—well, she wasn't going to confront him.

Mysterious employee deaths tended to stay out of the papers, so Lori did some research another way. She pulled up directories of everyone from her undergraduate years onward, looking for obituaries.

She was disappointed. Everyone since Silverman had lived to at least 80, and died "quietly," "at home," or "after a long illness." Even if she'd wanted to see something suspicious in Silverman's death, she couldn't pin it on Kuzno—it had happened five years before Kuzno was hired.

The department was back to its ghostly appearance. The students were lying low, and Lou hadn't been in since the meeting with Ben. Lori couldn't blame any of them, but wished they'd at least send her an e-mail to let her know what was going on.

They didn't. It wasn't until after her class on Friday morning that Sam came into her office wearing an even cheaper black suit than her own, and told her to hurry up, they were going to Marybeth's funeral.

Fortunately she still had the suit crammed into a drawer, and figured no one would notice or care about her sandals. "Betcha we're the only ones there," she grumbled, as they crossed the campus and headed up the busy street that would take them past the community college, the Mongolian barbecue, and the dentist to the Shadow Valley Funeral Parlor with its little sign that read "Drive carefully! We can wait."

It was a tatty little room with a few pews, a divider down the middle to accommodate two ill-attended funerals at once, and practically no one in attendance except Lou, his student Alex, and Kuzno and his teenaged wife. No one seemed related to Marybeth except possibly a couple of aging Angelenos sitting stiffly in the back row. The woman was as trim and blond as Absinthe, but the effort it took to maintain her perfection had left traces of pain on her lacquered face. The man was nearly as perfect and seemed manicured like a hedge, two tiny scars on his nasal bridge hinting at rhinoplasty.

A Catholic priest was already delivering the sermon and eulogy when Lori and Sam arrived. Lou was in a pew in the front row, sitting with his elbows on his knees and looking so dejected that Lori braved the glares of the priest and went to sit next to him. He turned his head slightly when he saw her, giving her a watery smile.

It was hard to imagine what he must be going through. He had survived hell by clinging to his work, but it turned out the one place that was his refuge had harbored the killer all along.

Even worse, the killer—or killers—was still running around free.

Lori hoped he'd just been hiding out in his parents' mansion in Malibu—taking pictures, writing screenplays, maybe hiring a private investigator to tail Kuzno.

One thing was obvious: along with whatever else he'd been doing, he had planned Marybeth's funeral. The only input to the eulogy had come from school, as it contained no dear daughter, dear friend, dear sister, but only words about how she had contributed to and "brightened" her group at the university. Wasn't that couple her parents, and hadn't they had anything to say?

From this close up, she could see that the coffin was little more than a cardboard box and that the flower arrangements were professionally respectful yet minimal.

More people had mourned Lori's evil, evil parents.

Certainly more people had mourned Roger, who had had at least four people at his funeral besides his mother who loved him deeply. It was hard to imagine now that he had ever existed, he was so linked in her mind to the cold and the snow and the twang of *joual* French, all now so remote and far away. The heavens had wept for him the way California skies could never weep, a wintry mix of rain that froze and snow that melted and thick fog boiling up from the icy canals. Radhika had flown out all the way from Oz to stand by the grave in her too-short black skirt (Radhika in a skirt!) and flip-flops under the horrors of a Montreal February, as out of place as a hibiscus at the South Pole. She had refrained from comments on the weather, or Canadians, or the omnipresence of Catholicism in the service, just took Lori's too-pale hand in her warm brown one and let their tears mingle with the elements.

Lori reached for Lou's hand now, and they both cried in silence for all they had lost, and for the vagaries of fate that could make someone otherwise so young and gifted be blighted with a personality that made her unlovable.

She wondered if Marybeth would have anything on her tombstone. If chosen by her group, it would probably read $\Delta S > 0$. Or not—perhaps they would get as maudlin as Lori and Roger's sister had, somehow in the depths of their grief settling on *Au revoir, cher ami,* even though they were both atheists and knew there was no *au revoir*, there was no *adieu*, there was just *bye-bye*.

"Are those her parents back there?" Lori whispered. "Because that might explain—"

"Shhh," Lou murmured patiently, interlacing his fingers with hers. "Those are *my* parents."

It would have been idiotic to get up to pay respects, since they were practically all in the same department, so she stayed seated next to him and watched the students mill around hypocritically. At least the casket was closed; Lori couldn't imagine having to see Marybeth's pigtails arranged carefully on a funeral pillow. Lou's parents came up and sniped at him a bit in annoying snobby French, telling him he was a fool to have paid for all this and to sit up straight. Then they left.

After that he spoke, disengaging his hand from Lori's so he could point incriminatingly at the coffin. "Things would have been different if we had listened to Marybeth. I can't express the profoundness of my regret. Please try to remember her for how she helped each and every one of us—this group would not exist without her."

To Lori's astonishment, the students looked immensely guilty, even tearful. She herself felt a pang: he had paid for Marybeth's funeral, but she was such a lousy advisor that she let her own people rot in Gitmo.

Guilt wasn't productive. Roger had spent his entire life feeling guilty, which had got him nothing but scars on his wrists and tardive dyskinesia. No, she should focus on trying to get Dim Bulb and Kuzno caught and convicted of their crimes. What had Marybeth claimed in her complaints to the police? Was it just her sexual-hysteric stuff or was there anything about blackmail or violence?

Why had Kuzno come to the funeral? Maybe just to make sure Marybeth wasn't faking her death, like her blindness and quadriplegia and child abuse and melanoma and irradiation and scurvy and black plague.

"Ready to go, Dr. Lou?" Alex asked at last, waiting for Lou to nod before bringing him his wheelchair from a far corner of the room (hiding it from his parents? she wondered. Bastards!). Lou climbed in, still seeming melancholy, rolled up to the priest and thanked him warmly, and then spoiled it by saying "Goddammit."

Lori wanted to laugh at the priest's expression; he'd never heard a good *hostie de tabarnak!* "What is it?"

"I just want to do some experiments. Let's go."

They and the two grad students left together and paused for a moment at the door, dazzled by the sunlight. Alex sneezed, and Lou and Sam both brushed locks of unmanageable, uncurling hair out of their eyes. Their run of Santa Ana weather was continuing with all of its slightly surreal atmospheric phenomena—December highs in the nineties, the smog pushed from the city into an ochre smudge above the ocean, and the air so dry that every sound was amplified and every spark caused a forest fire. The fan palms rustled and buckled in the wind, and fronds rolled and danced down the street, where leafblowers continued their infernal task that nature made futile.

It was too beautiful a day for Marybeth to miss, but not too beautiful a day to scheme in the basement with an electron microscope. "What do you mean?" she asked Lou as soon as they were out of earshot of the building. "Did you say *experiments*?"

"Not quite real ones," Lou admitted, trying to sound apologetic but clearly bursting with eagerness to tell her. "Not yet. It was supposed to be a surprise…You know the old fluorescence microscope in that creepy virus lab?"

"Sure I do. I used to use it every day, and I checked it last time I was in there. It still works, but it doesn't have a digital CCD camera yet, just an old 35 mm that takes film."

"Precisely," said Lou. "And where you are a phonophobic Luddite, I'm that way with photography. The camera you saw in the park is my first digital. I still have a darkroom at my parents' place."

"And so?" Lori urged, walking quickly to leave the students behind.

"And so, the microscope is almost ready to go. The camera wasn't parfocal with the eyepieces, so I fixed that with a test pattern. We'll need a bunch of optical filters to separate the wavelengths, but I think I can find the parts right on campus. Give me samples when you have them." He laughed at her amazement, doing a wheelie over a giant palm frond. "What, Barrow? Thought I was a p-brain, did you?"

"I—I thought you were off-campus," Lori managed. "Hiding."

"What could be safer than the BSL-3? There's a double entryway with a padlock and then a keycode. And Kuzno never told *me* not to go in there."

"So the project is still on?"

"Of course it's on! It has to go on—otherwise they've all won."

He's been talking to Ben, Lori thought. "OK. I'll get you samples. We can start with dyes, so you can check the wavelength. Because I'm not sure what colors—" She stopped herself, realizing she was starting to babble. "I'm kind of behind the curve here," she admitted. "Carol has a microscope, now you do, too. Why didn't you tell me?"

"Because," said Lou, "I was hoping you'd knock off Dim Bulb." His bravado finally failed, and he reached for a tissue too late to hide the tears that had filled his eyes.

It was upsetting to see a grown man burst into tears—especially when he appeared to be wiping them away with a Kimwipe from the BSL-3. Now we'll have a *real* lab accident, Lori thought. She had nothing to say, so they stood there outside the Mongolian barbecue—the gale-force winds blasted them with odors of meat and oil—and shed a few tears that might have been more sincere than those at the funeral but which dried instantly on their faces in the Santa Ana air.

"It's my fault," Lou sobbed. "I feel as though I killed her."

Sam, behind them, caught up and started to sniffle, too. "No, it's mine. I'm the one who made fun of everything she said."

"It was so cheap and abject." Lou wiped his face and hands on the Kimwipe and tossed it into a garbage can. "I wanted to give her a nice funeral, but Rose and van Gnubbern said it would be inappropriate. Why would they say that, Lori, why?"

They were just being sentimental and providing no information. "The real question," interrupted Lori, "is whether they suspect what we suspect."

There was a moment of silence, more thoughtful than emotional. "I don't have the slightest fucking clue," Lou said at last, making a retard-face at some people who were staring at them and then continuing rapidly down the street, with Lori jogging after. "It just seems too good to be true that Rose and Gerson have this great project they want us for. It seemed like such a great opportunity, but we're their cannon fodder."

"So you don't know any more than I do," Lori exclaimed, dismayed, trying to tug off her stupid uncomfortable blazer as she ran. They had left the students some distance behind, perhaps deliberately.

"Probably less. You were an undergraduate here, you know what makes this place tick. Fuckin' *a*, if anything happens to you I swear I will wring Solomon Rose's neck myself." They stopped for a traffic light on the border of campus, which allowed the students to catch up, and Lou changed the subject quickly. "I really don't like the idea of you rollerblading up and down that hill while this is going on."

"What am I going to do?" she asked. "Get Sam to follow me in a yellow go-cart?" She realized she was the one who was supposed to be paranoid and got an idea. "Actually, maybe you're right. I know the RA at Pasteur House and I can probably get her to put me up in a dorm room for a while. Then I'll be on campus to work day and night, won't have to go up the hill in the wee hours, and might be able to actually do something."

It actually was a good idea, she realized later that afternoon as she headed down to her old undergraduate dorm to ask if they had a spot for her. This way she wouldn't waste any commuting time, and could sneak around and use facilities when Kuzno wasn't around. The undergrads were all too young to know her personally, but some of the resident staff were sure to remember her. The brick path shaded by olive trees seemed so fresh and innocent—spattered with fallen fruit, crowded with hungry birds, and smelling of soil and leaves—that it made her skip like a little girl.

The House had been extensively remodeled, including losing the tree that had held their famous treehouse, but Lori had mourned enough for one day and tried to tell herself that the new rooms were clean and healthy instead of sterile and scary. There was a very nice spot for her, in a double where one of the students had dropped out after two months to transfer to UCLA, and she left some items on the empty bed and then went into the common room to call a meeting. It was time to recruit her army of little Buboes.

EIGHTEEN: THE FEW, THE PROUD, THE BUBOES

BUBOES DIDN'T HAVE ANY particular costume, like the Ferrets who dressed in black, or the Thorns from Calvin House who went barefoot, or the Snodgrass Snots who wore green athletic clothes. Still, no matter where they might be, from downtown at the grocery store to stalking the streets of Boston, a certain impalpable *je ne sais quoi* gave them away.

They stood there wide-eyed and elbowing each other in their eagerness. More than a dozen had materialized in the common room the instant Lori had mentioned a secret meeting. "You wanted us, Dr. Barrow?"

"Right," she said matter-of-factly. They looked so young; she felt a stab of guilt at the thought that she might be leading them into real danger. "As you know, we had a tragic accident in the cold room last week."

There were solemn nods. The Buboes' eyes started to glaze, no doubt as they anticipated a lecture on lab safety.

"Well," Lori continued, "some of us are pretty sure it was *not* an accident."

This woke everybody up, and she passed around some bad photocopies of Dim Bulb's staff photo, and even worse copies of a fuzzy cellphone picture showing his mittens. "He's supposed to work at the LEPERLab now," she told them. "He has no business being here on campus. If you see him, find me and tell me immediately. Don't try to confront him."

They all nodded vigorously. A tall guy with taped-together glasses raised his hand. "Question! What do we expect him to do?"

Lori was about to protest that she didn't know, but then she realized she did kind of know: a sliced elevator cable. A freezer door that came off and fell. A bad latch on a cold room.

"Infrastructure crimes," summarized another Bubo, clearly delighted with the concept.

They asked for video equipment, and Lori gave them the key to the departmental audiovisual supply closet, Kuznetsov be damned. Then they went scattering off as if on a scavenger hunt, plotting and theorizing and giggling.

"One more thing," Lori called them back. "Trust no one. Anything that happens, tell me and me alone. Everyone else is a spy. *Especially* Kuznetsov. Got it?"

They did. Or so they claimed.

Having delegated her pranks, Lori then went back to the department to delegate the real work. She called the "two who didn't suck"—Chi-Ming and Walter—into her office and told them to figure out how to slice the ice cores.

"Go next door to biology," she suggested. "Ask around. Tell people you need something cut very thin and mounted on a microscope slide. Once you've got that accomplished, let me know."

This time, when she finally settled at her desk to be a good little theorist, Lori's heart was in her work. She knew that her rebellion was humming away invisibly down in the BSL-3, being carried out by Lou and the Buboes, and slowly corrupting the latest generation of Walter Waddles.

She finished the paper on the Poincaré proof and sent it in. Then she sat down with Sam and tried to help him with his Feynman diagrams. Quantum field theory wasn't like riding a bicycle, and she wasn't sure how much she managed to accomplish. It did give her an idea of where Lou was going with his models, though, and an appreciation for why he needed data from the South Pole. She showed Sam how to submit to the *Physical Review Letters* on-line paper submission site, and suggested possible reviewers who would help him get accepted by the prestigious journal.

She took the theory students for coffee around nine o'clock, and as they came back to campus, two Buboes with flashlights and video cameras greeted them.

"All's well?" Lori asked.

"Affirmative," the Buboes replied. "Dr. K departed, nineteen-oh-five hours. Sworn enemy not sighted."

Sam and his pals looked confused, but Lori didn't bother to explain. The fewer people who knew the details, the better. Then the students left, too, leaving her alone on the theory floor to wait for news from her experimental cronies.

It was past midnight when a yawning Walter knocked on the door and brought her a tray full of labeled slides, each bearing a nearly invisible circle in the center, which was a thin section of part of their microbial community.

"The coverslips slide around," he complained. "I can't get them to be stable."

"We need nail polish," Lori mused, "but the pharmacy is closed."

And so it was that in the name of science she rifled Marybeth's desk the day of her funeral, not expecting to find anything of substance since the police would have already taken it. She did unearth a small bottle of clear nail polish that she handed to Walter. While he sealed the coverslips over the samples, she went through the desk one more time, sorting through hair clips and old photos for something interesting.

She was glad that Chi-Ming had given up and gone home, because Walter needed a little interrogating. While she rummaged she mentioned casually, "It's funny, Walter…I know your grandpa, and I know your great-grandpa, but no one's ever heard of Walter W. Waddles III."

"My dad's the black sheep of the family." Walter concentrated on his task, painting meticulously. "We're ashamed of him."

"He's a LEPER!" Lori accused abruptly, finding a small pencil bag and an old lab notebook underneath a drawer in Marybeth's desk. She didn't want to open them in front of him, so she threw them into her backpack for later inspection.

"In more ways than one," Walter chuckled, blowing the nail polish dry. "He thinks he'll get the Nobel Prize for finding life on Mars, but he's wrong."

"Just so long as he hasn't asked you anything about what's going on here," Lori warned.

"He hasn't, I swear."

Lori tried her sternest possible look, but Walter's gaze didn't waver. "What on Earth made him take a job at the LEPERLab, anyway?"

"Don't you know?" Walter glanced over his shoulder. "He was promised control of the whole Science Colony, and he got to…" He lowered his voice to an imperceptible whisper.

"He got to what?" Lori demanded.

"…to fire Kuzno," Walter hissed.

"That doesn't make sense," Lori announced loudly. "Your dad started at the LEPERLab while I was an undergrad. Kuzno's only been here for eleven years."

"Here on campus," her student corrected, standing up with the boxful of slides. "He was a LEPER for a long time before that. I'm pretty sure my dad was hired to drive him out."

Lori stayed seated in the rickety grad student chair, mind reeling. Kuzno had been here when Silverman died. Did a collapsing hiking trail count as an infrastructure crime?

Not wanting to rouse Walter's suspicions, she jumped to her feet and led him downstairs. Buboes met them in the stairwell, reassuring them that the building was empty.

The padlock opened with her standard master key. Once inside the staging area, Lori made sure to follow all of the BSL-3 precautions so as to set a good example for Walter. They put on lab coats, hairnets, booties, and one pair of nitrile gloves. She then punched in the code for the second door, which Lou had set to the excitation and emission wavelengths of fluorescein, something that evil LEPER scullions who feared biology weren't likely to guess.

White lights would ruin their visual sensitivity, so they avoided turning them on. The only light in the small inner room came from the scatter of the powerful blue beam of the mercury lamp that would excite their fluorescence. All Lori could see was the outline of Lou's head as he peered into the microscope, and a small green circle on the slide he was inspecting.

He didn't even bother to turn around, keeping his eyes on the eyepieces as they passed him one of Walter's carefully prepared slides.

Even without magnification, Lori could tell immediately that it was a disaster. A hazy green shot out in all directions from the slide, much too bright and not the color she had expected.

"Ugh," said Lou. "What is this?"

"I screwed up," said Walter hastily. "The sections are too thick."

"So did I," Lori added. "The dye is the wrong color."

"And me too," argued Lou. "The filter is too wide."

They all contemplated in silence for a moment, united in the disappoinment of a failed experiment.

"But hey," Lori reassured quickly, "at least it's a start. We're here, Kuzno doesn't know, and we're going to make this work. Right?"

The others nodded, seemingly without conviction. Walter yawned, and she screamed at him not to touch his mouth in the BSL-3. Then Lou reached around and snapped off the mercury lamp, plunging them into total darkness.

It was hot, cloying, and stinky. Lori fought panic, feeling with her feet along the edge of the wall, then slapping around for the light switch. "Why'd you do that, you bastard?"

"Huh?" Lou sounded asleep. "It didn't occur to me. Sorry. The light's right by the autoclave."

Lori found it at last and switched it on. The bulb was weak and yellow, but it clearly revealed all of the effort Lou (and his students?) had put into the lab since she had last been here. Everything was spotlessly clean. The drawers were all labeled—*Optics, Tools, Pipettes*, and even *Batteries*. On the bench by the microscope was a collection of microscope filters and mirrors in various stages of assembly; laminated sheets gave their specifications.

"This is amazing," she breathed.

"We're not there yet." Lou's eyes were red and looked unfocused, with creases around them where the rubber eyepieces had pressed. "I really don't know what I'm doing. I've been staying up reading this stuff, but…" He gestured at the optical components. "It's bedtime."

As if on cue, Walter's phone started to tinkle a few bars of *Macarena*. "No phones!" Lori yelled.

"Oh, OK," Walter shrugged, letting it play. "It's just my grandpa coming to pick me up. You know… in case it's not safe." He waited for them to nod permission, then dashed out through the inner door.

"Lab coat!" Lori called, in case he'd forgotten.

"Oops!" said Walter. There were more bangs and clicks, and he was gone.

Lou and Lori met each other's eyes, not needing to say it aloud: Walter Waddles Jr., endowed professor of physical chemistry, thought his grandson might be in danger on campus.

"Did you find yourself a place in Pasteur?" Lou asked, seemed very relieved when Lori nodded. "Good. Let me walk you back, I'm going that direction too."

She was going to object that it was only five hundred meters, but as she tugged open the door she remembered the gouges on the bottom caused by Dim Bulb's fingernails and was grateful for the company.

NINETEEN: I WILL COME LIKE A THIEF

IT ORDINARILY WOULD HAVE been funny to see Sam waiting outside of her office, tearing his massive amounts of hair, but they really didn't have time for another crisis. "Barrow," he whispered, glancing around, "*help.*"

She sighed and beckoned him in. She still didn't have any furniture, so Sam settled himself on the edge of her desk. "Our infrastructure grant specifically excluded furniture, mouse pads, and chalk," he explained.

"I figured something like that. What's the problem?" Lori opened her laptop and started scrolling through the image files. They were getting better with the fluorescence microscope, but the slices were still too uneven and thick. Whatever the microtome was that Walter had found in the biology building, it wasn't doing the job.

Sam took a deep breath. "*Phys Rev Letters* rejected my paper and they're accusing me of fraud. They say an identical manuscript was submitted the day before by a different group."

Lori half sneered. There had to be some mistake. "You should be telling this to Lou and Rose, not to me. They need to call the editor and find out what's going on. Who's the corresponding author?"

Sam's big brown eyes grew very round; she could see the edges of his contact lenses. "Me. I'm the only author."

"Their names aren't on—? Wow. You have a good advisor, Sam. You should call the journal yourself and find out as much as you can, but Lou needs to know what's going on pretty damn quick."

Sam leapt up and paced around the room. "I just know I did something wrong. How can this happen?"

"What did you do?"

"I don't know. I posted a pre-print to the Los Alamos site."

"That's fine, we all do that. That's how the Internet was invented."

He looked at her as if she'd just claimed to be Al Gore. "It is? Have you ever heard of someone stealing a manuscript?"

She thought long and hard. "More often it's grant proposals because they never go public, so it's easier to get away with. Manuscripts—yes, actually, once or twice, but the culprits got found out. Once the person was caught because it was sent to the original authors for review. The second time it went to press and then had to be withdrawn. Who all had copies? And were they hard copies or a electronic copies?"

"The only people I gave copies to are you and Dr. van Gnubbern."

"My loyalty is above suspicion, and so is van Gnubbern's. Call the journal. Talk to Lou."

Sam shook his head in despair. "He's going to kill me."

"He's not going to kill anyone. He wouldn't even kill Dim Bulb."

"Really?" Sam stopped pacing and looked hard at her as if inspecting her statement for irony. "Did he say that? He's got to be lying. *I* would kill Dim Bulb."

"So would I. With my bare hands. And fingernails."

"Yeah, but you, Barrow.... It doesn't take much."

"Despite rumors to the contrary, I've never killed anyone in my life. I just happen to be around when—"

"When people you don't like drop dead? Remind me to stay in your good graces."

With that he was gone, and she hoped not to see him again for the rest of the day. She couldn't help thinking about him, though, when Lou wheeled in a few minutes later with a bulging canvas bag on his lap. "Uh oh," she worried. "Severed head?"

"Yes," he replied with utmost seriousness. "They told me in rehab that I could do everything I did before. The serial-killer thing's still a bit tricky though, the heads keep rolling onto the floor." He dumped out what had to be a hundred boxes of prints and slides onto her desk, and they both stared at them for a long moment. "Actually, a severed head would be less daunting."

Lori fought panic. This whole approach was just so analog—and Kuzno was sure to catch them using the slide scanner.

"Can you tell if any of the pictures are any good?" she wondered.

"No," Lou admitted, "not really. All of the samples have these elongated, football-shaped things in them. I can't tell if they're organisms or minerals."

"Did you do a DNA stain?"

"Of course, but I couldn't see what it was stuck to." He shuffled through a box of slides, picking one and holding it up to the window for her to see.

It was more of that green haze. Green haze wasn't going to win them six hundred million dollars. "What does Ben say?"

"He says the answer will reveal the evolutionary history of the region—so keep trying."

"Oh. I see." Lori thought hard. Lou was staring at her, waiting expectantly like a graduate student or a puppy dog. "Well..." she tried, "what if they are organisms with a thick cell wall? You could try bursting them open and then using the DNA stain."

Lou's eyes lit up. "That's a great idea!" Abandoning the deskful of prints, he went off humming to his secret lab in the basement.

Lori was horribly jealous, especially since she couldn't even go downstairs for a pee without being collared by Sam.

"Is it safe?" he whispered, materializing out of a broom closet.

"It depends on who's the enemy," she replied impatiently. "Did you call the journal?"

"Yes, and I'm totally confused." He glanced all around, but the second floor was empty. "They finally gave me the name of the senior author on the stolen paper, and they say he's from STI, but he's not in any of the directories and I've never heard his name. Ellis D. Tripp?"

"Oh yeah, he's a LEPER," said Lori, and dashed into the bathroom.

When she came out, Sam was still there. "A LEPER? A LEPER stole my paper? I thought LEPERs weren't allowed to publish."

"They're not. That's why the high-ranking LEPERs get associate positions down here. It's something Professor Rose has been trying to stop because he thinks that they degrade the average quality of our research. I must say this will help his cause. They don't get listed in our directory, and the LEPER directory is secret, so you won't find him anywhere, but I've heard the name." In spite of herself, she was becoming intrigued. "I have a friend at the LEPERLab. Let's go to my office and give her a call."

"OK. Want to see how Dr. Lou used to climb the stairs?" He took a running start, grabbed the banister, and flew up the four flights three steps at a time. Lori could barely keep up, and they arrived at the theory floor gasping. "Then," Sam panted, "he would make fun of us for breathing hard."

"Yeah, he makes me run seven-minute miles in the gym, and if I touch the handles, he yells, 'triche pas'!'" Sam must have seen things, things she couldn't imagine—the thought made her abandon all resolve and interrogate him right there in the dusty stairwell. "Why is he so broken-hearted about Marybeth?" she demanded rapidly. "Did she really save the group?"

She wasn't going to let him shrug and change the subject, either. "Come on, Sam. I saw you cry."

"Not here, OK? Let's at least go into your office. What's *triche pas*?"

"'No cheating.' Remember it if you need to encourage me later this afternoon."

Lori did her best to grill him, but Sam didn't seem to know anything special. He described the Marybeth she knew, the attention whore with the terrible stories that couldn't be true.

"No idea why he hired her," he conceded, rolling his eyes. "She worked for Dr. Kuznetsov at first, but he told her to go away when she only got eighty on the qualifying exam. She didn't want to leave his group, but I guess Dim Bulb started harassing her—hey, do you think Kuzno was using Dim Bulb as a tool?"

"That's sort of what I had in mind. Was this when she was filing the police reports and everything?"

"Oh no, this was long before. I don't think Dim Bulb was doing anything serious then, just looking at her funny and giving her the creeps, but it was enough to make her leave Kuzno and start hanging around our group. Dr. Lou didn't have tons of money at the time, but we were sort of a group already: he was helping us write fellowships, and I guess he told Marybeth she could be a part of the group if he won the proposal or she got a fellowship."

"Why would he take someone with an eighty?"

"No idea. Pity?"

"Lou is the only person on Earth more pitiless than I am."

"Than you, Barrow? Not a chance. I'm sure you've clubbed baby seals."

"Did you know," Lori informed him meaningfully, "that Marybeth had a pencil bag stuffed with empty pill bottles with Lou's name on them?"

"Well, for sure Marybeth was a pill-head, and stole whatever she could find." Sam picked up a random pencil and tapped it on the desk, looking out the window. "But Dr. Lou said he wasn't in any pain, so we all just let it go. She was less annoying stoned than she was with her stories."

"'You call yourselves lepers, but I have *real* leprosy!'" Lori mocked, cackling. "'All my fingers fell off, but they re-grew in Chernobyl!'"

"Why am I telling you anything? Obviously you already know more than I ever will." Sam gave a short bark of mirthless laughter, but after that he spoke more freely, as if she were a fellow student. "She knew she had a problem. Once she even admitted it to me—'When I'm stressed, terrible lies come out of my mouth. It's like puking.' She tried taking real drugs for it, but I guess they made her slow and foggy, even worse than the painkillers…"

"What did she take?" Lori demanded.

"Benzodiazepines." Sam didn't try to hide his snooping. "Antidepressants. And a beta-blocker once."

"So was she any good at physics at all?"

"I told you, I don't really know. Dr. Lou must have had some reason to hire her, but you'll have to ask him. All I know is she was always a freak."

"It sounds as if Lou was too fucked up last year to know or care if his students were any good."

"He was *so* fucked up." Sam's olive complexion grew pale, and he grimaced. "Somehow I never imagined that he could die, though. Maybe that was because of Marybeth, in a way—he was always there to take care of her. He took her to the emergency room one night when he was only half alive himself. Can you imagine! He rolled with her to St. Vitus's while she moaned about some bullshit. I went along because I was worried about him, and they refused to treat her, they said she was a drug-seeking hypochondriac and kicked her out. I just feel bad because she was right about Dim Bulb."

"OK," said Lori, wishing she'd been taking notes. Hadn't the cops asked her something about Marybeth and drugs? She decided immediately that they had more important things to worry about. "Thanks for the info. Now let's call my favorite LEPER and see if we can get your paper back." She dialed Carol's number, putting her on the speakerphone so Sam could hear everything.

They quickly established that Tripp was Carol's (and Bob Drift's!) "colony manager," but the boson refused to see anything suspicious in that, protesting that there were only two LEPER colonies in the whole place.

"Look, Carol," Lori commanded, knowing that Carol was more logical under pressure, "this is a matter of scientific fraud. I don't much care who is responsible or why as long as those who did the work get the credit. Right now, Tripp's name is on the paper, and Tripp didn't do the work. I don't suppose you'd be willing to go into his office and look for a manuscript on his desk?"

Carol reacted as if she'd been asked to break out of Alcatraz on the backs of trained alligators. "And I can tell you," she added after freaking out for a solid three minutes, "that his office doesn't open with a key."

"Good to know. Would you at least be willing to get me an expedited visitor's pass? Or even one for Solomon Rose, if that's easier?"

What Carol said next made Lori swear in new and interesting ways but left Sam gaping in confusion. "*Hostie de* motherfuck *de tabarnak!*" Lori raged. "How can they do that?"

"I don't know."

"Do you know *anything*?"

That often worked on a boson. "I know his office opens with a passcode," said Carol, "and that he's a cosmologist."

Lori slammed down the phone. "All right," she declared, "I'm pissed now. This is your last chance to ask someone sensible for help. Otherwise, you're in for a Barrow Adventure."

Sam clapped softly. "Barrow, Barrow…What did she say? I didn't get the acronym."

"PNG—persona non grata. The LEPERs put me, Lou, Rose, *and* van Gnubbern on PNG status. We're not allowed to visit, and we're technically not even allowed to speak to LEPERs."

"Oh boy!" Sam laughed sarcastically. "Poor you!"

"But that means we have to sneak onto the LEPERLab to get your manuscript back."

"How?"

"I haven't the foggiest idea. But the days are getting short, so we're going to have to move fast." She stood up. "I'm going to go find some people, do a little research, and ask the Buboes what they know. Your task right now is to write down all of the constants that you think he may have used for his passcode. Do you have any non motorized vehicles?"

"Huh?"

"Can you skateboard? Rollerblade?" He kept shaking his head. "You *do* have a bicycle, right?" Sam nodded sheepishly. "Good. Go get it, and oil the chain and pump the tires—there's stuff in my office. I have a feeling it might come in handy."

TWENTY: THE INFAMOUS COVERUPS OFFICE

"Tell me one thing." Absinthe steered Carol towards a comfortable leather chair in the legal office. "What do you know about killer deer?"

All Carol could think about is how high up you'd have to be on the LEPER ladder to get a chair like that. "Deer don't kill people."

"At the LEPERLab they do." Abby slammed her briefcase onto the table, commanding attention. She turned to close the blinds, showing just how perfect her size 4 bottom was in its pinstriped pants.

They had sworn to each other in the first month of grad school not to let their bodies go the way the other first-years were doing, their lives nothing but studying and pizza. Every afternoon, before the rush began, they would walk through the tunnel that led from the physics building to the new gym. There they would change—Abby into tight shorts and a bra top, Carol into baggy sweatpants—and do forty-five minutes of cardio and a weight circuit (arms and abs twice a week, legs twice a week) or a class (aerobics, kick-boxing, yoga).

Men's jaws would hit the floor as Absinthe walked by, and not a single workout passed in which someone didn't say, "Is that your friend? She's gorgeous."

She still was. And now she was successful on top of it. She'd made Carol leave her ridiculous "technician" position in the middle of the day to come down here to campus to answer questions. It wasn't as if she was missing any work by leaving, but she still worried that the LEPERs would find a way to punish her.

Talking about killer deer was a sure way to invite retribution. "Oh, my," Carol murmured. "I don't think I'm allowed to talk about this."

"Carol, let me be the first to inform you that legally, the LEPERLab does not exist. You are managed by STI, you are technically STI employees, and the legality of your appointment and dismissal is handled by the STI legal office. Me," she added, just to underline precisely how thick she thought Carol was.

Carol never imagined the "killer deer" were anything besides a LEPER ploy to oppress the employees. She wasn't going to say that in so many words, but she did admit, "There was an accident, and after that the safety committee told us deer were dangerous and we had to avoid them. It became this big thing for a while, but now people have mostly forgotten it, I think."

"Uh huh," snorted Abby, not at all amused. "Just who is this 'safety committee'?"

"I don't know, but they made videos and everything, showing deer chasing and trampling people."

Without a word Abby sprang up, leaving her computer on the table, and pulled Carol by the hand through the door and down the hall.

This little Victorian building seemed too small and quaint to hold what they all only imagined existed, but here it was. In a small room in the back that looked like a psychologist's office were row upon row of rickety, overloaded filing cabinets containing the generations of STI Infamous Coverups. Carol sighed with an odd sense of pleasure, not hearing what Abby was asking her.

"Earth to the Dugong!" said Abby, snapping her fingers. "What got into you?"

"Are these it?" Carol breathed. "The Infamous Coverups?"

Abby laughed airily. "Oh, no, these are the things no one considers infamous, or at least not yet. The real infamous coverups are in another—don't get any ideas," she corrected herself suddenly. "Now, I want you to look at something."

She was clearly a pro riffling through the file folders, and Carol wondered how the coverups were classified. Did van Gnubbern have his own file? Did Kuzno? Did Lori? Were they sorted by degree of secrecy? She could spend days in here, she thought wistfully.

Abby crouched down and opened a drawer at the very bottom of one of the cabinets. "I don't know the name," she told Carol, "but I thought you might. Read these and I'll run back and get my computer so we can figure out who the guy was."

The files were definitely coverup territory, because the guy killed by a deer had been a young new-hire and his parents had sued the LEPERLab— or, since the LEPERLab didn't really exist, they sued the university—for all sorts of terrible things, including wrongful death. The deer seemed to have played a minor role. It had been a baby fawn, and the poor guy had crashed into it because his eyes were on the unmarked car chasing him as he left the lab on his bike.

Carol shivered in sympathy. She'd been chased by a go-cart, and that was bad enough. Then it seemed that the guards had deliberately avoided calling the ambulance or giving the guy any first aid at all until he was well and safely dead. His parents had asked for nine million dollars in a civil suit and she hoped they got every penny.

She had to agree that she would call that a murder. But what did it have to do with anything else…? She kept reading, skimming without full comprehension until Abby reappeared.

"Recognize the name?" Abby sat cross-legged on the floor of the tiny room, opening her small red laptop. When Carol shook her head, she smirked sharkishly. "Oh, really? Not keeping up with your theorists, are you? Before he went to the LEPERLab, he did his PhD in Chicago. Then he was a postdoc here on campus. With Kuzno."

"Kuzno?" Carol gasped. "So Kuzno is the one—?"

"I didn't say that." Abby took a deep breath, then dropped her bombshell cold in Carol's lap. "What I am saying is that everyone who's interested in astrobiology has had an attempt on his life. Or hers." Her perfectly controlled bun had come loose, spilling strands of hair over he face that she tugged at nervously as the talked. Locked in the closet and sitting on the floor, she was no longer a high-powered IP lawyer, but Carol's old friend from grad school.

"Our office knew something was up," Abby admitted in a shaky voice. "We thought it was a joke that everyone Solomon Rose tried to hire or promote ended up dead. We called it the 'Rose Blight.' Here, look at this one."

Carol took another folder. This one hardly counted as a STI coverup, since the person hadn't even made it to the interview—he'd died in a commuter van that flipped on Highway 2 from Palmdale. "You really think…?"

"I don't know," Abby groaned. "I'm not sure about anything any more. All I know is, Lou Maupertuis got the job because this guy died. And here's one more."

The next folder Carol didn't even understand. It was full of legalese and something about visas, and certainly didn't look as if it dealt with someone dying. But then she recognized the name: Fang Li. "Lori's postdoc!" she exclaimed. "STI is keeping her out of the country? Why?"

"Because Solomon Rose told me it was imperative," Abby whispered. "And look at what I found at the library archives." She clicked on her trackpad a few times, then turned the computer around for Carol to see. "Nobel Laureate Says Physics Must Change," said the pixelated old scan:

> Solomon Rose, STI Nobel-prize-winning theoretical physicist, claims that the days of "pure" physics are over. "Rutherford once said that all science is either physics or stamp collecting," Dr. Rose, 84, began at a recent symposium on the future of STI. "Today, all science is either biology or not funded." Rose was instrumental in the recent appointment of the Lobo Peak Research Laboratory's new colony manager, Jacob A. Silverman. Many refer to the appointment as a "regime change" as it replaces hard-line rocket specialist Ellis D. Tripp, who has served in the position for thirteen years. The LPR Lab currently has a budget of five million dollars for the recruitment of an "astrobiologist" to examine the possibility of detection of traces of extinct life on Mars and elsewhere in the Solar System.

"Jacob Silverman lasted a total of ten days after accepting that postion," said Abby. "Someone has been killing people in the physics department since 1991."

TWENTY-ONE: A FACE-OFF AT THE LEPERLAB

IT WAS WONDERFUL TO have an army. The Buboes made a map of the LEPERLab, showing possible points where unauthorized personnel (or killer deer) might sneak in. There were two high on the hillside by Lobo Peak, the ones that had been reinforced after the Twin Towers attack. The third was across the drainage pond, which was too shallow for a canoe and too toxic to wade in.

Another student took Lori's weight and maximum power and compared them with those of a go-tard, calculating the speed differential expected between her and the go-tard at different topographical points on lab. His conclusion was that she couldn't out-run them, so she needed her skates and she preferably needed to head uphill—she'd be four miles an hour faster than a go-tard on a 6% grade.

"That's assuming I can generate three hundred watts in the presence of the horrible fumes," she reminded him. "I'm not too sure about that one." But she packed the skates anyway, along with an assortment of hex and star wrenches, a lock-picking set, and a small crowbar, tucking the tools into tiny pockets inside her beloved orange backpack.

Yet another Bubo had plotted the projected trajectories of the go-tards with an estimated arrival time on lab of four o'clock and departure time between four-thirty and five. He didn't think that Lori would have any trouble sneaking into the buildings because the go-tards were expecting people to be leaving—the problem would be getting out. Around four o'clock, the go-tards all lined up outside the buildings, engines running, to shuttle employees to their cars. The yellow go-carts were actually for the plebes only, and headed to East lot; the silver ones took the managers to STUMP parking. Lori didn't even drive and the whole idea pissed her off. "Thanks be to God that I don't work at the LEPERLab," she declared as she pushed open the door to the HPV club, now carefully renamed the Human-Powered Transport Association to avoid any gross acronyms. Back in her day, no one had heard of human papilloma virus.

"You *should* thank God!" Mike the carbon-fiber guy was there, surrounded by a glob of Snots. "They banned bicycles from lab—it's like banning feet! Kids, Lori Barrow, former Bubo, holder of the California women's hydrofoil speed record, tester of all of my new creations, and—and what else?"

"And builder of the piece-of-shit pedal boat that you've been using to prop up your framesets. Think we can get it to work?"

It wasn't really such a piece of shit, she reflected an hour later when they delivered it to her, cleaned and overhauled and fitted with a clamp on the back so it could be attached to the rear axle of Sam's bike to get it up the hill. It would work in just a few inches of water and its plastic bottom wouldn't dissolve in the toxic solvent pond the way a rubber raft was sure to do.

Sam had wanted to drive the boat to the parking lot above the LEPERLab, but Lori nixed that idea. It would take them longer to find someone to lend them a car, that person might talk, and LEPERs or LEPER guards might see them parking and taking things out of the car. As long as they were unmotorized, the guards were not likely even to notice them.

Besides, she enjoyed kicking his ass. "Quit whining," she admonished, steadying the boat from behind as they started up the steepest part of the hill. "It's not heavy, you're just in too big of a gear. Shift down one and climb seated, it will handle much better that way."

Sam gave her one of those *All the rumors* are *true!* looks. "The boss says 'Hanging with Barrow is like rehab,'" he gasped. "At least you're not making Dr. Lou do this on one of your arm-powered vehicles."

"Oh, so you heard about those?" She skated up alongside. This was an easy hill. "I have at least two designs for him to try."

"Just don't get him killed," muttered Sam, cresting the hill at last ("Now upshift!" Lori commanded). "He says you threatened to take him seventy-two miles in one day."

"It's not a threat," Lori objected. "...Unless there are people lurking around trying to kill us, of course."

"I'd stay out of the wilderness until Dim Bulb is locked up."

"That's what I was thinking."

They passed up through Christmas Tree Lane, the giant deodars decked with lights reminding them that the holidays were almost upon them. It would be wonderful to have a few days off after the insanity of this proposal, to go back to her own house where fuzzy things had probably taken over the fridge. Thinking about Christmas was inconceivable, though. Montreal was Christmas and Christmas was Montreal; it was the one time of year she could forgive the cold, the streets were festive and full of music even as people hurried by with their coats tugged up over their faces. Her favorite bakery sent out a special catalog of holiday breads, the pictures almost as delightful as the chocolate-cranberry or maple-walnut loaves that she would buy on Sunday mornings and carry home in one hand like a baton as she skated, pedaled, or skied.

"Any plans for the holidays, Barrow?" Sam wondered as they finally came out of the tree-lined corridor and onto the street that would lead them directly west to the LEPERLab.

"You're assuming we're going to live." Lori felt exposed all of a sudden, on this wide street with the sun beginning to dip in the sky, even though there was very little traffic and no businesses except a Mexican grocery store and a poultry feed shop.

Sam started singing, pedaling with all his might. "Leper leper can't catch me, I don't wanna get your leprosy. Leper leper—" He froze as a black car pulled out of a hidden driveway on the left, came all the way across the road, and cut them off.

He slammed on the brakes. Lori tried to slow herself on the back of the bike saddle, missed, and fell butt-first into the boat. Sam looked back to see if she was OK, turned the bars, and dumped her and the boat out into the dirt.

The car roared away with a screech of rubber. It was a hearse.

"Oh no," moaned Sam. "What have I done? This is a bad sign!"

"You got dirt in my bearings, that's what." Lori crawled out from under the boat and tipped it rightside-up again. The hook where it attached to the axle was bent, and it took some wiggling to get it back on. "I don't think it's an omen, though—I think it's just the carpool going to get the zombie LEPERs to take them back to their graveyard for the night."

Sam shook the bike slightly to make sure the boat was still attached and then continued on at a much more sedate pace. "If you die, I am in *so* much trouble," he worried. "Why did you come on this yourself instead of sending a Bubo?"

"This is too important a matter for a little Bubo," Lori told him solemnly. "My methods may seem frivolous, but my motivations are not. What Tripp did is the worst crime a so-called scientist can commit."

Sam made as if to turn to look at her but realized it was a bad idea and kept riding. "Ah shit, Barrow, don't get serious on me or I'll start thinking we're really going to die."

Lori's left skate now made crunching noises as it rolled. "Leper, leper, can't catch me..."

They stopped singing when they got to the dirt parking lot on the hill overlooking the LEPERLab. As the Buboes had predicted, there were bikers and joggers milling around all over the place, so they were invisible to any prowling LEPER guards even with their boat. Lori eyed the trails up Lobo Peak and Mt. Hansen with envy and thought, I'll take Lou out here on the off-road handcycle as soon as the proposal is in.

No, I'll try it myself first, she corrected her thoughts. It might fall apart halfway up the mountain. Or worse, down.

She was getting soft in her old age. "Can you pedal down that?" she asked, pointing to the sandy ravine that led through the bushes directly to the drainage pond. It was at the very end of the East lot; no one could possibly see them except the poor LEPERs forced to park there.

Sam looked at his skinny tires, at the boat with its bent hanger, and at Lori as if she were mad. "No!"

"Then walk, and I'll sit in the boat and take my skates off."

She was still fighting with the laces when they got to the bottom. Sam refrained from asking how she expected to make a fast getaway on a vehicle that took her five minutes to get on and off, but she could tell he was worried. If only the Canadian national sport had been skateboarding.

They hid Sam's bike in the bushes so he could leap out of the boat and grab it as quickly as possible. Before starting across the pond, she checked her backpack pockets for the tools and re-read the map the Buboes had prepared. The only piece of paper she was going to bring was the suggested list of passcodes—there was no way she would remember them: they were weird things like the controversial value of the Hubble constant.

Skates in her bag, wearing the stupid blazer and what she thought was a pretty fake-looking LEPER badge—made by one of the Buboes and labeled with the name of Louise Pasteur—she got in alongside Sam and put her feet on a set of pedals. "*On y va?*"

"*Triche pas,*" said Sam, and they started across the pond.

The plan was for Lori to infiltrate LEPERLab while Sam waited in the boat to make ready their escape, and it was amazing how easy it was. There were no LEPERs anywhere near the pond or in the sandy area on the other side. A few hundred meters away, she saw the first string of yellow go-carts taking employees back to the East lot, but some scraggly prickly pears and manzanita hid her from their view.

Once onto the paved area by the cafeteria, she was just another LEPER. The few others that she crossed on her way to the colony manager's building looked equally furtive, probably because they were supposed to be riding in go-carts. It wasn't really necessary to sneak in behind the building through the rosemary, but she did it out of some sort of nostalgia, sticking a few sprigs in her bag just because.

No one was in the building. Three days remained until the Polar Institute Proposal was due, and there was no one there. Was this place really so huge that no one had to work very hard? Maybe Tripp wasn't really involved in the writing, but in that case, what was his interest in Sam's paper?

Just to make sure, she knocked on Tripp's door before pulling on a pair of nitrile gloves and starting on the list of passcodes.

It was the fifteenth one that did it, just as she was starting to panic, and it wasn't even a physical constant that she recognized.

No manuscripts on the desk. No manuscripts in the drawers. Username and password were both admin, and there were no files in the computer containing any of the title or keywords from Sam's manuscript. There were hundreds of megabytes of PowerPoint slides, spreadsheets containing budgets and budget reports, and a photo of him and his wife that confirmed that Ellis D. Tripp was none other than the fat man she had seen twice: once in St. Vitus's over the yellow fever scare, once in the guard shack as they had tried to leave with their ice cores.

This last thought made her check his Internet browser history, which contained enough to get lesser LEPERs fired but nothing that would embarrass any straight man. He had tried to erase the record of his visits to a racist forum and some kind of anarchist site; Lori thought both were childish.

Finally she gave up. Leaving a small branch of rosemary between the G and H keys of his keyboard, she cautiously exited the office (still no one) and peeked out the front window to assess the go tard situation. This had to be a management building because there was only one silver go-tard parked outside, idling in a cloud of fumes.

Taking a deep breath for both courage and oxygen, she strode purposefully out the front door and past the go-tard, whose driver ignored her completely.

Right. Louise Pasteur didn't have a management badge. The Buboes had told her that managers' badges were colored bright blue to indicate their right to STUMP parking and silver go-tards. *Thanks be to God that I don't work at the LEPERLab.*

She headed up the hill as discreetly as possible, not liking the idea of having to escape from the Drift lab. This descent would be terrifying on skates, and on foot she was at best two miles an hour slower than the carts, which could go twelve miles an hour before they became unstable. At least there were two doors into the building: the main one where all the go-tards were parked, and the one she had come in last time by the loading dock. A good flying leap off the loading dock might be preferable to facing the two-stroke horrors.

Breaking into his office would pose a variety of problems, primary among them the fact that she had no idea where it was. She started in the cold room because she knew it was there and that it wasn't locked. It was too scary to latch the door behind her, so she left it cracked but used her Bubo-provided flashlight instead of the overhead light.

All of the ice cores were gone. It was hard to tell what might have been disturbed by Tripp, since Dim Bulb had come first, apparently removing everything he could find. Only one shelf held office supplies, a pile of paper next to a very small laptop computer.

It was Sam's manuscript. The original with only his name on it, but that wasn't going to prove anything. She needed to have Word files showing changes. She started up the laptop, shivering due to both cold and impatience. It was dangerous to stay here so long—Bob might come by—but it would be no use coming all this way if all she got was something they already had. At least she had the crowbar so nobody could lock her in.

Opening his document files one by one, she felt a broad grin spread across her frozen face. They were all there, time-stamped, from the first scanned copy of the paper to the one where Sam's name had been crossed out and replaced with a handful of LEPERs, Bob Drift in first place and Tripp in last.

There were other things too. Lori's breath grew quicker as she saw her own name—it was a file of all the emails she had exchanged with Carol since she arrived. Then there was another file…

…But there was no time. Pulling out the star screwdrivers, she went to work removing his hard drive, leaving some rosemary in its place.

When this was done, she was feeling pretty cocky and decided to put on her skates and cruise out of the building off the loading dock and face the gnarly downhill. Hard drive safely in her bag, she pulled out her rollerblades and sat on the floor to lace them up.

She was in the worst possible position, one skate on tightly and one foot bare, when the door burst open.

The light flicked on just as she stepped away from the computer. Bob

Drift stood there, nodding knowingly, saying nothing.

If I were a real Canadian, she thought, I'd know skate fu and hop on one foot while knocking him out with my ultralight chassis.

There were footsteps in the hall, and it quickly became clear that not even skate fu would help her. Tripp the colony manager came in, and towering over him was the chilling figure of Alexander Kuznetsov. "My, my, my," hummed her department head, "it appears you were right, Ellis. Barrow, or shall I say, *Pasteur*," his laugh was unutterably vile, "could you kindly tell me what you are doing at the Lobo Peak Rocket Lab, unauthorized, in Dr. Drift's private space?"

She felt ridiculous, balancing on one skate and wielding a tiny flashlight, but she gave it her best shot. "I certainly can, Dr. Kuznetsov. These people are thieves of the very worst sort. They stole Samuel Roth's manuscript."

They all exchanged a *Yes, as we expected* glance. "Tell me, Dr. Barrow," purred Kuzno, "did you see Mr. Roth write this manuscript?"

Her mouth fell open like a carp's. They were going to try to pretend *Sam* was the thief? "Of course, I—" She couldn't tell them what she knew, or they would know she'd opened the computer and then might guess she had the hard drive. "I worked with him on it all last week."

"Yes," Tripp nodded smugly. "That was about the time Dr. Drift says it disappeared. You were right to be suspicious, Dr. Kuznetsov. Clearly no one would take responsibility for this manuscript at STI. There isn't even a senior author."

Lori wanted to smack that hierarchical leper upside the head with anything available. "It is not *our* procedure to put the 'senior' person on as a guest author," she practically spat. "He who does the work gets the credit. I was the sole author on at least half of my papers in graduate school, as was Louis Maupertuis—he's just following an honorable and honest tradition."

Tripp and Kuzno snorted derisively at her last two adjectives. Bob Drift finally spoke, though in a voice that sounded cowed. "Is it really honest to come into someone else's lab and play with their computer?"

Tripp took a step towards Lori. "We'd better let Security take it from here. Bob, make sure she didn't damage your laptop."

Lori staggered backwards on her one rollerblade and one frozen foot, almost tripping over her backpack. Her stomach was tied in knots and she wondered fleetingly if she could projectile vomit in self-defense. She should have sent a Bubo or anyone not on PNG status (why van Gnubbern? How could they PNG van Gnubbern?).

She should have done anything but pedal across the drainage pond in a boat that she built in 1988.

You're a pathetic loser, Barrow, said her brain unhelpfully. Thirty-three years old, and you still wish you were a little Bubo. Those days are over. Get a life!

"It's not booting," mumbled Bob. "Just a second—"

Everyone clustered around the computer. Lori thought she was doomed, especially when the door banged open and four burly security guards tromped in. She cringed, expecting to be slapped in handcuffs as they intoned, "We need you to come with us."

But it wasn't her they wanted.

It was Bob. They took him by the elbow, ignoring her completely. Deep voices murmured into his ear, words like, "Your employee," "second incident," and "electric shock."

Dim Bulb *ex machina!* Lori thought, mentally slapping herself to tear herself away. Slowly, quietly, behind everyone's back, she bent over and started lacing up her skate.

Security led them all out of the building. She followed as far behind as she could without attracting attention—but when Kuzno turned to look at her, she spun around and started down the hill as fast as her dirty bearings would carry her.

The Buboes had been wrong that her greatest speed advantage was on an uphill. She could go much faster than the go-tards on a downhill, she just couldn't stop at the bottom.

Now they were after her, with that tyrant Tripp screaming at them that she was a criminal who must be stopped. Her life as a false Canadian flashed before her eyes: *Pousse avec le talon!* they always said, and *Poids en arrière!*

She chanted the mantras aloud, thighs shaking as she descended in a seated pose.

Halfway down the hill, a silver go-tard was parked across the road. Her choices were to turn left and crash into the arroyo, which was a twenty-foot drop full of cacti, or to turn right.

There was a hard right turn in the Ottawa marathon. Every year she missed it, and every year she crashed into the grass, getting up to cries of *"Ça va?"* to start a humiliating and futile chase after the group that had dropped her. Every year she told herself that all she needed to do was hop, lift both feet up and once and turn them ninety degrees to the right.

Both she and the go-tard were astonished when that worked, and she sailed cheerily over the sidewalk. "Can't catch me!" she called. "I'm Canadian!"

Now there was a left turn back to the boat. This she could handle. She descended as far as she needed to and then crossed over carefully, hip into the turn. It was nearly dark by now, but she could make out the blue of the boat and a small red light where Sam's head should have been.

"Barrow!" he screamed. "Triche paaaaaas!"

He had a video camera, the little twerp. She was no more than ten meters from the boat, but if she didn't slow down, she was going to die.

Suddenly she remembered the sandy region through which she'd sneaked earlier. She could cut through the sand and the manzanita, scrub speed and destroy her bearings, and fling herself headfirst into the boat. This turned out to be a good choice—she could no longer see the go-tards puttering along on the paved road, but she could hear them coming closer, along with a good deal of shouting.

The manzanita was surprisingly sharp, but her wrist guards covered most of her arms, letting her clutch at every available branch without too much damage. At the last moment she decided to try feet first into the boat, but this was a mistake, and she crashed into Sam's outstretched right arm— the left still held the camera—and sprawled across the front of the boat. It swayed dangerously, toxic sludge lapping at their feet.

"Oooh, this is going to be Pasteur's most popular video," he rejoiced.

"Not for long," Lori gasped. "Just wait till we catch a serial killer. Come on, Sam, pedal!"

Lori pedaled for all she was worth, skates and all. They abandoned the boat on the side of the pond and ran for Sam's bike. As she had suspected, a car's headlights came on just as they emerged from the bushes. "Up the sandy part! Go!"

"STOP!" yelled the LEPER, revving his engine.

But they were already off LEPER property and into the wilderness trail. She tried to shield herself behind vegetation and the bike, in case the guy was a guard with a gun, hoping the darkness would help them.

There was a rustling in the bushes. The LEPER was chasing them on foot. "Barrow, they're after us!" Sam yelled.

"Tell me about it!" Even a fat LEPER was a match for a guy pushing a bike and a rollerblader in sand.

Sam hopped on the bike. "Grab on!" he yelled, downshifting all the way (yes) and tearing up the sandy hill as if it had been the smoothest pavement in the Tour de France.

Lori clutched his seatpost, too thrashed to assist, her skates completely useless in the soft surface anyway. She heard the LEPER give up, bellowing and wheezing like a hippo, but it wasn't until they were more than a mile into the four-mile descent to campus that either one could say a word.

"I got what we need, Sam," Lori breathed, still holding onto his seatpost. "You can call the journal in the morning. I think it was my computer that was the leak—they have all of my emails."

"You mean your laptop?"

"It's the only computer I own. Hold off on posting the video, OK? And don't say anything to Lou and Rose. Tell them you found Drift's laptop somewhere or something."

"Don't tell them?" Sam exclaimed. "You were brilliant! I want to give credit where credit is due."

"As long as I don't get the credit for what happened to Dim Bulb," Lori replied grimly. "Because from what I heard, it sounds as if someone has tried to kill him again."

TWENTY-TWO: THE ONLY FACT WE HAVE

Solomon Rose was standing right in the middle of the room, as far away from any surface as possible, refusing to take one of the BSL-3's freshly reupholstered, nonporous, and completely nonpathogenic lab chairs. Lou and van Gnubbern, on the other hand, were too blasé—elbows on the benchtop, holding cellphones, not wearing lab coats. They might not have had any yellow fever out, but it was still a hot-agent lab.

And it was also the safest place to talk in the building. "Well, Lori," said Sol, "it looks as if you've been vindicated."

He sounded as proud as if he'd killed Dim Bulb himself. "That doesn't make any sense," Lori objected. "I mean, I'm happy that the labs can re-open, but what does Dim Bulb have to do with Marybeth? Officially or unofficially?"

"Officially?" said Sol. "There is some old infrastructure in these buildings that needs repairing. It's no one's fault."

"Unofficially," continued van Gnubbern, "I think we can guess."

"No we can't!" Lori objected. "I thought Dim Bulb killed Marybeth. If someone killed him, it means there's still a murderer on the loose."

"No one says it was murder," said Rose soothingly. "It could have been suicide, a careless accident…"

"How did he die?" Lori wondered.

"You mean you don't know?" Lou was at his usual spot at the microscope, distracted with turning tiny screws on an optical filter. He wore no gloves at all. "You were up there. We thought you'd know everything."

"For once, the evil on this campus has completely escaped me."

"I'm the one who found his body," van Gnubbern admitted. "No more than five hours ago."

"Five hours?" Lori echoed. "But that's before I left—that's about the time I called Carol. Did they put you on PNG status because you found Dim Bulb dead?"

"Indeed," said van Gnubbern. "I had gone up there at the request of Bob Drift to fix a microscope. When I went into the room, our old friend was lying on the floor, inert. I tried to revive him, but he was stone cold."

"Not frozen again!" Lori shrieked.

"Oh, no." Van Gnubbern chuckled. "The temperature in the room was quite normal. They say he was electrocuted, although I couldn't tell you the basis for that conclusion."

"We expected you to fill in the details—unofficially." Rose no longer sounded quite so soothing. "It sounds as if you have some work to do."

"Wait, what?" Lori was starting to suspect all three of them of conspiring without her. "I thought I was supposed to slice ice cores. Let's cool down the room and I'll go to it."

"Oh, I can handle that," said Lou casually—too casually.

Lori whirled and glared at him. "No you can't! You're a theorist! I bet you don't even own a parka."

"I was captain of the ski team in high school, Barrow," said Lou.

"And I can certainly show this young man all he needs to know about sample prep," continued van Gnubbern.

"So what are you saying?" Lori still couldn't bring herself to yell at Rose, but this was outrageous. "Am I just your henchman, like Dim Bulb was Kuzno's? Or maybe we're all really on the same team? Who are you going to ask me to kill?"

"We certainly won't ask you to go that far." Rose had that comforting voice again. It was a good thing he hadn't become a pediatrician, because it was really phony. "Nor will we ask you to do string theory."

"We just want you to ask a few questions of the people who know too much," added van Gnubbern.

Lori knew when she was outnumbered. She couldn't even slam the door on her way out—it had to suck closed with its negative-pressure suction. Waiting impatiently, she noticed three brightly colored parkas hanging from the hooks in the vestibule.

"Ingrates!" she shouted, but of course over the laminar flow they wouldn't hear a thing.

She didn't know where to start, she realized as she ran up the stairs to her office. Her computer was suspect—apparently its entire contents had been leaked to Tripp, Bob, and the other LEPERs. She'd have to check it for spyware, but in the meantime, who was it who knew too much?

No one who would talk to her, that was for sure. Everyone she'd thought was on her side was hiding down in what was supposed to be her lab, doing experiments without her.

There were the four mini video cameras she'd given to Carol to install around the microscope—maybe that's what Rose had meant. She wouldn't put it past him to know all about that. Where had Carol been while Dimmy was being killed, anyway?

The trouble with Carol was that you had to make her believe you had called to talk to her, not just that you were after information. You had to make small talk and pretend you cared. It was a lot of work—especially when she started weeping.

"Bob is in trouble!" There were some noises in the background—it sounded as if Carol were driving in heavy traffic. "I thought he'd get punished the first time, but somehow he didn't, and now this time…"

"What do the LEPERs do to punish people?" Lori asked, genuinely curious.

"Oh my God," howled her old classmate, as if Lori had asked her to recall Pacific POW camps. "You have no idea…it's horrible. Once my boss got a parking violation, and they locked us all in a purple room with no windows for hours, asking the same questions over and over. It was over a hundred degrees and we got no food or water. Even after people started fainting, they wouldn't let us go. And what could we say? What do we know about our supervisor's driving habits?"

That was petty and stupid, not the life-threatening abuse Lori had been expecting. She tried to gently steer the conversation around to the microscope room, but all she got were more LEPER parking stories and wailing about Bob.

She could be more direct, and risk Carol clamming up—or she could take her out and get her drunk. "I think the best way to deal with Bob for now is to avoid him," she suggested. "Why don't we go to downtown and see $500 \ milliCoulumbs$?"

"I don't think I—" Carol swallowed hard. "OK. Fine. Let's go. I'll see you in a half hour."

It took Lori almost twice that to get to the club on her winter bike. Chaining it to a post and looking around both inside and out, she was dismayed to find that Carol wasn't there. Thinking her not-really-friend had changed her mind, she grew rapidly impatient with the noise and stench of the busy street, noting the time on her watch and vowing to leave after fifteen minutes.

It was six and a half before an unmistakable din added itself to the background. Abby never let anyone forget that she had owned her gray Porsche since she was sixteen, a present from her father who had owned it since *he* was sixteen. Somehow that gave it a smog exemption, or else she didn't care about paying the Gross Polluter tax, because the thing rattled and stank like a leafblower. Shouting at the valet, she leapt out into traffic, coolly certain that she wouldn't be run down like a squirrel.

Carol, on the passenger side, followed more slowly. It was clear that she'd spent the past hour trying to compete with Abby's office-to-nightclub little black dress and absurd teetering shoes. She was a bit overdone, wrapped in something metallic red that looked confusing to put on, like a tangle of interleaved scarves. Her bright red lipstick and blue eyeshadow only made her face look older and more tired.

It was annoying. Annoying she was late, annoying that she had dressed up to see some old loser classmate sing about how grad school sucked, and even more annoying that she had brought an enemy.

Lori braced herself for a wave of hissing as they approached, but Abby appeared relaxed and friendly. It was downright scary—the only thing that could make Abby stop hating her, she thought, was if her life truly were in danger.

"Come on, Carol," she urged, probably too hastily. "Let me buy you a tequila. You too, Abby."

It was just like old times. Old times where they'd had nothing in common but their gender and their quantum mechanics homework, and where each glared silently at the other wishing she could only understand.

At least then they could bond over trying to get good grades—tonight no one could find a word to say until the ethanol began to work on their GABA receptors. Lori worried that her soda water would make the others suspicious, but they didn't seem to care, slamming back drinks each containing more alcohol and refined sugar than Lori had consumed in her life. The club was noisy, and they were clustered around a tiny table just to one side of the opening band, but there was never any problem hearing Abby.

"In fifteen years," Abby raged, gesturing for a second (or third?) margarita, "no one has ever told me I made the right decision. Everyone thinks I left grad school because I was too stupid."

"That's not true. I always knew you were the most talented of any of us," Lori objected mildly, not even bothering to shout over the music.

"Ha! You're the one who kept telling me to come back and take the qualifying exam."

"Just to prove to yourself that you could do it. So you wouldn't stay angry for fifteen years. Look—you make twice as much money as I do, work half as many hours, and send my postdocs to prison. What do you hate me for?"

Abby contorted her face into a rictus of horror and fury, just as Kurt the drummer appeared and stood directly behind her—something she always used to despise. "I was sitting two feet away from a guy whose head was blown to pieces." She pushed her chair back as if preparing to get up, knocked into Kurt, and then leapt to her feet with a hand raised as if preparing to slap him. She let her hand drop as she recognized who it was, but spluttered with uncontained wrath.

"A blast from the past!" Kurt chortled, making as if to pat Abby on the back but stopping himself at her expression. He had aged well—probably better than those who hadn't dropped out, Lori thought, noticing his tongue piercing that glinted in the light when he laughed. His red hair was in a thick ponytail, and ape-like muscles stood out on his forearms. "Green-Eyed Monster and the Dugong! Suddenly I feel twenty-one again."

The sound of the opening band's last song died down, allowing Abby's voice to carry to everyone in the room. "Then you should remember that if you stand behind me, I will assume you're preparing a garrote and take appropriate action," she spat, clearly not too drunk if she could put together sentences like that.

"Chill out, ladies," chuckled Kurt. "I just came over to see how our class stars were doing. I hear you're all rocket scientists now."

Lori and Abby howled with scorn in unison. They had finally found something they agreed on.

"Rocket science!" Lori scoffed. "Those LEPERs don't build their own rockets anymore—they contract everything out because they're not allowed to touch sharp objects!"

"Their semi-official motto is *Brilliant Engineering, Mediocre Science, Shitty Management*," Abby added. "I spend my days covering up for two-bit tyrants who think they can lock their employees in the closet with no food or water as punishment for criticizing the system. Then just today Carol's dearly beloved Bob caused a scandal..." She clamped her mouth closed, and changed the subject by urging Kurt to play old classics that she had inspired. "Remember 'Gibber Ellen'?" she demanded for the whole room to hear. "Or 'Santa's Got Scurvy'!"

When the music resumed, Abby all but pushed Carol away to lean in and whisper to Lori. "Who would kill Silverman?" she inquired. "And why?"

"I don't know," Lori stammered, caught off guard.

"You hated him, didn't you?" she persisted, with a trace—but only a shadow!—of the old loathing.

She must really think I'm doomed, Lori thought. Wow. "Only because he was an arrogant fuckwad, but we all are—I mean…"

Abby chortled. "What did he think about string theory?"

"I don't know. I was only an undergrad. Is this really what you think it's about?"

Ignored and neglected, Carol got up and wandered backstage. Abby waited until the red butt had just disappeared behind the curtain, and said too loudly, "Did you see her eyes on Kurt? I'm gonna tell him that she needs to ditch Bob ASAP. Even if he's not fired, those LEPERs will make his life hell."

"Back to the killer," Lori urged, hating the way loosened inhibitions correlated with not making much sense. "Can we relax and work on our project now, or is Dim Bulb not the end of the story?"

For a moment Abby looked furious, as if she were about to respond in her usual hateful fashion. But the rage passed, and she leaned in again and spoke more quietly than Lori thought was possible for Shouting Abby. "If you're still planning to work on an astrobiology proposal, we're all going to need to watch your backs. I've got an idea for how to trap them—now listen carefully."

TWENTY-THREE: CALL ME WIGBERT

A MONTH AFTER DIM BULB was safely buried, they had all entirely forgotten the killer in the department in the frustration of trying to do cutting-edge science with an impossible deadline. Twenty-seven days of nonstop work, and they still didn't have the data they needed. Some of their images were beautiful, from both the electron and fluorescence microscopes, but they still didn't know what any of it meant. Lou had spent all Thanksgiving weekend trying to caption the pictures, not coming up with anything much better than "Unidentified microorganism from fifty centimeters depth in an Antarctic ice core."

That wasn't going to cut it. But he needed a break—they both did—or someone was going to melt down completely. His fingers were stained with dyes of seven different wavelengths, and when he shut his eyes, bacteria and fungi and algae swam across his retinas. The cracks in the road looked like mineral structures, or patterns in broken ice.

Lori's little outing was probably going to kill him, but Lou didn't care. It was the best adventure that he had had in years, and honestly, being left for dead in the desert was probably more pleasant than writing six hundred million dollars' worth of budget pages.

He pulled the rental car into a spot next to the empty nature center and rolled down the window. There was a cute little adobe building right in front of them, with various types of cacti and other desert plants growing in strategic locations on the walking path that branched out in all directions. The sand in between the plants was fine and light grey; a black willow, heavily infested with dodder, shaded their parking place. "I didn't expect it to be so wild and deserted here," he exclaimed. They were no more than a twenty-minute drive from campus, and just off the major freeway that ran south to Long Beach. "This is beautiful."

"I used come here almost every weekend," Lori informed him. "But this is the first time I've made it since I've been back, thanks to you and Sol and your project."

"We're in the home stretch now," he promised, but didn't believe it himself. "It feels weird not to have a cluster of Bubo bodyguards cataloging our every move."

"Mad killers won't find us here," Lori promised. "You'll see what I mean."

He could already see what she meant. The adobe nature center had boards on its windows, and the asphalt in the parking lot sprouted with Bermuda grass and dandelions. She'd said they could go on this trail all the way to the beach, thirty-five miles out and thirty-five miles back, but Lou had doubts on every count: her home-made vehicles, her description of the terrain, and above all his own stamina.

Lori had a reputation for dragging people off on near-death adventures in unlikely pedal-powered craft. The most famous story involved Radhika—who had an incurable case of acrophobia—an ultralight airplane, and a cliff. Lou would have thought the story exaggerated if he hadn't seen the pictures in Pasteur House, apparently taken at Lori's ten-year reunion. There was also a rumor that none of her students graduated unless they survived at least one test of endurance in the wilderness. More extreme versions of the rumor said that not all of them emerged alive.

As if reading his mind, Lori admonished, "This route is perfectly safe. You know my adventures are dangerous when I invite more than one other person to be sure of having a witness."

He laughed. It was nice that she treated him just like everyone else, even though it was done with the insouciance of a small child or a psychopath.

They'd learned an incredible amount in the past weeks about astrobiology, about teamwork, and about how to put together a six hundred-million-dollar proposal. But they had learned next to nothing about each other, and Lou still relied for most of his information about Lori on Bubo legends. It was hard to reconcile the image of the daredevil criminal mastermind with this soft-spoken little genius who was so nondescript that she had to shout in shops and restaurants to even be served.

Lori's career was all over the map, but Lou had come to the conclusion that people who criticized her for that were fools. She just plain knew everything and seemed to have a finger in every pie in the science world, from green fluorescent protein to robotic mice to heavy-ion collisions. There was no doubt that she had deserved her position and that most of the senior people would fight to keep her; but there was a dark side to the story that he still didn't fully understand. Kuzno and Rose appeared to be engaged in a final battle, but whether Lori was the queen, a knight, or a pawn was yet to be determined. He had managed to convince himself that the war was merely a symbolic one, that anyone capable of actually shedding blood was safely six feet under. But somewhere, down deep in a part of himself he didn't even want to acknowledge, he had to wonder if Dim Bulb had himself been only a minion. The Buboes swore that Kuzno had been on campus dawn to dusk on the day that Dim Bulb had died, and had video to prove it, so it was hard to even imagine who the evil puppeteer might be.

This was the second weekend in a row that they'd been brave enough to do something together off campus. Lori hadn't known that there were hand controls that just snapped on to the steering wheel of a car; she had especially not known that you could call up a rental-car company and request them. She'd learned this last Sunday when he had called to ask if she wanted to go for a drive, and they had gone up the Angeles Crest all the way to the snow line. It was early for snow even at seven thousand feet, reminding them both that with the approach of the holidays came the approach of their deadline, which sent them scurrying back to work.

Lou, for his part, hadn't known that handcycling had been invented at STI or that Lori had come five hundred meters from being the 1988 forty-kilometer champion. "The problem was that the fairing that made me fast also made me too hot, and I passed out just before the finish line," she explained as she got out of the car. "By the time my friends noticed that I wasn't moving and ran over to reanimate me with a water bottle, three other people had passed me."

"Sorry to be a theorist, but what's a fairing?" Lou opened the car's rear door and slid his bike out from the back seat. It was a weird and awkward shape but light as a feather, and he held it easily in one hand.

"A plastic lid that closed over me to make me aerodynamic," she explained, going to the trunk to get her own vehicle. "I threw it out long ago, but it's the same bike. Yours is infinitely cooler."

"Carbon fiber?"

"Single-piece carbon fiber design made by a guy in STI's own Human Powered Vehicle club. All the old-timers remember me. Half that stuff hanging on the wall is from when I was an undergrad—the hydrofoil, the pedal boat, the airplane..."

"What should I bring?" Lou asked before leaving the driver's seat, reaching for his bag. "Camera? Food and water?"

"Definitely food and water. There's nothing between here and the beach. If you haven't been here before, you might want your camera. There are some pretty spots." She sat down and her seat immediately fell to one side, spilling her onto the pavement. "And the tool bag. And my rollerblades, in case both bikes fall apart and I have to run back and get the car."

"The road goes right along the bike path?"

"I think so," Lori shrugged, but she clearly had no idea. Well, if she ended up dragging him home, it was her own doing.

Lou was much more impressed with the handcycle than with Lori's organizational skills. The crank was about shoulder-width, and had a huge assortment of gears and shift levers that you could operate without letting go. He'd never been much of a gadget freak, but as gadgets went, this was pretty awesome. He spun around the parking lot while Lori finished loading all the wrenches and hex keys and tubes and pumps they might need. "I didn't quite understand at first why the cranks are parallel rather than perpendicular," he mused. "But it's faster this way, isn't it?"

"Unless you're going up a very steep hill. There is only one hill on this ride, when we climb over the reservoir."

"Anything else I should know?"

She scratched her head, thinking. "When we descend the other side, there's a sharp left turn at the bottom. The turning radius on these things sucks, and remember you're on homemade carbon fiber, so try not to crash."

There wasn't much to see in the first five miles, apart from the little desert park with its interpretive signs, stunted sycamores, and elderberry trees that they left very quickly in order to climb the massive edifice of stone that was the dam over the reservoir. The late-November day was clear and hot, and they were exposed to a merciless blue sky and an infinite expanse of concrete until they came over the crest and saw laid out before them Los Angeles in all its glory. The areas closest to the dam were industrial, but farther on they could see wooden houses and horse trails, still farther the lush green expanses of a golf course, and running through it all a fifty foot deep chasm of pavement that was the San Gabriel River. Spindly palm trees emerged from the cement, towering to absurd and crooked heights, casting twisted shadows in the oblique winter sunlight.

"Caution, gnarly downhill," Lori warned, about to start descending. But Lou called for her to wait and pulled out his new camera and the telephoto lens he had never even had a chance to try. From their vantage point he could look east into the foothills, all the way to the telescopes of Mt. Hansen, or west along the river to the Pacific. He rarely saw such an incongruous panorama of wild neglected nature and slabs of black pavement.

"If only I had known you were into photography from the beginning," Lori mused.

"When I was a kid, I wanted to be a wildlife photographer," said Lou.

"What we do in the BSL-3 is kind of like that."

"It is, isn't it?" he agreed, laughing. "Stare and scroll around and stain and hope you catch the bacteria doing something good." He started re-packing the instruments carefully into their black leather bag, glancing at his phone when it started to ring.

"Oh god!" Lori grumbled. "I hate cell phones."

"I have to have one, because I don't trust you." He glanced at the number. "And because of my students. Hello, Sam, what's up?"

"The paper just came back with requests for revisions," Sam revealed in a plaintive tone. "Can you look at them?"

"No, I'm not in right now." Lou said something he'd been waiting to say for a long time. "I'm on a bike ride with Barrow."

"Uh huh," said Sam, blasé. "I suppose you visited her miracle stem-cell lab first?"

"You got it. It's right by the BSL-3. I'll be in by five or six, I think, right?" Lori shrugged, then nodded reluctantly. "She says yes. I think. You could show it to Bert first."

"Who? Dr. van Gnubbern? You call him Bert? I thought his first name was…"

"Right, Dr. van Gnubbern. Do *not* call him Wigbert, or I guarantee he won't help you. I'll be in this evening for sure. Bye. Excuse me," he apologized. "Sam's paper. Ready for the gnarly downhill?"

Lori gaped as if Lou had said something inexplicable or offensive, and refused to go downhill.

"Lori?" he prodded gently. "What's wrong?"

Her mouth still hung half open. "Van Gnubbern… His name is *Wigbert*?"

Lou burst out laughing. "Wigbert Aloysius van Gnubbern—all these years and you didn't know? Watch out, Lori, if we fail in our Plan you will not only be doomed to haunt the campus in your skinsuit and rollerblades, but you will have to change your name to Wigbert."

They started on the short, steep hill, traveling faster than they should. Lou had to lean hard coming into the turn and he heard Lori swear, but neither crashed. They pulled up to what was promised to be the only road crossing of the entire trip with a squeak of brakes and a shout of laughter.

"I can't believe how easy and intuitive this is," Lou exclaimed, taking the lead across the street onto the smooth bike trail that would take them twenty-five miles west to the ocean.

"Like riding a bike," said Lori, passing in front of a Mexican rodeo and pointing out a cell phone tower disguised (quite well) as a palm tree. He had to stop to get a picture of that one, with the timer on and both of them sitting in front of the plastic palm complete with false dates and trunk scales. It was the first picture he'd taken of himself since he'd been hurt, and was having so much fun he didn't even realize that until three miles later.

"Do you have any hobbies other than strange nonmotorized vehicles?" he asked as they left the smooth black pavement and started along a rutted ledge along the river.

"No," she responded automatically, but then reconsidered. "Unless you count learning to be Quebecois. I did a bachelor's degree in literature at a French university there. Tell me, how does a spoiled Westside brat like you end up with a Parisian accent?"

"Because my parents are from Paris, and I'm such a spoiled Westside brat that they sent me to the *lycée français* for six years. After the baby-Einstein kindergarten." So much for getting to know each other—the last thing he wanted was to start talking about his parents. "As you can imagine, they're difficult to deal with. My God, what is this?"

An oasis of green had appeared inside the paved river, cattails and duckweed and water lilies sprouting in what was no more than a puddle of water. Ducks with bright blue bills swam in a tight circle, and a single pelican perched dinosaur-like on the metal railing, four webbed toes per foot gripping tight.

She didn't have to answer, because there was a wooden sign describing the mini-nature preserve and its creation almost by accident after the mandate to pave all of L.A.'s rivers had been carried out. Lou photographed the sign and then crawled off the embankment in pursuit of the pelican, which flew away every time he pointed the camera in its direction.

"Are you almost done down there?" Lori called. "We won't get home before dark at this rate."

Lou was determined. It was quite a bird. "Could you pass down the wide-angle lens? But shhh! I think he's landing."

There wasn't a whole lot to see after that, which let them cover the distance as fast as they could go with only a couple more photo shoots. Many miles of cement-lined river, with a rivulet of water running down the center, hosted a few ducks and the occasional egret probing the unpromising trickle for food. There wasn't a single other soul on the bike path; the only other people on this hidden slice of Los Angeles were golfers on the course off to their left and a couple of kids on BMX bikes in the river. On the opposite side of the river were long stretches of plant nurseries displaying potted palms, climbing vines, and pallets of snapdragons. Occasionally they passed through a narrow, dark, scary tunnel, and in one of them a desiccated rat lay splayed on its back, bicycle tire tracks creasing its belly.

The last stretch to the beach was bumpy with a headwind. Lou's arms were killing him, but he would never admit it, instead focusing up ahead on the roofs of the mini-mall where they could stop for lunch.

Naturally peeing had to complicate everything, as usual. He hadn't thought to pull off the trail in a deserted spot, and somehow it had entirely escaped him that this enormous vehicle wouldn't fit into any public bathroom. So he had to park outside the gas station bathroom and scoot inside with an empty Gatorade bottle, and then was mortified to discover he'd forgotten his catheter kit and had to ask Lori to reach it from his bag.

With all of her usual tact, she demanded, "If you're shy in front of *me*, how will you ever find a girlfriend?"

"Goddammit, I just want to piss," he replied irritably. First his parents, then his bladder! Could it possibly get any worse? "Get out of here."

By the time he came out, she'd already gone to the grocery store for sandwiches, power bars, and lemonade. She showed him the spot on the grass where she said she always had her lunch, right by the pier next to a lineup of sailboats. They weren't quite at the beach here, but they could see the dunes and the waves, and after a few minutes Lou recovered enough from his snit to be able to take a picture.

"How do you know I don't have a girlfriend?" he asked, curious as to how she would answer.

"Isn't it obvious?" She dumped the contents of the shopping bag out in the grass. "You spend your weekends with me. Have a sandwich."

He took turkey and left her with the veggie burger. "I don't know, you're kind of cool. You're like the living embodiment of Pasteur House."

Lori remained silent. They ate ravenously, almost not chewing, and leaned against the grassy hill, which was chilly even though the sun beat on their heads from behind.

Lou was astounded at how great he felt. He'd been so sick for so long, and struggled so hard through so much physical therapy, that he'd forgotten what it was like to exercise as hard as you could just for fun. Now his lungs felt clear and the food tasted better than anything had in years. Even just lying in the grass was a forgotten joy—he could feel the ground with his back and with the hand not holding the sandwich, reveling in the sensation, tempted to roll around like a dog to let every part he could feel touch the earth.

He wanted to thank her for bringing him out here, but he didn't really know how, settling for giving her his sweatshirt when he saw she was shivering. There was no one around but a seagull begging for crumbs, and the intimacy made it tempting to ask personal questions—why had she left

Canada, why did she flinch at any mention of suicide, what were her hopes and dreams. But he figured she'd just say something glib and that would be the end of it.

One thing he knew: Radhika had told him on the phone that Lori was a total prude in English, and a complete libertine in French. "I know why *you* don't have a girlfriend," he taunted in his best Quebecois accent. "Your breakup with Radhika is a nice bit of legend—they say she slapped you at the March Meeting when you said you were taking a faculty job in a place with snow."

"It's been five years," Lori replied without elaboration, but at least she managed to speak French without crying.

"So, you'll never find another woman as smart and beautiful as Radhika." He tore open a power bar with his teeth and grinned at her.

"It doesn't have to be a woman," Lori informed him, throwing a crust of bread to the seagull. "All I ask for is someone who doesn't believe in God, thinks marriage is evil, and knows enough science not to annoy me. I'm also turned on by correct use of the accusative."

"Well, Lori!" He was taken aback by her candor and chewed in silence for a moment, offering her half of his power bar, which had a horrid icing. "Just between you and me, I'm not sure what the intersection of those sets is, but it's a small fraction of the population to be sure. Am I disqualified for having been Brian's best man?" He thought she'd been kidding, or just playing with his head, and was taken aback when she announced that anyone who would take part in a wedding was an *ostie de vendu*—presumably a sellout. "Awww, come on, it was cute! The poor guy is such a nerd that the only person he could find was his thesis advisor."

"I don't understand how allegedly smart people can live such conventional, conservative lives," she griped, pulling out handfuls of grass. "Swallowing all the gender stereotypes and doing what their parents tell them, buying and trading each other like chattel, it makes me sick."

"I'm just starting to realize how conservative physics is," Lou admitted. "My friends here were all movie people, and during grad school in Chicago I hung out with the art crowd. They sometimes annoyed me by not knowing much about science, but hey—once I got to calculate a parabolic motion problem for a Hollywood blockbuster, how funny is that? They were all surprised when the equation worked."

"Hmph. Are you saying I should ask you to introduce me to your spoiled rich Westside friends?"

"They're not my friends anymore. At least not that I know of." He lay back in the grass, gazing at the sky and eating from a bag of trail mix open on the ground between them. "All I have now is this job. My bargain with the gods is that they can take everything else—my freedom, my health, my sexuality, the love of my friends and my parents, everything—but I will keep this job if it kills me."

It was an unexpected confession, but what came out of Lori's mouth was even more surprising. "You know how the guards who almost Rodney-Kinged us kept talking about an anonymous tip and a white SUV? Who would associate that SUV with any of us? Did you drive it a lot?"

"That beastly thing? Are you kidding? Twice in my life, and only on the Westside."

"So who would know it was yours, except maybe your parents—and the person who saw you drive it last."

Lou choked on a peanut and had to sit up and reach for a bottle of lemonade. "Do you mean Dim Bulb?"

"It could be," Lori acknowledged, picking at the grass. "He was at the LEPERLab that day, or should have been, at least. My video camera that I put in the elevator shaft was found at his place; the cops just gave it back to me. He was involved for sure. But..."

"But what?" he wondered in spite of himself.

"But I'm starting to understand how the LEPERLab works, and I doubt anyone would have listened to an 'anonymous tip' from him. He's just a flunky, a new-hire, a leper."

"So you think someone else was involved? Dim Bulb was a henchman for a LEPER?"

"Who rewarded him for killing Marybeth with his own position, maybe?" Lori suggested.

A cold breeze came off the ocean, making Lou shiver. The grass was dank and cold, and the sun dropped ominously down towards the sea. "Why don't we go home now?" he suggested.

Lori reached for her bike, but not without a parting shot. "Lou, I realize you have advanced powers of denial, but at some point you're going to have to think about these things."

"Why?" he demanded, scooting down the grassy hill to where his bike was parked. "As far as I'm concerned, the killer is dead. And every minute spent obsessing about him is just another piece of my life that he's taken." She made a face and he was annoyed. "Oh right, no TMI. You can handle any pestilence or revolting medical procedure, but no mental anguish permitted."

"There's nothing revolting about having to pee."

"It's revolting that I can't do it on my own." He held up a hand before she could interrupt. Did she think he was a font of pathological horrors? He hated those more than she did. He just wanted to be normal—but he supposed he'd already failed miserably at that.

"It's all right, Lori, I'm not going to burden you with horrible stories. Want to know why my girlfriend broke up with me?" He waited for her to assent. "Old highschool sweetheart from Malibu. Tolerated me going to Chicago to do a PhD, but only barely. When I came out here for the interview, I studied all night without even asking her how her half-decade had gone. Then in the morning I took a shower, tripped over the litter box, and ran off leaving cat poo everywhere. It went on like this for three days, she couldn't even call because I had the cell phone off, and she finally said I clearly loved STI much more than I loved her." The bike was low to the ground and should have been easy to get into, but for some reason he struggled with it. Maybe his arms were tired.

"Duh!" said Lori, watching his effort critically. He didn't mind; no doubt she was thinking about how to modify the bike. "What a bonehead. I hope she at least had big tits. Want to know what Radhika told me about you?" He nodded, finally getting his butt over the edge of the cushion into the seat. "She said that the one time she presented to the theory section, you leapt up, ran down the aisle to the audience microphone, wrested it away from some poor old guy and said that her multi-exponential fitting routine was garbage."

"It was," he said simply. "It doesn't mean her data weren't any good. She told you about that?"

"It was obvious that it turned her on."

"Damn!" He punched the grass. "I miss my strutting arrogant ways."

"I'm not sure that you've lost them."

He sighed to indicate he was being serious. "I feel as if I have no body language anymore. I'm afraid to go to conferences because I'm just not me."

"Just be glad you have arms," she reminded him. "If you were a quad, I would have to build you a tongue-cycle."

"Christ." Lou was amazed once again by the depths of her flippancy. "Fuck the bike—give me a tongue-powered sniper rifle."

She enjoyed that a lot. Too much. After laughing long and hard she kissed him on each cheek, Quebecois-style, and strapped herself in for the journey home.

"Just you and me against the world," she announced. "And maybe Solomon Rose, if we can trust him. *On y va?*"

The sun was getting low over the water, so they didn't linger or try to go to the pier. The wind was picking up and it would soon be very cold.

The wind was at their backs, though, and they raced each other across the river valley, surprisingly well-matched in speed and equally stubborn. They arrived at the dam in under an hour and a half, Lou completely out of breath and Lori screaming that her arms were going to just plain fall off. The gnarly downhill was worse in reverse, and Lori almost slid backwards from laughing when Lou muttered, "*So* glad I'm not doing this with my tongue." After that they had nothing but a long sloping descent all the way to the park.

It was getting dark by the time they left the trail, but Lou sensed that there was something wrong the instant they pulled into the parking lot. The car somehow seemed too clean, as if it had been polished, and he was sure they hadn't left the passenger window cracked.

Sure enough, the doors were unlocked and everything inside was gone, including Lori's backpack, their extra clothes, and the small bag of Doritos they had stashed in the front seat for after the ride. "I guess we forgot we were in L.A.," he remarked, trying to sound casual although he hoped the thieves were far away by now.

Lori, though, seemed very upset, much more so than he would have expected from an empty backpack and a bag of chips. He couldn't think too hard about it, because he'd just learned to drive again and it took all of his concentration to navigate up the narrow winding streets to her house.

When he remarked innocently that her neighbors had a nice jellypalm, she whirled on him with a strangled rabid hiss.

"Are you OK, Lori?" he asked at last, as she prepared to get out of the car. "You had your wallet and your skates and everything with you, didn't you?"

"Call me Wigbert," she replied, tears sparkling at the corners of her eyes. "There was a CD with a copy of the proposal in the pocket of my backpack."

TWENTY-FOUR: UNCLEAN

CAROL SHOULD HAVE BEEN relieved to see Bob animated again after almost a month of depression. Instead, she was just worried.

He hadn't lost his job over Jim Kalb's electrocution, but he had received the lab's two worst punishments short of being fired: his office had been reassigned to the trailers, and he had lost all his parking privileges.

Not that they lived all that far away—he could walk or bike to work. But parking at the LPR Lab was about much more than where you put your car. Spaces were assigned by rank, in concentric circles centered on the primary management building. The lab director parked in front of the building, the chief scientist and chief engineer right behind it, and VIP visitors (Nobel laureates, president of STI) in the Visitors lot. The next nearest parking lots were a good ten-minute walk from the building but still on lab property, and they housed the highest STUMPs: colony managers and principal scientists.

The great unwashed, including Carol herself, all had to squeeze into the East lot, usually referred to as the Beast lot because of all of the raccoons, skunks, possums, and occasionally foxes and coyotes that would gather there after dark. It was off the federal property, belonging officially to the County of Los Angeles, but still patrolled by LEPER guards. Physically it was separated from the main lab by a swath of desert and a drainage ditch feeding a shallow runoff pond that was still contaminated from the rocket-fuel experiments of the twenties. Every once in a while, dead animals or even people would wash up there after slipping off trails in the mountains. Carol had heard stories of a physics professor once found there, but the most she had ever seen had been a poor old mallard floating on his side. Lured no doubt by the sparkle of water in the desert, he had been swiftly poisoned.

For the duration of his punishment, which was still undetermined, Bob wasn't even allowed to park in the Beast lot or to ride in with anyone else. In order to distinguish him as someone not permitted to be a passenger, his ID badge had been revoked and he had been issued a paper one with a dot-matrix image of his face and "LPR" stamped across it. Carol was even afraid to walk with him, thinking it would be forbidden.

"I'm unclean! I'm unclean!" he wailed constantly, ashamed even to meet with his managers or to go to lunch in groups because he was sure everyone was staring at his punishment badge. Their colony manager didn't make things easier for him, more than once announcing in public that Bob was a fool to have hired someone from a known "loose cannon" like van Gnubbern.

Weekends were better since they were spent away from the lab, so when he got up that morning full of energy, she had attributed the improved mood to the fact that it was Sunday. The furtive phone call in the bathroom was a bit weird, though, and he had grown increasingly more agitated throughout the day. Around three o'clock he drove off without saying where he was going, but was gone less than an hour and returned with a canary-swallowing look that he couldn't wipe off no matter how he tried.

"Just because he has a Nobel Prize doesn't mean he'll win," he muttered several times, along with several dark comments about either destroying or saving the LPR Lab. The direction of his allegiance was unclear, and Carol was worried.

"I'm not sure I should be hearing this," she said.

"You probably shouldn't be," Bob agreed. He gripped his cell phone tightly and went into the bathroom.

She thought of Lori as she pressed her ear to the door.

Bob was insisting that he himself hadn't done anything "too" illegal—her breath caught in her throat—but that he had gotten what he wanted.

"If STI submits and wins a Polar Institute Proposal, it will destroy the LPR Lab," he was saying. "They've already threatened to take away our special status and make us civil servants. You think we're militaristic now! Just wait until we can't submit any of our own projects or choose who works for us."

She still couldn't tell which side he was on. The call ended and she prepared to tiptoe away, but he called another number.

"I need to be able to get this to someone who can move fast," he said in a very different voice, one that verged on a nervous giggle. "Obviously I can't go running to the chief scientist myself. I'm not even a manager, and with my punishment badge! Besides, no—the chief scientist would be a mistake.

Remember how he stood up during the proposal kick-off and said that LPR employees weren't allowed to do biology? He's still in bed with Gerson. Yeah, that was all a disaster, never should have hired a biologist! Trouble is, I have no standing at the Lab right now. People at STI who'd like to see this thing stopped? ...*How* do you spell that? That's an impossible name...Why would he help us? I suppose 'Hates Solomon Rose' is enough for me. Guess it has to be at this point."

The door flung open, and Carol managed to eclipse herself into the neighboring bedroom just in time. Bob closed it immediately, no doubt suspicious, and she again heard the beep of the cell phone.

She was relieved in some ways that it sounded as though he wanted to protect the LPR Lab rather than destroy it. Still, getting involved in intrigues was always a bad idea, and to do it when you were on Unclean status was suicidal. If he were even seen in the same building as Ben Gerson, his career would be over.

She knew that when Bob got an idea in his head, it was no use arguing with him. Still, it hurt when he said he was having "some professors from STI" over for supper and that she was not invited. He even went so far as to tell her to make herself scarce.

"It's just to protect you, baby," he said. "I see it as my only way out right now. If I don't do something to redeem myself, they'll keep me on Unclean status until I quit. But you have a career there. I don't want you to hear things that might hurt you."

It's my choice, she wanted to argue, but he was blowing all of this out of proportion anyway.

But now she had no one to talk to. Lori was furious that her video cameras had disappeared from the microscope lab where Kalb died, and blamed Carol for it. She claimed those cameras had to hold the key to everything—whether the death had been a murder, a suicide, or just a very unlucky accident coming at a really bad time.

No matter how much Carol tried to explain that she hadn't been on campus, and that the LEPERLab had locked down the microscope room right after the incident, Lori wouldn't listen. She didn't understand that sneaking into a cordoned-off room, after hours, when you were married to the person blamed for the incident, was not just impossible but literally dangerous.

Carol didn't believe that there was some "second murderer." She was sure that Kalb had been trying to booby trap the room to kill someone else—probably her. How someone could die of electrocution in a room not supplied with electricity was a mystery, but maybe he had just managed to get Facilities to turn the power on. He'd probably hoped Carol would try to plug in the ratty old microscope and die.

Of course Lori didn't want to hear any of Carol's boson theories. She could be insufferable, but Carol was used to it. Besides, Lori was the only one in L.A. who had known her almost all the way through grad school. Lori had seen Carol struggle to succeed, studying by herself because the top students didn't want her and the bottom ones had ulterior motives: they wanted to get in her pants or for her to help them get in someone prettier's pants, or else they were trying to convert her to their religious cult. The more stressed she was, the more her bulimia took over her life, making her obsess about weight and calories rather than quantum mechanics and electricity and magnetism.

Still, through all of that, she had had passion, and Lori was the last person left who could confirm what Carol feared: that the LEPERLab had stolen her zeal. She had everything she was supposed to want, but she would be forty-two this year, and life was passing her by. She had never slept with anyone but Bob Drift. She had never traveled outside of the country; even inside the country, she had been only to conferences in Miami, Minneapolis, or Washington, DC. Her greatest triumphs at work were filling out her time card and getting to leave early. Lori and Radhika, although they had also stayed in science, seemed to lead lives that were much more exotic and exciting.

Carol had started to have her doubts about her job and what it had done to her, but she didn't want to be forced to leave unprepared. She had worked her entire life for this position. It had taken Lori a week to pass their qualifying exams in graduate school, but it had taken Carol two years; Lori four and a half years to complete her PhD, and Carol eight, and she was lucky that it hadn't taken her even longer.

After that she had done a postdoc in Indiana, where she had worked with radiation physicists who were trying to develop new treatments for brain cancer. A couple years into it, Bob Drift had joined their group as a theorist, and when he left for a second postdoc two years later he had asked her to marry him. They had ended up splitting a salary, since Northeastern University didn't want her, and although she loved Boston she would always remember that year as squalid.

Even though the LEPERLab hadn't wanted her right away either, Bob's position was enough to get her a one-year temporary assignment. It was little more than a postdoc, but for once they both had real salaries. When she was made permanent a year later—the colony manager loved her!— she had at last begun to relax, allowing herself to hope that she had truly seen an end to the days of ramen noodles, trading off a single bus pass, wearing coats in the house, and painstakingly balancing the checkbook every month. They had gone a bit overboard in the other direction, with the plane and everything, but it seemed that their savings always grew.

She had so many friends who were still postdocs. In their forties, often with kids, they went from position to position with little hope of permanence. They said only two percent of physics PhDs got faculty jobs. If she had to leave the LEPERLab, where could she go? She could never be a professor since LEPERs weren't allowed to publish.

"I'm a LEPER!" Carol cried on the phone to Abby.

"Can a LEPER change its spots?" Abby wondered rhetorically. "I think a LEPER can...but maybe the LEPER needs to stop associating with the Unclean."

Carol knew the call was a mistake when Abby started talking about the date she'd had last Friday. She had always been able to make Carol blush, and now it sounded as if she was trying to make her come along on some kind of women's stag night.

"Abby," Carol spoke in a whisper, even though Bob wasn't home. "I can't betray Bob like that."

"What about Kurt?" Abby leered. "I saw you ogling him all night." Did people truly never grow up? Carol didn't find any of this amusing or titillating in the slightest—it just gave her flashbacks.

No one Carol dated was ever good enough for Abby. Abby didn't seem to realize that Carol couldn't hope to attract the same sort of men who went for six-foot blonde supermodel types—and didn't necessarily want to.

Her first date had been in graduate school, if you could even call it a date, with a fellow boson named Paul. They had gone bowling, and for coffee, and studied for exams together. Both raised Lutheran, neither had ever considered any physical contact beyond a side-hug.

This didn't stop Abby. Poor Paul was only five-foot-three, with awkwardly short limbs, so Abby lost no time in teasing Carol about *Paul-with-the-short-arms* or from asking if other things were short, too. Pretty soon the whole class was teasing them, and the relationship fell apart.

Carol, who had not gone all the way with Paul or anyone else in grad school, who had known Bob and only Bob, couldn't really understand any of Absinthe's jokes or her practiced cruelty. It had taken her years to even understand what "other things" even meant.

Maybe she was naïve, but she wasn't a bitch and she wasn't a cheater.

"Can you just help me get Bob out of trouble?" she wondered now, trying not to sound as lost as she felt.

Abby gave a disgruntled sigh. "You're the only one who can keep him from digging in even deeper than he is. I'd keep him on a tight leash if I were you—there are things he's messing with that even I shouldn't know."

TWENTY-FIVE: THE PARIA PROJECT

IT WAS NEARLY NOON by the time Lori rolled up to the physics building on Monday. Every muscle in her body ached. She'd ridden her winter bike as some form of penance, wearing the Roller-Montreal skinsuit that really wasn't made for the skinny saddle but which had symbolic value.

"Uh oh," said Lou seriously when he saw her in it.

"Yeah. Bad things. Very bad things. We need to find Rose. I need to teach my class. I need to take poison."

"One thing at a time. Go change and teach, I'll see if he's free this afternoon."

"Not going to change. This is my outfit for the next sixty years." She parked her bike in her office and slunk off, afraid of encountering Solomon Rose before she was ready to break all the bad news.

They were both waiting for her when class got out, and they dragged her downstairs to the BSL-3. Even if they never managed to do any real science in there, it was the safest place on campus for a private conversation.

Lori didn't even make fun of Rose when he went to extremes not to touch the benchtops or walls in the yellow-fever lab. Besides, she was not in a laughing mood. The PIP was ruined and it was all her fault. Carol, Abby and the Buboes had all confirmed that her backpack had been stolen by none other than that punished LEPER, Bob Drift.

"Why would Bob do something as idiotic as steal our data?" wondered Lou.

"No doubt to redeem himself by passing it on to LEPERs," said Lori.

"He's a fool." Rose seemed reluctant to speak, but they whirled on him, practically frothing with curiosity.

Still standing in the middle of the room, scared to touch any of the furniture, Rose explained, "Bob only got hired because Gerson left. But the

LEPERLab hasn't given up on the idea of doing astrobiology—they think they just need more money and to recruit someone more compliant than Gerson. That's why they're pulling out all the stops to win this PIP. If we win it instead, it's business as usual for the LEPERs. But if the LEPERLab wins it, Bob—" He drew his finger across his throat.

"Can't we just tell him that?" Lori wondered. "How could he and Carol not know?"

"It's a bit late to tell him now," Rose sighed. "I'm sure by now the data are all over the LEPERLab."

"I have no excuse to have been such a moron as to carry that CD in my bag. It's all my fault."

"Yes, it kind of is," Solomon Rose agreed. "What are you going to do about it?"

Change my name to Wigbert was the obvious answer, but looking at each of them, those goofy theorists trying to learn to work with pus, she realized that they weren't angry with her but were simply looking for a solution to a problem. "I don't know," she exclaimed. "Are they going to try to stop us from submitting, or just steal our data?"

"I can't think offhand of how they would stop us, at least not using legal means," mused Rose. "Stealing our data would be the most effective approach. None of us is a recognized astrobiologist, and if we go up against each other with the same data, the LEPERs will win."

"I suppose there's one thing I can do, then," Lori said, resting her head in her hands so that her lips came a mere three inches from the bench. "Redo all of the ice core data and make them even better this time."

A small smile played at the corner of Rose's mouth. "If you can do it, then that's what you need to do."

"OK." Lou still didn't seem too convinced. "I can take more pictures of ice cores, I guess. But there's still so much to do. I haven't even started on the management section."

"Pah." Rose strode over to the microscope where Lou was sitting. He looked at the computer somewhat skeptically, then nodded thanks to Lori when she handed him a pair of gloves. Slowly, hindered by the latex, he typed out

```
The Superior Technological Institute Polar
Antarctic Research In Astrobiology (PARIA)
project is organized along the Galley Slave
model. The PI, because he is old and has
a Nobel Prize, will play the time-honored
role of Figurehead. The Co-Is will serve
as Slave Drivers. Slaves will be recruited
```

by press-gangs operating at the American
Physical Society March Meeting, the Lunar
and Planetary Sciences conference, and the
Geological Society of America.

"There's your management section," said Rose, stripping off his gloves and handing them to Lori as if they were a dead mouse.

"It's pretty good," she admitted, "but the acronym needs an *H*."

"I say no *H*," insisted Lou. "That way it's French, and it is also the past tense of *parier*, 'he wagered.' Lay the odds, my friends, *les jeux sont faits*."

"Recruit your students, train them as much as you can, and see what you can do," Rose continued. "You still have ten days."

Lori thought about Chi-Ming, and Walter, and the Buboes, and was not reassured. They just weren't efficient enough, and they were occupied with so many other things. Then there was Carol, who was probably a spy for Bob and the LEPERs.

She got up from her bench and strode around the room, thinking. "We need to maximize everyone and everything we have. Lou, you might have to learn to use the electron microscope as well as the fluorescence. If you can do that, Chi-Ming can slice and stain, and Walter…" The ideas began to crystallize in her head. "Then Walter can do ribosomal RNA analysis! We can characterize the communities completely. With the fluorescence, we can even do FISH."

"Uh oh," worried Rose. "Animal experiments?"

"No, no—fluorescence *in situ* hybridization, F-I-S-H. It tells us what kinds of organisms are living in the samples. I took a molecular biology class when I was a senior here, just for fun—it was with Jerry Pine, remember him?—and all the reagents are available from the stockrooms on campus. It will make the first version of the proposal look completely unsophisticated, if not downright wrong."

A gleam appeared in Rose's bunny-like liquid brown eyes. "Speaking of which, could you please make me a CD of the old version of the proposal, one where you may have inserted, here and there, a couple of egregious and embarrassing errors?"

"I can do that," said Lori, "while Lou is helping Sam with this paper revisions. Then we can get started in the microscope room. Get your parka, and I'll meet you at five."

It was a relief to put on normal clothes, and adding the egregious errors to the proposal was highly amusing. She replaced "Antarctica" in several places with "Australia," referred to the ice cores as "meteorites," and added a sentence describing the microorganisms that ended with "...similar to those life forms known to be found on Mars."

The last few errors were more subtle, ones that would escape a nonscientist reader but which any technical reviewer should catch, no matter how jet-lagged or hung over he might be. She changed the scale bar on the figure from "nm" to "km," she referred to a transmission electron micrograph as a "scanning" electron micrograph, and made reference to the "two-kingdom" taxonomic model, which had probably been out of date when Rose was in elementary school.

Then it was time for some real work. Pushing a two-tiered aluminum cart over to the BioBar, Lori loaded up on all of the molecular biology kits she could find that might help them. There was something called "community whole DNA extraction kit," of which she took a few, and a couple for RNA as well. She got the special reagents needed to work with RNA without degrading it. Enzymes that broke up RNA were everywhere in nature, especially in those bodily fluids that seemed to flow freely in the lab: sweat, tears, saliva, and snot.

Finally, she ordered three FISH probes, each targeting a seprate kingdom of life. Any bacteria in the samples would be labeled a turquoise blue, fungi a deep red, and archaea a bright mac-n-cheese orange. She'd chosen those colors so as not to overlap the dyes she knew Lou was using for other parts of the cells.

The FISH probes wouldn't be ready for a couple of days, but everything else just needed hands, eyes, and to a lesser extent, brains. Lori walked into the first-year student office and told them all that they could get extra credit for a "real live" project of which she revealed no details. Each team of two had a specific kit and a specific experiment with a specific result, and she said that whoever got the best data wouldn't have to take any finals at all. STI's exams weren't known for their cruelty, but they were long and grueling, and she figured this would be incentive for something

She debated whether to make a team out of the two best first-years, Chi-Ming and Walter, or whether to distribute them. Finally she put them together so that they could have the most sensitive part of the operation, the one where they actually saw and touched the ice cores. The other students might have had loyalty to Kuzno; it was impossible to tell, but as long as they were delivered nothing but small tubes of clear liquid, there was no way they could know for sure what was being done.

Feeling considerably better, she had time to jog into town and have a sandwich and a triple latte before heading back to meet Lou at the microscope. It was going to be a long night.

It was funny to see him all tan and blond from their outing yesterday but wrapped in a black winter coat and carrying mittens and a fuzzy hat, ready to be an electron microscopist. The room was cold, dangerously cold, and parkas or no, neither of them could stand more than half an hour at a time. They did alternating slices of the cores, one thick and then one nanometer thin, sliding each section onto a numbered and labeled slide or electron microscopy grid. The thick slices were for optical microscopy, and the thin ones for electron. Keeping them in order, they would be able to directly compare the images they got using each technique.

When it got too cold to endure, they would take a break and go into the BSL-3, where Lou had set up a station for fluorescent staining. They had dyes to show cell walls, DNA, membranes, and active metabolism. Each dye was supposed to stick only to its target on the cell and nowhere else, but this was where they ran into a lot of problems. Most of the dyes also stuck to rocks and minerals, making it sometimes hard to tell what was a bacterial cell and what was just a piece of rock. A bad enough problem here on Earth—but a disastrous one for any instrument that was supposed to land on Mars. No one would think you were crazy for seeing bacteria anywhere on this planet, even in Antarctic ice, but on another planet the burden of proof was just that much higher.

With the problems in mind, Lori put on all her warm clothes and went back next door. She hoped that the higher resolution of electron microscopy would help resolve some of the ambiguities. Even though it was essentially impossible to make an electron microscope small enough to send to Mars, they all hoped that someday a Martian rock would be brought back for examination by all of Earth's most sophisticated techniques.

The key was to figure out exactly what to look for. How did a rock that once harbored bacteria differ from a rock that had never seen traces of life? So many blebs and particles of mineral looked like cells that the shape and size alone could never be proof.

Many of the rocks Lori looked at seemed to have "shadows" of cells, imprints where bacteria had once sat. She used the X-ray spectroscopy feature of the microscope to get an elemental analysis of the imprinted areas compared to areas without the patterns. This used the electron beam to make atoms emit characteristic X-rays that identified the element. Unfortunately, it only worked for the heavier elements, so key components of cells—namely carbon—didn't show up.

Most of the imprint-looking areas came up high in sulfur. Maybe, she thought, the sulfur minerals around living cells were different than those in purely mineral areas?

She tried to call Ben Gerson, but couldn't reach him. So she stayed until late in the night taking images and spectra, hoping that somewhere on the ice lab's hard drive was an explanation of the only known habitable planet's most remote life forms.

TWENTY-SIX: DRIFT TOWARD CATASTROPHE

Bob WOULDN'T LISTEN WHEN she said that going against Lori Barrow and a Nobel laureate spelled nothing but trouble, but maybe after a few hours of questioning in a hot room with the cops, he would start to get it.

Carol wasn't going to lie to protect him. That orange backpack was obviously Lori's, and Bob had definitely shown interest in it lately. He had stolen it and he had been caught.

A minor crime by any standard, maybe, but if Bob spent so much as a night in jail, his days at the LEPERLab were over. He knew himself about the LEPERLaws: he had used them to tell James Kalb as soon as he was hired that that no one could protect him from dismissal if he got any police reports filed against him.

She didn't need to waste her Monday here at the station, in this hard wooden chair, in the heat, with flies crawling up the wall. There was work to do in her lab—real work, with Lori's SLAP and a microscope that had finally been plugged in—so she left a note and headed back up the hill.

She spent the afternoon happily photographing what Lori called the "footballs," tiny minerals that might have been simply rocks, or might have been the outer coating of some kind of very tough bacteria, nobody could tell. Analysis was not her job; she just had to take the pictures and pass them on.

A loud slam of the door broke her concentration and she leapt up, swallowing a scream. She let out her breath when she saw it was just Bob, and was about to walk over to him until she realized he was furious. At her.

He called her a traitor for doing work for the STI group, shouted that he could get her fired, and demanded she turn over all of the images on her computer. Pacing in rage, he nearly tripped over the thick extension cord going to the microscope—which he then tore out of the wall and waved above his head as if he'd slain a dragon. His eyes bulged with fury and he growled low in his throat like a pissed-off duck defending its nest.

She'd never seen him like this, and had to close her eyes and count to ten before she could respond calmly. "Bob," she appeased in her best logical tone, "you know it's illegal for me to work without a charge number. Lori is the only one who's given me a SLAP."

"I'll give you a slap if you don't hand over those data!" roared Bob.

Carol stood up slowly. Now she was getting mad, too. "Are you threatening me?"

"Maybe I am!"

"How dare you threaten me! Are *you* even doing any of this work legally? Who's paying for your time to bug Lori's computer and steal her data?"

He wouldn't tell her, just bellowed and stomped some more like a complete Neanderthal. Carol couldn't believe that the LEPERLab had done this to her dorky, mellow Bob, but she wasn't going to put up with it.

"You need to go now," she said firmly, urging him towards the door. "Don't make me call Security on you."

He screamed that she was the one who'd be punished, that he could get her fired on the spot for her treachery, but it was an empty threat and they both knew it. Finally Bob left, eyes wet with wrath, or remorse, or both.

The first thing Carol did was upload all of her new data onto an FTP site and tell Lori that they were there. She knew what side her bread was buttered on, but she wouldn't be surprised if Bob got some idiot to come in here and shut her down.

Vigilantism was not regarded positively at the LEPERLab. Bob didn't have a SLAP on the PIP, so he had no right to think about the proposal or to try to help in any way. There were already more than twenty people on the waiting list for SLAPs of any kind, which Carol knew because she was one of them, willing to make copies or collate or even fly out Friday morning to Washington, DC to deliver before the deadline so they didn't have to rely on a delivery company. If Bob didn't watch out, he'd find himself bitch-SLAPped, forbidden to work on the project under penalty of dismissal.

Carol sat and thought for a good, long while before deciding what to do next. The LEPER phones wouldn't dial internationally, so she reached for her cell and looked up the country code in the phone book.

There were so many numbers to dial that she was amazed to hear the tone come through so clear, and the voice with its American intonation unmarred from five years Down Under. "Kameakaloa lab, Radhika speaking. Hello? Is someone there?"

"Hi, Radhika," Carol finally managed in a wee small voice. "It's Carol, you know, Carol Dugoni from graduate school. Um…what time is it there?"

"Nine o'clock on Tuesday morning." The thought, Why would you call me, you *boson*, traversed the Australian continent and two thousand miles of Pacific ocean. She called out something to her students, something about laser power.

"I'm calling because my husband and your ex-girlfriend have gotten into something way over their heads."

"Hah! I can't speak for Boson Bob, but Lori's a big girl. I've never seen her in over her head."

"This isn't funny. She's trying to bring down the LEPERLab."

"The LEPERLab?" Radhika laughed cruelly. "Let me tell you something: I interviewed there while Lori was interviewing at STI. And even though I love her more than I do all of the other six billion humans put together, all I wanted to do afterwards was put as much distance as globally possible between me and that hellhole." She took a breath to recover from that sentence, then continued, "The human resources rep was off his face at ten in the morning and lied to me about the scientists being on soft money. The researchers were broken and cowed and talked about nothing but parking. If she can do something about that place, then more power to her! …And to the 488 line, guys—13%, OK?"

Physics was such a small world, Carol reflected. Everyone knew each other and there were personal feelings behind everything they did. "The problem is, it wasn't her idea. I think she's being used."

"By who? Rose and Maupertuis?" Radhika made a *pfft* of disdain. "Carol, mere mortals like us cannot understand Lori. Lori was born and bred at that university. She knows STI better than she knows—*knew*—her own mother. She has been wrapping Solomon Rose around her little finger for twenty years. As for Maupertuis, from everything I could find out, he's nothing but a spoiled rich playboy. He has a degree in drama, for fuck's sake, and when I met him at the March Meeting he cared more about surfing than physics—as do I, incidentally. Here in Oz, we have our priorities, and it's summertime."

"Radhika, could you please just give me fifteen minutes to explain?"

"You have half an hour. After that I'm going to the beach."

Carol started off totally wrong, telling about the data and Bob. Of course Radhika just sneered at her, calling Bob all sorts of names and saying that he deserved to lose his job if he was taking Lori's data. Carol had to shift gears, mentioning Jim Kalb, the cold room, and what she knew—not much—about the grad student who had died.

There was definitely a quaver in Radhika's voice when she repeated, "Someone *froze* to death?"

"Marybeth and Jim both got stuck in cold rooms, but Jim didn't die. I think he was trying to cover up what he did to make himself look innocent. But then he died, too, playing around with electricity in my lab. We don't know if he killed Marybeth or what he was planning when he died, or if he'd committed other crimes, like steal money from Maupertuis or even shoot him."

"Shoot him? What is the body count now? Dammit, Carol—this isn't about a proposal or some stolen photos. Hang on, I can barely hear you with this pump, and we need some privacy. I'm going to go into my office and call you back." She put her hand over the mouthpiece and called, "Take the rest of the day off, guys—lie on the beach, get a tan, wade in the ocean. Don't get a PhD, it will ruin your lives. Run away while you still can." Then she hung up.

The last phrase echoed in Carol's head while she waited for the phone to ring, and when she had Radhika back, she asked as casually as she could, "When you met Maupertuis at the March Meeting, was he normal?"

"What do you mean, normal? He's a freak like Lori, obviously. Reminded me a lot of her, in that hyperkinetic geek way."

"No, I mean…I mean was he *able-bodied* normal?"

Within two minutes, Carol had Radhika exactly where she wanted her—on the verge of a heart attack. "All right. Let me get this straight." Radhika took several deep breaths, no doubt of air scented with honeysuckle and jasmine. "Lori is sleeping in Pasteur House because she's afraid to go home, even though the madman who maimed her colleague and killed his graduate student is dead, because they all think this is part of a larger plot centered around the proposal they are writing that will bring down the LEPERLab?"

Carol had always envied Radhika's powers of synthesis. "That's about it. Oh yeah, and her postdoc can't enter the country for some reason related to the project as well."

"Carol, my boson friend, either you have been promoted to manager and experienced your first Executive Crack Hour, or Lori is telling me *nothing*."

Carol couldn't help rubbing it in a little. "Well, obviously she's not answering her phone since she's living in Pasteur House."

"All she said was that the three of them were writing a big proposal and were very busy! I'm tempted to fly out there to slap her, except that I want no part of any more physics department psychos. That's why I moved to Darwin in the first place." There was some kind of noise—opening a window, maybe, to gaze out upon the sea. "What's wrong with these maniacs? They'll never have a faculty job no matter how many people they kill. Remember that creep in grad school? Abby's lucky she wasn't mutilated or slain."

"I'll have to remind her of that," Carol mused.

"Yeah, is she still a bitch? Don't answer that. I'm worried now."

"Mmm-hmmm," Carol agreed, letting the hint sink in. "The proposal goes in next Friday."

"Yeah, Carol—but I'm in Darwin. It's forty-eight hours by donkey to the nearest town, and then we have to ride kangaroos across the desert to the airport."

"Really?"

"No, of course not. I could be there tomorrow if I have to. Let me check, OK?"

"Wait, Radhika—" Carol had almost forgotten her original aim. "Just a second. What do I do with the data that Bob wants?"

Radhika's recovery from her panic was marked by her ability to *pfft* again. "That's easy enough. Fill them with errors, then give them to him. He'll be the big hero with his purloined pictures, but any reviewer with half a brain will laugh his ass off and the LEPERs will lose like they deserve."

The phone buzzed and she was gone, back to her world of sun and sand and hundred-degree Christmas days. Adding the errors was easy, but Carol felt terrible delivering the material to Bob. Now she, too, was on the list of those who had betrayed him.

She didn't feel so bad when Ellis D. Tripp came storming in a few minutes later, demanding her hard drive. He was so stupid he didn't even know how to take it out; Carol showed him because she knew that otherwise he would stay, trying to figure out how to humiliate her while they waited for IT support.

But now she was officially forbidden to do anything for STI under penalty of being fired. When she told Tripp that she needed a SLAP, he said that this was a problem so far beneath him that he couldn't possibly consider it. She needed to go through the ranks of "line management," from a group supervisor to a deputy section manager and so on, three more layers before they got to the heights of such as him. The fact that her immediate supervisor, Kalb, was dead, did nothing to change the rules.

Lori was always acting outraged at Carol's stories, but it was hard to believe that there was a workplace that was genuinely free of abasement and humiliation. Grad students and postdocs certainly got treated like slaves;

how could Lori forget that? Was it really so different when you were the star?

TWENTY-SEVEN: THE PORTALS OF DISCOVERY

HALFWAY THROUGH LORI'S CLASSICAL Mechanics class, the door opened discreetly and three men in black entered. They stood at the back of the classroom, wearing sunglasses, arms folded like geeky FBI agents.

She dismissed the students immediately and ran forward, wondering if Sol no longer even walked across campus without Sam and Alex protecting him.

"I got the signatures," whispered Rose as soon as the last student had closed the door behind him.

For any proposal, getting the signatures from all the institution's responsible parties was always the most harrowing part. For a proposal of this magnitude, they had needed the department head, the legal office, and the president himself to sign. "No muggings?" Lori asked, only half joking. "No one tried to run you over or drop a piano from a window?"

"I'll let the kids come help me put it in the safe, just to be sure." The Great Man winked, tipped his hat and was gone, and Lori knew that he considered his part of the PARIA project complete. It was now up to her and Lou to finish the data analysis—and then print, collate, copy, and ship before the deadline. They couldn't come crying to Sol if they screwed it up.

Taking a deep breath for courage and energy, she ran up the stairs, but screeched to a halt outside Lou's closed door as bangs, crashes, and shouting issued from inside. Finally she pushed the door open carefully, only to find a team of Buboes wrestling a beautiful new color laser printer onto the desk.

"We'll need fifty hard copies to submit," Lou was instructing them while typing on his laptop, "plus one copy on CD, and one copy for each of the offices on campus."

Lori waited to hear if he was going to explain about the fake proposal being used as bait for psycho killers, but he didn't breathe a word of that. No doubt that was wise, since anything known by two or more Buboes would immediately have its own website.

"Lori!" he exclaimed when he saw her. "You need to help Walter a bit with the Materials and Methods. He's doing his best, but he's inexperienced and I know nothing about molecular biology."

"I'll find him. What else?"

"I'm finishing the Facilities description, trying to make your lab sound like Plum Island. Then that's it apart from the color figures."

"We'll have to go downstairs to check on the progress of that. I have to say, this is the most traumatic proposal-writing experience I've ever had." Too late, she realized that this was kind of a tasteless comment.

Lou, however, was laughing along with some of the Buboes. "I think it's only my second-most. Although by a narrow margin."

"I'm not sure that's funny." Lori looked both ways before exiting his office, and they made their way to the creaky old elevator that seemed to have miraculously fixed itself since Dim Bulb's demise. Maybe, Lori thought hopefully, Dim Bulb really was the only homicidal maniac on campus. "OK, prepare for a nightmare: six theorists trying to do molecular biology."

To their astonishment, all of the students—Buboes included—had done an incredible job. They were busy plugging in their data as they got them, and someone had even drawn up a phylogenetic tree. All Lou and Lori had to do was watch like proud parents as the different teams put their individual pieces of the puzzle into place.

Walter, armed with an array of slides and a half-dozen bottles of nail polish, had prepared a boxful of sections for fluorescence microscopy. Some were stained with a single dye or FISH probe, others with an array of combinations designed to separate and identify all of the different organisms in the sample. There were hundreds of slides, and they all knew that this was their last chance at identifying the organisms for the proposal.

Walter was the only student permitted in the BSL-3, and he'd gotten the prep routine down: lab coat, booties, and first pair of gloves in the entryway, second pair of gloves at the microscope just before beginning work. There was barely room for one person in the tight spot between the bench and the autoclave, and while Lori was hopping with excitement, she reminded herself of her duty as an educator and let Walter do the honors.

First he installed one of Lou's multiple bandpass filters, which seemed to take him an eternity of fumbling with latches and screwdrivers. He was nervous, no doubt afraid of looking inept, and spoke to them with that first-year shyness where he wasn't sure yet if profs were normal people or if they would bite his head off.

Lori finally told him he could take his second pair of gloves off, and Lou tried to put him at ease by talking about flying. "Did you get your instrument rating yet?" he wondered, wordlessly pointing out the metal tab that had to be lifted to insert the filter.

Walter nodded eagerly, peering into the microscope's innards and feeling around where Lou had put his hand. "Yeah, just last month! I haven't done any real approaches yet, you know, ones with weather. Maybe over Christmas if we have fog but not too much rain." He eventually snapped the filter into place, then sat on a stool and placed a slide on the stage, reaching to open the shutter to the mercury lamp.

Lori had heard Walter mention a glider, but she didn't know he flew airplanes, too. "Do you want to be an astronaut?" she wondered, thinking of all of her undergraduate friends who had tried out for the astronaut program. Most had been turned away for bad eyesight, but Walter didn't seem to wear glasses or contacts.

"Not since I rode in the Vomit Comet," he replied, scanning across the section at increasingly higher magnifications. "Besides, astronauts are crazy and kill each other wearing diapers. But my dream is to have something I built land on another planet."

Lou and Lori exchanged a glance in the scattered light. "Win this one for us, and that's practically guaranteed," they said together.

"Really?" he murmured doubtfully, clearly not too encouraged by what he saw. "I dunno, Dr. Barrow. I see some bright spots."

She could stand it no more and all but elbowed him out of the way. Bright spots there were, spots of green and yellow and red through the magic filter, spheres and rods and footballs of color. "Oh my," she breathed. "Oh my God. This is amazing."

Lou was a patient guy, but even he had his limits. "Come on, Lori, let me see."

She scrolled one more time through the visual field just to confirm what she had seen before stepping out of the way.

"Well, the filter works," said Lou, as skeptical as Walter had been, "but help me out on the biology here. The red are the fungi. The green are bacteria. These orange ones with the annoying wavelength to resolve are archaea?"

"They're archaea," Lori confirmed, "and they're the footballs. Gerson told me that it's a huge controversy. If they're archaea, it changes the entire evolutionary model for the region. Many people say they're not organisms at all, that they're just minerals. In the first draft, I said they were minerals. So we have a provable error."

"And Walter has a paper that will bring him fame and fortune."

Walter had stepped back to a respectful distance. "I do?"

"You do," agreed Lori. "It's one step away from life on Mars, but don't say that to your dad. Go upstairs and start printing, and do a happy dance on your way out—it might bring us luck." She leaned her elbow on the bench. "I'm exhausted and starving," she admitted after Walter had gone. "In principle the fluorescence is stable for days. What do you think?"

Lou remained glued to the eyepieces. "I think if we turn off this lamp, we're fucked. I'm going to stay here until we're done even if you need to feed me through a straw slipped under the door."

"I might at least try a thin-crust pizza," Lori promised.

They were there until dawn, taking turns imaging now and then to give the other a chance to eat or pee. At dinnertime Lori bolted a burrito at her desk while finishing the Materials section with Walter, staining everything with Cholula sauce. Then she gave Lou a break and tried some tricks with the filters while he was gone, photographing one color at a time and merging the channels in a software program.

They finally came to the last slide, a control with nothing on it, snapping a single blank image for comparison. The desktop was littered with slides, rolls of film, used gloves, lens paper, and filter parts. Afraid to take the precious film to their respective residences, they wrapped the rolls in paper towels and hid them in a scary-looking biohazard bag by the containment hood. Everything looked blue in front of Lori's eyes, and she was infinitely grateful that she didn't have to face the hill.

You weren't supposed to high-five someone in a BSL-3, but they did anyway. For the first time since the project began, it was starting to seem as though they could win it.

Chilly without their gloves and lab coats, they exited the lab into the first light of morning. All of the Bubues were safely in bed, so Lou accompanied Lori across campus to Pasteur house. As they passed the library, descending down the narrow path past a large pond croaking with bullfrogs, she asked bluntly, "Lou, are you afraid to die?"

"I don't want to die," he replied, then admitted with a catch in his voice, "I want to see everything. All of the scientific discoveries, social upheavals, climate change. I want to see evolution."

"We are about to, in a way," Lori mused, waiting until they had entered the canopy of olive trees to elaborate. "Ben's ice-core organisms ruled the world for billions of years and survive essentially unchanged. Do you realize there are no pathogenic members of the kingdom Archaea? They evolved without us."

"I would have liked to see that world, too," he remarked, stopping just before the short brick path to the dorms. "Imagine how alien the colors would have been without photosynthesis: no grass, no moss, no trees, no green, just mats and plaques and towers of microorganisms."

"You should draw a picture of it," she suggested.

"I wouldn't do it justice." He shook his head. "There's so much to learn. Good night, Barrow, and take care of yourself."

Safely inside the colorful halls of her old House, she realized he had been lying about his place being in her direction—there was nothing east of Pasteur but the botanical gardens and a few movie-star mansions. It was all too much for her tired brain to process, the death and the data and the hope and the fear, and she hoped he didn't have too far to go because they would have another long day tomorrow.

TWENTY-EIGHT: THE WICKED FLEE

WALTER W. WADDLES, JR. was the grandfather of Lori's graduate student, Waddles IV, and the father of the LEPER chief scientist. He himself was a full professor of physical chemistry, and looked a bit different from the other living members of his family. His hair was actually white, not just platinum blond, and he was a few inches shorter than both his son and grandson. At the moment, he was also dressed in a FedEx uniform.

"You don't actually have to make fifty copies of the fake proposal," he lectured pedantically, approaching Lori's desk. "We don't expect them to open the box."

"I know—but it's hard to stop the Buboes," said Lori, trying not to pause in her rapid collating of the massive pile of papers on her desk. "I certainly don't want them to know what we're up to."

"No one knows?"

"No one apart from us, Lou, Abby, and Walter—er, your grandson," said Lori, wondering what the Waddleses called each other since they all had the same name.

"Hm," Grandpa Waddles sniffed. "Perhaps that's as it should be. But I would like to get started as quickly as possible with the lure."

Lori was unclear on all of the details of the "fake proposal" scheme, which had been worked out by Abby and apparently the Waddles clan. "What do you expect the bad guys to do?"

"There's no telling," he muttered. "They might try to steal the box. They might try to have it removed from the truck, claiming it's suspicious-looking. They could even hijack the driver—who knows?"

He hushed up quickly as the door opened, but it was just Lou, with an armload of prints. Lori was about to ask him questions when she noticed he was talking on a Bluetooth. "Not yet," he advised solemnly. "We're not sure…will give you the word.

"That was Ben," Lou told the others, unplugging the device. "He's ready to tie up traffic between here and the airport in case we need to intercept a FedEx truck for any reason."

"Excellent." Grandpa Waddles rubbed his hands.

"How are the wildlife?" Lori asked Lou.

"Oh, they're just great." Lou grinned broadly, looking happier than she'd ever seen him. "Exotic and colorful." He held up an 8×10 glossy, where orange ellipses nestled among a tangle of brilliant-red, nucleated strands.

Waddles Jr. couldn't resist. "May I?" he asked suddenly, sweeping down on the photos. "Aha! Phycoerythrin, isn't it? I spent much of my early career studying dyes, you know…"

That was the problem with faculty. Waddles Jr. seemed to have completely forgotten his task as he rambled on about his patents on special dyes for pens and paints and microscope slides, developed back in the seventies "and still used everywhere!"

Even Lou appeared a little impatient, rolling his eyes towards the door a few times as if pleading for an interruption.

When it came, it was in the form of a rather subdued and business-looking Absinthe. "Hello, colleagues," she said with no trace of sarcasm and without shouting.

"Hello, Mastermind," said Grandpa Waddles. "We're moving right along here with the plan."

"Yes," she murmured, sounding distracted. "That's very nice…But I'm here to deliver a bit of bad news."

"Naturally," said Lou and Lori at once.

Abby looked quickly back and forth between them, then at Waddles Jr. with silent inquiry.

"Walter W. Waddles, Jr.," he clarified, offering her hand. "Pay no attention to the, er, costume."

"Right." Abby swallowed a disdainful snort. "At any rate, I'm here because there was a question raised about the validity of the proposal's signature page—namely, that of the department head's signature."

"That fucking Kuzno." Lou laughed demonically. "I figured he'd pull some stunt like that."

"I'm not sure he's entirely wrong." Abby took a step backwards and averted her eyes from all three of them, looking at Lori's only piece of furniture—a bookshelf containing all of the textbooks that had tormented

Abby for her single year in graduate school. "He claims he never saw the signature page, and that Professor Rose falsified his signature."

"You believe this?" Lori demanded, talking to Abby's back. "Rose is the most famous person in the department."

Abby turned around and smirked. "It's not whether I believe it—it's whether the University president does. There appears to be a little history between him and Professor Rose."

"So what are we supposed to do?" Lori wondered.

Abby spoke in a stiff voice. "The legal office wants an attorney—a position I happen to fill—to witness all of the signatures on a new page. The investigators, collaborators, and department head need to sign in my presence, then our office will sign, and then, if you're lucky, the page will go back to the president."

It sounded simple at first. Then all three of them simultaneously shouted, "Oh, shit!"

"Fucking Kuzno is on his way to Denver!" Lori recalled.

"It had to be his idea," grumbled Grandpa Waddles. "Making oneself scarce is the best way for department heads to suppress projects they don't like."

"And he went one better—he made us think we had what we needed," finished Lou. "That *butthead*."

In an instant they all had their computers on, searching for flight schedules and wondering if they could chase Kuzno down in the terminal. Abby took part as if she were one of them, making Lori increasingly suspicious.

"Do you have his cell number, or do you think he'll hide if you call him?" Abby wondered.

"He'd crawl into the cargo bay if he had to," said Lou. "We have to go out there and tell the gate agents there's been a family emergency. We already know what a convincing liar you can be, Dr. McRae."

Abby had a JD, but no one ever called her "doctor," and Lori noticed her flush slightly and smile as if that had been a compliment. "It's Burbank, and he leaves in forty-five minutes," she mused, leaning over Lou to get a good look at his computer screen. "I know a shortcut, and I drive fast, but I only have a two-seater."

"Oh, no, now wait a second here!" Lori stomped her foot to get their attention. "Lou, if you are so deceived by her wiles as to actually get into her stinky Porsche, that's your choice, but I'm going to get your signature on my own copy of the front page before you go." She sent two copies of the critical front page to the her printer, copies of the same page Rose had locked in his safe but menacingly blank in all the important places.

Lou took them out and signed both, shoving one across the desk to her. "You have a Porsche, Abby?" he asked, eyes gleaming.

She seemed momentarily surprised that he would dare to speak to her directly, but the love for her noisy, smelly car got the better of her and they wasted at least three minutes talking about various parameters until Lori could stand it no more. "If you guys are going to Burbank, then *go*! You don't need me. Find Ben afterwards, and I'll make sure Sol sticks around. Lou, here—take my copy of the cover page, get Kuzno to sign it, and FedEx it to me from the airport. Then when Abby murders you, I'll still be able to get this in."

For some reason this seemed to be the funniest thing those two had ever heard, and they both grinned at her with perfect, white, carnivorous teeth.

"I've learned a few things since yesterday," Abby offered by way of explanation for why she was acting as if she were on their side. She still gave Lori a wide berth, though, and backed away nervously from Lou as he headed for the door. "I'm not sure…" she began.

"That I'll fit in the car? My dad has a Carrera, I'm a pro." He held the door for her, which seemed to reassure her a bit as she stumbled out of the office with her open laptop still in her hands. They resumed their Porsche conversation as they hurried down the hall, Abby squealing that she had to see Lou's parents' car.

"If you really want to, we can spin by after we see Ben," was the last thing Lori heard Lou say. "I'd like to grill Gerson a bit while we get his signature."

It was quite a relief not to be involved in this particular adventure. Lori forced herself to focus, sending Grandpa Waddles next door to collect the fake proposal and swearing that she wouldn't move until the writing was done.

TWENTY-NINE: NEW MEXICO, USA

HE WAS IN A vintage Porsche with the top down, next to a beautiful woman under a beautiful blue sky, and Lou was more uncomfortable than he had ever been in his life.

It was clear that Abby despised him, so why was she doing this? If she had her own personal reasons for hating Kuzno, she wasn't sharing them—in fact she wasn't doing much besides spitting like an angry puma at the traffic jam backing up the freeway.

"You can take La Tuna Canyon," Lou suggested, fishing for his iPhone. The traffic map showed a web of red all the way through to downtown L.A.

"WHAT?" bellowed Abby. (*Shouting Abby*, Lori called her. Yep.)

"Take the surface streets to the airport, there's less traffic."

"How do you know?" she demanded.

"I'm from around here," he replied, at last able to break the conversational embargo with giving directions. In a few minutes they had escaped the city and embarked on a winding mountain road that led through small farms, horse pastures, and plant nurseries to the Burbank airport. It was old-fashioned and scenic back in the chaparral-covered hills, with teenagers galloping by on horseback and a flock of Pekin ducks quacking at them from their pen in an orange grove.

Abby broke the speed limit just enough so that they might conceivably catch the enemy's plane, but even she noticed the anachronism, and cooed "Oooh, cute" at a girl riding a long-haired black and white pony.

"This is how Southern California used to be," said Lou, still determined to engage her in some sort of small talk besides directions and growling. "Even when I was a kid twenty years ago in Malibu, we went everywhere on horses—up in the mountains, down to the beach, everywhere."

"You're from Malibu?" cried Abby.

Success! "It's less glamorous than it sounds," he explained. "No one liked the coast in the early seventies, when my parents moved there from France. It was cold and plagued by landslides and forest fires."

"I did my JD at Pepperdine, and I thought Malibu was heaven. The only other places I'd lived were Minneapolis and New York."

"I hate Manhattan," Lou agreed. "It's like an alien settlement, with a purple sky and green clouds."

"It also smells like urine five months out of the year, and everyone including little old ladies assaults you in the street. *And* I was married to a jerk who didn't care how much I hated it."

They emerged from the canyon and the small miracle evaporated. Burbank was squalid and vile, with cheap apartment complexes bordering fast streets and a constant roar and stench of traffic and airplanes. Just before the turn to the airport, they saw a small white poodle dash into traffic and get obliterated by a semi.

They both groaned in horror. "It's an omen," Abby said solemnly.

Lou was not superstitious, but he had to agree it wasn't good. He was also pretty sure they were too late—it was nineteen minutes before the flight was scheduled to take off, and they probably closed the doors ten minutes before that. "Why don't you leave the car with the valet and run in," he suggested. "I'll be there as quickly as I can."

Abby opened her mouth to protest, then shut it, then opened it again. "You think that's the fastest way?" was all she asked.

"Yes. Valet parking is right out front." He was surprised that she didn't know where it was or how quick they were. Back in the old days, when he ran fast and security hadn't gone Nazi, he'd showed up for his flights from Burbank with seconds to spare. It still had the feel of a tiny airport, with only three airlines and a small parking lot right by the entrance to the terminal.

After Abby took off and the valet parked the car, Lou sat for a few minutes with his eyes closed, considering the options. According to STI's Honor Code, Kuzno could not refuse to sign unless he had real proof that the content of the proposal was fraudulent. All he could do was try to hide—but if they caught him, there were no excuses. So as long as Abby was genuinely on his side, if one or both of them hopped a plane to Denver...

"Do you need help, sir?"

"NO!" Lou was astonished at his own anger, finding himself screaming at the valet who had sneaked up and was standing right by the passenger-side mirror. "Go away! Leave me alone! I want to think!"

No doubt he appeared deranged, and the valet refused to leave until Lou got out his iPhone and pretended to be surfing the web. These things were God's gift to dorks. Almost by reflex, he went to the Southwest Airlines site and started browsing for flights to Colorado. He was just getting to the first of the severe-weather alerts when Absinthe showed up, seething.

"It had already pushed back from the gate," she grumbled. "I did my best—I said his parents had had strokes, his house was on fire, everything I could think of—no dice."

"I wish I could have heard that." Lou grinned for a second at the thought of Kuzno's imaginary misfortunes, then came back to reality and showed her the screen. "We may be in even bigger trouble than I thought. They're about to cancel all the flights to Denver because there's a storm blowing in."

"The gods are against us," Abby reiterated, shuddering no doubt at the memory of the Omen of the Bloody Poodle. "How about the other airlines?"

The web sites were all slow to load, so finally they decided to split up and look at the departure screens at all three airlines, and call each other if they found anything. Before he was even out of the car, Lou could tell that it didn't look promising. There was a long line of people for taxis, all of them disgruntled-looking, some with skis and others with surfboards. The words *by Christmas* floated by several times, and he realized that they were only five days away from the holiday that was supposed to mark the end of their ordeal.

If we get stuck in Denver, he thought, I won't have to visit my parents. Christmas with Abby and Kuzno! Oh boy.

The terminal was packed, and everyone was shaking their fists at the "Departures" screen. CANCELLED CANCELLED WEATHER DELAY CANCELLED, declared a list of flights to Denver, Boise, Omaha, and Salt Lake.

He found a spot in line and logged in to the Southwest website at the same time, not sure which would be faster. The people at the checkout were all refusing to leave their places even though the answer would continue to be the same: no flights in or out of Denver. Clinging to the luggage scale and crying was not going to help, though it seemed to be a popular approach.

The closest place they could get to on short notice appeared to be Albuquerque. Two years ago, he wouldn't have hesitated—fly to New Mexico, rent a car, drive through the storm to Denver and get a room in the conference hotel where Kuzno was staying. Now the whole thing seemed like a recipe for humiliation and disaster. When you couldn't even pee on your own, everything took absurd amounts of planning...he had never been any good at planning.

But really, what was the worst that could happen? They had pharmacies in Albuquerque. If he couldn't get an accessible hotel room, he could always crawl into the bathtub. And surely between him and Absinthe, they could put snow chains on a car if they had to.

Feeling as if he were breaking all the rules of a game he didn't even know, he signed in to his Southwest account and bought two tickets, then called Absinthe and told her.

Naturally she arrived shrieking, "WHAT?" but surprisingly, didn't seem all that put out. "Can you drive?" was all she wanted to know.

"Yes," said Lou, without bothering to provide any details. "I just don't want to do it alone."

"No, I don't either." She laughed nervously. "If the weather gets too gnarly, we turn around."

"Of course."

Suddenly she was stern again. "And I hope to all that's good that you didn't pay for those tickets with your grant. Because…" She clamped her hand over her mouth in an excessively obvious fashion, *Oh I shouldn't tell you, I know something you don't know.*

Lou shook his head dismissively. Barrow was right, Abby was a pain in the ass. "Of course I didn't. Because what?"

She snorted. "You're lucky not to have been fired ten times by now."

Now it was his turn to screech "WHAT?" but she refused to elaborate. "Let's go through security first," she declared smugly.

Cursing her silently for distracting him, he sifted through his bag and tried to figure out what he could carry on, and what to do with all the tools that needed to be checked. It was a stroke of luck that he'd been carrying the portable hand controls, so they could rent any car they wanted—and this was only because he hadn't cleaned out his backpack from the outing with Barrow on the River Trail. That meant the bag also had nasty crumpled power bar wrappers, along with old CDs of various versions of the proposal, torn journal articles stained with lunch items, and several things that were completely unrecognizable. He pulled stuff out in handfuls, making piles of Check, Carry-On, and Trash.

"Why don't you just go and I'll meet you at the gate?" he grumbled, nervous at the way she was staring.

But she refused, enjoying making him uncomfortable, or maybe curious about how he was going to go through the metal detector. It was not much fun being a spectacle for the amusement of the biggest bitch on campus.

He reminded himself that he didn't have to like her as long as she acted as an effective weapon against the real enemy. Finally he was ready, checked his backpack at the kiosk, and fought through the angry throngs of thwarted ski vacationers and stranded Coloradans to the nearly empty security line.

Absinthe looked doubtfully at the TV screen above their heads. The flight to Albuquerque still read ON TIME. "No one else seems to be doing this. Think it will work?"

Lou only shrugged. He doubted it would, but it was better than going back to face Barrow and Rose empty-handed.

They had only until tomorrow night to get the signed proposals to FedEx. If they didn't make it by ten o'clock, someone would have to fly the package to DC in person—and given what had shown up on the weather maps, that was an even sketchier proposition than what they were doing now.

Abby passed first through security and he lost her, but things went pretty quickly with nothing but his silly little plastic bag of stuff. He found her waiting at the gate, holding some kind of repellent blended coffee drink and a newspaper. Buried in the Local section, she of course continued to keep him in suspense about his reputation at the legal office. "They're about to start boarding soon," she muttered without looking up. "Don't you have to do something special? How does this work?"

"What, flying with a mutant? It's easy," he replied cheerfully, wondering how it was that appalling lies could come out of his mouth so easily. In secret he pretended to be immune to PC, but in public he would say whatever they expected, like an automaton speaking without will.

He didn't want to introduce her to his private hell, could barely stand to think about it himself. He could never remember what he was supposed to do. Some airlines expected you to stand in line to register to pre-board; come to think of it, maybe Southwest was one of them. Back in the old days, his girlfriend dealt with everything involving bills, tickets, or reservations, and Lou happily played the role of idiot savant. Then it was maybe cute— now he was just a retard. Fortunately, Abby was paying him no attention, so he sneaked off and went to see the gate agent.

They gave him a pre-boarding card and told him to wait. Southwest *was* easy, he recalled, since there was open seating so he could just sit in the first row by the window and not have to get into that frighteningly tiny and rickety aisle chair that they used to move the mutants through the plane. But no more Burbank Trick, where you sat at the back of the plane because you knew they'd put a staircase there and you could be the first one off. Come to think of it, would there be stairs onto the plane?

The agent didn't mention it so he didn't ask, returning to rejoin Abby and carefully subtracting the Arts section out of her newspaper. "So, when are you going to tell me what you promised?" he wondered.

"Huh?" She lowered the paper. She was wearing reading glasses— Barrow was right again, Abby was over forty and lied about it. She snorted in disdain. "Meh. Come on, Lou, you can't pretend you don't know you're the most financially irresponsible faculty member in the university."

"Me?" he exclaimed, honestly surprised. "What have I done?"

"What *haven't* you done?"

"Anything! Give me an example."

"Well…there was the time your students spent a week at a five-star resort in the Bahamas."

"I had made the reservation for myself and I couldn't go. So what?"

"So, they got drunk as lords every night and bragged about how they could spend all the money they wanted. Sam flew home in First Class."

"The grant didn't pay for that," he objected. "I had upgrade points."

"Well, you're not supposed to do those things. Then Sam didn't want to teach, so you doubled his salary so he wouldn't have to. That *was* from your grant."

"He can't do research if he has to teach full-time. No one told me I couldn't do that."

"They tried, but whenever the financial office calls, you tell them to eff off—or you pass them on to Marybeth. And speaking of Marybeth…"

He felt his face grow hot and he wished Abby under a bus. "She told me she was homeless," he muttered. "What could I do? I wasn't going to let her go hungry."

"How much did she take you for, before you figured out that everything she said was a lie?" Abby smirked.

Now he was getting mad. "Everything she said was *not* a lie. Maybe your office should have cared less about where her salary was coming from and more about the fact that she was being harassed."

"We had no reason to believe it was real." Abby got a closed look, and he knew she knew things that she wasn't telling. She was truly the dark side. Her office was the origin of the STI infamous coverups, and who knew but that she wasn't the author of some of them herself.

If Hitler and Stalin had come in at the moment and sat on either side of Abby, Lou would have been hard pressed to say which of the three was the most evil.

"What do you know that you're not telling me?" he hissed.

"Nothing I'm at liberty to talk about," she sneered back, slurping the last drops from her plastic cup.

They read the paper in silence until the pre-boarding call, and Abby seemed relieved that they weren't the only ones to pre-board. She hung back and helped a young mother with a toddler and a baby, which was good, because Lou knew he looked like a freak trying to get into the window seat. He'd got used to Barrow staring, but that was mostly OK because she was usually doing something equally clumsy at the same time. Abby would never crash into the rosebushes, or wallow in the mud, or pick her way through sand on rollerblades.

By the time the young family was settled, he had managed to at least make it into the seat and retrieve his cushion to sit on, deflating it a little so it wouldn't explode in the reduced air pressure of the cabin. He was becoming quite the expert. Abby hesitated a moment, then finally sat down next to him, hissing into his ear, "What a repulsive spoiled brat. If it pulls my hair again, I'm going to put it over my knee and smack its heinie."

He choked out a surprised laugh. Her evil was kind of funny when it was aimed elsewhere. "Since you're so pissed to be here, and I'm such a loser, tell me why you agreed to do this," he asked casually.

"Because Kuzno is a thousand times worse," she replied as if that were obvious.

"In ways you aren't at liberty to describe?"

"Certainly not. Got a pencil?"

He was a theorist—of course he had a pencil. Abby folded the New York Times crossword into a neat square and the conversation came to yet another end.

Lou was getting pretty sick of the silent treatment. He pretended to read a journal article for a few minutes, but then he could stand it no more. "Never mind Kuzno," he dismissed. "It's Rose who is up to something."

Abby did a very unexpected thing. She burst into tears.

He had limited sympathy. If she was crying, it meant she felt guilty—and if she felt guilty, it meant she knew something she wasn't supposed to.

"Everyone seems to know it but me," Lou persisted. "He tried to recruit Gerson, who refused, and he'd been trying to get Barrow for years before she finally agreed to leave Canada."

Abby pulled herself together quickly, shaking her head. "Not sure if that's part of the pattern. She only agreed to leave Canada because of Roger."

"Who's Roger?"

"Who's Roger? Oh my gosh. She didn't tell you who *Roger* was?"

Lou listened, half in disbelief, as Abby told him that one of their old graduate school colleagues had been the only reason Barrow had gone to Canada and certainly the only reason she'd stayed, and that she'd left after he killed himself last winter by jumping into the St. Laurence river. So there was the suicide thing—why hadn't she told Lou?

He sat speechless as the drinks cart came by, barely able to ask for orange juice.

"Roger was always manic-depressive and a little weird," Abby explained, blowing her nose into her napkin before sipping her Diet Coke. "He'd tried to become a Catholic priest when he was a teenager, but they kicked him out when he ODed on psych drugs. Then he went to get a PhD, but he was always kind of ethereal and otherworldly, if you know what I mean. He did all sorts of volunteer work helping old people and sick children and things, and was a hopeless virgin, I don't think he'd ever even been kissed. When he graduated he went back to Montreal to live with his family because he needed stability in his life. *She* didn't see him for fifteen years, and then she showed up on the doorstep and wanted to be his friend again, but you can imagine that it was less than heartwarming—you don't believe a word I'm saying, do you?"

"It's not that I don't believe you," Lou addressed his cup. "I just think you're attributing an awful lot of emotion to someone who, well, face it… has something missing in that department."

Abby sprayed a mouthful of ice chips in a shriek of demonic laughter. "Finally someone says it! I can't believe you can stand working with her."

"Barrow's a genius," Lou said loyally.

"Bleah!" Absinthe made a cat-with-a-chicken-bone noise. "Let me ask you something," she declared finally. "Did she ever express the slightest sympathy over what happened to you?"

"She's very nice to me," Lou said quietly. "She takes me on bike rides and to the climbing gym."

"That wasn't the question. Did she ever admit that your life was ruined by going to grad school in physics?"

"No, of course not." He was scandalized. "You can't expect that of her. This university is everything to her." He had been waiting for a safer moment to bring up the story, but he couldn't resist. "She did tell me that you left grad school because you were about six inches from being like me, or worse."

"More like two feet—but yeah." Abby snorted and crumpled her plastic cup. "Whose fault did she say it was?"

"The Missionary's, I think."

"Pfft! Typical. The Missionary was the one who died. He was a stuffed shirt and everyone hated him, but he didn't deserve that."

"Lori said you were blackmailing the Missionary," he prompted.

"I wasn't exactly blackma—oh, all right," she acknowledged. "He had it coming. So we would always meet in this one room and sit on a bench, and the killer decided he could mount his hunting rifle outside the building to aim into the window and shoot me. Instead, as you know, it got the Missionary. I wasn't looking at him, because he had this nasty little moustache and this annoying mouth like a cat butt, so I was looking the other way when I heard kind of a plopping noise and something wet hit me."

"Eeew," was all he could think of to say that didn't involve taking the Lord's name in vain. Barrow always said that you must never swear in front of Abby because of the things she had been taught in Sunday School.

"Worse than eew! I thought he'd spit at me or something, so I turned around to slap him and saw that there was a hole in his head, and that the wet stuff was some brains."

"*Tabarnak*," he exclaimed, trying out a way to blaspheme that couldn't possibly offend her.

"Yeah. I just sat in shock for a minute, and he put his hand up to his head, saw the blood, then grabbed the bench and slid down slowly, slowly to the floor. Then I started screaming."

"Weren't you afraid the killer was still there?"

"Of course! I thought if I screamed he might run away. I didn't know the gun had been programmed and so the murderer was sitting in class when it happened. A fifth-year grad student found me—us—and called the police and the ambulance."

"Did they catch him right away?"

"No—it took *months*. We went to class with him all the rest of the year, and then they let him finish his degree in prison!"

"Holy crap." Lou started giggling hysterically. "Physics graduate school. I had *no* idea."

"You think I did? I had flashbacks for years. Even now I still wake up screaming—but I don't need to tell you," she finished kind of sheepishly, not looking at him. "I don't know how you stand it."

Lou looked out the window at the relentlessly blue sky. "Sometimes denial can be a superpower," was all he could find to say, as the plane dipped down to land with the horizon visible as far as the eye could see.

THIRTY: SLAP-HAPPY

CAROL FINALLY GOT HER SLAP. It wasn't one she would have asked for, but beggars can't be choosers: she was supposed to take all fifty paper copies of the completed proposal, plus fifty CDs, on the red-eye from Los Angeles to Washington, DC to deliver the precious cargo in person. If she arrived one second past four pm EST on December the twenty-first, all of the lab's hard work would have been for naught.

She couldn't help thinking that there was an element of punishment in this task. It was one of the very worst. The completed proposals would weigh more than a hundred pounds and would barely fit, with massive effort, into the largest possible wheeled carry-on plus two smaller "personal items." They greatly exceeded the carry-on weight limit, and so the designated deliveryman, if caught, was supposed to say "Urgent space research secret government business!"

Some people (Bob) enjoyed doing this, but Carol couldn't imagine herself trying it, even less getting away with it. She wasn't aggressive enough, or imposing enough, and—face it—didn't believe strongly enough in what she was delivering.

How could she? It was riddled with embarrassing errors. Besides the ones she'd inserted in the data she gave to Bob, there were various other things that even she knew were ridiculous. "Organisms like those known to be found on Mars"? Were proofreaders forbidden to give scientific input? Still, how did that get past the scientific review?

Things between her and Bob had degenerated so much that she couldn't even tell him where she was going. She wasn't even sure if he was still on Unclean status. They passed like alley cats in the night, growling at each other.

She just wanted this all to be over so everything could get back to normal. She ordered a new hard drive for her microscope computer, hoping that the technical groups would be able to pay her as soon as the PIP ended. But then the scope itself started acting up—she suspected Bob had shocked it when he yanked the cord out of the wall. She couldn't get it to function reliably, and the LEPERs adamantly refused to take van Gnubbern off PNG status.

She knew she was riding the ragged edge at the LEPERLab, so she didn't even dare call van Gnubbern from work. Instead she waited until she got home and had had her dinner. Bob had still not appeared, so she left a message on van Gnubbern's voicemail and started packing her suitcase.

Her phone rang right away.

"Um, Dr. van Gnubbern?" Carol asked cautiously, afraid that Bob would return and interrupt their conversation. "I would really like to talk to you—about the microscope and, well, some other things. Are you free this evening for a coffee?"

Her spirits sank as he mumbled and muttered, but finally he said something that revealed he was a man after her own heart. "I'm actually trying to lose some weight," he confessed, "and pastry always ruins me. I think the rain has stopped; what do you say to a hike up Henninger Flats by moonlight?"

He was a man after Lori's heart, too, because he had no car and Carol had to pick him up from his house halfway down the hill and take him back up to the National Forest. It was kind of cramped in her car, with her stuff for the trip the next day—all but the proposals—but he tucked himself in amidst the baggage with a cheery grin.

Wigbert van Gnubbern was such a jolly, lovable old man that she didn't even laugh at his walking stick and green lederhosen. He was definitely paunchy and jowly, but his legs were sturdy and he started up the incredibly steep slope at a faster speed than she could maintain, talking all the while. The microscope was the last thing from his mind, no doubt he was flattered to be asked his opinion about things at last. She didn't even have to prompt him.

"You're a friend of Lori Barrow's? Good. I have always specialized in misfits and marginals, and perhaps you could say that she was my first. You knew her in graduate school? Yes? Well, the thirteen-year old Lori Barrow was quite another beast. And I mean that literally."

Blessedly, he stopped for breath just over the first rise, waiting for her to catch up. Carol had never been here at night, and had never imagined it could be this beautiful. The steep east-facing slope was miserable and dusty in the morning, but in the light of a rising almost-full moon was pleasantly cool and refreshing. There were wildflowers opening all around her, ones that hid their blooms from the heat of the day and released their subtle scent as the sunlight faded. The yellow and lavender both stood out against the surrounding hills in the moonlight.

"She had been raised by criminals," continued van Gnubbern, punctuating the word with a bang of his walking stick against a piece of granite. "Lie, cheat, steal, kill—why not, if they would benefit you? I can easily tell you that this is the only university where she would have survived. You were an undergraduate here?"

"No, of course not," Carol exclaimed.

He understood that immediately. "Nor I. Not nearly intelligent enough. Well, STI is unique in two ways, both enabled by the fact that we accept only students in the top half of 1% of their graduating classes. The first is of course our House system, which was established in the school's infancy when our first president decided fraternities were inappropriate. The second is our Honor Code. We have no exam monitors, no tests for plagiarism, didn't even have locks in the gym lockers until the math department hired that kleptomaniac. There is only one rule for our students and faculty: 'No member of the Superior Community shall take unfair advantage of another member.' Well, this young Barrow could understand, and she learns quickly. We do not steal because it inconveniences others. We do not lie unless absolutely necessary. I also believe that she was aided by the calming effect of electron microscopy, which takes a good deal of patience and rather more creativity than you might imagine. Do you play an instrument?"

For once she wasn't a total boson. "I play the flute."

"Yes, so you understand. So, quite quickly Lori became a contributing and productive member of our community. I am very proud of the way she turned out, by the way." He paused again, breathed deeply, and bent to sniff a flower. "California lilac. Rather a stunted member of the species, I'm afraid. Do you know that the true lilac only develops its intoxicating scent if exposed to a winter frost?"

"I do," said Carol. "I'm from the Midwest and it's the thing I miss the most. That, and maybe a white Christmas."

The L.A. Christmas wasn't white, but as they climbed the hill they passed from desert shrub into the beginnings of an evergreen forest, and Carol could forgive California its failings. Above them, they could see the peaks of Mount Hansen and the shadow of its radio astronomy array.

"I wasn't so lucky with some of my others," continued van Gnubbern solemnly. "I have been sued a total of fourteen times, and it is thanks to

STI's team of lawyers that I have only once had to appear in court. I have been punched twice and severely beaten once. I spent two weeks under the protection of a private bodyguard."

"Your students did those things?" Rather pointlessly, Carol found herself asking, "Why?"

"Why the misfits? I cannot tell you. Perhaps because I was so lucky with Lori. Perhaps because I am eccentric myself, and have always felt excluded because of my terrible name."

That seemed like a very strange excuse, but Carol prodded gently, "And Jim Kalb?"

"Ah, yes. As you can see, nothing really out of the ordinary for me. I knew he had had serious problems in graduate school, particularly problems with women. But we had only one woman in our department—the unfortunate Marybeth, who even more unfortunately had an advisor who also had issues with the other sex."

"Kuzno?"

"I can see that you are not a stranger to our intrigues. Yes, sadly our new head has certain old-school prejudices that we have recently come to consider unacceptable. He does not believe that women should be physicists, much less theorists. However, there was no other advisor willing or able to take on Marybeth for the first two years that she was here. When Jim arrived, Sasha—Dr. Kuznetsov or, if you will, Kuzno—saw this as an opportunity to try to drive Marybeth away."

Carol remembered what had happened to Abby in grad school, and a long shiver ran through her. The night no longer seemed refreshing, but cold, and clouds were beginning to shadow the moon. "What did he do to her?"

"That I'm afraid I cannot tell you." Dr. van Gnubbern paused for breath again. "Not because I am not willing, but because I do not know precisely. I can tell you that none of us took it particularly seriously."

Yeah, Carol thought, typical. "Why not?"

Van Gnubbern resumed walking, taking the steep left turn around the ridge onto a trail that was less well-illuminated by the moon. "Marybeth was special," he said at last, picking his way slowly through the rocks. "We all believed she was exaggerating, if not downright imagining things. We had all seen such things before, and we knew how it would end—with a quick and quiet lawsuit, she would take a year or two worth of salary to depart quietly and pursue her career elsewhere."

"Yes," said Carol more bitterly than she wished, "Absinthe McRae, of the legal office, says that happens all the time. The harassers stay and the victims are forced to leave."

"Unfortunately, this is generally the case. However, Marybeth did not leave after filing her suit. Instead, she tried to find a new advisor."

"Maupertuis?"

"You know Lou?"

"Not personally."

"Ah, well, he was a phenomenon. We don't often get professors his age nowadays, what with the demands of grant proposal writing and publication. Unfortunately for everyone involved, he seemed to take Marybeth as his personal project."

"Like a pound puppy," said Carol.

"Like a pound puppy," echoed van Gnubbern. "He and Sasha disliked each other from the start. It began as a professional rivalry, but Lou seemed to think that if he could make something out of Marybeth, it would reveal Sasha as a misogynistic bastard not worthy to be an advisor. It didn't help that Sasha always felt as though Lou had stolen all of his students. Kuznetsov hadn't had any money to hire anyone that year, so Lou got essentially the entire first-year class, and I must admit the whole bunch of them put on quite a show. They had group meetings on the beach in Malibu, and rumor has it that he paid them all out of his own pocket until he got a grant."

"Was Marybeth part of this?" Carol remembered the picture of Marybeth with the horse and the BMW.

"For a while she was, but I think Lou eventually realized he wasn't going to get any work out of her. I tried to help out, but to tell you the truth, she wasn't much use to me, either. It was one excuse after another: she was too scared, or too blind, or too weak to do what I asked her to do. I think she was afraid to try, maybe afraid to risk failure or to face her true limitations rather than her imagined ones. Who knows?"

"So you kicked her out of your lab, too," said Carol bluntly.

"Yes, I did," van Gnubbern affirmed matter-of-factly. "Things escalated from there. Jim became more horrid to poor Marybeth, she became more hysterical, and Lou and Sasha downright hated each other. Then, as you may know, Lou was injured."

"I didn't know, until recently," Carol admitted.

There was a bench around the next bend, giving a view over the city and fully exposed to the half-shrouded moon. "This may have been enough climbing for me tonight," puffed van Gnubbern, and Carol, relieved, went to sit beside him. The clouds quelled the city noises and shielded the Westside and the ocean from their view. "Where was I? Yes. Lou was gone off and on for months, and Marybeth, well, she just lost her mind. It seemed she was at the police station every week, filing a complaint against Jim or, more rarely, Sasha."

"Did she say that Jim had shot Lou?"

Carol regretted her brutal question as soon as she spoke, because van Gnubbern seemed to clam up. He said nothing for a long while, rocking back and forth, looking at the city. "Yes," he admitted at last, "but we could scarcely believe her. She was incoherent and histrionic. But I must admit, although we may have suspected such a thing, we all agreed on some level that it was better if this did not get out."

"What?" Carol had heard Lori speak of the infamous STI coverups, but this was ridiculous. "You had a dangerous maniac in your department!"

"Yes—but imagine how Lou would feel if he knew it. He was trying to get his life back."

"But there was still a killer running around!"

"I know," van Gnubbern admitted, "I know. But we had no way of knowing anything else would happen. We thought that if we shuffled him out, quietly, to a new position, he would think of it as a triumph and essentially disappear."

"You were *rewarding* him for being a killer!"

"It wasn't a particularly desirable position—" van Gnubbern began, but then he stopped suddenly, no doubt recalling that Carol was a LEPER too.

"That's OK, Dr. van Gnubbern," said Carol. "I hear from Lori all the time that being at the LEPERLab is worse than being in San Quentin. Now I realize she means it literally. But if he got away with what he had done, and got the position he wanted—" she shuddered to think of them planning to palm this guy off on her husband— "*why* did he kill her? Unless it wasn't Dim Bulb who killed her—maybe it was Kuzno all along."

"I have been saying all along that Jim was not acting alone," said van Gnubbern proudly. No doubt having a captive audience for his crackpot theories was the highlight of his evening. He lowered his voice, making his British accent more pronounced somehow, and placed his hand on her knee to whisper into her ear. "I am sure he was the tool of someone more desperate than himself, someone who is trying to stop both Lou and Lori from doing what they are doing. Because you do understand that they are changing the department irrevocably, and that the manner in which Marybeth was killed was...symbolic. Lou made his reputation saying the universe will expand forever without re-contracting—that is, that it will die a slow, cold death."

"Doesn't that have to make it Kuzno?" Carol wondered. "Who else would care all that much about the direction the physics department takes?"

He didn't answer. The bank of clouds coming over the hill suddenly seemed menacing. As they got up to go, Carol took van Gnubbern's arm for some purchase on the slippery granite, and he lurched and fell backwards against her. Pinned under him by the edge of the cliff, she screamed once in shock, then again as he raised his walking stick up over her head.

She managed to slither out from under him, still screaming as he grabbed at her, and ran away down the hill in the darkness with the moon covered by clouds. A heavy rain began to fall.

THIRTY-ONE: THE BUBO TANK

THE FAKE PROPOSAL WAS safely in the hands of Walter Waddles, Jr., Professor of Chemistry, Bubo class of 1967. The real one was still being printed and collated, just twenty-eight and a half hours before the 10:30 p.m. FedEx truck that was the last guaranteed on-time delivery to Washington, DC.

The Buboes and Walter Waddles IV were in charge of all of the black-and-white pages. Lori, locked in Lou's office with Buboes standing guard outside, was using the new printer to spew out all twelve of the pages that had to be in full color. Their months of work were condensed down into two eight-panel figures with light micrographs, three with electron micrographs and spectra, and one foldable pull-out showing a phylogenetic tree.

She was only about half done when two fat cops burst in and arrested her. The charge was idiotic: they were arresting her for taking Bob's hard drive from the LEPERLab. It was petty theft, and they intended to lock her up. The problem was, they only had to hold her for one day and all would be lost.

"Keep printing!" she cried to the Buboes as she was led away to the police station. "You know what to do!"

They gave her blank looks. Of course they didn't know what to do, and neither did either the junior or senior Waddles. The only other person who knew as much as she did was trapped in a rental Jeep in a snowstorm somewhere between Albuquerque and Denver.

Lori couldn't believe that Lou and Abby had both been so foolish as to go chasing after Kuzno. They should have known that bad things would happen here. They were the only ones she could think of who were respectable enough to bail her out—except maybe for Solomon Rose, who was supposed to be guarding the University president to make sure he didn't skip town on them, too.

She was starting to feel abandoned and forgotten when dinnertime came and went and she was stuck in jail, staring at the tiles and clutching a scratchy old blanket to keep warm.

Some Buboes showed up, just to inform her that Wigbert's mattress full of money was a myth, so there was nothing they could do. Typical behavior, which was why she hadn't sent them to fetch Sam's paper in the first place.

The old Lori knew perfectly well how to get out of the Bubo tank with a 2.5 mm hex key. The new Lori had forgotten her hex keys in her office, had rich friends, and was worried about her tenure review. So she sat sitting on the bunk like a good girl, counting the tiles in the floor, listening to the rain, and trying not to sniffle.

She very nearly used her one phone call on Ben, knowing he was in town and could put the proposal together, but at the last second she changed her mind and called Abby.

In response she got horrible heavy breathing and little moans of pain. She immediately envisioned the worst—Jeep flipped, trapped and dying in a snowbank.

But then there was a clink of silverware and a glugging noise. "Oh oh oh!" said Abby finally. "It's *sooo* spicy!"

Lori's stomach rumbled, and a 3D vision appeared in front of her of the last meal she had had in New Mexico: huge chicken enchiladas, smothered in green chile and a blanket of cheese that stretched across the plate.

Lori interrupted the gastronomic orgy with a flat, "Dammit, I'm in jail."

"Mmmph mmph…" Abby kept swilling some liquid, probably a glass of milk. "Call the legal office and ask for Jim."

"Now?"

"No, of course not tonight, but first thing tomorrow." Crunch, crunch—tortilla chips. "And I mean *first* thing, seven-thirty. The LEPERLab does not legally exist, and all STI faculty have the right to be there at all times. Do not post bail, don't risk your time or money. Jim will get you out in half an hour."

"But I did steal Bob's hard drive," Lori admitted.

"Pshaw. I'd get you out tonight if we weren't stuck in Bumblesnore, Colorado."

"Why did you both have to go? There's no one left here with a clue."

"There's a terrible storm in the mountains—neither of us wanted to be alone."

Great, Lori thought, so you'll die together. "No one here can even post bail. Rose is hiding, and the Buboes tried to find van Gnubbern, but he's disappeared too."

Abby swallowed a few times, and her voice lost its eternal anger, sounding—if such a thing were possible—even pitying. "Lori...I'm sorry."

"You're sorry? Sorry for what?"

"I'm sorry I thought bad things about you all these years. I know now that it wasn't you."

"Huh?" Lori's first thought was that Lou had somehow convinced Abby during their long drive that Lori was merely a victim of circumstance, a feral child who knew no better. She was completely unprepared for what came next.

"You were always there because you were his student," Abby continued, in the same strained, almost weepy voice. "It's van Gnubbern. He killed all those people. He just attacked Carol in the woods, and now he's taken off."

Lori pulled the Bubo tank receiver away from her ear. It was sticky, seeming to stretch, filling her with nausea as she was forced to hear what she couldn't accept but which she knew was true.

Unable to listen to any more, she hung up and prepared to go back to her cell. One of the cops suggested food, but she robotically waved him off, her hunger at the enchilada vision seeming universes away.

They led her back to the Bubo tank and she lay down, wrapping herself tightly in a blanket. The cops made fun of her—she didn't have any friends who could come up with a thousand bucks, she was acting like she had been booked for murder instead of petty theft, maybe they should look her up to see she if had done something more serious.

She ignored them, lost in the horror of what she had always suspected but chose to ignore. Of course it was obvious. She had been willfully blind for more than sixteen years.

Infrastructure crimes: all of the infrastructure had been van Gnubbern's. The door that fell on Lori, Marybeth's freezing room, and the microscope that zapped Dim Bulb were all his, all structures that he alone had touched for decades. The only part that wasn't his was the LEPER cold room, and that hadn't killed anyone. He had been right there when Lori found Marybeth, and had himself "found" Dim Bulb's body—maybe even the LEPERs had seen something fishy, putting him on PNG status so he couldn't come back. Lori had been led astray by her own PNGing at the hands of that stupid Bob.

Van Gnubbern's motives were painfully obvious. Everyone was always trying to get rid of poor old Wigbert—he was barely a physicist at all, just a guy who took pictures. Silverman ranted about "cleaning out the deadwood," and that's what led to van Gnubbern's lab being mostly abandoned in the first place, as the department heaped administrative tasks on him.

Wigbert had been forced to hire Marybeth, the department's most hopeless student, because his work was considered worthless and easy. She had been incompetent, even worse than she would have been as a string theorist, filing complaints against him for making her do microscopy when she couldn't see.

Then there was Lori, blithely showing up to take both of his labs away forever.

She'd been oblivious to it all because she didn't even want to consider the possibility. Even more horrible than the thought of van Gnubbern as the killer was the thought that he would be caught—arrested, tried, sentenced, off in San Quentin, a memorial to what academia could do to the soul. When his appeals ran out, they would all have to protest his execution, camped out in front of the prison with banners and candles.

Or maybe he was gone, across the border in Mexico where he'd shave his beard, ditch the lederhosen, and live out his years in a cabin on the beach. He could grow fruit and catch fish and regale the locals with made-up tales from his native Groningen.

Run, Wigbert, run, Lori thought, as she drifted off into a fitful sleep on the cot of the Bubo tank.

THIRTY-TWO: MIGHTIER THAN THE SWORD

THE SAME DENVER HOTEL had been hosting the Particles conference for years. Lou had been here twice in years past, but had never previously managed to score the business suite on the thirty-first floor. There were two bedrooms separated by a living room with an entertainment center, a full-sized bath, a separate shower, and a Jacuzzi surrounded by mirrors. On the coffee table in the living room were an espresso machine, a jar of pretzels, a box of chocolates, and a fancy ice bucket.

It was kind of a shame that they only intended to stay for six hours, the last four of which he had spent staring at the ceiling and tossing with insomnia. He finally gave up and got out of bed, rummaging through the stuff they'd bought in Albuquerque so he could shave.

Apart from not quite daring to get into the bathtub, Lou relished that the trip had gone off without disaster. He and Abby had outfitted themselves well before leaving. He had plenty of pee supplies, and there were blankets and food in case they ended up in the ditch. Abby had demanded snow tires on a beautiful, clear day, insisting that she was a Minnesotan and knew snow. With that and the four-wheel drive they hadn't had to stop, just plowed on through the snow for hours, silent in the concentration of winter driving.

Lou was pleased with himself for this bit of spontaneity, and for not disgracing himself in front of Abby. He'd done his fair share and she hadn't had to scrape him out of the gutter. He'd have to take off on more last-minute trips—ones not involving Kuzno. Brain still filled with images of dancing flakes and headlights, he held cold towels over his eyes until they could open properly.

Then he tried the espresso maker, which wasn't bad at all, the grounds black and fresh. By the third double he was almost out of his zombie-like state, and realized that thanks to Barrow, he knew exactly what Abby had for breakfast every morning. The data had been delivered with a layer of snark—*All that NutraSweet's going to give her a brain tumor*—but the facts were there: plain bagel, diet cream cheese "half as thick as the bread," and coffee that was one-third warm skim milk with two packets of Equal. He made the coffee in the room, then went down to the lobby cafeteria for the rest. Abby had eaten almost nothing in the New Mexican restaurant the night before, and Lou knew from bitter experience how skinny girls acted when they didn't eat.

"Rise and shine," he called cheerily, knocking on her door.

After a minute she stumbled out, hair sticking out in all directions, seemingly unable to form words. She reached for the coffee cup, found it warm, and cradled it for a minute before taking a tentative sip. Her eyes lit up when she saw the bagel and she reached for the upper half, still seeming dazed. "What time is it?" she mumbled.

"Just past eight. I thought we could nab him as he comes in to breakfast." Abby was cute in her morning disarray, Lou thought in spite of himself. If she were a physicist, she'd come to work like that, instead of groomed and made up and scary-looking. Her eyes were definitely absinthe green, and he wondered if it was just a coincidence, since surely babies weren't born with green eyes?

"Mmm," Abby mumbled, chewing on her bagel. A strange mix of emotions flashed onto her face—fear, pity, guilt. "Are you OK?"

"I'm all right," he replied, embarrassed. "Do you think I'm nuts?"

"Hardly. I feel like I am the one person who can even begin to imagine what you are going through. In fact, I had the same kind of episodes you seem to be having now. I'd forget about what had happened, sometimes for days at a time, and then I'd have these flashbacks. And I'd go to the police with my new 'information' that I was sure would lead them to the killer. They were kind enough, in a distant sort of way, but I could tell they thought I was just hysterical and a pest. It was horrible, and it didn't get better until they caught the killer."

She sounded insincere and full of shit—but maybe he was just grouchy, after twelve hours of driving through the snow and a night with no sleep. Not even the exhaustion of the trip had been enough to let him forget. He stared at the bottom of his empty coffee cup so he wouldn't have to see that unnerving expression that probably mirrored his own. "At least it will be easier to confront Kuzno knowing he's not a mass murderer."

"That's right!" Abby exclaimed with false cheer. "Regular buttheads, we can handle." She drained her coffee without saying anything, reached for the second half of the bagel, pretending to be lost in chewing. "I just never would have thought…"

"No," Lou said firmly, "never."

"They haven't caught him yet, either."

"I know."

Abby popped the last bite into her mouth and sighed. "This was perfect. How did you know?"

"I'm psychic," he replied with just enough irony so that she'd figure out what that meant. He wondered how she would react if he asked her to dinner—at a restaurant, obviously, since he couldn't have anyone visit him in that hovel in Postdoc and Visitor Housing. There was only one burner that worked and the stove had a tendency to explode. Abby had probably even heard the story of him almost burning the place down trying to make chocolate-chip cookies.

Someday I'll need to buy a house, he told himself without much enthusiasm. Just another task that needed to be done to return to the land of the living.

"Aren't you eating?" Abby wondered.

"No. I'm too nervous."

She nodded as if that made sense, stood up and went back into the bedroom. When she re-emerged, she looked professional and scary again. "Are you ready? Good. I'm just going to brush my teeth, and then we can go."

The diner had been empty when Lou came for the bagel half an hour earlier. Now it was filled with nerds who mumbled to themselves and drew vectors in the air. The booth at the very back was unoccupied, though, and he concealed himself behind the crowd with a cup of coffee and a camera. The Bubo website needed to feature Kuzno's expression when he came in and saw Abby there, ready to pounce, standing on the edge of the bar so she would be able to look him straight in the eye.

They didn't have to wait long, but Kuzno didn't seem to react at all at the sight of Abby. He gazed straight through her as if she didn't exist, went to the bar and ordered himself the deluxe glutton breakfast. He continued to ignore her when she stood beside him, pretending to check his e-mail on a small laptop; she finally had to say loudly enough for the room to hear, "Good morning, Sasha! I'm afraid you flew off yesterday without having a chance to finalize some paperwork."

Sasha evoked a gaspingly adorable golden retriever with long floppy ears—one puppy name that would be ruined for Lou forever.

Kuzno turned around, but didn't see Lou until Abby steered him towards the booth. Lou just had time to hide the camera under a cloth napkin.

Kuzno took a step backwards. "If you spent federal funds coming out here, Maupertuis, I will personally see you fired."

"I knew you were lame, Kuzno, but that's a dumbass threat even from you." Lou found he was enjoying fighting with his old nemesis again. "I could get you fired for interfering with my work."

"In cases of fraud, I can refuse to sign," Kuzno declared confidently. "And I think forging my signature counts as fraud." He tried to turn to stalk away, but Abby blocked him, urging him into the booth opposite Lou. She then sat down next to him, impeding his exit.

"No one forged your signature," said Lou and Abby together.

"Oh no?" Kuzno's lips folded up over his scraggly teeth, making him look like one of those squished-face dogs. "Neither of you actually saw me sign."

Lou kept his mouth shut, because this was Abby's job—and he really wanted to hear what she had to say about Rose's honesty.

Sadly, it wasn't much, apart from "Professor Rose has the Nobel Prize."

Kuzno continued to grin evilly, scaring away the waitress who had tried to approach with the coffee pot. "And why do you think that he has never been allowed to head the department?" he beamed. "The old man has been shady for years. He also has no business writing an experimental proposal. I would have refused to sign even if he hadn't pulled this ridiculous stunt." He sat back in triumph to allow another waitress (one older and more jaded, maybe) to deposit his glutton plate in front of him. Hunching over the mound of greasy eggs and meat, he slurped and snorted like a goblin for a few minutes before raising his head and pointing at Lou with a sausage. "Maybe *you* should have thought a little harder before trusting him."

"Writing this was not Rose's idea," Lou rejoined easily. "It was mine."

"Oh, I know," Kuzno replied, returning chompingly to his meal. "That obviously wasn't what I meant."

Lou slammed his hands down onto the formica table with all his might. It shook a little, making some scrambled egg jump up and stick to Kuzno's nose. "If you know something that you're not telling me, you motherfucker, I will rip your goddamn head off right here in the restaurant."

Kuzno sat back smugly, wiping at his nose. "I think that was a threat," he suggested in Abby's direction, then went back to eating.

"I wouldn't know, I only do intellectual property," Abby replied coldly. "What I do know is that if you know something, it's called *accessory to murder* and it gets you in even more trouble than being forced to marry nineteen-year-old undergraduates after seducing them in the conference room and getting them pregnant."

"Me, accessory?" Kuzno gave a brittle laugh. "I'd say it's the old man who has some problems in that department. Everyone he hires ends up dead— or at least halfway there," he added with another gesture of the sausage in Lou's direction.

"Fortunately, I'm tough to kill," Lou replied. "As Barrow once pointed out, there's nothing in my chest but a lump of stone."

"Yeah," Kuzno leered, "but what's it like knowing you'll never have a woman again?"

Don't point your sausage at me, Lou thought. "It gives me that many more hours every night to dream about hating you."

"Kuznetsov, you're disgusting," snapped Absinthe, forgetting her own injunction. "If you refuse to sign with Rose as the principal investigator, I'm sure the proposal works just fine without him—right, Lou? So you have two choices for PI: Maupertuis or Barrow, neither of whom has forged your signature."

Kuzno gave a bizarre, high-pitched squeal, something you'd hear in the woods just before getting chomped, or maybe gored. "That is even worse. Maupertuis is incompetent, inexperienced, and untrustworthy. Doubly so in accomplice with a known troublemaker, who was forced to go to a third-rate graduate school when the things she did here and as a child became public after *your* office leaked them."

"Watch out, Kuzno," Abby sneered—no more "Sasha"!. "Now you've insulted my home state. Maybe Minnesota is third-rate, but it's a lot better than where you'll end up if you persist in your stubbornness. Not only are you the most scandal-plagued department head ever—and yes, that includes the mathematicians—you also are going to have to back up any claims you make about these investigators and their alleged 'irresponsibility.' Professor Rose, if you recall, was offered your position several times but turned it down, and your personal vendetta against him is well-known. And you're going to look really evil in court trying to say bad things about a guy who went back to work a month after being shot in the spine. Not to mention a poor little orphan girl whose only home has ever been at the Superior Technological Institute."

She was just getting warmed up when her cell phone rang. It was now past seven-thirty back home, so Lou prayed it was Barrow and gestured at her with his eyes to answer it.

From the little "Eep" on the end of the line, he knew it wasn't Barrow but Walter Waddles IV, but he couldn't hear any of the rest of the conversation. Abby shrieked "WHAT?" a few times, then got up and tore out of the restaurant without even promising to return.

Lou was left alone with Kuzno, who was wiping the traces of his breakfast grease off his plate with a nasty-looking piece of toast.

"So which is it?" Lou asked him, hating to have to do this part himself. Nerds were not made for confrontation. "Sign or be sued?"

"You can't sue me, Maupertuis," Kuzno sneered. "You lost any credibility you might have had when those moron students of yours refused to leave. You had two of them, may I remind you—and that pathetic woman was not the worst."

"Keep talking, Kuzno, and you'll end up in prison," Lou replied with exaggerated politeness. "Marybeth is more than pathetic, she's dead."

Kuzno seemed to actually react to this. He wiped his plate with his second piece of toast, but didn't eat it, just wadded it up in fury and dropped it into the middle of the dish. "Fine, Maupertuis, you win," he snarled. "Make me a new page with Barrow as the principal investigator and without the old man, and I'll sign it."

Was it a trick? Or maybe, as Lou hoped, Kuzno thought that this would be a difficult task. Thanks to electronic gadgets, though, he was ready in seconds.

"There's a printer in my room," Kuzno offered. "Let's get this over with."

They wended their way through a bunch of string theorists, several of whom had very clearly been eavesdropping. Lou thought he recognized a couple of them, and thought about asking one to come up and witness Kuzno's signature in case Abby didn't arrive on time—but in the end he didn't. How absurd could this get, after all?

It took a while to make Lou's computer communicate with Kuzno's folding dot-matrix printer. Lou had to pay for hotel Internet access, log in, and download a remarkably large driver. Despite Kuzno's claim, it didn't work wireless, and the evil man sorted through a mass of cables for what seemed a ridiculous amount of time. Lou was starting to get suspicious that he was stalling for some reason, but they finally managed to get the page printed twice. Kuzno then made a big deal of selecting a writing implement from among his collection, which appeared to be everything from quill pens to artist's brushes.

Somehow this was the one thing about him that made him seem a little bit human. All theorists loved their pens and pencils, but Kuzno held his in special monogrammed boxes, some initialed in Russian, arranged in a padded mini briefcase. He had an inkwell—something Lou had only seen in art class. The ink was not black, but a deep violet.

The pen he finally chose was an ordinary ballpoint, though. He was just holding it over the page when there was heavy knocking on the door, shouts, and a woman screaming.

Abby dashed into the room, flanked by two security guards, and knocked the pen from Kuzno's hand. "You are in so much trouble now," she hissed as one of the guards bent to retrieve the pen with his rubber glove.

Lou could see the blood drain from Kuzno's face, and amusing though that was, he really didn't understand it. There was a bit of commotion as Abby produced her own pen, one of those very ordinary ballpoints made by blind people. She forced Kuzno to sign both copies of the form, duly witnessed by the two of them and the guards. They then got up and left, leaving Kuzno sitting on the bed with the look of a man awaiting a visit from the KGB.

"Good news," Abby declared once they were back in the lobby. "The sky's clear over Denver. I got us tickets and we'll be home before lunchtime." She whispered something to the security guard, and retrieved Kuzno's pen, safely enveloped in the glove. "I'm going to need to check a bag," she told Lou conspiratorially. "Certainly not going to bring *this* in my carryon."

He looked into her eyes for signs of the brain tumor, thinking that either the NutraSweet got her at last or there was something Walter Waddles IV had said that would put a new twist to everything that was going on.

THIRTY-THREE: WIGGING OUT

LORI HAD BEEN AWAKE for an hour, and was just starting over again counting the seven hundred and twenty-one little tiles when the guy from the legal office came to get her out. As Abby had promised, it went smoothly, and on the way back to campus she asked the question that had been tormenting her all night.

"Have they caught Wigbert van Gnubbern?"

The lawyer looked blank. He seemed to have no idea what she was talking about. When he asked for an explanation, she muttered incoherently and sped up the pace so she could eclipse herself into the physics building.

No one appeared to be in yet, not even any Buboes. Her office was exactly as she'd left it, with about half of the proposals printed and collated on her desk—the only difference was that Walter Waddles IV was dead asleep in her office chair.

"Wake up, Walter!" she shouted.

"Huh? What? Aah!" shouted Walter, head snapping up. "Barrow!" He looked infinitely guilty.

"What's wrong?" Lori demanded immediately.

"The president has left for his Christmas vacation. Professor Rose stalled him as long as possible, but he had to leave, and he wouldn't sign without Kuzno's signature first."

"Where's Rose?"

"I don't know."

"Oh," said Lori, not really giving a shit. "So I guess we've lost."

Walter jumped slightly, clearly expecting a much different response. "But—?"

"No, I don't give a good goddamn. Go home and go to bed. It's over."

He sidled out the door, probably afraid that she'd gone mad and would hurl a javelin after him or something. Left alone, she stared for a long while at the mountain of paper on her desk, but couldn't face it right away.

Instead she went downstairs and entered the BSL-3 (no gloves, only a lab coat that she didn't bother to button). Someone had forgotten to turn off the mercury lamp on the microscope. The lamps were supposed to be replaced every 200 hours of use, and this one now read 257.14. She snapped it off, wondering if the instrument would ever be used again, or if that number would sit for years as a testimony to this horrible day.

She wouldn't blame Lou if he never came back. But in case he did, or in case someone else came along in another seventeen years, she carefully boxed up all of his optical components and put them away in their labeled drawers. Then she gathered all the trash, put the bag in the autoclave, and wiped down the benches with ethanol.

Next she went over to the ice lab and did the same housekeeping chores. Buboes in the hall avoided her, eyes downcast. They clearly knew what had happened, and they all knew van Gnubbern, who had been the undergraduate advisor to every physics major since Walter Waddles III.

As a final act, she raised the room's set-point to room temperature, 70 degrees F. The remains of the ice cores would rapidly melt as the room warmed, leaving nothing but damp brown paper.

She felt no hunger or thirst, but was starting to get the twinge of a caffeine headache, so as soon as she was done she took off her lab coat and headed down the Rose Walk to Peet's. Kicking away stray grapefruit, she thought of the first day she'd met Lou, and wondered what he was doing now. If he was lucky he was dead in a ditch in Florence, Colorado.

It was almost noon and the bagel shop was hopping with ordinary people, ones who drove flashy cars and wore business suits, and always had a Bluetooth tucked behind their ears. She got the largest coffee they sold and sat out under the trees, sipping it as quickly as her roiling stomach would allow.

The moment of peace didn't last long, because some asshole had to rev the engine of his stinking car right in front of the patio. Lori picked up her stuff and prepared to move inside, wondering if the shithead would even care if she flipped him off.

"Lori! HEY! LORI!"

The only thing louder than Abby's disgusting car was her voice.

Lori was embarrassed to be associated in any way with someone who drove a car like that, and she wanted nothing to do with Abby right now. How had she managed to get back from Colorado so quickly? Lou was with her, too, looking much too cheerful for the circumstances.

"Come to my office!" he called, and they peeled away in a plume of stench.

Lori took her sweet time finishing her coffee and walking back to campus. Fuck Abby and the Porsche she rode in on, she thought.

Pages were spewing out of Lou's new printer when she got there, and he and Abby were both stacking and collating like mad.

"I had to remove Solomon Rose, but Kuzno signed with you as PI," he explained excitedly. "We were lucky that the storm ended last night, so we flew straight back from Denver."

"So what?" Lori snapped. "The STI president is on his way to Gstaad. It's over. We lost."

Abby smirked. "I bet you didn't know that when the president is on vacation, the LEPER director can sign in his place."

That seemed even more hopeless than catching a plane to Switzerland. "So? How do we find the LEPER director and bring him over to our side, when we're the competition and it's four days before Christmas?"

Abby plucked a sheet off the desk and held it up like a proud mama. "He owed me one," she grinned.

Lori thought about ripping it up and throwing it in Abby's face. "So what? I'm not going to sign as principal investigator. Give it up, already—the horse is not only dead, its guts are all over the road."

Lou and Abby exchanged some kind of glance—Lori knew exactly what kind. It was a *Poor twisted little bitch had no one to look up to but Wigbert van Gnubbern* glance.

"Fuck you both," she went on. "If this job turns people into killers, then I don't want it."

They both laughed some sort of laugh. She wasn't sure what kind.

"Barrow," said Lou cautiously, "we just had a long conversation on the plane, and we're not really sure van Gnubbern did anything terrible. Bob Drift's wife, what's her name, just called the police last night and claimed that he'd said something about a 'slow cold death' and then waved a stick at her. He could have been talking about particle physics, for all we know."

"Are you on crack?" Lori screamed, kicking his desk so hard that the printer stopped with a burp. "Of course it was van Gnubbern this whole time! He probably hired me as an undergrad to take the fall for him when he murdered Silverman. But then he got clean away because we were all so stupid we thought it was an accident. Notice he always keeps a freak or two around him when he's killing, though, so they're the obvious first suspects."

"Honestly," said Lou with a deep yoga breath, "I don't see—"

"You won't see anything when Wigbert's done with you!" she yelled. "He probably put eyeball-eating amebas on the microscope already! If you have contact lenses, take them out and throw them away right now."

"Jesus Christ, Barrow." Lou banged through a couple of drawers, finally coming out with a bottle of eyedrops that he applied liberally to each side. "Thanks for scaring the shit out of me. No contacts, but still…" He added more drops, blinking them onto the desk. "That's just loathsome."

"No worse than the things he's already done! Letting someone slowly freeze while she bashed her head against the door? Showing up at the LEPERLab with some kind of mysterious electrodes, and clapping them across Dim Bulb's temples? I could go on, but I think you get the gist."

The door squeaked shut, and high-heeled footsteps echoed down the hall. Abby had made a discreet escape while Lori was shouting.

Lori didn't really care. She leaned over the desk and peered into Lou's well-washed eyes. "You know what else? That incident report wasn't filed by Marybeth at all. I have her notebooks—her signature is printed, and I remembered that she told me she couldn't write cursive for some bizarre-ass reason. The report has a loopy cursive 'M,' that when you look closely, is just like an upside-down version of Wigbert's 'W'!"

"I suppose we were being stupid," Lou admitted, carefully putting away the eyedrops, then washing his hands with sanitizer. "I mean, thinking he could be innocent. If he had really just been misunderstood on the trail, why is he hiding?"

"Exactly! Because he's in Mexico already." Lori was damned if she would cry, so she kicked the desk again. This time her foot made a distinct dent in the crappy old wood. "I quit, and you're a moron if you don't quit, too. In fact I don't know why you've stayed as long as you have."

"I don't know either." Lou gave a helpless shrug. "But what else can I do in life? This is the only place I feel normal."

See how normal you feel when your eyeballs rot out, Lori thought, but decided that was a bit much. After all, Wigbert wasn't a biologist and wouldn't know how to culture the eyeball-eating amebas.

But if he learned, watch out.

"We're all exhausted," Lou continued, in his wooden Denial-Man way. "I agree, let's let the proposal go. But I wouldn't do anything else until we know the truth."

"We already know the truth. I should have guessed sixteen years ago. I can only blame myself for everything he's done since."

"Lori, calm down." The door clicked shut. Abby had returned—hands empty. "Now that the signature page is somewhere very safe, I want you to listen to me. I think it's Kuzno after all."

THIRTY-FOUR: BE THOU CLEAN

CAROL HADN'T MADE IT halfway down her driveway before she swore to herself that she would never go back to STI or the LEPERLab again.

What did one call an ex-leper?

She was still going to deliver the proposal to DC, because she'd promised to do it and because she didn't want to start her new life off on the wrong foot, so to speak. After that, she didn't know what she was going to do, but dragging out her days fixing typos for mad killers wasn't it.

It was a long drive through residential streets to the freeway. People were scurrying about campus like cockroaches, and she had to slam on the brakes to avoid hitting someone. At first she thought it was the chief scientist, but fter a second realized it had to be his son; those Walter Waddleses all looked alike. Oblivious to his near-death experience, Walter IV tore off towards town without even glancing in her direction.

She cut through the movie-star neighborhood, still shaking from the close encounters with Wigbert and Walter, and merged onto the freeway where she came to an immediate and total standstill. It was a good thing she had five hours before her flight. After a painful ten minutes without moving an inch, she followed a growing train of other cars in making a highly illegal U-turn the wrong way down an on-ramp, finding herself on a charming street decorated fifties-style and strung with Christmas lights.

Not wanting to face the surface streets to the airport without sustenance and a map, she pulled into a diner with big glass windows and red barstools around a soda fountain. Words she knew only from books of her childhood, like "egg cream" and "malted," swarmed in her head as she pushed the glass door open against a blast of warm air. The diner was crowded, and she took the last place at the bar, opposite the TV set.

Fighting her impulse to order one of everything, she finally settled on a tuna melt and a chocolate egg cream (who could resist!). Most of the people around her looked and talked like STI professors, reminding her that she hadn't made it very far from campus and that she'd need to get back on the road pretty soon. Fragments of familiar names reached her ears, which she ignored until a phrase leapt from the TV set in undeniable clarity.

"Celebrated microbiology professor Benedict Gerson remains unable to explain how he found himself travelling down the freeway in the wrong direction, at the tail end of downtown's morning rush hour," the newscaster announced brightly. "The 110 remains obstructed between the 10 and Pasadena…"

Carol tried not to react, hearing others guffaw around her and imagining that they were the villainous spies of Lori's tales. But who, really, are the bad guys? she wondered, sipping slowly at her soda to savor the chocolatey taste. Abby was right that as soon as Lori showed up, terrible things started happening. Ben Gerson was allegedly on their side, and he sounded like an irresponsible space-head. Not to mention that horrible van Gnubbern, who'd hired their department psychopath and then foisted him off on the LEPERLab once he got sick of him.

As she ate, she calmed down a little and asked herself if she'd misjudged van Gnubbern on the trail, feeling a little guilty for leaving him to walk several miles home in the rain. Still, he was far from innocent, and she couldn't help but wonder if his choice of the LEPERLab for Jim Kalb had some additional sinister motive that he hadn't dared express. The LEPERs wanted to get rid of Bob—were they hoping he'd be murdered so they didn't have to fire him? Was that why Tripp had deigned to interview someone as lowly as Dim Bulb?

The food warmed her belly and helped her to suppress those thoughts. She felt cozy and protected from the elements as she climbed back into her car, clutching a napkin scribbled with detailed directions for getting to the airport along the surface roads.

It was more than just Ben Gerson who'd tied up the freeway, she realized as she cut through the foothills, the 110 off to her side. There was a knot of police cars and fire trucks around a van that had been almost completely devoured by flames.

Carol hadn't really prayed since the Bible study group in grad school drove her off, but she bowed her head at the sight and murmured a few words, knowing that anyone inside the van would not have survived. She prayed not only for the bodies and souls of those involved, but also that the incident *please* not have anything to do with the LEPERLab.

THIRTY-FIVE: HOPE DIES LAST

ABBY STOOD AT THE back of the room, arms folded as if daring anyone to interrupt her. No one did.

"Kuzno could have tried to make everything look as if van Gnubbern was responsible," she began unconvincingly. "Remember, Kuzno has been here for *exactly* sixteen years—he showed up, then Silverman died. The guy killed by the deer was Kuzno's postdoc. He had known grudges against both of you for trying to change the department.

"And finally," she concluded with a conspiratorial glance round the room, "Walter called me this morning and said that Kuzno had something in his writing pen that was very dangerous. I thought you would have a mass spectrometer to check it out."

"Waddles Jr. has a mass spec," said Lou.

Lori whirled around and stared at him. They were just manipulating her.

But she was so easily manipulated. All it took was some mention of chemical analysis, and a funny-looking pen, and she was running off with them to the lab. Never mind that she wouldn't have minded seeing the whole university burn to the ground, she still couldn't resist the lure of the "poison" pen. Abby's hatred of scientists seemed to have volatilized like a low-molecular-weight solvent, and she followed Lori across campus babbling about gas chromatography-mass spectrometry and how it could identify any toxin in the world.

Grandpa Waddles wasn't in his lab, but Lori had a running invite to use any of his instruments. She started with the mass spec, breaking open the pen and extracting its dark blue contents, wearing gloves only because Abby insisted. Everything she did she noted carefully in the latest of the Waddles Jr. notebooks, arranged in perfect order over the benchtop back to 1975, the year he was hired. Back in the day, Grandpa Waddles had been Lori's favorite professor. He made every class seem like a voyage of discovery into the secret life of atoms and molecules.

Lou and Abby babbled absurdly as Lori worked, urging her to identify the peaks almost before they came spitting out of the old, Internet-unfriendly instruments.

Lori almost threw up when she saw they were holding hands. What the hell had gone on in Denver? she wondered, taking the rest of the ink to the back of the lab so she wouldn't have to see the revolting spectacle.

The ICP-MS gave the elemental analysis, and she also did an absorption spectrum and visible Raman. All of these tests led to a single, inescapable conclusion.

The pen was a gel pen.

Pasting the graphs carefully into the Waddles notebooks, she explained to Lou and Abby, "There is a mixture of three solvents of different boiling points, including butyl alcohol and the butyl ether of ethylene glycol. There is some zinc. And then a cyanine dye that makes up about half a percent of the compound."

"Cyanine?" Abby wondered. "Sounds like cyanide. Is it dangerous?"

Lori and Lou shook their heads at once. "We use cyanine dyes all the time in the lab to label things," said Lou. "Is there anything special about the pen?"

"Well, I'm sure it flowed freely and smoothly and was a joy to write with," Lori snorted, stripping off her gloves and lobbing them at the trash. "In fact, we could test that, there's plenty of ink left."

Abby looked completely baffled. "But then why—?"

Her question was cut short by the out-of-breath, door-slamming, screaming appearance of the youngest of the Waddles clan. "Grandpa?" he called out desperately.

"Do I look like your grandpa?" Lori wanted to know.

Walter seemed incapable of words. His mouth opened and closed several times and his arms waved, but none of this appeared to be under conscious control. "Tripp..." he squeaked.

"Walter," said Abby with great patience, "you have to expel air when you speak."

"Tripp, from the LEPERLab," Walter managed at least, his breath ragged. "He put a package on the FedEx truck. We're all sure it's a bomb."

"Who did you say put a bomb on a truck?" Abby moved towards Walter Waddles IV, cornering him.

"It's Ellis D. Tripp." Walter went and leaned against a lab bench, staggering a bit as if his knees had gone weak. "The engineering colony manager at the LEPERLab. But it's too late to do anything."

Lori, Lou, and Abby all stared at him, like three cats examining a fallen baby bird. No one said anything, and after a moment Walter began to talk.

"My dad took the fake 'bait' proposal and made sure all the LEPERs knew you were really submitting after all. Then he brought it down to me and I took it to the FedEx just before the 1:15 truck. But apparently Tripp had been there just before me, and the Bubo spies didn't recognize him." He stumbled over the words, seemed confused, and added, "Or maybe they were just watching for Kuzno? Anyway, they said everything was fine, and the bait went out. But then my dad went back to work and found out that Tripp had left just before me—sneaked out while Dad was taking me the box. Dad then rushed down to the FedEx and showed the Buboes a picture of Tripp, and they realized he'd been there, wearing some kind of huge raincoat and umbrella to hide himself. They tried to stop the truck, but it was already too late."

"Well for God's sake, call the cops!" yelled Lou.

"Don't be an idiot," Lori snapped. "They'd just call him a Bubo and threaten to arrest him."

"That's exactly what happened," Walter admitted, with a scared giggle. "They said they'd had enough of our troublemaking, and asked if I'd like to spend a night in the Bubo tank like my boss."

"If the cops don't listen to you, we have to find another way to stop the truck," Lou interrupted before Walter could finish. "Call in a bomb threat to the airport! They'll tear the place apart."

"Ben Gerson promised to do that," said Walter. "He also said he'd try to stop traffic, but..."

"You believe him? Ben Gerson is flakier than a good croissant!" Lou rummaged around in his bag for a moment, finally extracting his cell phone. "We're just talking and someone's life could be in danger! I'll do it myself." He dialed three numbers—they all knew which ones.

The others stayed silent out of excitement, or embarrassment, or maybe a bit of both. Walter looked hopeful, but Lori just wanted to see Malibu-boy learn what dumbshits cops were.

"Yes, a FedEx truck," Lou explained patiently. "Yes, of course...No, no I haven't. Why? WHAT? Oh. Yes, of course. Thank you." He stared at the phone for a moment before closing it. After a very long pause in which no one spoke, he said, "They already know. Apparently the bomb went off on the freeway about fifteen minutes ago."

"So there *was* a bomb…" breathed Walter.

"How could the Buboes fail?" Lou sounded furious.

"Because they're just kids." Lori took off her lab coat and hung it up, then replaced the Waddles notebooks carefully on their shelves as she spoke. "We can't expect them to understand evil. We should have given up this project the instant Marybeth died."

Abby turned away from Walter and stood beside Lou, gripping his shoulder. "We were busy chasing the wrong leads. We thought it was Kuzno, or van Gnubbern…"

Deep down, where she didn't dare to trust it, a tiny flicker of hope sprang up in Lori's heart. "So maybe it wasn't van Gnub—"

"Lab coats! Gloves!" Grandpa Waddles burst in, pushing them all out of the way. "What are you all doing here?"

"Your grandson told us Kuzno's pen was dangerous!" Abby accused.

Walter IV turned bright pink. "Well, maybe I exaggerated a little. I wanted you to test it."

"So I tested it," said Lori. "It's a gel pen. And so?" All of a sudden she thought of something. "Dr. Waddles, what will zinc chloride do to cyanine dyes?"

"Decolorize them, of course," said Waddles Jr. "Now out of here, all of you. You have some friends waiting in the physics department."

"But the bomb?" Lori wondered.

"Well, the bomb," said Grandpa Waddles slowly, not seeming to notice the others hopping with impatience. "No harm done. I must say I had the time of my life—it was like being a Bubo again. Go back to your office and you'll see what I mean."

Abby and Lori glanced at each other then sprinted out the door, with Baby Waddles hot on their heels like a badly imprinted duckling. Lou followed more slowly, clutching his cell phone as if it would tell him something. It was raining hard, making Lori think of the old physics problem: do you get wetter if you run in the rain than if you walk slowly?

Reaching the physics building, she dashed inside and immediately damned Grandpa Waddles to the depths of hell. The place was swarming with police. There were two cops right at the entrance, and she passed a third in the stairwell, coming down as she was going up.

She was out of breath from stairs and the beginning of panic when she reached her office—only to find that there was a cop there, too. Not just a cop: a cop, Radhika, and Wigbert van Gnubbern.

THIRTY-SIX: DISAPPEARING ACTS

WELL, WELL," VAN GNUBBERN was chuckling, "I hope that clears everything up." He shook the cop's hand.

Lori pressed herself against the wall to let the policeman slip out the door, and Abby and Walter slip in. They all gaped in utter confusion as Radhika and Wigbert collapsed on each other's shoulders, dissolving into nervous titters.

"Oh!" Radhika gasped. "I was sure we were going to get busted for what we did!"

"Oh, no, quite unlikely," Wigbert replied, but he looked mighty relieved, mopping his forehead with a tissue from Lori's desk. "The police just wanted to clear up a little misunderstanding from yesterday. I doubt we'll be in any trouble for our antics; after all, we saved at least one life."

Lori looked at each of them in turn—her childhood hero and the only person who had ever loved her—and prayed they would give a reasonable explanation.

Radi was wearing nothing but a lime-green camisole, a pair of board shorts, and her eternal rubber sandals—she probably owned no other footwear down there in Darwin. She was soaked and shivering but looked tremendous, strong and tanned and without a single white hair in her frizzy chocolate-brown curls. Her hair was longer than Lori had ever seen it, down past her shoulders, and her unlined face looked the same as the day they had met seventeen years before. Lori thought her heart would break.

"I got here yesterday evening, expecting to find all of you in your offices," Radi began. She suddenly seemed to realize she held a coil of copper wire, and turned to place it carefully on the desk. "But all I found was a soggy man in lederhosen who appeared hysterical."

"That would be me," said van Gnubbern unnecessarily. "I'm afraid I frightened Carol Dugoni on the trail, and was forced to walk back here in the rain, worrying that I would miss the excitement surrounding the false proposal."

"We stayed discreet and watched the action," Radi continued. "It became clear pretty quickly that the effort was disorganized, and that all the key players were unavailable for one reason or another."

"I was in Denver," said Abby.

"I was in jail," added Lori.

"Right. And Wiggy here asked me when you'd *last* spent a night in the Bubo tank, which gave me a genius idea." Radi picked up the copper wire and waved it meaningfully.

"Oh no," Lori wondered suspiciously. "You didn't—?"

"—Use railroad tracks to broadcast a warning on all radio frequencies? Yes, we did." Radi chuckled fondly. "How could I forget the only real crime you ever committed?"

She was so familiar and sweet and warm that Lori wanted to cry. She suddenly realized that she had given up so much for such a small amount of success, only to find that it wasn't really success at all. The "best department in the world" was scraping the barrel because everyone they hired tended to die suddenly.

"So we saved the driver's life and didn't even go to jail for it," concluded van Gnubbern, who didn't seem to mind at all being called "Wiggy."

Everyone still seemed incapable of response. Finally Walter echoed himself, "So there *was* a bomb…"

"Yes, there was," Radi affirmed. "But we warned the driver with the railroad-tracks radio transmission and it just exploded in the empty truck."

Wigbert van Gnubbern slowly, deliberately looked at his watch. "So now that the bad guys are in jail, you have some work to do. There are still two hours and fifteen minutes before the last FedEx truck."

This should have been good news, but Lori was exhausted. The thought of printing all those color pages, collating them, and then running to the FedEx suddenly seemed overwhelming.

Abby, on the other hand, was ready to rumble. "Hear that, Barrow? To work!" she commanded, prodding Lori in the back. "Where on Earth is Lou?"

Going towards Lou's office, they heard heaving and thumping noises and all of them froze.

Walter burst through the door first, playing the conquering hero, and when he let out a squeal of relieved laughter the others followed.

Lou's left hand and a part of his forearm were completely covered in cyan ink. The front of his new printer yawned open and the poor machine appeared to be gasping its last.

On the table in front of him were massive stacks of paper. "I heard what I needed to hear, and decided to finish the printing while you all gabbed," he explained sheepishly. "But there was to be something wrong with the cartridge, and when I tried to replace it, it exploded."

"Theorists should not touch tools," Lori snorted. "You can wash it off with ethan—" the word stopped in her throat as suddenly she realized the implications of Grandpa Waddles's data. "Ink!" she yelled, turning to Abby. "Kuzno's ink!"

"What about it?"

"It contains a bunch of solvents that evaporate at different rates, and zinc chloride, which Dr. Waddles said will decolorize dyes. As the solvents evaporate, the zinc compound reacts with the cyanine dye. It's *disappearing* ink! But not the usual Bubo kind—it's a very clever formula that will no doubt disappear at a precisely calculated rate."

"Kuzno tried to sign our proposal with disappearing ink?" said Lou. He handed the broken cartridge to Walter, who fumbled it like a football.

"But I interrupted him," said Abby.

"Right." The corner of Lou's mouth twitched as he recalled what had no doubt been a ridiculous scene. "Maybe that's why he insisted upon using his private printer. Could the ink require special paper?"

"It might," Lori agreed, making a mental note to get the recipe from Grandpa Waddles.

"He's not going to go to jail for that, though, is he?" Lou sounded disappointed.

"I kind of doubt it," Abby replied, smirking.

"But it's something I would do," Lori admitted. "It certainly isn't murder." Actually kind of funny, she thought with the beginnings of reluctant admiration.

"Not a killer, just a butthead," Abby agreed.

"Could have fooled me," Lori admitted. "But then, I spent a whole night and half a day thinking it was Dr. van Gnubbern who'd killed people."

"I've never killed anyone in my life, and don't intend to try," Wigbert promised.

"So then…" Lou looked exhausted and bewildered. He spoke as if the words caused him pain. "Who exactly was it, then?"

"It was Ellis D. Tripp," said Radi and Walter together—then the latter squealed with glee that he had been right.

"The engineering colony manager at the LEPERLab," Walter added by way of explanation. "The safety Nazi who came up with the killer deer."

"So are we going to kill him?" Lou persisted in the same voice.

"The State of California will do that for us," Radi declared confidently. "In fact, you can see him get Tased on the evening news. When we're done here, we can go to Bubo House and watch the show."

"I think we're almost done here." Lou peeked out over the mountains of paper, gesturing at Lori with a pink page. "Principal Investigator, you need to sign this. There's one more page that mentions Rose that we need to replace—and I think it looks pretty good in magenta, don't you?"

THIRTY-SEVEN: NOT WHEN THE NIGHT IS DARKEST

FOUR HUNDRED AND SIX dollars and seventy-eight cents at the FedEx, and it was over. All Lou wanted to do was take a long, hot shower and then go to bed and pull the blankets over his head. But the phone would not stop ringing, interrupting the instant he turned on the water, continuing to beep and ramble as he shook down the shampoo bottle for the last remaining drops.

He didn't want to go to Pasteur House to watch Bubo videos, but he did have to call Barrow to assure her that the proposals were on a new, bomb-free truck. Then when Abby rang for the third time, he figured he'd better let her know he was alive.

To his surprise, she asked him to come over. It was raining, and he was exhausted, but he knew that nothing awaited in the bedroom but another night of horrified insomnia. Abby seemed to understand that, for which he was vaguely grateful, and spent some time looking around to see if he had anything that would serve as a Christmas present for her.

She lived only a couple of blocks away, but in a fancy apartment building nothing like the squalor of Postdoc and Visitor Housing. He had never had a guest over here, and never would, unless maybe it was someone like Barrow who wouldn't notice. The place was repulsive, and even the Housing Office hadn't pretended otherwise, saying it was the "most historic" unit—which probably meant Einstein had once upchucked in the corner. Most of the appliances, paintings, and books he'd brought over when he moved out of his ex's place had never been unpacked; a plump spider hung between the two largest boxes. The old couch had a few sketchy stains and sagged in the middle in an obvious pattern of dog. It looked like the apartment of someone who had died months before, probably of scurvy.

In contrast, Abby lived in luxury, though a rather overdone and cheesy version of it that was somehow pitiful. There was a doorman, chandeliers, and ornate wooden carvings in the walls, and it was above all perfectly accessible, but it was still just an apartment building and it made Lou sad.

Abby had clearly spent her time showering, smelling nice, and braiding her hair. She answered the door in a cherry-patterned party dress (how Freudian *was* that?) and quickly gave the tour of her seventeenth-floor one-bedroom. It was well laid out, with a view of the foothills, and everything was in good taste if not particularly clean. She apologized for the bare Christmas tree propped against the wall and the needles all over the floor, and the fish tank without any fish that smelled of recent floating tragedy. Everything was light-colored: the sheepskin rug, the linen couch and matching drapes, the cute little pine storage cubbyholes, and the upright piano. There was a ficus in a pot attached to one end of the couch, and it was only after wondering how it possibly got enough light that Lou realized it was fake. There were also stuffed animals, books, and papers and documents scattered everywhere.

She asked if he wanted a drink, and came back from the kitchen with two glasses of a cheap red wine so vile that Lou wouldn't use it to decolorize stains. He took a polite mini-sip and set it under the ficus. "Why don't we finish your Christmas tree?" he suggested, handing her his present, which he'd wrapped in a maroon bag from the STI bookstore.

"Oh, sure." She took the box but didn't seem all that enthused, mainly because the poor blue spruce was almost dead. She filled the tray underneath anyway, and tugged a box of decorations out from under the couch. Last year's tinsel, some bulbs, homemade ornaments he thought she might have made as a little kid until he saw the themes on some of them.

"Grad B = 0?" he demanded, laughing. "Even *I* don't have Maxwell's equations on my Christmas tree."

"Oh, honestly." She snatched it away. "That must have been Lori. We always had parties together, you know, back in first year. Once we had an ornament-making party." She gazed back and forth between the ornament and the tree, as if trying to decide what it deserved, and finally graced it with a central location.

That was even more symbolic than the cherries, Lou thought, and hung bulbs and slung tinsel for a few minutes until the tone of Abby's voice made him pause.

"So," she began. "…Are you leaving?"

"Why?" he asked, alarmed. "Do you think I need to?"

"I don't want you to," she blurted in the same strange voice.

Lou was confused. He had been expecting terrible tales of killers in upper management. Maybe he was just too tired to make sense of anything. "Do you think we finally found the right bad guy?" he wondered at last.

"It's almost obvious in retrospect, isn't it?" Abby grumbled. "Tripp pushed Silverman off the mountain, and then he was able to take over two billion dollars a year of funding. Technically STI runs the LEPERLab, but there was no one here with the desire or status to oppose him."

"Only Rose," Lou prompted.

"Professor Rose created the Science Colony," Abby explained, fiddling with a branch of the tree and making more needles fall. "Immediately afterwards, Tripp tore out all the rosebushes at the LEPERLab, claiming they were 'dangerous.' At first Rose was going to get Kuzno to run the colony, but he realized that wouldn't work—so he hired Walter Waddles III. Tripp knew what Rose and Waddles were up to, of course. If the Science Colony and STI could get the NASA money for the big projects, like the ones at the South Pole, then his regime would come to an end."

"So anyone Rose recruited who was interested in the South Pole had to die," concluded Lou.

"So it seems."

"He can't possibly have suspected. He would have at least warned us to watch out."

"I don't suppose we'll ever know, now that he's gone."

"What?" He tried to stay calm, but belied his emotion by squeezing too hard on the bulb he was holding, which shattered into thousands of green-and-silver fragments. "What happened to Solomon Rose?"

"Nothing." Abby gave a sarcastic laugh. "He's retired as of three hours ago, and on his way to Honolulu."

"Oh." Lou looked stupidly at the broken ornament, shards twinkling in the bad light.

"Stay still!" Abby commanded. She ran to the closet where she took out a small hand-held vacuum with a funny nozzle like a tapeworm's mouth. She sucked the fragments off his hand and the carpet, not looking at his face and making an exaggerated effort not to touch his pants.

"It's OK to touch me, you know," said Lou.

"Oh! I'm sorry...I wasn't sure." Abby cautiously put the vacuum onto his leg.

"I know. It freaks me out too, not knowing where my feet are unless I look at them." He sighed, barely speaking loudly enough to be heard over the appliance. "I can't believe that Rose is really evil enough to set Lori and me up to be killed—more than once. He was probably naïve and in denial the way I was. After all, if I hadn't been so clueless, I could have saved Marybeth."

Abby's attempt to use the tiny vacuum on pine needles ended in a sputtering mechanical cough, and she threw it to the ground. "It's worse than the Blue Code of Silence," she raged. "No one wanted you to know what was going on because they just wanted you to keep working. No one cared about Marybeth because she wasn't one of the brilliant ones."

He started to say something, then stopped because no argument was possible. "Marybeth was actually very talented," he managed.

"That's even worse!"

"I suppose it is." He removed the last three strands of tinsel from the package and hung them, one by one, on the tree. "Why don't you open your present?"

She seemed surprised, but reached for the box and tore away the maroon wrapping—then dropped the contents as if they were sticky and gross. Her face was bewildered, even hurt. "What the…?"

He realized, a bit too late, that the blind incestuous cannibal dwarves might have sent the wrong message. "It's a movie," he explained. "Marybeth's favorite French comedy. I scoured Paris for that film." Suddenly it all seemed comic somehow, and he laughed. "Marybeth loved B movies. She knew them all by heart. I think her crazy stories were just scenes from old films she was reciting, and it never bothered me at all."

"She was a freak."

"We're all freaks."

Abby nudged the vacuum out of the way and went to sit on the pale couch, sinking deeply into the soft cushions. Lou made a mental note to fear that couch. "I shouldn't tell you this…but Marybeth had been addicted to drugs for years. Prescription drugs, painkillers, anything she could get."

"No big surprise," he responded. "I knew someone was stealing my pills. I didn't really need them, so I never said anything. I never even filled most of the prescriptions."

"That's not the awful part." Abby put her face in her hands. "She *wasn't* the one stealing them. It was Dim Bulb and Tripp. Tripp once got busted at the pharmacy with your prescriptions and your driver's license, trying to claim he was you. Our office had to cover it up, but none of us ever made the connection."

"Are you saying that he was controlling Marybeth?" Lou squinted at her, but she wasn't looking at him. "Trying to make her hurt people by sabotaging things, maybe, like the freezer door? And when she failed, he whacked her." He remembered Barrow's rant about the curlicued M, so unlike Marybeth's block letters. "I bet he forged the incident report. Marybeth must have refused to sign it."

"She probably suspected." Abby stared down at her feet, planted in front of the couch. For someone six feet tall, she had very tiny ones, with high arches and little nails painted red. "Maybe she tried to stand up to him. Poor girl."

"And apparently he tried to kill Dim Bulb twice," Lou continued. "The first time Dimmy lived, and Tripp tried to silence him with a promotion, but it must not have been enough because he tried again. How could he get away with this?"

"He hid his tracks well," Abby scowled. "You can cover a lot under the guise of the Safety Office. It all fits—Tripp was confiscating the chemicals at the LEPERLab so he could use them to build bombs without any of the materials ever being traced to him. Brilliant, really."

"*Tabarnak.* If your goal was to make me afraid to go home tonight, you've succeeded." Lou clenched his hands together and pressed them against a sudden sharp pain in his belly.

Abby jumped up. "Are you hungry?"

"Hungry?" he echoed, the thought of food so far away that it took him a long moment to realize the pain came from a stomach that had seen nothing since toast and coffee at 7 a.m. Mountain Time.

"I'll make us some grilled cheese," Abby declared, marching into the kitchen.

The kitchen was white. So were the bread and the cheddar. Rain pelted against the small window, making Lou think of Minnesota and snow, and a large pale family around a large pale table piled with pale food, bowing their heads for grace. "Are you going home to your family for Christmas?" he asked, which couldn't possibly be interpreted as an invitation to anything.

"Oh, lord no," Abby spat with surprising vehemence. "It's cold out there, and they all treat me like a slut since the divorce." She banged a pot onto the stove and reached for a can of tomato soup.

So far Barrow was ten for ten in her description of Minnesotans, but somehow Lou found himself liking Abby anyway...hopefully not just because they shared the dubious distinction of having been shot at by deranged physicists.

She slid the sandwiches onto plates, served the soup, and poured them each a glass of chocolate milk. Lou felt as if he were back in nursery school, but he ate without complaining. The bland food was about all he could endure at the moment, anyway, and even it tasted like sawdust.

"What are you doing for Christmas?" Abby wondered.

"Calling NASA headquarters," Lou replied promptly.

"Oh, right." She was suddenly businesslike. "You want to make sure your proposal is the only one with your names on it, if you know what I mean."

"I sure do. Then I suppose I'll hang out at my parents' and take care of the horses while they're in France for the holidays."

To his surprise, Abby moaned, "Oooh, I forgot you had horses! That's what I miss most about the farm."

"You're welcome to join me," he offered, "if you don't mind the wet and the cold and the mud."

"Are you kidding? I still have my overalls and rubber boots."

That was enough for tonight, he thought, thinking he should quit before he said something that would end up on the Pasteur House web site. "I'm going to stay at STI," he decided after finishing the sandwich. "If we win this thing, we'll run the place. And no one else would hire me—you heard them all, I was completely unqualified for this position to begin with, and now I've done sweet fuck-all for the past two years."

"That's hardly your fault," Abby objected.

"In this business, it doesn't matter. And if Kuzno quits, we'll have managed to purge all the villains."

"Except Lori and Wigbert," Abby reminded him, but even she appeared to be laughing now. She cleared away the dishes, went back into the living room, and sat at the piano. There was a book of carols propped up there, and she flipped through it, playing a few bars here and there.

"Roger used to tell us something funny," she remarked after a while, plinking out the first notes of *Minuit Chrétien*. "He said the Quebecois Catholics believed that if you weren't in church on Christmas Eve, and you looked out the window, you'd see leaves and flowers and be forever accursed."

It wasn't quite Christmas Eve, and it had been three generations since any member of Lou's family had been to church. But he figured it wouldn't be a bad idea to draw the shades and sing along with her—after all, they needed all the luck they could get.

THIRTY-EIGHT: LET'S LICK THE LEPERS

PASTEUR HOUSE WAS DRAMATIC in the night and the rain. A rickety wooden staircase led up among the branches of three large olive trees, and the lights of the common room shone through as if the house were perched in the treetops. Triumphant laughter issued from the open windows.

"Wow," Radi breathed.

"To soothe the beasts within," Lori explained, leading the way up the slimy stairs.

Once inside they realized how wet and freezing they were. They stood dripping for a few seconds, and then a parade of Buboes appeared—one with maroon towels, the next with cups of tea, the third with a bag of popcorn and a blanket. The fourth brought Lori her suitcase, and she realized that maybe, just maybe, she would make it home tonight.

Various Buboes arranged themselves on the shag rug in front of the thirteen-inch TV, drinks and snacks in hand. One of them, shrouded in covers, was sunk deeply into a beanbag chair with a beer. Heads wrapped in towels and cuddled under the blanket, Lori and Radi took their spot of honor just in front of the screen.

They could see the flames and fire trucks before the newscaster's voice began. "An unorthodox and illegal warning saved the life of a truck driver on the Pasadena Freeway this evening," it began, and Lori scooted closer to see the delivery van gutted by fire, a huge hole blown in one side.

"Wiggy and I were afraid to tell anyone what we were planning," Radi admitted. "Especially Waddles III. He might have been on our side, but interfering with radio communications is a felony, and he's…"

"He's a LEPER," boomed a voice from behind them.

They jumped and turned around, finding that the "Bubo" in the beanbag chair was a highly amused Ben Gerson. "Isn't it a Bubo rule to check under the blanket for spies?" he wondered, with a wink at Lori and Radi.

Lori inched away from Radi, embarrassed to be caught snuggling. "Ben! What are you doing here?"

"Looking for answers, of course. This morning your IP lawyer showed up at my house demanding a signature, then zoomed off without explanation. A bit later your graduate student called and told me to block traffic, and next I know there's a bomb on the news. I want the story." He gestured to the Buboes with an empty beer can, and they rushed over with a fresh one and a bag of popcorn.

"We'll just let that graduate student tell you, then, because I don't know any more than you do. I'm assuming you mean Walter?"

"Did I hear my name?" A blond head poked into the common room. Walter Waddles IV looked so longingly at Lori's empty popcorn bag that a Bubo finally brought him one of his own. "I've just been with my dad, but I still don't understand everything," he admitted, digging into the popcorn like a starving man.

They all turned toward the TV as the Buboes hooted. An image flickered on the TV of Tripp being arrested in his home in the foothills, followed quickly by a landslide warning and a bit of Christmas cheer. It was less than informative.

"The rest of us don't understand *any*thing," said Lori. "Tell us about your dad. Why did he become a LEPER? To oppose Tripp?"

"No one could oppose Tripp," Walter muttered through his mouthful, volunteering nothing more until Ben rose from his seat and gestured for him to speak. Walter's voice grew bitter as he described how his father and others had been helpless to prevent the implementation of LEPER policies to investigate the employees, and to fire them for visiting suspect websites, drinking alcohol on lab, or making mistakes on their time cards.

During his tirade, Buboes were busy all around them—removing the TV, setting up a projection screen and some speakers, occasionally rubbing their hands and cackling.

"The policies were bad enough on their own," Walter continued, paying no attention to the students around him, "but Tripp was apparently a racist, too." He described the lawsuits he'd heard about during in the thirteen years that Tripp was colony manager. Some were just silly, like a black female speaker being sent away because she "didn't look like a STI professor," but others were much scarier: drivers and pedestrians chased by armed guards, people locked in "interrogation" rooms for imaginary infractions of what they called the LEPERLaws, and of course the famous episode of the killer deer. When the lawsuits became too expensive even for the LEPERLab, Tripp made up the list of VIPs that Lori had seen on their visit. This had been passed around to all the guards and managers to make sure that those they abused weren't famous enough to fight back.

Perhaps most surreal of all, the mere mention of the incidents could bring punishment, and whole ranks of managers were hired to pretend that none of it was happening. Lori wondered if it was all of this and not the Vomit Comet that had destroyed her student's dreams of being an astronaut.

Even Ben, who would rather break rocks in Siberia than be a LEPER, looked surprised. "It was measurably less bad in the Science Colony. We weren't actually physically abused."

The Buboes decided this was time to make their move. They stepped in between Lori and Ben and between Radi and Walter, clapping their hands. Walter slunk off to the back of the room and sat on a stuffed purple cube, scrounging in his popcorn bag for the last remaining kernels.

"We have a show for you, eh," said a tall redhead who could have been Canadian. "I hope you didn't think you came all the way here for a silly clip on the television."

As he spoke, the video began. It showed an overdone foothills neighborhood, speckled with mini-mansions. Videotaping Buboes slunk through the perfectly manicured landscaping, knocked on a door, then ran.

Ellis D. Tripp came out, glanced around, and shouted, "I see you!"

"Hands up!" yelled a Bubo in a phony, too-young voice. "You're under arrest!"

"You kids get offa my property!" bellowed the LEPER.

But the Buboes' timing was nearly perfect. Tripp had barely finished shouting when a real cop car appeared, and a real officer shouted at him to keep his hands visible.

"I will personally see you expelled—" Tripp bellowed, taking a step towards the cop.

So they Tased him.

He fell to the ground, shrieking as they Tased him again, kicking his head and gut as they rolled him over to cuff him.

The Buboes played the clip over and over again: "expelled—" ZAP! "Aaaah!", "expelled—" ZAP! "Aaaah!" until Lori couldn't stand it any more.

She hadn't known Tripp, and nothing that happened to him would undo any of the horror of the past decade and a half. "All right, kids, that's enough," she grumbled.

"One more time!" pleaded Ben.

They obliged, of course. "You won't get us expelled, will you, Dr. Barrow?" asked the redhead.

"Of course not. I'm just surprised the cops didn't catch you."

"Should've seen me sprint just after that scene," he admitted. "The video ends there, I'm afraid."

Lori was almost relieved. The last thing they needed was more violence. "So what about Kuzno?" she asked to change the subject. "He's been so evil all term—then it turns out the worst thing he's done is to try to sign our proposal in disappearing ink?"

"Well, not the worst thing. He's still a child molester." Walter got up from the uncomfortable-looking cube and moved over to the VCR, playing the Taser scene one more time for his own personal enjoyment.

Ben let him wallow in it, then pursued, "I imagine Kuzno was traded down to campus to weaken the department, keep it closed and provincial. When Rose tried to recruit me here after I quit the LEPERLab, Kuzno said I couldn't be hired on campus because I wasn't a string theorist."

"That may be part of it," Walter agreed. "The LEPERs only agreed to take my dad if the department took Kuzno. It also may just have been to get rid of Kuzno, who's a pain in the ass on all counts. But I have to say, in retrospect, Kuzno was on our side—he was calling attention to the reign of terror. He was *furious* that the guard let his postdoc die, and the whole business with the killer deer was designed to cover that up. LEPERs could be fired if they said anything or anyone besides deer was involved. Kuzno, of course, would not be silent and apparently at one point called the security guards 'murderers' in public."

"Wow," Lori breathed. "That doesn't sound like him."

"Maybe the guy was a great postdoc," suggested Ben, chuckling.

"Then why did Kuzno let Rose hire Lou and me?" Lori wondered. "Unless he knew we were doomed to die, of course."

"I'm sure he just figured you were too young and naïve to oppose him," replied Ben, wadding up his empty popcorn bag. "The LEPERs thought they could bend me to their will, and they were wrong. I'm just grateful to be here in one piece."

Walter swallowed nervously, then turned around and let his backpack slip from his shoulders. "There's some more," he admitted. "Dr. Barrow… these are yours."

When Walter made no further movement, Lori stepped forward and peered inside the pack. The recording unit for her mini video cameras was there—minus the cameras, but that didn't matter. All she needed to do was plug the recorder into the TV and see what was there.

A long, cold shiver ran from her toes to the top of her head. "How did you get this?" she whispered.

"My dad," Walter whispered back. "He got it from Tripp's office just before all hell broke loose."

"I've been asking you to look for this for *weeks*. If we'd known it was in Tripp's office—"

"I know," Walter groaned. "But Dad wouldn't take me seriously until this afternoon. It is what I think it is, right?"

"Yes. It's a recorder that took videos from four tiny cameras placed all around Carol's lab. Did you look at any of the recordings?"

He shook his head violently. "We were afraid to."

Lori packed the recorder back into the bag and zipped it. "This is evidence. You need to take it directly to the cops."

The Buboes booed. Walter and Ben objected loudly.

"I actually think we need to look at the videos," Radi argued. "Because what if...?"

"What if what?" Lori demanded. "...What if it was Wigbert all along?"

No one acknowledged her question, but she allowed herself to be out-voted against her better judgement. Certainly anyone, tenured or not, could be fired for subjecting a roomful of undergraduates to a snuff film.

The disks were filled with snapshots of Carol's electron microscopy lab from all different angles, motion-triggered and date- and time-stamped. One day showed Carol sitting there reading journal articles. Once Dim Bulb came in, and she stuck her tongue out at him as he left.

The next day Dim Bulb was by himself, going behind the microscope. He seemed to have something in his hands—a cord.

When Tripp entered the room in the next frame, the audience grew very quiet. A she-Bubo shielded her head with a towel, and Walter responded by covering his eyes. So did Ben—but he was peeking.

There was no sound. They all saw Tripp talking to Dimmy, seeming calm. Then Tripp looked up, saw one of the cameras, and was furious. He knocked it down, eliminating the view of his face, but erasing none of the recordings since the recorder still sat safely on another shelf. They saw him jump and holler a bit, and then the image changed.

Dim Bulb was still there. Unmistakably alive. Still playing with his cord. And in the next panel. And the next. Once he had bared a long blue nail to scratch a zit at the back of his neck.

And then, just as certainly, he was dead...stretched out on the floor with the electrical cord still in his hands.

"Wait!" Lori yelled.

"What!" Ben added.

"It looks as if Dimmy died by accident," said a Bubo, unnecessarily.

"Damn you for throwing us off the trail!" squeaked Walter, shaking his fist at the frozen image of Dim Bulb on the screen. "Could Tripp have sneaked back in between frames?"

"I suppose so," Lori replied doubtfully, "but we don't have any evidence." Relieved that the contents at least hadn't corrupted the youth, she went to make sure they'd seen everything, and then turned the video off.

Walter seemed massively relieved, too. Clearly he had been terrified to see what was on the recorder. "Shall I take this to the police, now, Dr. Barrow?"

"If you think they'll take it from you without calling you a Bubo, then yes." Lori handed him the device. "…I don't suppose we'll ever know everything," she concluded, disappointed.

"I'm more confused than when I arrived," admitted Walter. He gathered up the materials and prepared to leave—Lori stopped him at the door and confiscated the videos to watch again later, still bothered.

"Find Rose, then you'll know everything. The old man skipped town before we could kick his ass." Ben put his hands on his knees and got to his feet, none too steadily. "Now, would you ladies like a ride home?"

Lori looked at the circle of beer cans around the beanbag. "Er, better to let me drive, Ben," she suggested. "Or else we could all spend one more night here in Bubo House."

The Buboes cheered at that, and one dutiful soul came to lead Ben off towards an empty dorm. The she-Bubo who shared Lori's room promised to sleep in the common room, leaving her and Radi and the unpacked suitcase alone at last.

"Oh boy!" said Radi. "Bunkbeds!"

Lori didn't want to sleep in bunkbeds. She wanted to go home, unpack her dirty clothes, and have enough room to tell Radi that it was silly to sleep on the couch. She sat down on the bottom bunk and sniffled, but found she was incapable of actual tears.

Radi noticed, at least, and sat next to her. "Are you OK?"

"No," Lori replied, staring at a spot on the carpet that looked suspiciously like scrubbed blood. "I gave up everything else in life to get where I am, and they didn't even really want to hire me. I was just cannon fodder." She took a deep, shuddering breath. "I'm so alone. No one loves me."

Radi put her arm around her. There was a faint, long scar along the underside of her arm—no doubt the souvenir of some horrid Australian jellyfish. "I do. You know I do, and I always will."

"But you're far, far away."

"Not so far as all that, if I move to Honolulu. Rose wants me to help him start a company."

Lori sprang up, remembered the bunkbed just in time, and whacked her head only a little. "Not that madman!"

Radi seemed to remember something, unzipped her fanny pack and rummaged around in what seemed to be an infinite supply of odd things. Then she handed Lori a letter in a small envelope, addressed in a shaky old hand to her and Lou. "He gave this to me this morning," she admitted, trying to smooth out the fold down the center. "Just before I came to get you."

Lori took the envelope and stuffed it under the mattress. She didn't want to see the old man's excuses—not now, maybe not ever. She just wanted to stay here with Radi and pretend she never had to go back to work. Wrapping her arm around Radi's waist (how did she get obliques like that?), she murmured, "Thanks for coming out here."

"It's no problem, once you get past the kangaroo ride through the outback." Radi shivered, planted a chilly kiss on top of Lori's head. "I'm going to take a hot bath, and then we can figure out if there's a way to survive without freezing in a cold place or being surrounded by maniacs."

Lori nodded mutely, watching Radi go off and hearing her footsteps go first the wrong way, then the right way towards the Bubo communal shower. Unable to be alone with her curiosity for more than a few seconds, she tugged out Rose's letter and began to read.

> Dear friends and colleagues,
>
> This is difficult but it must be said. I imagine that you are thinking that I have fled. Indeed I have, but not from your disappointment or wrath, as justified as those might be. When Walter Waddles (pl.) told me of the concerted hunt for a departmental killer, I feared for my life and for that of my wife, Chava, who is recovering from heart surgery. Rather than appeal to the police, we decided to take our retirement several days early.
>
> Louis, you probably don't know or recall all of the details of what happened the day he attempted to kill you. All I will say here is that I am now fully convinced the murderer tried to kill me that day as well, and that only chance kept him from succeeding. While I realize that my apology

will in no way make up for all you have lost, please believe me when I say that I knew nothing until this very moment. I am sure that we will meet again someday, and I will tell you the entire story, should you wish to hear it.

We spend our lives fighting ignorance and insisting that it is no excuse, and I am no exception. When my scheming leads to actual bloodshed, it is time to admit I am a senile old fool and take my retirement. I am sure that you both will prove worthy of the principal investigatorship of this and many projects to come. I wish you all the best.

Yours sincerely,

Solomon A. Rose

Professor Emeritus of Physics, Mathematics, and Astronomy

Superior Technological Institute

Los Angeles, California

December 21, 2007

P.S. Let's lick those LEPERS!

THIRTY-NINE: FIVE HUNDRED MILLICOULOMBS OF HAPPINESS

THE CARRYON BURST OPEN when the TSA prodded it, and proposals flew everywhere. Carol had to crawl on her hands and knees to retrieve the loose sheets of paper, being berated for the size of her luggage, completely unable to say "Secret LEPER urgent space business." She was x-rayed, groped, and relieved of her Altoids, toothpaste, and jeweler's screwdriver.

But they finally allowed her to board the plane with all of her paper and no damage except to her already well-battered pride and dignity. She held back tears, wanting desperately to have a drink and a Benadryl but knowing she'd need all her energy and wits once she got to DC. The flight was supposed to get in at six-thirty in the morning California time, or nine-thirty EST, giving her in principle plenty of time to drag the proposals through the terminal, find a taxi, and make it to the government office. But given how everything else had been going, she was sure to encounter delays and other obstacles.

She wasn't being fair. The STI team was even worse off, if her suspicions were right that their proposal was on the truck that exploded. They probably wouldn't get to submit at all.

Carol knew it was mean, but the best way to describe her thoughts in their regard was *Cry me a river.* They could always write another proposal, whereas she was on the track of losing her job and her marriage.

His time on Unclean status had brought out the worst in Bob. He'd become secretive, grumpy, and downright mean to her and everyone else. He had always been—at least Carol had believed he had always been—a sympathetic and kind boss. Now she knew that he had tried to get the people in his group to bear the brunt of the punishment for Kalb's "accidental" death, firing a young guy just because he was in his first six months and so easiest to dismiss. He had stolen Lori's backpack and confiscated Carol's data, getting her into trouble with the management even though his actions couldn't possibly benefit him in any way. It was hard to imagine going back to their ordinary lives after that.

She finally managed to doze a little in her seat, kicking off her shoes and curling up against the window. In economy class it helped to be short. When she woke, she saw bare branches and scattered patches of white, which reminded her that it was almost Christmas and that the East Coast had been hit by a particularly severe cold snap. A "wintry mix" pounded against the airplane wings as they came in for a landing, drops illuminated by the flashing lights, a million tiny comets in an extraterrestrial sky.

There was no point in hurrying out of the plane. She had hours and hours before the due date and could imagine herself dropping the illegal hundred-pound carryon on someone's head and causing a disaster. She watched the other passengers exit in a steady stream, continuous yet discrete like photons, and then asked for help with the bag and lugged it behind her.

Her struggle was not yet over for the day. The taxis moved through the city at a crawl, the Southern drivers unused to anything resembling snow. While she sat there, watching the minutes tick by on her watch, the cabbie turned on the radio. First there was a bunch about the storm, which they called "Snowmageddon." Then something about the layoffs at the local NASA center. Finally, in a voice that sounded somehow smug:

"...In other NASA news, the manager of the Lobo Peak Rocket Laboratory's Engineering Colony was arrested yesterday evening for murder in connection with the death of one of his employees. A large quantity of explosives was removed from his home, and he is also being charged in connection with a car bomb that snarled L.A. traffic for over six hours, though no one was injured..."

Carol gulped so loudly that the cabbie turned around with a suspicious glare. "I...I know that guy," she managed. "He's my boss."

The driver just laughed as if that were the best story he'd heard all week. Maybe it was, but Carol was stunned into silence.

And then she was furious. The thoughts coalesced in her head as the taxi inched forward in the slush, stopping and starting, squealing its brakes inches from other cars' bumpers.

She had spent the past few years of her life being abused and humiliated by a murderer. Now that she knew the truth, there was no denying any more that the way Tripp had treated people was criminal. He had turned the LPR Lab into Leavenworth, and no one had dared to fight him.

Some people had even enjoyed it—and sad to say, those "some people" meant Bob. He had let himself be manipulated, acting like a coward—or, worse, letting his vanity blind him to the fact that he was being used.

Bob had been so flattered that Tripp showed an interest in Jim Kalb, way back almost two years ago, that he'd never allowed himself to ask why. So many things were wrong: Kalb wasn't really a student of van Gnubbern's or a student at all. He hadn't gotten his degree from Chicago as he claimed. He had no one willing to write him a recommendation.

Tripp had known that Kalb's presence on Maupertuis's proposal was not legitimate and had done everything to make sure the contract went through without both sides ever being in the same room. He had accomplished that, making his control over Kalb complete. When Kalb had tried to fight back, Tripp had murdered him.

What outraged Carol the most was that Bob too had fallen under the control of Tripp and, worse, had enjoyed it. Tripp had obviously rewarded and then punished Bob so that Bob would have to try to redeem himself. Tripp then never missed an opportunity to suggest that all would be forgiven if Bob stopped the STI proposal from going in using any means necessary. Bob had been foolish enough to think that all of his scheming was his own idea.

Now that Tripp was on his way to prison, it was hard to say what would become of Bob at the LEPERLab. He could almost certainly get off Unclean status, claiming his punishment was a spiteful move on the part of a killer. When all was said and done, Bob would probably stay there—and it was that final submission that Carol could not forgive. After a year or so he would have forgotten all about the drama, erasing his own sins from his conscience and denying his role in Tripp's little killing spree. No doubt Tripp had killed Marybeth, as well, and probably even Silverman.

When she finally got to the government building where she was supposed to take the proposals, she was ill, and leaned over to retch into the gutter before even paying the cab driver. Then she went inside, found a bathroom, and threw up again. Glancing in the mirror afterwards, she was horrified by her red eyes and swollen cheeks, and took a few minutes to clean herself up with whatever toilet articles remained after airport security had decimated them.

The women's room was empty, but the rest of the place was a maze crawling with people who were either slow-moving zombies or panicked howler monkeys. Carol took the wrong elevator several times, once getting stuck on a "secret" floor where guards prevented her from getting off, before she finally found the little room where the proposals were to be delivered.

It appeared that the LEPERLab wasn't the only institution delivering their proposal in person. Someone from another government center—oily and arrogant in a three-piece suit—squabbled with the secretary for a good half hour about getting proof of delivery. In the meantime, Carol looked around the room and saw it: *Polar Arctic Research In Astrobiology (PARIA), a Proposal Submitted by the Superior Technological Institute, Principal Investigator Lori Anna Barrow* was sitting on the table just behind the secretary's left shoulder. She didn't know how they'd done it, but they had.

Still waiting for the pushy man, she pulled out her laptop to check her e-mail. It was a mistake.

No fewer than ten messages from Human Resources, Finance, and her layers of line management told her that she was under investigation for "time card fraud" for having taken a SLAP from campus. The best-case scenario, they all warned, would be a demotion and a few weeks Unclean. The worst case…

The images were dated yesterday. One of them was from Tripp. The LEPERs had thought nothing about bullying and threatening her while she was serving them, traveling across the country to do her job.

She looked down at the sack of proposals at her feet…then hauled back and gave them a swift kick in their error-filled innards. Jamming her laptop back into her briefcase, she wheeled the carryon out of the room and into the elevator (the correct one, this time). Deposited in front of Headquarters in a flurry of wet snow, she stomped along the sidewalk, dragging the luggage behind her, until she found what she was looking for.

It took all her strength to heave the bulging bag into the Dumpster, but she managed it, and then she was free.

Light as a feather without her burden, Carol took a taxi to the Mall and went to the Museum of Natural History. She saw everything except the planetarium show, which somehow was less than appealing right then. Then she visited the café and read the local paper while drinking a very large cup of coffee.

She felt a thrill of excitement when she saw that *500 MilliCoulombs* was playing at a club that night in town. It would be so much fun to show up and surprise them here in DC right before Christmas. They weren't going to be performing until much later that night, which made her hesitate a moment before she remembered that she was rich.

A fancy hotel room and a nice nap later, she felt almost human again, and went to do some shopping. It felt so good to shed her nasty, scratchy business suit and try on dresses for dancing, lycra shorts and bra tops for working out, and shoes by the dozen. In the end she bought two complete outfits: one for spending a couple of hours in the nearby Gold's Gym on the treadmill and in the aerobics class, and the second for going to see the show afterwards.

After her workout she had a facial and then ate a fruit salad and a turkey panini, and finally it was time to take a taxi to the club. *500 MilliCoulombs* was opening, and she was planning just to go for that, stay for a quick chat, and then go back to her hotel to seriously plan her future.

Talking with Kurt was like being home again, and she didn't even drink a full martini before she was telling him everything about what brought her all the way across the country in a snowstorm just before Christmas. The proposal, the murders, the rivalry she still couldn't grasp between the LEPERs and the STImpies, her history, her hopes and fears, and Bob. As they talked and drank, he moved closer and closer to her, finally slipping his hand underneath the tiny table and placing it on her thigh.

Carol, who at forty-two had never even kissed anyone but Bob Drift, leaned in close and whispered, "I have a room at the Wyndham."

EPILOGUE: SIX MONTHS LATER

Lori and Lou won their proposal, but because of the small size of their team, their budget was reduced to five hundred million dollars. They are not complaining.

Lori gave up her house in the hills, which she never saw anyway, and took a position as Residential Associate in Pasteur House, where she is part den mother and part cat lady.

Lou bought a house about halfway up the hill, and although Abby kept her apartment, the pale furniture and a new baby grand piano adorn his living room. They subscribe to *Dog Fancy* but they still don't have a puppy.

Solomon Rose lives in Honolulu, running an astrobiology consulting company with Radi's help. Radi took the precaution of making sure she was also offered a tenured position at the University of Hawaii.

Kuzno stepped down over the incident with the ink, and took a tenured position at another local university, where no one knows the story.

Carol left Bob and fled to Canada with Kurt, the drummer from *500 milliCoulombs of Happiness*, which he tried to recreate as *500 milliCoulombs de Bonheur* in Montreal. But they quickly decided that learning French was too hard and installed themselves in Toronto.

Bob Drift denies all knowledge of or responsibility in anything except the theft of Lori's backpack. He lives alone in the foothills and keeps waiting for Carol to get cold and come back.

The trial is scheduled for the end of summer, with only Tripp up on murder charges. He has pled Not Guilty to everything. The videos of Dim Bulb's death vanished and were never seen by the police.

Lou and Lori dread the trial for the time it will take away from their ability to concentrate on Lori's tenure review and the interviews for the two senior positions that will find replacements for Kuzno and Rose.

Wigbert van Gnubbern is the most senior remaining member of the department and the acting department head—a position he is singularly unsuited for.

Ben Gerson is still at the Enemy School, where he continues to win awards for research and teaching.

Fang Li took a faculty position in China.

Sam published his paper and passed his qualifying exams, advancing to PhD candidacy.

All of the Walter Waddleses are continuing as usual. Waddles Jr. still teaches Chemistry, Waddles III tries to protect his scientists from LEPERs, and Waddles IV has become the department's best student. He is beginning to show a remarkable talent for molecular biology—but that is a story for another day.

CAST OF CHARACTERS

STI professors and students

Alexander Alexeevich Kuznetsov, Professor of Physics
Solomon Ahab Rose, Professor of Physics
Wigbert Aloysius van Gnubbern, Professor of Physics
Walter Wilson Waddles Jr., Professor of Chemistry
Louis Alain Maupertuis, Assistant Professor of Physics
Lori Anna Barrow, Assistant Professor of Physics
Samuel Benjamin Roth, Physics Graduate Student
Walter Wilson Waddles IV, Physics Graduate Student

The LEPERLab

Walter W. Waddles III, Science Colony Director
Ben Gerson, former Principal Scientist, Science Colony
Ellis D. Tripp, Engineering Colony Director
Bob Drift, Engineering Colony/Earth Science Sub-Colony/ Group E2/ Cell E2_C1/Meteorology sub-cell/Engineer Grade V
Carol Dugoni, Engineering Colony/Earth Science Sub-Colony/ Group E2/ Cell E2_C2/In situ instruments sub-cell/Engineer Grade IV

GLOSSARY

Tabarnak = strong Quebecois swear word; equivalent to "fuck"

Câline de binnes = euphemistic Quebecois swear word; equivalent to "golly gosh darn"

Qu'est-ce que c'est que ça? = What's that?

Grandes écoles = part of the French educational system

Crisse de tabarnak = strong Quebecois swear; "fucking Christ"

Le grand méchant loup = the Big Bad Wolf

Hors de combat = out of service

Les produits de chez nous = local products

On se vouvoie = roughly, "we're not on a first-name basis"

Ma (pe)tite maudite = Deary, sweetheart (sarcastic)

On s'en vient chez vous = we're coming to your place (Quebecois)

Cet après-midi = this afternoon

Tcheke = Quebecois Anglicism, "Check" (instead of *vérifie*)

Pour qu'il y ait pas de neige dans ton stationnement = that there's no snow in your parking spot

Triche pas = no cheating

Le microbe n'est rien, le terrain est tout = the microbe is nothing, the terrain is everything (Pasteur)

Quelle horreur = the horror!

La voiture maudite = the accursed car

Du calme = relax!

Je m'excuse = sorry

Joual = Quebec slang French

Au revoir = until we meet again

Cher ami = dear friend

Adieu = goodbye

Hostie de tabarnak = really strong (blasphemous) Quebecois swear; like "goddamn it to fucking hell"

Je ne sais quoi = I don't know what

On y va = let's go

Pousse avec le talon = push with your heel

Poids en arrière = weight in the rear

Ça va? = are you OK?

Ostie de vendu = fucking sellout

ABOUT THE AUTHOR

Susy Gage is the pen name of a physics professor who hopes to remain anonymous until tenure, retirement, or death, whichever comes first. In her scholarly life, she has published over one hundred papers on condensed matter and particle physics and traveled from pole to pole. Hobbies include ultra-marathons on human powered vehicles of all descriptions. Susy is currently in training to attempt the women's 24-hour cycling record, and hopes to take the summer of her tenure year off in order to in-line skate across the country. No, not *that* country—Canada, of course! Other hobbies include good food, live theatre, and gardening. Her favorite rose is Lavender Pinocchio.

www.ingramcontent.com/pod-product-compliance
Lightning Source LLC
Chambersburg PA
CBHW071255250626
47159CB00004B/1198